THE WEAPON

BAEN BOOKS by MICHAEL Z. WILLIAMSON

Freehold
The Weapon
The Hero (with John Ringo)

THE WEAPON

MICHAEL Z. WILLIAMSON

THE WEAPON

This is a work of fiction. All the characters and events portrayed in this book are fictional, and any resemblance to real people or incidents is purely coincidental.

A Baen Books Original

Baen Publishing Enterprises
P.O. Box 1403
Riverdale, NY 10471
www.baen.com

ISBN-10: 1-4165-0894-5
ISBN-13: 978-1-4165-0894-6

Cover art by Kurt Miller

First printing, August 2005

Library of Congress Cataloging-in-Publication Data

Williamson, Michael Z.
    The weapon / Michael Z. Williamson.
        p. cm.
    "A Baen Books Original"–T.p. verso.
    ISBN 1-4165-0894-5
    1. Human-alien encounters–Fiction. 2. Undercover operations–Fiction. 3. Fathers and daughters–Fiction. 4. Fascists–Fiction. I. Title.

    PS3623.I573W43 2005
    813'.54–dc22

                                                        2005011259

Distributed by Simon & Schuster
1230 Avenue of the Americas
New York, NY 10020

Production & design by Windhaven Press, Auburn, NH (www.windhaven.com)
Printed in the United States of America

10   9   8   7   6   5   4   3   2   1

This one's for my children,
Morrigan and Eric:
For equal parts pleasure,
aggravation, motivation
and education.

APPRENTICE

CHAPTER 1

The first time you suffocate, it's terrifying. It doesn't get any better with practice.

The airlock chuffed open, atmosphere hissing away in an increasingly sibilant, ever quieter sound that was familiar. The two goons grabbed us and tossed us out. I was already in the standard safety position, mouth and nose open to let the air roar out of my lungs. My ears were stabbing out of my head, and gas pressure shrieked unheard out of my guts through the obvious orifice. My eyes began to throb and flood with tears, and I spun myself around, grabbing quickly for a line, a stanchion, anything. Nearby, my buddy Tom Parker already had hold of a line and reached out an arm to me.

It's hard not to panic as the blood starts to boil in your lungs. Tom looked like a gaping fish, and scared. I assume I did, too.

I saw the two goons grinning through their faceplates, feet tucked under stanchions on the dark gray hull of the ship. I swung around Tom, snagged the line and jerked to a stop then ricocheted back toward them. They reached to grapple with me, and I snuck my left hand down and behind my back, slipping a knife from the tape sheath I'd built and stashed inside the belt of my ship coverall. It wasn't much of a knife. Just a bar of steel

3

with a crudely ground and serrated edge with a chisel point ahead of a tape-wrapped hilt, but it would suffice for this. And I'd been in a hurry.

Goon One looked shocked as I ripped it through his braided oxygen hose. He gaped like a fish, then gulped as I had while Tom caught him from behind and tangled with him. As Goon Two approached to see what the problem was and lend assistance, I swung over him and jammed the armor-piercing point into the edge of his faceplate, near the gasket. He imitated a carp also, and I twisted over him and back into the airlock, clutching for the safety bar. Tom was waiting, having levered the first goon out into space while I dealt with the second one.

As air roared into the lock from soprano to basso, the sweetest music anywhere, I heaved several deep breaths, the blotches in front of my eyes fading along with the twanging in my ears. I then opened the inner hatch, we swam inside and waited for the inevitable response one gets for outwitting the instructors.

They both tumbled back in a few seconds later, coughing and gasping. They proceeded to verbally ream us meter-wide rectums. I was worried it might actually turn into a real fight, when Captain Ntanga swam in from his observation post.

"Brace up!" he snapped. We did. It looks odd in microgravity. "I'm disgusted," he said. "How in the name of God and Goddess did you two screwups let a student get a blade in here?"

As they looked stunned and sheepish, he turned to me and said, "Chinran, you are a devious, non-regulation, bloodthirsty, vicious, murderous little bastard. You'll go far. If you live long enough." Then he left and it did turn into a real fight. I'm sure he knew it, he just pretended not to see it.

Higher praise a student cannot get.

It always bothers civilians, and more than a few military personnel, that it is a required part of our training to practice suffocation, drowning and surviving torture. But they're just exercises. We cannot, *ever*, panic in an emergency. We've made a career field out of hypoxia and pain.

Let me start at the beginning. This will be graphic, so don't read it if violence and human suffering bother you.

Everyone has heard of Black Operations, the utterly clandestine division of Freehold Military Forces Special Warfare. You probably know how badly we beat up Earth during the war. However, virtually no one knows what actually goes on within our ranks. This narrative is of course, *not* complete, since there's far too much that you as the reader have no need to know, especially about me. I'm the man who destroyed most of Earth.

I went into the military to get away from home. I suppose, looking back now, that my home life wasn't that bad. At the time, however, it seemed interminable, oppressive and objectionable. So I went into the military. The inconsistency in that should be obvious to all readers.

The recruiter I spoke to was honest, but did have a quota. He tried to get me into a slot in missile control. I didn't want missile control. It had few civilian applications and little activity or travel. I chose combat communications, which had some technical transference to the civilian world and lots of travel. A tentative date was set for me to depart and I took the battery of standard tests.

Less than a week after that, I got a phone call. "Is Kenneth Chinran there?" the caller asked. He was military, in uniform and looked sharp. In fact, he was huge. He'd make a good recruiting vid actor.

"That's me," I replied.

"Mister Chinran, you recently enlisted in combat comm. I'd be interested in offering you a different slot, with a bonus," he said. "Can we meet?"

"Sure," I said. I didn't figure I'd be interested in switching, but I'd give him a fair listen.

He flew in, dropped and landed on our apron a short while later. I walked outside into the glaring summer Iolight and met him as he left the vehicle. I really didn't want him to meet my parents. They'd be polite, hospitable and a bit condescending. They like to think they've done it all, but they come across as insecure.

"I'm Sergeant Washington," he said. He was as tall as I, had fairly obvious African ancestry with some of the local influx of

Hispanic, Indonesian and American. His muscle tone was incredible and he was obviously very competent, deadly and self-secure. I knew I'd never look like that, skinny, gawky kid that I was.

We left as soon as I strapped down and we chatted as he flew. "You blew the tests off the scale, Ken. May I call you Ken?" he said.

I love hearing about how smart I am. I'm still waiting for someone to offer me money commensurate with my brains. "Sure. Or Kenneth. I don't mind," I replied.

"Good deal," he said. "Sure you want to go into combat comm? Can I ask why?"

I shrugged. "It has a bit of travel. The technical training is good, and it gets me out of here," I said. "Here" was New Rockville, a small suburb ninety kilometers south of Westport. It's an okay town, but hardly the center of Freehold culture, much less of the galaxy.

"I have a position available that's better. Not to put the combat comm guys down, I mean, but—"

"What is it?" I interrupted. I didn't want to hear a spiel, just the facts.

He shifted drive ratio fast and said, "Special Warfare. We get to travel too, and sometimes first class and in high circles. We get a lot more training, some of which has civilian applications, even though people might not realize it. If you want action, then we're your people."

I started thinking. I knew of Special Warfare, of course. I'd heard lots of stories, and had no idea which were real and which were rumors. The idea was appealing, but . . .

"I couldn't possibly pass the physical," I said. Not a skinny guy like me.

"Sure you can," he said. "After Basic, we have our own course. You'll be in adequate shape then, and we'll build you up from there. You'll be hardcore by the time you're done."

Now that sounded good. I had no illusions about huge muscles, but strength and agility appealed. I loved gymnastics and dancing and I never backed down from a bully. The idea of being able to actually clobber them instead of being splattered gave me a warm feeling.

"Let's go to your office," I said. It didn't take much convincing to make me agree to switch over. I held out for the bonuses they offered, though. He scheduled me for another battery of tests, mental, physical and psychological, that made the standard military placement look like an elementary school assessment test. I was worn out when I finished.

My parents were convinced I was making a huge mistake. When I got home, my mother started in on me. "I thought you wanted to work with comms? That was the whole reason you signed up; for the school."

"I can still go to that school. I get to do other stuff, too," I said.

Then my father hit me from the other side, "There's very few real world applications for any of it, unless you plan to be a rescue tech in the Dragontooth ski resorts, or an evac vertol medic. There's no real money in it."

That was his gig: money. Money only concerns me as a means to put a roof over my head. As to career goals, I had already jumped in headfirst. I planned on being a military careerist. I wasn't interested in civilian applications anymore. I was convinced of my own immortality, and wanted to be a badass. I knew they'd never understand that. Besides, after building a few bombs in the back lot, I loved the idea of working with real explosives, and that did have civilian applications with all the inland construction going on as we developed the continent.

They tried to talk me out of it, and called the recruiters, but I was a sworn adult and they couldn't do anything to stop me. They did wish me the best and follow me to the port, where I was almost late from mom's hugs and kisses. While appreciated, it was a bit embarrassing.

There were other recruits on the flight, and we got along variously, from reserved to riotously righteously fun. I hadn't been on a ballistic flight in a couple of years, but the thrill of a spine-grinding lift was tempered by the fear of what lay ahead. Or maybe it was the booze. Still, high Gs, microgravity, swooping back to increasing Gs and a thundering rollout are never dull.

We debarked, were met by a sergeant in uniform, and marched out to a bus, then taken to a hotel.

I had expected to be treated like a number. I also had my own ideas on how to avoid that. I was a jokester, a goof, and had smuggled along a couple bottles of liquor. It made me popular with some of the recruits, avoided with headshakes and wary glances from those who thought me "strange." I never worried about people like that.

Shortly, I was the center of a party of about ten recruits. They were younger and older, men and women, including a few cute ones. I had no illusions about bedding any of them. Not only was I unsophisticated, with no idea how to approach a stranger, but we were all there for basic training. I admired a couple of them, though. There was a striking redhead with sapphire blue eyes who was on the slightly elfin side. Nice! I could only wonder what she was training for. We chatted briefly, but didn't really have much to talk about except our upcoming ordeal. We didn't want to talk about that. Her name was Denise ("Call me Deni. Everyone does.") Harlett, and she hit all my buttons for lean women. Her lion's mane of red hair was gently restrained by a static band behind her ears, her tattoos were temporary nanos, not permanent ink, so she could change styles without surgery, and what body art and makeup she did wear was quite restrained for her age, which I put at about my twelve, or eighteen Earth years. She seemed a bit odd; her clothing didn't match her style and was rather plain. It was as if she'd studied makeup and snuck some with her, but hadn't been able to afford clothes. Well, some people do get dressed by their parents until they escape.

We retreated to the only two chairs, in a corner of the room, and tried to talk for quite a few segs. ("Seg" is local time measure, 100 seconds.) Neither of us mentioned training. We discussed music and camping. It was safer.

It turned out she was another fan of Cabhag, at least a closet one. "My friend has a huge collection," she said. "I love the way they mix ancient and modern instruments."

"You dance?" I asked. Gymnastics had got me into dancing. I'm pretty good. And women love a man who can dance.

"No," she said. "Well, I've never really tried. Logan's a small town and pretty far north for any real clubs."

Miss. Damn. I looked her over again while trying to come up

with another topic. Then I noticed one of the strange things about her: no ear piercings. None. Not even a pair of basic studs. "You don't wear jewelry?" I asked.

"No," she said. "I'm—"

Right then they came by and did a bed check. Some sergeant came through the door, filling it as he did so, and said, "Everyone to your assigned rooms, it's lights out." They were ensuring, already, that we were where they could keep us reined in. I guess it made sense, especially after we tried to remove a drunk from the room I was sharing with a military firefighter-to-be. It took both of us and the local sergeant, and Deni, who held the door and helped shove him through. She seemed to enjoy it.

I got a brief chewing out over the liquor, apologized, and watched as they dragged off the struggling body. His career was over already. They threatened to write me up, but at this point, I was still a civilian, a legal adult, and they couldn't do much except refuse to take me. I knew they wouldn't do that.

The next day, we moved officially on base, into another holding cell, basically. We sat there for hours as they called names, checked paperwork, etc. It took far longer than it should have, and I'm sure it was done on purpose to annoy us. What was even more annoying were the idiots who couldn't follow simple directions. We were told, for example: "We'll call off your name. If we mispronounce it but you recognize it, come on up. Don't try to correct us, because we don't have time and it doesn't matter."

Naturally, they pronounced mine "ChinRAN," instead of "SHIN-rahn." I answered "Here, ma'am," and stepped up. A moron shortly after me heard, "Chuvera" and said, "That's 'Kuvera.'" He received a good reaming.

Let me be honest. I was not the most self-secure person. That evening, we wound up standing in loose formation, bags by our sides, waiting for our Sergeant Instructors. I was a bit shaky. I was also tall enough to be in the front rank, and could see four of them gathered just inside the "ADMIN" door to the huge barracks. I knew they were professionals here to do a job, and I also knew that this was designed to be intimidating. I also knew my legs were twitching like a rabbit in the sights of a shotgun.

My stress level went through the roof a few moments later. One of them kicked the door open, and they came out screaming. I didn't get one of them in my face, which was good. I did see the guy next to me—with peripheral vision, as I was not about to turn my head—get torn apart for having his bags on the right side. The staff who dropped us off clearly had said "left side" as they departed. I saw how this was going to play out. Despite that, my legs were still shaking from involuntary reflex. I was glad I'd worn loose pants.

I did as I was told. I didn't stand out. I tolerated the mindless exercise, the blistering days, the nights colder than the Outer Halo, and bugs, snakes, rocks, and the rest of the drill. It was almost two weeks into it, nineteen days to be precise, before they even knew my name to go with my face. Unfortunately, it fell apart after that. I felt perfectly comfortable talking back to an instructor who was being (in my mind) unreasonable.

She was bitching me out for not having "enough" uniforms in my locker. I was protesting that several were dirty, I was awaiting laundry detail, and that those I had were arranged as prescribed in the recruit training manual. I proceeded to quote from memory about "spaced equidistantly or 10 cm apart, as is feasible, shirts buttoned and facing the right, pants hung folded at the halfway point lengthwise and seam-to-seam along the legs . . ."

She claimed I'd simply dumped my extra uniforms into the laundry bag to avoid having them inspected. She was right. There was nothing prohibiting that, however, and I wasn't about to accept a gigging over it. She swore and threatened, I replied that she was violating regs. Another instructor came over, and it got louder. Then I was written up.

I refused to sign it. They could impose any punishment they wished, but I wasn't going to acknowledge it as legal. Shortly thereafter, I was standing shaking and terrified in front of the battalion first sergeant. I'd look like an idiot if I backed out now, so I made it clear I'd take it through the chain of command to the Marshal if I had to. He hemmed and hawed, but agreed I'd committed no violation, merely been a smartass. He agreed the instructors had no authority to act as they had. I was dismissed back to my section. I won the battle.

And that lost me the war. They knew who I was. They knew

I was a smartass. I spent the next six weeks (we have ten day weeks, twenty-eight plus hours to our day) regretting it, being nailed for every tiny infraction (it's impossible not to make them) and cheerfully accepting the punishment. Wasn't I the recruit who liked to go by the book? What did the book say about dust? Wasn't that a dust mote on my locker?

It was a valuable lesson. A little extra work would have saved me a lot of grief. I never saw an off-base liberty, and damned few on-base libs, either. I spent my time polishing furniture and shoes, scrubbing latrines and floors, and hating the instructors. The only time they left me alone was survival training, and that was brutal enough on its own.

I made it to the "Wreck" (Recreation Center) for one evening, for a whole half div, about 1.5 hours. I knew I couldn't get any-one to dance with me, we weren't allowed to touch if we did, and I didn't like pop music. All I wanted was to get away from everything for a few segs.

While standing there, getting a sugar high off a single mug of chocolate, I was confused by a face almost nose to nose with me. The eyes twinkled and looked happy to see me. I stared at them and tried to place the rest of the face.

Deni. Hard to recognize in shapeless camouflage and with a shaved head, but it was Denise, the redhead from the hotel. "Hi!" we both said together, and laughed.

We sat and talked, ran late, hurriedly swapped unit and contact info on paper, being forbidden to use our comms for personal matters ("All soldiers must carry a manual writing implement and notepaper at all times, in case of comm failure." Thank you, Freehold Military Forces!) and parted ways. I cheerfully took the bitching I got and the extra half div of guard detail.

Deni was in the barracks next to us, which might as well be light-years away rather than a mere 200 meters. There were sixteen platoons in each blocky barracks building, and we were on adjoining sides. Occasionally, I'd see her across the drill field during PT, or while doing details. It was frustrating.

I had a normal sex drive. I still do. After thirty days, I needed an orgasm or I was going to die. There were plenty of naked women running around my platoon for me to think about, and some were quite hot, but it was Deni in her shapeless goof suit that I thought about while carefully jerking off under the covers at 0200. I really hoped to meet up with her later, although I knew it was highly unlikely.

We covered much more than the silly minutiae I mentioned above, and those aren't really part of the training. Those are designed to get the mind *thinking* about the petty details that must be dealt with to keep one alive. The real training was what you would expect, and then some. We shot, practiced first aid, field sanitation, perimeter security, orienteering, concealment, support weapons, recognition of air and space craft of our own forces and others, communication methods, order and discipline, the laws of war, and unarmed combat. I excelled at swimming. I'd competed in several events at school, and was totally comfortable in water.

I loved unarmed combat. I got my share of bruises and then some, but I learned to dish out much more than I'd ever managed against bullies. It was a far cry from the rudiments in school gym. The FMF form is a combination of various styles, predominantly Northern Shaolin and Indonesian Pentjak Silat, if you want the history. It has some jui jitsu, hapkido, and a smattering of tai qi quan and mantis quan, but it's mostly a hard, external form. We were told we'd be doing it every day in training, and every other day the rest of the time. I had no problem with that; I loved it.

We covered survival in water, arctic, desert and jungle environments. That was brutal. I lost five kilos, and I was a skinny bastard, barely 65 kilos at 185 centimeters. That and our final exam, trudging around the Sawtooth mountains performing sundry tasks, was a rite of passage like no other. It was the defining moment. Why other militaries don't require as tough a test is beyond me.

At graduation, we marched through a classical Victorian-era parade. My parents couldn't make it, unfortunately. Some people had family there, most not, so I didn't feel too left out. I cleared the field and fell back into route march with the rest of the platoon and felt much lighter. That part was over. I wasn't thinking as to the weeks ahead, just to the present sense of relief.

Some troops were shipping to other bases or a few remote specialty schools. Some were going home to reserve units. I would be staying here with most of the rest, and prepped my gear to sign out and move across base for further training.

While waiting for a shuttle bus, I was joined by another graduate—Deni, looking exceptionally good in a perfectly tailored uniform. She was as cheerful as I was, and we decided to walk so as to be able to talk longer. That meant shouldering our rucks and our duffels, grabbing civilian luggage in the left hand so as to be able to salute officers, and trudging several kilometers. Yes, we were gung ho and stupid. Weren't you at that age?

"So what are you training for?" I asked as we left the barracks area. I felt good. I was a soldier, I kicked ass, and I was about to become better.

"You won't believe me," she said.

"Try me."

"Mobile Assault . . . then Blazer . . . then Black Ops if I can," she said.

Holy shit. "Me too!" I said, surprised and thrilled. "Skiffy!"

"I don't think we can choose our buddies," she said. Then she gave me a sidelong glance that was far too sophisticated and sexy for her age. "But we'll have breaks and leave time."

That was a hint. I knew a hint when belted with one. "We don't have to stay on base the next three days," I suggested, fluttering inside and with a rushing water sound in my head. "We can go into town." I needed sex in the worst way, and she seemed to feel likewise.

"Good idea," she said.

We were both desperate for contact after eight ten-day weeks of stress and no socializing. I had more sex in the three days that followed than I'd had in my life. That wasn't saying too much, as I'd only had three ladyfriends, and wasn't able to do more than the usual fumbling one does as an adolescent. A couple of one-shot encounters were nothing to write home about. Deni and I stayed in bed those three days except to eat, and tried every position either of us could think of, all over the room and the balcony.

She floored me the second day when she casually admitted to having been a virgin until we met.

"I was raised in a Seeker community. Obsessive parents. One reason I left. What can I say?" she said in explanation.

She didn't have to say anything. So her parents were primitive religious types and she wasn't. I didn't have much basis for comparison, but I knew talent when I encountered it, and she was evidently a quick study. Add in a delectable body tightened by exercise and I wouldn't have traded her for any three vid stars. Even after I acquired more experience, my opinion of her in any fashion never dropped. She was bright, thoughtful, strong, sexy and had those eyes that seemed unnatural. Most redheads have green eyes, hers instead were a blue like a high-latitude eastern sky at sunset. I'd never realized until then that eyes could be sexy.

Mobile Assault Training was fun. The instructors were strict without being anal-retentive, and good-natured. They used sick jokes to reinforce safety. I recall one, where the sergeant teaching Initial Parachute Landing (Lecture) explained, " . . . for an emergency landing during a total equipment malfunction, cross your left arm over your right and right boot over your left and remain at full extension." She demonstrated as I tapped furious notes with the rest of the class. I drew up short as she finished, "It won't do you a damn bit of good, but when the rescue crew shows up, they can just unscrew you from the ground." Very funny, especially the morning before you hang on the side of a VC-6 as it lifts straight up, then fall off as the rail is yanked from under you.

There were no cancellations of pass unless you *really* screwed up. We had a two-day break at equinox, and I hung out with Deni. She insisted on temple, which I rarely do, but I went along gamely. She'd called ahead and arranged with the priestess, so we were greeted cordially. It was temple, I hadn't been in a while, so I agreed. It was an actual temple, too, not a grove. Cozy little building, all wood and angles with flying beams and buttresses. I took a glance around and stopped, because all I could think about was this bundle of power sitting on the ground next to me. Deni, meanwhile, seemed to be unfamiliar with ritual. She hesitated over the invocation and I could tell she was watching me for cues.

After the service, we let our noses find food and walked a block over for lunch. It's forbidden to touch in uniform, at least in anything that might be considered a sexual fashion, so we made a game of bumping shoulders. Our booted feet clattered on the walk and it was all fun until her weapon dinged my elbow. We eased up then.

I'd skipped breakfast to sleep late, so I was ravenous. The restaurant was neat, clean and packed, mostly with regular military in civvies. We were acting maturely enough, so they nodded and left us alone. The server found us a booth at the back and I at once ordered enough ham and eggs to fill me, while Deni got fruit and pancakes with a side of bacon. I *hate* pancakes and said so, as our server stuck thick, bittersweet chocolate in front of us.

"So I'll eat all yours," Deni said, grinning.

"I'll throw them away," I said. "Haven't been to temple in a while?" I asked over the clatter of dishes.

She sipped her chocolate, shook her head and said, "Never have."

"Huh?" I replied brilliantly.

"Seekers are Naturalist Wiccans. My folks are obsessive about it," she said. "I've always wondered what a Druidic service was like. So I went."

"Okay," I said. I tried to be casual, but I wanted to ask a thousand questions.

She appeared to figure it out from my expression and said, "That's why I don't have any piercings, hardly own any makeup, or much in the way of clothes. Seeker sect. They even made us keep all our body hair. Rough natural fabrics to wear, 'whole' foods to eat . . ."

As she trailed off I said, "Hated it?"

"Despised it," she agreed with a nod. "I have makeup, I'm working on a wardrobe, and first chance I get I'm getting at least my ears pierced. I'm thinking about a tattoo."

"Lots of sex, too?" I asked, feeling a thrill from a simple flirt.

"Pay your tab and grab your weapon," she said. Then she gave me *that* look.

I never pulled cash out of my pocket so fast in my life.

We went back to training the next day, goofy grins on our faces. It was obvious to everyone what we'd been doing, and I got some jealous ribbing. It felt great. My previous lovers were certainly attractive. I'd had few because I am picky, even when desperate for sex, and my abrasive personality was an additional hindrance in that regard. Deni seemed to like my personality, however, and we meshed. As to looks, she went beyond attractive to flaming. I loved the comments from the guys who'd spent two days doing nothing in the barracks, hiring basic escorts or jerking off alone.

I didn't believe Deni at the time when she told me that she was getting similar comments. I now accept that I'm handsome in a way, although I still think I'm awkward and gawky. At the time though, it was a huge and needed ego boost.

We finished our instruction block, jumping out of spaceboats, starships, stations, fixed-wing cargo craft, vertols and specialized vehicles, and sliding down ropes from cliffs, buildings, vertols, and doing controlled falls like spiders on a line. We swam, climbed, swung, crawled, and generally found all kinds of ways to get where we were going. I loved it. And on weekend passes, I had a budding, experimental nymphomaniac. Deni was coming out of her shell, with military discipline being just enough to stop her from being stupid. She even kept me from a few mistakes that would have screwed my career. She was much more mature than I.

There was a week delay before we were due back for Special Warfare, and we had some funds. I wanted to show her off to my friends. Well, I wanted to show me off, too. She agreed to go with me.

"Are you sure you don't mind?" I asked. "What about your family?"

"I'm not going back anytime soon," she replied. "We don't get along well."

I called ahead to let my parents know. My mother answered.

"Hi, Mom," I said.

"Ken! Oh! How good to hear from you!" she said. I'd only called a couple of times a week. She'd been pushing for daily reports. Parents.

"I'm done with assault school, and heading home. I'm bringing a friend, if that's okay," I said. She sounded really excited, far more than I was. It seemed odd.

"Of course. Now, make sure you negotiate a good rate for the flight, and call if you need help. And don't forget to carry a water bottle, just in case of delays—" she was saying when I interrupted.

I said, "Mom, I'll be fine. I've had survival training, okay?" I knew she meant well, but it was embarrassing to have her repeat the obvious. Besides, I had several hundred thousand kilometers of civilian air and space travel under my belt anyway. I knew all this.

"Just making sure you don't forget, dear," she said, "and call . . ."

The call ended after another hundred seconds of lecture. I love the lady, really, but she can be so annoying.

The flight home was uneventful, except for Deni and me teasing each other. That and a few stares from young civilians jealous of our status. Dress black-and-greens are designed to be impressive, and we were in top shape and knew it. It came across to others as an aura. We were on our feet as soon as the craft stopped rolling and were out the hatch at a brisk pace, rucks and rifles shouldered. We caught a cab and I paid to have the driver take us in on the ground, so I could get a look around.

Would you believe the town looked different in twelve weeks? New construction, dress style changes . . . even the traffic patterns seemed odd. I knew it was I who'd changed more than the town, but I didn't *feel* different. This brought it home. Still, a hundred and twenty days is not a short timespan, I thought. I kept switching between the two thoughts.

We pulled into the apron and I tipped the driver. We spent a few seconds adjusting our uniforms as the cab left, then swapped grins and headed around back where I could smell dinner.

The grass and rock garden looked the same as I recalled, but it was no longer neat, now that I could compare it to military facilities. Well, I'd never cared that much about gardening and my parents had less free labor now, with me gone. The house looked good, familiar and comforting, sprawled out and relaxed across the lot.

I turned the corner and saw that Dad had the grill going, and a pile of assorted dead animal flesh alongside it to convert into deader animal flesh in the flames. I got cheered by the crowd, which I took gamely, and I introduced Deni to my friends and family. Mom wanted pictures, which was fine, and my sister Jacqueline came up and hugged me. "Hiya, big brother!" she said.

"Hiya, squirt," I replied. It was really good to see her. She was skinny in a healthy seven-year-old way (seven of our years, ten and a half Earth years), had styled her hair into a double cat's tail in back, and moved much more surely than she had before I left. I guessed she was taking her gym classes seriously. While my 'rents got things ready, she took Deni and me over to meet her group. I went along politely, even though they're all in the six to nine local years range. I recognized a few of her classmates and tried to keep track of names as an exercise, as I knew my memory would be tested when I got back to school. Oddly (it seemed to me), her friends made less of a deal and acted more normally around us than the older kids and my friends and classmates. Deni was a heroine to the girls, but I intimidated the three boys. All these social things I'd never noticed before were hitting me.

Jackie had made up a banner for me, and the quality was good—the colors fluid, the blending even and not muddy. She had a miniature vidcam on a float platform that hovered near her head unless she sent it off to get images from another angle. Occasionally, she'd dictate a note to it. She was still pursuing her goal of being a videographer or director.

"Where'd you get the floater, Jackie? I don't recognize the make," I asked.

"I built it from a component kit," she said proudly. "Even the lift fan."

"Really," I said, impressed. I knew she was growing up, but to me she'll always be the two-year-old, left behind by the bigger kids and wanting to "snuggwe" on the couch. Dammit, my mind was still switching drive ratios. I drifted back over to the other adults, as I thought of myself now. Deni nodded as I moved, no words spoken. We communicated in gestalt fashion.

Deni and I both wore the Mobile Assault qual badge prominent on our chests, and people were impressed. I was also a bit bulkier and much stronger than I'd been when I left. I heard comments about Deni from friends, and even got a wink from my father. My mother was gracious and didn't embarrass me much, and Deni was just as courteous in return. All in all, it was great. I drank far too much, and stayed awake late enough to avoid a hangover.

There was only one vet among the group; this was after our independence but before the buildup to give us our own armed forces really got under way. Joe Tanaka had been in the UN forces back when we were still a colony and serving with them, and had been in the New Jerusalem system while it got over its problems. He asked a lot of questions about our training. "That's better and more intense than what they gave us," he commented. "Sounds like a good course."

The visit seemed odd to me in another way. Deni and I wanted to talk about weapons and craft and gear and camping, and my parents wanted to talk about civilian jobs. That was years away, but we seemed to stumble over the issue. I felt a growing gulf that I was sure would never close. I was right. I have to wonder what they'd think of me now.

CHAPTER 2

Special Warfare Candidate Training is organized hell. Nothing I'd read or been told could have prepared me for the reality. The reception was cordial enough, but the first morning began not at 2 divs, but at 1:50. Let me convert that—we'd been awake until midnight because we were young and stupid, and woke up four hours later instead of five and a half. It was like recruit training all over again, only more so. After all, they knew just how much punishment we could soak up, and they started there and got tougher.

It hardly seemed worth the pay raise to E-3, Trooper. We would be considered Troopers until we qualified as Blazers or Operatives. Still, it was a raise, it was a qualification of sorts, and it would have to do. To take my mind off the pain, I calculated time left as a percentage and as seconds, breaths, and heartbeats, and the money I'd make per each. It really didn't seem worth it.

Physical conditioning was a huge part of our early training. It was done both out of necessity—it's a job requirement to be strong, and to both find out if we had the mindset to stick with the program through pain and to teach us to deal with discomfort.

I'll bet most readers think they're in pretty good shape. My guess is, if you're a surface dweller on Earth or another urbanized planet and reading this, you can't bench press more than 20 kilograms. Want to know how much I can push?

One hundred eighty. And I can do them in Grainne's or Novaja Rossia's gravity. Deni, being female, has less upper-body strength. She could only do 100. I do 150 reps every day. I leg press 500 kilos. That leaves you with the myth of physical strength and mental ability being incompatible. Please continue to think that; it's a weapon we can use that we don't have to carry with us.

Do you want to know how that type of prowess is achieved? It's very simple. You have to want it. Hurt for 2000 seconds every morning, and you'll be this strong within a year or two. That's all it takes. Or is that bowl of pseudofood you're munching while you read more important to you?

Guess we can rule out you having more willpower than I, then can't we?

Of course, we aren't superhuman. A lot of people would like us to be, so they can feel comfortable not being on par with us. The reality is, we are mortal humans, simply at the far end of the curve. When we show up and kick your ass up around your shoulders, it means that in the evolutionary state of existence, we're better. If that bothers you, tough. I proved myself to Senior Sergeant Yeoh. I didn't have to prove anything to anyone else then. I don't now. My record speaks for itself.

I'll tell you one thing: I don't *ever* want to meet Sergeant Yeoh's grandmother. That first day, I must have done a thousand pushups, and he kept screaming in my ear from six centimeters that his grandmother could do better than that. She must be the vac-sled bitch of the century, and her virility clearly explained his testosterone overdose.

He wasn't the worst. The worst was Sergeant Irina Aleksandrovna Belinitsky, immigrant from Novaja Rossia. She was decent-looking, but with huge boobs three sizes too large for the rest of her leopard-lean, muscled body. To describe her in one word, she was a sadistic bitch. And that's what we called her when she couldn't hear: "The Bitch." She was a runner. How she could run as far as she did without stopping still amazes me.

I was matched up with Trooper Tom Parker as buddy. Tom

was . . . a character. He was blatantly bisexual and flaunted it as jokes. He loved to talk about "ze Revoloooshun!" that was coming someday. Brash, loud and not much of a runner. But he could do pushups. I can run, I just hate it. I could do pushups, too. He'd keep me company by reciting the manual for the M-5 Weapon, Soldiers, Individual, from memory, page after page. "Disassembly is accomplished by: One: unloading the weapon. Two: squeezing the trigger to disengage the firing mechanism. Three: rotating the takedown lever down and to the rear. Four: Withdrawing the takedown lever . . ."

Pushups. Situps. Pullups. Leglifts. Jumps and jerks and running. I thought it would never stop. Then I found out that they'd lied to us. No one was allowed to quit. If you wanted to quit, you had to race for this bell at the admin building and ring it. If you moved toward it, the instructors would beat the snot out of you. All you had to do to quit was suffer worse pain than we already had. It was unfair, I was pissed off, and I started screaming at one of the instructors—Corporal Vic Daniels—about how I'd have his ass in detention. He laughed in my face, punched me in the cheek and hit me in the guts so hard I puked. While I was puking he shoved me back into my slot in formation. The Training Center commander, Captain Ntanga, just watched from the deck of his office and made no move to interfere. So that's how it was to be played.

"Is it time yet for ze Revoloooshun?" Tom asked.

"I'm beginning to think so," I gasped, swallowing bile.

We actually got a hot evening meal, a hot shower, and two divs of sleep. The next morning, they gave us a friendly lecture, and I decided it had been a test. I was right. And wrong.

After breakfast, we got screwed by a three-meter dick. I'm not joking. They dragged up this three-meter-long penis carved from a thick bluemaple trunk and told us it went everywhere we did for the duration. We were required to heave it onto our shoulders and run with it. Anytime we weren't doing something else, we were carrying the dick. It hurt the collar bones, it splintered into our arms and ears and abraded the skin over the bones. It made our weapons bang into our shoulders and spines. Sometimes, the instructors would ride atop it. Belinitsky would crack jokes while she did so; that might have been funny under normal circumstances. Tom cracked a few jokes back, and we all got dropped for pushups. If anyone dropped out for exhaustion or injury, that just left the rest of us with more to carry. We started at Iorise, carried it through our calisthenics and around an obstacle course from hell, took shifts holding it while eating, then carried it to class. We tumbled it end over end on runs, did pushups and situps by squad with it lying across our chests or spines. There's not a millimeter of that log I don't remember. Though it may have changed; seeing scars left by the last victims, we spent every moment we could unobtrusively picking splinters off it with our fingernails. It couldn't have reduced the mass much, but it was the only way we had of fighting back, so we did it.

Class wouldn't start until everyone was present at the chosen location. Each squad had its own dick, and sometimes the riding instructor would beat on us. Whichever team arrived last had to do pushups in mud while being beaten until someone collapsed or threw up. All our comms had clear waterproof covers, because we were all filthy, all the time. We took class sitting on logs while the instructors used a comm and screen under an awning to protect it from the weather. Note that I didn't say it protected us from the weather. We got Iolight, rain, a freak snowshower, hail, birdshit and everything else that came from above. We'd sit there, burning and blistering, teeth-chattering numb and frozen stiff, pounded senseless by drops, straining to hear the voice of an instructor who more than likely was sitting in a lounge chair sipping a soda and munching cookies, neither of which we could have. Sometimes they'd grill lunch for themselves, upwind of us. The aroma of marinated venison or turkey would waft down over us. Bastards. There is worse torture than mere pain. I learned that then.

Beyond the bruises, splinters, scrapes, UV burn from Iota, bugbites, feet blistered and ground into sausage and aching, oxygen-starved muscles was the cold. Water has a better thermal transfer rate than air, and so sucks the heat right out of you. That's true of "warm" water in the 30 degree range. "Cold" water in the 20 degree range is brutal. Mirror Lake is fed by mountain streams, and is in a deep fault valley. It averaged 5-10 degrees, just barely above freezing. A few seconds in it gave me a pounding headache from the chill effect on my ears and neck. My muscles shrank up even tighter than my gonads, and I was so tooth-rattling numb I could barely stand. Then the coughing started. Skinny runts like me have no insulation to slow the effect.

We found a way to alleviate that, sort of. Body heat. Someone reacting to the chill would pee as they swam. The next person would feel the slight warmth, and they'd pee. By the time twenty people had done so, there was a substantial volume of water that was three to five degrees warmer. It was a few seconds, but it was relief from the vampiric cold for those few seconds. Tom would be just behind me, and I'd say, "Ahhh!" when I hit the spot.

"Why, thank you . . . Ken. I look forward . . . so much . . . to you peeing . . . on me every morning."

"I could . . . do it late . . . at night in . . . your rack," I offered.

"I have a . . . better way to keep . . . warm," he replied. "Maybe you . . . and that lovely redhead . . . what's her name?"

"Trooper . . . Denise Harlett." It was seriously hard to breathe while swimming and talking, but any chat was a welcome diversion.

"Yes . . . you two could . . . join me in my rack . . . and . . ."

"Only if . . . I can sell . . . tickets."

"See, I was . . . going to have you . . . be behind me . . . so I wouldn't have . . . to look at your face," he said. We went on like that whenever we had enough breath to spare. I have no idea how much of it was serious, or if it was all persona. But it was bizarrely amusing, now that I think back. Tom's dead now. He was annoying and strange, but a first-class troop. His griping was always cheerful, and he always got the task done. I miss him.

We'd spend all day splashing along the shoreline, our sand-filled uniforms rasping our skin off and wicking away heat as they dried, only to be soaked again. If you want an idea what it was like, fill a tub with cold water and add about ten trays of ice. Then lie in it for most of a day, fully clothed, getting out periodically to step into a walk-in cooler. Refresh the ice as needed. Peel out of the clothes and sandpaper the joints of your legs, behind your knees, anywhere skin meets skin, and rub dirt into the abrasions. Put the wet clothes back on, run a few kilometers with rocks in your boots then get back in the tub. Now, imagine that goes on all day, every day, for weeks.

Why did we stick with it? Probably because we were ornery little bastards who took personal offense to the often-stated theory that we were all geeks who couldn't do it and would run home crying to our mommies and daddies. They made us mean and determined, and we were going to go through hell just to prove these assholes wrong. Which was, of course, exactly what they wanted. You do this because you have something to prove to yourself. No one else will notice.

Then we hit Week Three.

Sorry. Did I capitalize that? I meant WEEK THREE!!!

I don't remember much of week three. I don't want to. Week three was the first of several plateaus we had to cross. They woke us at one div (2.8 hours after midnight), and dragged us out in the cold rain wearing only our shirts and shorts and boots. We formed squares, linked legs over shoulders and did tabletop pushups until we collapsed. They beat us around to be sure we really had collapsed, then they made us throw our dicks over our shoulders and run. We ran until people dropped out and fainted and puked to more beatings, then we ran some more. That extra 25 kilos of dick per person became 30, then 35, then 40 as bodies fell out. Eventually, someone was bound to get squashed as it fell, and I was determined to make sure it wasn't me.

Finally, we dropped our dicks and did our calisthenics to warm up for exercise. While we did them, they doused us with a fire hose. It not only stings like hell in the face, it makes it impossible to breathe. If we turned our heads, we got slapped. If we ducked, we got kicked. We dealt with it, did our 300 pushups, 300 sit-ups, 50 pull-ups, our ten kilometer run, and the obstacle course. Then they brought us back and told us we'd be exercising until breakfast.

Breakfast was at noon. Belinitsky tossed a box of crackers into the mud in front of a group of us and the fight started. I hurt three people getting to them. I think Deni was one of those. Screw her if she couldn't hack it. I managed one pack of about ten crackers from the box, and had lacerations and bruises all over from the fight. Tom and I shared what we had, and handed a couple of spares over to the others in our squad, so Deni got hers anyway. It was very confused.

That afternoon, I felt the twinges that told me my lower back was about to go. I asked Yeoh for sick call and he nodded. A hand wave brought a medic over, who did a quick scan, asked me about it, then told me, "It's superficial. It isn't actually a permanent danger or incapacitating. You can deal with it, it's just pain." I expressed my own obscene opinion of what pain was. I don't know if you've ever had nerve injuries in your lumbar region, but they hurt like a dogfucker, and they *are* incapacitating. I found out you can deal with the pain, if you are desperate enough. It's no harder than holding still while someone stabs you repeatedly with a red hot needle.

The rest of the week was a daze. We ran, jumped, hauled weights, swam across one arm of Mirror Lake (which, I remind you, is fed by frigid mountain streams) that was more than five kilometers wide at that point, hauling a heavy rock in one hand with our weapons slung across our backs and fighting off instructors in boats who thought it was the height of humor to run an inflatable boat over us to hold us under. The swimming was the worst. I could swim for whole kilometers. I'd been on the school team. Ever tried it in frigid, choppy water? It curls you into a gasping, struggling ball. The bottom is too deep to touch. Clothes, weapon and a rock weigh you down. I was absolutely terrified, and more so after I watched someone else sink from exhaustion. They brought him up gasping and choking. Eventually. It had to be a hundred seconds or more they just watched the water, waiting to see if he would learn how to breathe it. They dosed him with oxygen and tossed him back in like a too-small fish. Tom kept cracking jokes to encourage me, about what he'd do with my corpse.

"You can . . . do me if . . . you get them to stop," I told him. I think I meant it.

So the crazy son of a bitch asked them.

Three thousand pushups for us both later . . .

We were taunted by civilian gawkers from town, crawled across hot, sharp rocks, got beaten, abused, flogged, ate perhaps once a day—and at the little we were given and the metabolic rate we were running, that was not enough—and slept perhaps ten divs total (that's 28 hours in a 280-plus-hour week). The "sleep" was hardly worth it, because we were put on watch. The watch duration was 100 seconds. After 100 seconds on watch, the first person thus assigned grabbed the second and formally was relieved. "TROOPER, I RELIEVE YOU!" and "TROOPER, I STAND RELIEVED!" shouted every 100 seconds is not conducive to sleep. Even worse is that it was an alphabetical rotation, so you had to try to sleep on your back so you could be identified, assuming your shirt was clean enough they could read your name. When you were on watch, you were on a dead run to find your replacement, not caring who you stepped on to find them. We finally figured out that we should sleep in alphabetical order. But by then, day three, we were too exhausted to decide what that order was.

Note that I didn't mention showers. Note also that I didn't mention latrine breaks. Again, I'm not kidding. We were cold and wet enough all the time that my clothes smelled only of dirt and mildew when we were done, not sweat, piss, or shit. They sure felt dirty, though.

The tenth day, Belinitsky ran us until noon, probably thirty kilometers, then told us we were done and to rest. I fell asleep on a pile of rocks and didn't notice until I woke up with blood blisters and Ioburn. They let us shower and clean up then, and eat a full meal. I think I ate about 10,000 calories. My uniform was in rags and I tossed it. The medics stretched my back back into shape, handed me a bottle of basic painkillers, and told me to get back to it. I'd spend the rest of training with that "minor scoliosis" they'd discovered during my physical leaving me wincing and teary-eyed in agony.

We run up to ninety-five percent of applicants out in training. It's efficient compared to some. We're very picky about who we take, and hold them as long as possible before even giving them the option to quit. Of course, a few do wind up in giggle wards for restruct. We'd only lost sixty percent so far, although ten percent more needed medical work before resuming training.

The beginning of week four, they doubled our PT requirement. We didn't notice. No amount of physical distress could bother us now. The classes were the tough part, and we covered space physics (the effects of microgravity and various atmospheres on the human body) in paranoid detail, because mistakes would kill us. We'd covered it in Basic. We covered it again. I was glad to see that Deni was still with us, and she didn't seem to hold the pasting I gave her against me. It came to me that I had a really good friend cooking in her, as well as a great sex partner. Then I stopped thinking about it, because I had more to do.

We moved to space the next week, and the ride was in a stripped cargo shuttle at high gees—I found out later it was seven—without padding. I gripped my harness in terror. I wasn't in control of the vehicle, couldn't see out of the vehicle, was at the mercy of others. I've never liked that. I *don't* like violent rides, I *don't* like chaotic maneuvers and I *don't* like being a bug in a box. The docking was bumpy and designed to make us puke, and I did. After I cleaned the mess up, I made my way to the lock, and was cycled through with three others.

What they hadn't told us was that we weren't docked. I assumed we were and that the lock was a safety measure. As soon as we got in, the air vented fast, and we were in a panic state, beating on the inner hatch as we gasped at nothing. Ever seen a fish out of water? Ever wanted to know what that's like? As the atmosphere cleared, the outer door popped and there was a vacsuited instructor with a large sign that read, "GRAB THE LINE AND MOVE ACROSS QUICKLY."

I moved with what you might call alacrity. The stabbing in my eyes and ears and nose and chest was not fun, and I was sure I was going to die. I snatched the rope, swarmed across hand over hand into the station, then pounded my fists on the inner hatch there waiting for Tom and the other two to cross. It was eerie, to hit so hard and hear not a sound besides your heart galloping. I think I actually heard my adrenal glands working. I gasped for air and got nothing. It affects the brain at a fundamental level and is disorienting and almost hallucinogenic. I got smart, snatched the handle and heaved, trying to let myself in, but nothing happened. I passed out from hypoxia while doing so.

They dosed me with straight oxy to wake me up. It was all part of the plan. I coughed and hacked and wheezed and wasted the oxygen swearing up a storm at the instructors, the asshole who was last across, the military and the human race in general. The instructor just laughed, slapped me and told me to shut up.

It became a daily ritual to Cross the Gap. The instructors made it worse by using retch gas and tear gas (they work even better when they have no air to hinder the spray projection, and your membranes are unshielded), "harassing" us (a fancy way of saying they beat anyone who was too inefficient), and then requiring us to stay tethered and fight our way back in. After twelve days of that, I found a way to grind myself a knife in the ship's shop and conceal it on my belt, which is where we came in in this story. I got points for that, for being creative and devious. That was always the goal. I also got beaten to a pulp by the two instructors in question. Although some of that likely had to do with me fighting back (we were encouraged to), and breaking Yeoh's arm.

I suppose a lot of this sounds extreme. I'm told the exposure wasn't injurious, long term, in those small increments, and we were examined regularly and dosed with reconstructor nanos to repair any micro-lesions. It was all supervised, within strict boundaries, and designed to make us willing to take abuse and stress. When in combat, we'd be used in squad-sized units at most, usually smaller. The mission cannot be aborted because an Operative gets a minor injury like a lost finger or broken ribs. He simply has to continue and accept the risk of exacerbating the injuries or dying and plan on getting patched up after the fact if possible. Extreme? Of course. All Operatives are extremists. Someone has to define the boundaries.

We continued unarmed combat training in emgee. Beyond the basics we'd learned, we acquired skills in grappling with the body as the base, rather than the floor; in using bulkheads, overheads and stanchions for leverage; and in crawling through the rat maze piping and skeleton of a ship. It was fun, and gradually became an automatic response to be aware of the surrounding in case of an attack, which we got several times a day. Tom wasn't as flexible as I, and he made sure to joke about my ability to put my head between my legs, but he had a broader build and could take more abuse. I joked about being right behind him in combat. I was almost sad when we had to return dirtside and to gravity.

At this point, we split into two groups—Blazers and Operatives. Our morning routine remained the same, but the afternoon classes differed.

If you are a religious person, I'd like you to remember this. Two hundred and forty-seven Operatives have died in the line of duty. At the end of time, the forces of evil will form ranks and march to the last battle. When they reach the gates of Heaven, they will find those Operatives guarding it. And if the legions of evil have any brains at all, they will about face and leave.

Arrogant mythological babble? Yes. You have yours. I have mine. I've lost a lot of baggage over the years, and accepted that I am mortal—brainwashing only lasts through so many life-threatening encounters before one grows up. But I still believe with all my heart that we are special.

During skill training, we were required to research and report on one of those two hundred and forty-seven. I was given Rowan Moran, and I recognized the name, but I wasn't sure from where. I got to work.

I started reading and it clicked. He'd been the ambassador's bodyguard on Caledonia in 186 (2521 Earth calendar). Yes, *that* Rowan Moran. Briefly, for those of you who don't recall, he escorted the ambassador to a formal Crown function. Caledonian law prohibited foreign nationals, and almost all Caledonian citizens, from being armed in the royal presence. Hard to believe, I know. Who'd want to live in a society where the rulers don't trust the ruled? But it was their law, and he reluctantly went along with it at the ambassador's request.

Luckily, they assumed his sword was merely ceremonial, like theirs.

This was when the attack by the Common People's Action Group terrorists occurred. They swarmed past the palace guards, got amongst the Crown Princess and her siblings, and made a standoff. The guards couldn't respond quickly enough, as they were worried about unacceptable collateral casualties. To whit: the Royals.

Moran put the ambassador down, stood up, and "boosted"

with chemicals (I'll explain later). He took three terrorists apart with his sword, snatched a weapon and killed four more. Facing the last one, who had the princess in a death grip and as a human shield, he found himself out of ammo. He charged with the sword, drove the point bare centimeters past the princess' face, through the chin of the terrorist and up out through his medulla oblongata, killing him instantly and preventing him from shooting the princess as a last act. During the rescue, he was hit nine times and died right after his final thrust. Please note that it *took* nine hits to put him down. It took about a week to mop up the blood and assorted pieces of disassembled terrorists, and there was utter shock throughout the system.

Immediately after that, the Queen demanded, and got passed in Parliament, a law recognizing the right of Freehold soldiers to be armed in the Kingdom and Freehold diplomatic guards to be armed even in the Royal Presence. That's also why Freeholders can always run to the Caledonian embassy in an emergency.

I didn't realize the significance of this until much later. More than death, most people fear oblivion. Operatives know that, whatever happens, we will remember our own. And when it comes down to it, the respect and remembrance of your peers is more important than any fleeting fame in the public eye. It doesn't make death any less scary, but it provides some comfort while facing the process. Rowan is my comrade, though he died when I was a child.

Research, history, and physical conditioning didn't stop us from having more technical training, and we started at the bottom. The very bottom, as in spears, bows, crossbows, thrown rocks, sticks, knives, and swords. This was above and beyond what everyone does in Basic. We even used primitive firearms for a few days. It was fascinating to compare the weapons to the lectures on strategy and tactics, and then compare that to modern hardware.

If any of this narrative has made you queasy, you should probably skip the next section. Special Warfare Operative Survival Training is not for the faint-hearted. The good news is there's nothing you can scare me with after that ordeal. The bad news is, it's the most painful, disgusting, terrifying thing you can ever go through. Keep in mind that we underwent the most intense training possible before we were subjected to this. I don't recommend doing it to your friends as a gag. You'll kill them if you're lucky. If you aren't, they'll survive. Sort of.

First point, it had only briefly been mentioned that this was going to happen. We had no idea when it would occur or how long it would last. When we were dragged out of bed, retch gas smoking up our nostrils and batons clubbing us, it was a shock. When we were hauled outside, shackled and hooded and cuffed and kicked about, it was scary enough to send rippling adrenaline shivers racing along my spine. Then they unbound us and stripped us of all but blindfolds, and started getting nasty. . . .

We were run along, jeered at, spit on and pelted with rocks and garbage. Whoever they were using as actors for this were taking perverse delight in it. I veered to the side at one point, sensing an obstacle ahead through the bare slit in the tied blindfold I could see through. As I did, someone jabbed me with a shock baton. I was urged back into line, and just managed to see the 2cm cable strung at shin height in time to trip over it rather than slam my legs into it. I sprawled, skinning the heels of my hands and grinding burning sand into them.

While I was trying to recover from the searing pain, I was jabbed in the ass several times with a shock baton and screamed. One shot caught my scrotum and I stopped screaming. That it was dogfucking painful doesn't begin to describe it. I barely held back from vomiting my stomach onto the ground in front of me, and I do mean the stomach, not the contents. My abdominals and diaphragm locked up, and I had what felt like a concrete block in my belly. I realized afterwards that the instructor had slipped and done that unintentionally. However, he could *not* break from his do-it-or-we'll-kill-you persona for anything less than a life-threatening injury, so he kept jabbing my ass and thighs while I staggered from the gravel and sand and began running again. He gradually backed off and found other victims to share my ordeal.

I was burning from his ministrations, from the gravel and dust driven into my skin, from the burning Iolight. I was afraid to even consider what might happen next in case I was right or in case it was even worse. Then I didn't have to wonder.

I was crammed, blindfolded, into a tight cage. My knees were jammed against bars, my toes wrapped painfully around mesh, and my shoulders were bent across a frame. Moving hurt. Not moving hurt, until I went numb. It was cold. No sooner would I go numb from inaction, someone would jostle me and I'd start to hurt all over again. My nerves were tingled, itched, burned, frozen, and variously tortured in ways I can't describe. Won't describe. I wasn't fed. I was hosed with incapacitating and hallucinogenic agents.

Extreme? Disgusting? Inhuman? Are those the words you're looking for? All are inaccurate. Nothing can describe it. Nothing can compare to what we were put through, except real torture. A captured soldier can expect abuse, Conventions and Laws of War notwithstanding. An Operative can expect to be tortured slowly until betrayal or death. Sexual abuse and torture is so common most places as to not be remarkable. I'm sure you think you live in a civilized society and that that *never* happens. I sincerely hope you never get apprehended by your local police as a "guaranteed dirtbag" or any other term meaning they're sure you're guilty. There's maybe four systems where you won't be sexually abused, and we're one of them. Yes, that includes men. Believe it. Yes, even on Earth.

We took this as psychological training, and as a test to see who really didn't have the nerves it takes to deal with it. It was a week. It was the longest, most terrifying ten days of my life. I'd been buddied up with Tom for weeks, and now I was alone. That didn't help my state of mind, either. He was a freak, but he was a freak I'd learned to depend on.

All alone, I recall hearing a conversation between two instructors that went approximately:

Belinitsky: "Isn't that the little fuck who smashed your helmet?"

Daniels: "Yeah. Is anyone looking?"

Belinitsky: "Nope. Why don't you do him? Break his neck and claim it was an accident. I'll cover for you."

Daniels: "Nah. I'll settle for a minor injury. Got any broken glass?"

Belinitsky: "I'll find some."

Then they laughed, held a pistol up to my head, and fired nothing. Then they fired a blank off next to my ear. Then I got beaten while my head was still ringing.

I spent the week receiving "accidental" trippings and elbowings, and expecting a lethal incident at any moment. It wasn't vengeful, as everyone got similar treatment. Our incident in space was simply an excuse for them to build an act on. I had no idea at the time, of course.

I became sure I'd survive the course on the third day, when Daniels told me that I'd have my legs broken and my teeth pulled if I moved a muscle. He clacked a pair of pliers suggestively at that last comment. I was left standing naked at rigid attention for three divs, almost nine Earth hours, not moving, barely breathing. My back was out again and every wiggle was shrieking agony that I couldn't let to the surface. Occasionally, a thrown rock would smack me, and I'd wince the slightest bit. Iota Persei, our star, was cooking the skin off me, I was half blind from glare (we were on the lake shore), and it was cold enough after a while—remember it is at altitude, and Io has substantial ultraviolet, so you can burn even when it's quite chilly—that I should have been shivering. I was too scared to do so. I stood stock still as mosquitoes and hoverers and other nasties crawled over me, stung me and bit me, taking the chill and dreading the breeze. And mosquito bites on the face and crotch are worse than boiling acid.

After all that, he came over. Standing in front of me, he made an elaborate show of fitting detonator and timer into a one kilo demolition block. He sat it down on my toes, struck the fuse and stepped back. Then he made an aside to Yeoh. "When he moves, crack his shins for me. Then we'll go to work on his jaw. Don't damage his ribs until we're done," he said, then turned to me. He told me, "We're allowed a certain number of deaths and injuries for this, Chinran. You're one of them. Stay still, you die in less than three segs. Move, and we pound the snot out of you. You're too eager to fight authority, and it's time you had a lesson the rest of them will never forget."

I knew he was bluffing. I also knew I had a kilo of HE on my feet. I also knew he *was* allowed a number of injuries, and that he held a grudge over my cracking of his faceplate. I also knew that I wasn't going to give the prick the satisfaction of moving. He'd get me out of the way before it blew. I also knew that I couldn't plan on that, and the charge was real.

About that time, my molasses-slow thoughts were interrupted by him glancing at his chrono, muttering, "Holy shit!" and running as fast as he could away from me, while Yeoh sprinted past him. I closed my eyes and waited for what I knew intellectually would be a training charge to blow my toes and balls off, and was afraid at gut level was a real charge that would blow my brains into orbit. I pissed myself, which hurt nothing since I was naked. It even warmed my right leg as it dribbled down.

He was back a few moments later, after the fuse burned to nothing, muttering, "Chinran, you are one seriously insane dog-fucker." He removed the "explosive" and led me away. He then PTed me until I puked, for not trying to save myself.

Don't ever try to psych me out or stare me down. I don't take bluffs worth a damn. And I play poker.

It's not hard to imagine that I got sick with the flu. I wasn't the only one. Our bodies were being given a test that pushed to the limits of human capability. That does weaken it, and viruses are always present. The fever was horrid, making my head spin. I felt weaker than I already was, and a few times I threw up hard enough to black out. I won't describe what my ass was doing, except to say it was bleeding afterwards. Then the sinus infection moved into my throat and lungs. I cannot recommend a wracking cough as a complement to pinched nerves in the spine.

You know the worst part? Listening to the women scream in agony. I was pretty sure I could pick Deni's voice out of it, but it affected me about the same with the others. Gender Unification crap aside, men and women are *not* the same, and we are motivated differently. Seven million years of evolution has branded into the human male animal genes to protect women and children so the race will survive. Inquisitors love to use that for advantage while seeking intelligence from prisoners. It's been a fact for centuries that the easiest way to make a tough, uncrackable man break is to torture a woman where he can see, or worse, just hear. Usually, information is forthcoming quickly. Operatives have to learn to be immune to that.

I can't be persuaded by the sounds of a woman being strangled, raped and beaten. I don't like it, though. Not even when I know it's a fellow professional. A civilian woman's suffering disturbs me at my core. That's as may be, but I won't talk.

When they finally let us out, we were haggard and worn. A quick, final hosing was a relief for the relative cleanliness it brought. We slept on a pile of (quite comfortable) quilts right there, and awoke to thin soup and crackers. It took an entire day to return to something that felt remotely human. They were very gentle with us that day, so we could start recovering. We'd lost another handful of people, some of them damaged psychologically from the stress. My spine was killing me, and I could barely walk. The docs stretched me out, hit me with electrostim and ice for the soft tissue damage, adjusted me as best they could, slapped me full of muscle relaxants and reconstructor nanos and told me to take it easy. One side effect of muscle relaxants is to reduce erectile reflex. I gave Deni as much attention as I could that weekend, lying flat on my back, but was frustrated in my own desires. Not that it mattered much; we were both beat to hell.

Mountain Training was next, and we met back up with the some of the Blazer trainees. We all adjourned to a remote site in the Dragontooth range and started on a near-vertical face. They didn't believe in babying us; we started climbing that day. The instructor went ahead, and as he climbed he shouted a lecture about handholds, toeholds, crevices, the dangers of cracks and mossy areas and more. He went up like a spider. We followed very gingerly. Too gingerly to suit him. Out came the tear gas. Ever cling to a wall while being gassed? It's horrible.

Climbing is painful. Not traumatically so, but it hurts in a steady, aching way. My fingertips got abraded raw even through the gloves I wore. My arms and legs cramped up from stretching at odd angles. The insides and caps of my knees were bruised and bloody in short order. Every time I slipped, I'd take skin off my face and off my shoulders, right through my shirt. It's draining in adrenaline, calories burned, sweat in the eyes, aches and sheer concentration. You try not to think about the drop below you, and how a fall will either grate you to slivered meat on the face on the way down or smash you like a falling melon if you bounce clear. Tom and I didn't make any jokes. We just clung to the rock and muttered to ourselves.

We had one serious casualty, and one death the first day. Someone slipped and fell, twisted and landed neck first. The severe trauma made regeneration impossible. The other shattered his hip and a chunk of spine. I watched him fall right past me, and gripped the rock tighter. Yes, I cried. I wondered why I was there, as he screamed and screamed until they doped him and took him away for regen.

I didn't stick with it from sheer bravado. I stayed because I was afraid to admit I was scared. Had anyone else quit, I would have joined them. Looking back, I think we all felt that way. No one wanted to be first. We even joked about "bouncing" and how "a sucking chest wound is the universe's way of telling you you screwed up."

We did climbing with equipment including the usual anchors, pins, ropes, explosive-set shanks and all the other goodies. Then we did free climbing, barefoot and barehanded, just as an exercise. It was good for our confidence but sheer hell on our bodies. Our final exam was in boots and gloves only, but one hundred plus meters straight up. I barely made it through the course and wet my pants several times, but I *did* make it through, so don't even think about kidding me about it unless you can do the same. A lot of the smaller men and women just didn't have the upper body strength. Even with protein enhancing muscle builders, which everyone was taking after our stress-test of qualification training, they simply weren't strong enough. Reluctantly, we transferred them back to Mobile Assault.

Each lesson, they'd add another item to our gear until we were carrying full assault packs. We lost a few people in this part, sheer physical overload. Most of them were near the bottom of the cliffs, but we had two more serious injuries requiring regen.

We have few women in Special Warfare as compared to the regular forces, only about three percent, and they drink daily doses of protein enhancers at triple the rate of most women soldiers.

We do infiltration and more sheer brute battlefield work. We carry heavier loads. This rules out most women physiologically, even with enhancement chemicals. Don't like it? Hey, reality. Deni is an Operative, but I'm fifty percent stronger than she. There's a reason we teach women in unarmed combat training to grapple—punching it out with a large man is a quick route to suicide. If the opponent is smaller, use brute force. If they are larger, grapple, evade, and outthink. But I digress. More than half who'd made it that far failed the climbing course.

We had VIPs visit during the latter part of that course (it's four weeks), and we shocked them senseless. We started our daily climb, after having been informed that we were putting on a show for guests, and figured to be mistreated. We weren't disappointed.

The instructors atop the cliff began dropping small pebbles on us, which stung the hands, chipped flesh even through fabric and clattered on the helmet. Then they threw flashbangs. The booms echoed through the valleys, *BANG! bang ang rumblerumbleumbleble . . . BANG! rumblerumble BA-BANG! bang ang . . .*

Through that, we could barely hear the shouts from below. The VIPs were shocked and outraged that this was being done to *students*, forgetting that we were student *killers*. Not licensed to kill yet, but we had our learner's permits.

They were silent a few segs later, when instructors below us began shooting rifles at us. Well, not at us precisely. They were shooting near us, and as we couldn't move very fast, there was minimal risk of them hitting us. If we panicked, however . . . but no one did. We were going up that 100 meter face as if it were a garden wall, and apparently we did impress them, even if the training outraged them.

We snapped on harnesses, anchored ropes and fast rappelled down, shooting at targets as we went. We hit better than 80% of our targets, and were down the face in fifteen seconds. The hubbub from that told us they were beyond impressed. We went to a meet-and-greet.

We were camo-painted, dirty, sweaty, grimy, propellant-drenched from the firing and generally not the type of people one would want in the parlor. These diplomats and politicians, with a few almost real military officers scattered in, were rather bothered by our presence. Rabbits. We gave our best grins and put on the rest of the show. Instructor now-Sergeant Daniels had me grab a tree branch and do pull-ups. I did thirty-five, even after all that exertion, and while wearing a twenty-kilo assault pack. And remember that our gravity is 118% of Earth normal. That's a heavy pack, and I even impressed myself. The desk-sitting sheep I was introduced to had to be awed. At his request, I shrugged off the ruck and handed it straight-arm to one of the colonels from the UN. He reached for it, I let him grasp it, then I let go. It hit the ground and staggered him over with it. There were a few chuckles, but I'd impressed, no, terrified these people. My face was an emotionless mask and they thought I was something other than human. It showed in that they never addressed me directly, but always as third person to Daniels. "Can he—," "Would you have him show us—." They were afraid to talk to me. Good.

Then Daniels threw them a curve. He left, and they *had* to address me. I loosened up my demeanor, and took the questions as they came. They were very slow to start.

Finally, the colonel I'd used as a dummy broke the silence. "Private? Jelling is it?" he asked. He needed a rank to place me in his world. "Jelling" was one of many cover names I'd use whenever identified publicly as Special Warfare and not a normal soldier.

"Blazer, sir. All of us are addressed as Blazer. The idea is that lower echelon troops are not distinguished by rank so as not to question their capabilities. Any Blazer is suited for the task at hand. For the upper echelons, not using rank denies the enemy knowledge of who the actual team or squad leader is." I was taking a slight liberty; I was not a Blazer or Operative yet. I didn't think anyone would mind. And I'd never be IDed as an Operative in public.

"I understand," he replied. "Can you tell us about your weapon? It's different than our issue, and I'd like to compare."

He'd even picked a subject on which I was an expert. I could have kissed him. For the next few segs, they all stood slack-jawed as I gave the full, personally annotated lecture on individual weapons. I yanked back the bolts, dropped the clips, locked the receiver and passed my weapon, "Joseph," (after Joseph Merrill, the designer) over to him.

I started to lecture: "The concept of the assault rifle dates back to World War Two, from 1939 to 1945, Earth calendar. During it, the Germans developed the Sturmgewehr 43 . . .

"The Soviet Simonov and Kalashnikov designs proved effective, simple and popular . . .

"Eugene Stoner's work on the AR series, AR-10, AR-15, AR-18 specifically, then showed . . .

"The US Army battle lab speced and tested, in the early twenty-first century, a unified weapon combining both rifle and repeating grenade launcher. While flawed in many ways . . .

"Most nations have gone to a design of electrically fired cartridges, however, we find that the mechanical system is only marginally less accurate, and less prone to failure in the field. Now, on to the M-5 Weapon, Soldiers, Individual . . ."

After that, they no longer thought me a dumb grunt. I'd detailed historical facts that most of them could barely place in a time-line, and they nodded the polite nods of people who are out of their depths. Looking back, I wouldn't have made our capabilities known, but I presume it was an attempt to send a message. We were shown to them as a warning of what capabilities would be unleashed in a war. How sad it didn't work.

We resumed mountain training, moving up to the high plateaus and glaciers. We didn't do much alpine skiing; we did do a lot of cross-country. We also trained with snowshoes, which are much harder to use than one would imagine, especially when humping a ruck. You have to swing your legs wider to avoid bumping your own ankles and take long steps. I much prefer skis. Actually, I much prefer snow skimmers. Actually, I prefer a warm hotel room with Deni's painted lips wrapped around . . .

Well, never mind. All I could do was think about it, and it did keep me warm. That's rules one and two of both mountain and arctic survival: Stay warm and keep busy, both physically and mentally. Boredom and slow metabolism will kill you.

Of course, Tom had comments about that. We dug and piled a snow shelter around our rucks, then crawled in with our cloaks. Body heat was the only way to stay warm.

"Now, can you imagine if we had a woman in here—"

"Yes, quite well, Tom. Goodnight." I didn't tell him which woman specifically I was thinking of.

After that, we actually spent some time in the tropics. We'd covered jungle survival and cold ocean in Basic, but not warm water. What they gave us was basically a class rather than an activity, and then we got on with the matter at hand, which was dive training. You know: air tanks and snorkels.

Actually, it's a lot more complicated than that. Space has one pressure: effective zero. Under water, the pressure goes up quickly as you go deeper. You must balance oxygen, CO_2 and inert gas different ways for different depths. Mistakes there, as with everything we do, will kill you. We did deployments to colder waters, rivers, and even harbors. We swam for kilometers a day, and even "warm" water sucks the heat out of you. Choppy, rolling ocean waves are a bitch to swim through, effectively tripling the distance at least, worse if they're heavy.

Don't rule diving out as archaic. All human planets have water. We can use that water to move about unseen. We'll use anything we can. We trained on vehicles, basic aircraft, maneuvering sleds and thruster harnesses in space, horses and camels, more parachuting, any way to insert you can think of and a few you can't.

We had yet another survival test after all that. This one had a difference—it was the "Practical Escape and Evasion Tactics Examination." All they told us was to expect anything. It was scheduled rather than sprung on us, so we knew it couldn't be that bad. At least, we thought so. They had a lot of aircraft on hand, which made me wonder exactly what they had planned. I Found Out Soon Enough, as they say.

I was prepped in a fashion I didn't like (which I'll come back to), driven across the flightline at the AirFac and stuffed onto a VC-3 Hummingbird, which has just enough room for six passengers. Four were already there, Yeoh and I were the other two. We lifted fast and headed north. On most recently settled planets, and at 200 Earth years, Grainne is recent, north is bad. On Grainne, north is even worse.

So, we flew across the Hinterlands, all low scrub and rough ground with interglacial puddles and swamp, and I knew this was to be one hell of a test. I shortly found out just how sadistic the military could be. I was already wondering what the plan was, as the uniform I had been issued at prep had no laces, zips, mesh, or buttons. I'd had to hold it together with my hands as we boarded.

The pilot slowed and hovered, then brought us down. Sergeant Yeoh grinned a sick grin at us, and said, "This is it. We'll drop you here. The test lasts up to ten days."

He continued, "Now, pay attention. In one div, the rescue students will begin searching for you. Pilots, as soon as you are found, you will be pulled and pass."

Then his grin turned downright vicious. "Operative, you must stay hidden for ten days. You must also keep the pilots hidden for ten days. If one of them escapes and is recovered, you fail, and you know what that means."

God and Goddess. I didn't ask if he was serious. I knew he was. I thought furiously as the vertol dropped, touched, and the door popped. We were chivvied out and it started.

First, I grabbed the nearest two pilots and smacked them senseless as the vertol powered away, blasting us with cold breeze and debris. I hobbled them with their flightsuits over their boots and tied the sleeves together as tight as I could manage. Then I took off after the other two. The first one wasn't that far away, but I was hindered by my clothes trying to fall off. I got close and kicked him in the shin hard enough for him to scream. I followed it with a stiff one to the guts and the scream turned to heaves. I pulled his sleeves down and lashed them to his right thigh. He wouldn't be going anywhere for a while. I ran the other way to catch the last one.

He was a sneaky little bastard. He'd headed off at a sprint in the farthest orientation and had dropped low to crawl. Worse, he seemed to be fairly decent at evasion; I didn't see a trail to start with, and I *had* to find him soon before the others got free. There was a slight drag through the tall, spiky weeds, but it could be any animal, not just him.

"I have a deal for you," I yelled. "Show yourself and I'll make sure it's a comfortable ten days. Stay hidden and I'll beat you when I find you, and for the duration. It makes no difference to me."

No response. I hadn't expected one. I dashed out farther, and began a zigzag back toward the landing site. I figured he couldn't get past me, and would be easier to catch if he headed back in.

There he was. Coarse grass was rolled over him from both sides, which was easily visible to me, but he had been in a hurry. I ran over and dove for him.

He fought. He was good, too. I got nailed in the nose and the ribs, and it took a few seconds to beat him into submission. I hoisted him to his feet, twisted his arm into a hold he couldn't break, and marched him gasping back toward the others. I started with the one I'd crippled in the shin, and swiped laces to tie them back to back by their thumbs. Then I grabbed the other two, now struggling free, and repeated the procedure after thumping them again. Then back to the first pair. I was panting by the time I finished, and it must have looked ridiculous—one man with his pants falling off getting intimately close to lash four other people together.

I dispensed with formal introductions, but did get their names as I worked. Shortly, I was wearing a flightsuit that fastened, the four of them weren't, and their hands were lashed behind them. Spaceboat Flight Engineer Plante was wearing my uniform, which was two sizes too big for her. Close Support Vertol Pilot McKay had her suit, far too snug on him, I wore his, and the other two (Spaceboat Navigator Sereno and Spaceboat Offensive Weapons Systems Operator Hickey) wore each other's. They couldn't go far like that, as their suits would either fall off and hobble them, or were too tight to allow good movement. None of them had bootlaces.

But I had a deadline to keep to have them hidden. I had them restrained, now I had to cut the deal. I faced Rob McKay, who'd hid and fought me, and kneed his balls up into his throat four or five times. He collapsed and curled up, retching. "I offered you a deal and you refused. I'm a man of my word," I told him.

"This can be as hard as you want it," I told them. My voice was raspy from exertion in the cold, dry air. "I plan to keep us hidden for ten days. If you go along with it, you'll be mostly comfortable. Mess with me and you'll get back half dead. Or all dead. I really don't care. I'll kill you if you look at me funny.

Now, we walk toward that scrub over there," I said, indicating a low spot that had heavy growth, "heavy" being a relative term. It was about five kilometers, and the fact that I could see it that far away gives you an idea of the terrain.

They walked sullenly through the stalky grass, stepping along as their boots flopped, almost falling off. I prodded them to urge a little eagerness and we made it to the depression. Step three.

"I'll cut one of you loose to help build a shelter. Try to escape and you'll all be freezing and miserable tonight." I found a lone tree near a wet spot that would serve my purpose and lashed them to it with clothes and laces.

They didn't fight too hard over that. I left McKay wrapped and used Sereno, supervising while holding a rock. I didn't really need it, but it was an authority symbol, and a primal one. We used reeds and grass and a few precious sticks to lash a lean-to together, and I turned to fetch the others from the knot I'd tied them in.

Plante had been struggling, trying to break free from the trunk. She stared defiantly at me, until I grabbed her ankle and twisted it in a most unnatural direction. She grimaced, snorted breath through her nose and finally growled as she winced. I kept at it and twisted a bit more to make sure she got the hint. Then I put a stranglehold on her, watching her thrash in instinctive terror until she passed out. I threw her uniform open and left her like that for the night, shivering and cursing quietly. At least, quietly after we had a discussion of the risk noise posed for discovery.

I stayed awake. I figured one complete day wouldn't hurt me much. Besides, I had things to do. I improved the camouflage slightly, although I didn't plan on staying long in one place. Then I gathered some twigs heavy enough to build a small fire, and tinder and kindling. Next, I expended a few thousand calories patiently scraping ignition compound from a rescue flare to get the fire started. Fire has a primal effect on people, and any camp becomes "Home" psychologically once there's flames. Cooked food was a luxury I could offer them that would dull their desire to leave. I'd make it better for them here than alone and that would make it easier for me. To that end, I had adequate material supplies, having liberated everything the pilots carried. That didn't, for training purposes, include any knives or weapons. A few segs with a flake of rock (damned hard to find) and a stick got me a frog spear. I found not only Earth frogs, dull and slow in the cold and easy to catch in the shallows, but a couple of pseudo-manders and some tricky, skinny local frog analogs, the ones we call michigans. I have no idea why they are called that, as they never saw Michigan, which is in North America. They sing loudly, but shut up as soon as anyone comes close.

They roasted nicely on the coals, and I mean *on* the coals. I kept the fire small and virtually invisible on sensors, I hoped. To further hide it, I had it under tall grass to break up the image, and doused it as soon as I was done. No, frogs don't taste like chicken. Similar, but that's because they are white meat. I ate enough to keep me going, peeling meat off bones with my teeth, and saved the legs. John Sereno and Pete Hickey woke up, and I let them dig into the rich, tough meat on the hind legs. McKay and Plante gave me murderous looks, but they'd struggled, so they didn't eat. Punishment and reward was how I planned things. I could hear them coughing all night as the cold, now damp, settled into their lungs. They weren't any happier when I gave them their morning thumping, either. McKay got the gonad treatment, Plante got a boot in the belly until she screamed and dry-puked. They were somewhat mollified when I assured them that good behavior would get them dinner and no more beatings.

After that it wasn't too hard. We all had diarrhea from water-borne parasites, of course. I kept us all fed adequately if not in gourmet fashion, and I released one of them at a time to help build shelters when we moved. I wanted to stay as far ahead of any trackers as possible, so as to delay the inevitable past the deadline. Fires were small and buried, dead brush was used as far as possible and we stayed bundled in our clothes for heat. By the end of ten days, we all stank and were only too grateful for the pickup. I'd wrung what information I could out of my captives and the instructors seemed satisfied. As soon as we debriefed, I was posted to Black Ops Team Three. Tom and I said goodbye and hugged. He was headed for Team One. Deni was posted with me to Team Three and would arrive later, after a stop at Small Arms Repair School.

CHAPTER 3

I arrived on base at Heilbrun feeling only slightly cocky. I knew I was the new guy, and knew they wouldn't let me forget it. Still, I was determined to make a good impression. I managed, but not in the fashion I intended.

One of the huge advantages of SW is that we don't exist. I don't mean in the secretive sense, but in the hassle and admin sense. We aren't in chain of command for either the Combat Operations Battalions or the Base Battalions. We're "tenant units." This means no hassles in the pecking order, except that sometimes out of the blue, one of our officers will decide he's too old for ops and snag a regular command. This is done the way Operatives and Blazers usually do things—in a fast, brutal and unexpected fashion. A slot will open up, a bunch of aspiring officers will vie for it and, while they're congratulating themselves on their marvelous performances, an SW officer will magically appear in the desk. Next morning, the regulars find themselves reporting to a new commander, with no idea where he came from. Needless to say, this causes some friction.

Such was the case the day I got there. The commander of Black Operations Team Three, Captain Alan David Naumann, had just grabbed the command slot for 3rd Mobile Assault Regiment, to whom we were usually attached. This had two repercussions. First was that all the company and duty section commanders in 3rd Mob were pissed at SW again. Second was that we had a hole in our own chain of command to fill. There was a shuffle to do so, and I didn't realize this was all advantageous to my career.

So I reported in instead to Captain Juletta Maron. The driver for the base taxi (junior troops except SW soldiers rotate that duty) gave me a quick tour and dropped me at 3rd SW Regiment HQ. I appraised the area as I would any combat zone. It was old but clean in minimalist fashion—grass and bushes perfect, one single pair of flamebushes a riot of crimson and orange aflank the entrance to the plain paneled building. I dropped my duffel and ruck inside the door and went about becoming known. We do this from the top down, so as to ensure everyone is familiar with the chain of command.

I checked with the orderly, got my new commander's name since it wasn't "Naumann," knocked on her office and heard her bellow, "ENTER!" There was nothing wrong with her voice.

I stepped in, snapped to and said, "Operative Kenneth Chinran reports as ordered, Captain." My voice didn't crack, and I felt confident. I looked her over. Short black hair, slightly graying, trim, slightly above average height for a woman and clearly self-secure.

She saluted back, dropped it, and I raced her down, trying to be back at attention before she was. I made it, but her age was not slowing her down yet. It seemed we both had something to prove, being new. "Do you have an attitude problem, Chinran?" she asked.

It was a bolt from the blue. What had I done to come across as non-reg? I was here less than one hundred seconds and I was being hit with that routine. What in the name of God and Goddess had I done?

I decided, instantly and without conscious thought, to go on the offensive. I had nothing to be ashamed of and wasn't going to grovel. That would be the worst possible response. So I said, "As often as I can, ma'am."

She nodded and said, "Good. I like that." It had been a test. "What do you go by, Chinran?"

"Ken or Kenneth is fine, ma'am," I said, still quivering slightly from that first question.

"And what's your hobby?"

"Shooting, ma'am," I said.

"Good hobby for an Operative. Let's get you up to speed."

I met our First Sergeant, who would handle all my personnel issues. Senior Sergeant John C. ("Call me Sergeant Jack") Hayduke would almost qualify as a recruiting vid icon, taken from the neck down. His face was on the craggy side, which matched his office. He had imposing cliffs of rams, paper and folders, and his comm was idling. "Welcome," he said, all grins. "Good to have you." He ran me through a chart on his wallscreen, gave me a ramchip for reference on inprocessing, and sent me to our logistics element.

SW troops are required to maintain all their gear at all times. We may deploy on short notice to almost anywhere in space, and our gear is specialized; it can't be acquired locally most of the time. This sounds smart theoretically, and is, but do you have any idea what it means in the real world?

I already had my standard-issue weapon that I would keep for life. SW issued me a Merrill automatic carbine and an Alesis pistol, both in 7mm, sealed packs of clips, magazines and ammunition, grenades, demolition blocks and detonators, body armor, another knife and riot gear modified for use in clandestine takedowns. I got lock picks and coders, detection gear ranging from DNA sniffers and programs for my comm to binoculars and goggle/contact lens displays that worked on a variety of frequencies. There was a vac sled, an emgee maneuvering harness, a skintight suit with recycling gear and extra oxy bottles. Diving gear and more bottles, wet and dry water suits, chameleon camouflage and exomusculature gear, climbing gear, parachutes, ropes, tens of ramchips of documentation and training volumes, repair kits and a tool pack, along with harnesses, rucks and canteens rounded it out. Then I got dated food and water packs that I would consume on missions, or else they would be turned in when expired. I would use them on exercises, but only after replacing the amount expected to be used.

All this fits packaged into a one-meter cube mounted on the sled, but to repack it requires warehouse facilities. I was warned not to open it to show off (much of it is stuff we hope is secret in detail, unlikely as that is), as unnecessary repacking would be charged to me. It was mine for the duration of my career, and when not on leave, it would be within short reach of me at all times. Freehold soldiers are armed at all times with at least a pistol, and my orders were to have a pistol on my person and my standard weapon with me or in my vehicle as well. I would need to buy a vehicle post haste. I didn't relish carrying the combo everywhere I went, which is why I'd already bought my own Taurus 8mm sidearm, smaller but as effective as the larger issue weapon.

Being assigned a team did not mean I was trained. I had the basics, certainly, and was capable of chopping a typical foreign squad into sushi with my bare hands or any weapon. I was a trained killer from top to bottom, but I was not yet a specialist in the surgical skills of covert operations. That would take more time and in fact I'm still learning now, ten years—fifteen Earth years—later. That should scare you. It scares me. I could be more dangerous than I am.

First, I had to have surgery for a CNS bioplant. Combat Neural Stimulant was secret for years, and isn't widely acknowledged now. Slangly known as "Boost," which I mentioned earlier, it is a combination of oxygenating compounds, adrenaline and other hormones, and glucose and other sugars, and I'm being deliberately hazy as to the ingredients. First of all, I don't know for certain what they are, but I can recognize it in use and tell the signs in an autopsy or blood analysis. Second, you don't need to know.

The implant is a small artificially grown biological mechanism, implanted you don't need to know where, and can be recharged with additional doses fairly easily with a syringe or, ideally, by a nanocarrier if you have a modern hospital. The artificial organ doesn't show on most X-rays, CT scans or enzyme traces and is hard to see by eye even during an autopsy. Some nations give their troops extensive surgical enhancements, as we do for certain Blazer specialties, but that defeats the purpose of being "covert." Boost enables me to nearly halve my reaction time and increase my strength and speed a considerable percentage. Add that to my training and its physical enhancement is exceeded only by its psychological effect on an enemy.

After that was real generalized specialist (pardon that phrase) training in the art of Black Operations. We'd qualified to be ammo humpers and bullet stops, to get there and set up shop, now we had to learn to dish it out when we got there. I hope by now none of you thinks of us as "dumb grunts." We were all better than Olympic quality athletes, more stubborn than mules and with intelligence ranging from borderline genius to right off the charts.

Deni arrived and was promptly sent back out to Sniper school. I went to Advanced Demolitions. For six wonderful weeks I studied and planted charges on everything from starship hulls and planetoid installations to aircraft and house doors. Want to know how to take out the window on a 75th floor penthouse suite without scattering shards on the hostage two meters inside? I can do it. How about cracking the center spine on an *al Jabr* class Ramadanian cruiser without breaching the hull? Yup. You name it, if explosives can do it, I can set the charges.

We met up again at NCO Leadership School. All Operatives regardless of rank go to NCOLS. We need to know how to plan operations for insurgents and lead them in battle. After that, we split again, she going to Russian Language School, I to Combat Medical. We moved around a lot, adding skills to our expertise in killing. As we traveled, we'd read up on the course basics for whatever we were to study and be prepared to test out of as much as we could. It saved time and was encouraged. I skipped three of six weeks of Combat Med, two weeks of Specialist Welding/Machining, and most of Basic Electronics. I bogged down in languages. My mother speaks ten, but I apparently don't have her aptitude for grammar. Vocabulary and accent was no trouble, so comprehension wasn't my problem, just diction and my comprehensibility to others. I was adequate for combat, but not for the finer points of clandestine work. I cursed and studied and took hypno and more RNA learning boosters than "normal," which was a lot.

Leadership School had the added complexity of having to learn the reorganized operation and personnel system. Briefly, until then, the FMF used 16 troop squads composed of three teams of four troops and a support pair with a machinegun, and two leaders.

That was a good system, which I still heartily endorse, because it made for two buddy pairs per team and a third team for backup. The then new (and still current) doctrine called for twenty: three teams of six, the third being the weapons team, and two leaders. This added the third buddy pair to each team. Another plus was that we added two more support weapons in the hands of those extra pairs. The third team had an anti-tank gunner and assistant, a heavy machinegunner and ammo humper and a pair of combat marksmen (SpecWar teams get bona fide snipers). Thus split, we could do more damage. I'll work with either approach, as they both have their pluses and minuses.

I did fine in the Technical Physical Security course, which is a polite term for breaking, entering, lockpicking, code bypassing, and other rudeness. It's taught by Operatives and by contractors of two types. The first type are either veterans or professionals who take a test whereby they crack a security perimeter. The second type are criminals who eventually got caught doing the same thing unofficially. Both were good, they just had different approaches.

The most fun was the class in Manners and Etiquette, slangly known as "Pie With A Fork," which I'm told is a literary reference. We had to learn how to be polite, make small talk, dance, eat cake without making crumbs, sip wine and dine at a formal event. Keep in mind that while doing this, we are staking the place for its security provisions and plotting a way in or out, or else swiping as much overheard intelligence as possible and grilling other guests for data while being courteous and saying nothing. I can eat appropriately to any culture known, and fake well in an unknown circumstance after a few seconds of surreptitious observation. One of our tests involved a "drunk" host who played with his food, wiped his nose on the tablecloth, drank until the booze spilled over his lips, and was generally a slob. So were his other "guests," and the trainees were graded on how long it took us to fall into the routine. We also ate raw rat and rancid yellow roe at that one, without making faces. I can't recommend either as a delicacy. I can suggest a wine, order an appropriate meal from start to finish in six languages, and charm the thongs off lady diplomats, politicians, officers and wives. I can even fake it and charm male types or ladies' husbands, if the mission calls for it. I prefer not, but a mission's a mission.

Operatives train constantly. I can't stress that enough. There is always something else that can be used in combat, or as a cover persona, or for infiltration. New tools and techniques are developed all the time. From waking until retiring, I read updates, studied manuals, worked out, practiced operations, shot and jumped and took things apart. Sometimes, I even put things back together. I lived, breathed and dreamt warfare. You probably wouldn't want me in your parlor at a diplomatic banquet, although you'd never know which one of your guests I was, but you certainly want me on your side when SHTF—Shit Hits The Fan.

There were several of us from about the same cycle of training posted at Team 3 (3rd MAR had one squad of Operatives and Blazer squads in Combat Air Control, Combat Pioneer, Combat Rescue and Recon attached to it). We were encouraged to be friends, as it gave us needed socialization at minimal security risk, increased esprit de corps and let our competitive natures urge each other to learn better. In short, it made us easier to control. The thought of a rogue Operative defecting to an enemy, the private sector, or even going freelance is enough to give us nightmares. Anyone this powerful *has* to have iron discipline and control. We're more dangerous than nukes—we can't be detected until after we go off. So we keep a good eye on each other, and why would we associate with regular people anyway? It made dating rough. I was lucky enough to have a fellow Operative, but there were few women. Mostly, we dated other soldiers at least. The relationships with civilians tended not to last long. We just weren't compatible. And let's face it: we were egotistical punks back then. We wouldn't grow up for years. But that attitude sometimes meant the difference between death and life.

So it was that after six months (fifty-day months, remember) of tiring skill training, Frank Lutz, Tyler Jones and I were assigned to audit the Chersonesus Army Advanced Combat Assault Course and report back on what we found. Whenever possible, we swap with "similar" units from other nations. This is to trade secrets for dealing with terrorists and insurgents, practice working with unknown allies and assets, and of course to spy on their capabilities.

This was at least a slight change from our training so far—we weren't being graded, we were the assessors. I had slightly more time in service than either of them even though we were all E-4 Senior Operatives, so I was in charge. There's no real significance to relative newbies like ourselves going on the mission. We do this at all ranks to get different viewpoints.

Tyler Jones was a cute but mousy woman who kept her brown hair bobbed in what was called a dyke cut (I'm not sure why it's called that; fashion is not my strong suit), measured about 160 cm and massed about 60 kilos. At the time, she was twelve. Don't let that fool you, as she was inhumanly strong and could outwrestle me about half the time. She was also a bloodthirsty little killer who delighted in starting fights whenever someone made a derogatory comment about her, which happened not infrequently. During our advanced training, she lugged an M23 Heavy Machinegun (20.6 kilos with tripod, plus ammo) without any complaints or assistance. I hated carrying the heavy, personally. I do love the firepower, though.

Frank was taller than me, slightly softer with curly hair and had a wicked sense of humor. His idea of entertainment was to use a pressurized can of solvent and a lighter to torch any bug that landed within range. He only caught a fellow drinker's hair on fire once. He was working on Combat Air Control and Meteorology and had a stack of rams with him.

The three of us were cut orders to ship as supernumeraries on a UN military transport pulling routine rotations among embassies and remote sites. It was departing in two days. I screened a quick message to Deni, telling her I'd miss our planned encounter for the weekend, and grabbed gear and ran. Mercifully, we were not required to ship our full package. We'd be detached and unavailable. Still, what I had to carry was plenty.

The shuttle that was our first leg launched less than a div later. It was a nice flight, I must admit. We were stuck on a contract flight to save time and the only three spots available were in First Class. Seen through station ports as we entered the gangtube, the craft was a brilliant red, polished and glowing in Iolight. The cabin inside was rich leather, real nuggetwood paneling, and had enough legroom even for lanky bastards like myself. As military in uniform (which is rare for Operatives, but we were dressed as Blazers and officially acting as Blazers), we were treated to complimentary booze and snacks, and the meal was lovely—shredded chicken quesadillas with sweet jalapeño peppers, tomatoes and four cheeses. I highly recommend Barchetta Shuttle Service, if you have the means to travel in such fashion. It was a personnel shuttle only, and we climbed until the nacelles could no longer duct enough air. Then the real thrust kicked in—reaction engines. Those took us to Skywheel docking altitude.

We switched to one of their intra-system ships in the odd centripetal and real gravity of the Skywheel, whipped off at the outer arc and headed for Transfer Station in Gealach (our satellite) orbit. Yes, "Transfer Station" is its corporate name; after all, that's what they do. We had berths nicer than any in a military training craft. In less than a day, the shuttle clanked and connected, and we had to rush to transfer to the UNS *Paris*.

We bumped through the passageways of Transfer, apologizing to civilians and bouncing off the mostly bare metal walls of the military terminal. There were a few framed prints to break the monotony, and they looked interesting at a glance, but we had no time to dawdle.

We weren't last aboard, but did reach the lock with only fifteen "minutes" (60 Earth seconds each, roughly 60 of ours) left. We saluted the flag ("ensign") as we'd been briefed, even though it stuck in our craw to salute a foreign flag, and were ushered aboard. We had our bunkroom assignments and map already loaded into our comms, saluted the Officer of the Deck and swam aft.

We needn't have rushed; they didn't thrust on time.

This is one of many cycles of positive feedback in the UN Peace Forces. They don't actually punish soldiers for being AWOL. As a result, people are under no real urgency to get where they're supposed to be on time. This means the commanders call troops early and plan to commence operations late. Knowing it will commence late, the troops sleep in or goof off until the last moment they figure they can get away with, which is after the official deadline. This delays the start even further, so to compensate, the commanders give earlier deadlines. As military craft, they get priority slots in UN and colonial space, so they aren't in any real hurry to do anything about the problem.

This is actually beneficial to the companies that run docks in the Freehold. Since neither they nor the Citizens' Council take orders from the UN, they don't have to give priority to UNPF ships. So if the ship misses its slot, they have to pay a premium to bump the schedule and be fit in. They whine about it, and accuse us of not respecting their importance, but if they can't have their troops stick to a schedule, it obviously isn't that important to them.

A Freehold military vessel would leave on schedule, and anyone who had not cleared ahead with the chain of command would simply be left behind. When he did eventually catch up through civilian ships at personal expense, he would be dragged up for AWOL charges, too. It almost never happens.

We had time to examine our bunkroom while we waited. We lucked out, and there would only be the three of us in the six person bay. That was a rare occurrence, and we made the most of it. We could take turns with some small privacy (a luxury in the confines of a ship), and run through some training sims. It kept us busy, but as a plus, we wouldn't have to deal with snoopy questions.

It's probably a good thing we could keep to ourselves. That evening, we went down to the centrifuged deck that serves various functions including exercise, certain labs and dining, and joined the line for chow. I was early in line for food, as always.

A soft, ugly spacer ahead of me turned and asked, "You're the Colonial troops we picked up, right?"

It was an obvious rhetorical question. Who else would we be in these uniforms? We weren't "colonials" either, but it was a friendly enough inquiry, despite the ignorance. There was no need to make an issue over it.

"Freehold Blazers, yes," I agreed.

"Marines, basically then," he nodded.

Frank wasn't thrilled by that comparison. "We aren't Marines," he said. "Mobile Assault troops pull that duty, among others. They don't fall under a space force authority, because we have a unified military structure."

"So what are you, then?" he asked. He seemed to be prodding a bit from his tone, despite the innocuousness of the question.

Tyler answered, "We're like your Special Units. Only we're better." The expression on her face was not a smile.

He snorted. "Got a bit of an ego there?" he asked.

"Yes," I said. "Because we're that good." I will always back my people up, even when they go overboard. Especially then. But dammit, they understood diplomacy. They simply were choosing not to exercise it. I sighed.

He carefully ignored us through the rest of the line. I knew we'd hear about this later, though.

The next words I spoke were to the server, who was a civilian contractor. Yes, on a warship. I found that to be bizarre. "What's good?" I asked him.

"It's all good!" he said, smiling.

"What do you recommend?" I asked, correcting my question.

"The Thai chicken with green sauce is *very* good," he said with a smirk. He obviously thought to play a trick on us. I knew exactly what trick, and went along with it.

"I'll take it," I said. Frank and Tyler did, too.

We sat down with steaming trays and got settled. It actually looked to be adequately prepared, and it was still steaming. While the crew awaited our surprise over the "hot" food, we grabbed our utensils and dug in. We could hear the conversation volume drop in anticipation as we outsystem hicks each took huge mouthfuls.

Actually, I'd give it a 7 of 10. It wasn't bad. The next thing Frank did, however, was to produce a bottle of Crowley Osbourne's Satan Pepper Sauce and pass it around so we could dose it to a higher plane. The bay was silent at that. I really don't care for Satan Peppers. They're too bitter for my taste. But I can eat them, and a point had to be made.

A nearby diner gestured at the bottle, and Frank nodded. Mister Curious took a whiff of the fumes and handed it back fast. His reaction made it seem he'd sniffed a plasma torch. We'd won this round.

Of course, it got better from there.

Three days later, I was working out in the gym. Frank was

running on the centrifuge track, outpacing those few UN troops who bothered to exercise. That gave Tyler two "hours" to listen to music, or talk to herself, or masturbate, or whatever she chose to do with her precious privacy.

We were at 1 standard G in the centrifuged gym. It's lower than Grainne's gravity, and I had the mass boosted to compensate. While I pumped, some tendonhead from the ship's Marine force came by to razz me. "I hear you said you're better than us?" he started without preamble.

"I'm sorry," I said. "I didn't say that."

"One of you did," he pushed.

"Nope." I wasn't going to let this start, and I wasn't going to be misquoted, either. "Different, yes. We aren't Marines."

So then he took the machine next to me and tried to push more mass than I. He was obviously from a high-G homeworld too, although I couldn't place the accent at that point in my training. I did the best thing I could think of; I ignored his challenge of constantly rising mass, and asked him about home. He was from Thorkel, I found out, and gave me a brief rundown on it. By the time I was done, he was quite happy to drop the testosterone challenge. It seemed like a good start to me. Real warriors (which I am and he was at least trying to be) always like to team up against spacer pukes. We agreed to meet up again and spot for each other.

We were five days out when we hit Jump Point One and flipped through to Earth, from where we'd jump in another fifteen days to Alsace, and from there to Chersonesos. That's when the encounter I expected to happen actually happened.

I left the gym, having said goodbye to Fremont ("call me Monty"), the Thorkel-based Marine, and took the companionway aft toward the bunks. I slipped through a side passage that would take me further out the radius, and there they were.

"Hello, friend," one of them said.

"Hello," I replied, looking at the group. There were eight of them. I counted six men and two women and they were the burliest, ugliest-looking pack of goons I'd seen so far. One of them was the troll from the chow line that first day. I felt flattered. "Companionway party? Where's the beer?" I asked, hoping.

"It's a party alright," the leader said. "A jump party."

"Am I invited, then?" I asked. I could see exactly where this was going. Okay, I cheated: I'd read about it beforehand. Tactical knowledge of the enemy and all that. But I waited patiently for him to proceed. I also checked out the environment, which I should have done earlier. It was a late-night low-use passage with a few stanchions for gripping in an emergency, and precious little else. That had the disadvantage of little for me to use, but the advantage of little for the higher-numbered enemy to use. And yes, I'd already pegged them as enemies before the alpha weasel spoke again.

"The way it works," he said, "is that slimy little spaceworms, which is you, go through the Spacer's Ordeal, and become real spacers. It happens to everyone on their first hyperjump. You come with us to the Court of the Space Queen and make nice to him, er, her, rub up, drink some Space Goat Juice, and we get a few photos." Such rituals were officially banned. Good commanders let them happen anyway. Bad commanders were clueless. The rituals persisted.

"I've jumped before," I told him. I wasn't interested in playing games. I'd been through far worse than he could imagine, but it was my stubborn streak. I had no need to play, no desire to play and wasn't going to play. And no one took photos of Operatives, even if it meant destroyed equipment.

"Not on a UN ship you haven't," he said, grinning. He probably thought his size would intimidate me into his silly hazing ritual. "You do it, or you go through us to get out."

Well, he hadn't mentioned *that* option before. That seemed fair.

My kick caught him toe-first in the balls, knocking them up into his abdomen. He *whuffed*, curled up as I expected and gave me a handhold in the emgee. I used my left hand for leverage, with his head as the fulcrum. It incidentally bounced off the bulkhead, which was fine with me.

That swung me toward one of his buddies, and the edge of my right hand caught him across the bridge of the nose. He grunted as it cracked. As I recoiled the other way, I caught the third one with the same hand, jabbing hard under her ribs, then grabbing a tit and crushing it as I bounced. I pulled my foot free of the first thug with another kick, twisted around her right tit as she screamed, and planted my feet on the overhead to soak up momentum. I straightened, pushing her toward the walkway and blocking another geek with her body. She gave me a good base from which to punch one in the side of the head. He spun into the inboard corridor side as a few drops of blood drifted past, alerting me that number two was trying something else.

I jackknifed and pushed off, then yawed right, getting my feet onto the outward corridor side. I brought my left foot up behind his head, hooking him with it and driving my right boot heel into his ear. Then I scissored it back and caught another woman dead center in her crotch with the instep of my foot. You may think that without testicles that doesn't hurt, but the reactions I've seen tell me it does, and she howled in appreciation of my form.

I jabbed fingers into a convenient throat, pivoted around an arm as I used my feet to push the attached torso the other way, thus dislocating it with a satisfying rubbery feel, and bashed my head back into the face of the person trying to get a stranglehold on me. That made me a bit dizzy, but I wasn't about to show it. With feet against the walkway, I grabbed the nearest body and dove straight "up."

Remember that I can leg press 500 kilos in 1.18 gees? There was a satisfying thud as we hit, and my brains shook in my head. My victim probably didn't feel a thing, but would upon waking. Someone interrupted my satisfaction by grabbing me, so I slammed a foot into his head, then drove my other heel back into his face. I stopped my forward momentum by kicking the first woman in her left breast to give her a matched set, and gracefully hiked my toe under her chin, clacking her teeth closed on her tongue. She gurgled a scream as I twisted and threw a stiff-fingered hook into an exposed solar plexus, male type.

There was a lot of blood drifting through the air now, clogging the vents and splattering the deck and sides. It was good blood, i.e., not mine. I swam through the moaning, grunting and retching bodies, turned and said, "I trust that this satisfies the ritual requirement?"

I took a slight wiggle of a head as "yes" and went to find food. Exercise makes me hungry.

This incident had two additional payoffs. The next "morning" by ship's clock, Frank, Tyler and I came to breakfast. We entered the centrifuge (which was spun to create G when not under pseudothrust. As we were currently under thrust, it was stationary, but still in use), grabbed our trays, and I led the way to a table. I didn't see any obvious spaces where the three of us might sit, but as we—I—approached the nearest, a space five seats wide cleared out, the spacers grabbing trays and falling over themselves to make room. Apparently, word of our escapades had gotten out. Tyler, I found out, had also been hazed and had gone for joints—three spacers had broken elbows or wrists. I told you she was a bloodthirsty bitch. Frank had been asleep in his bunk and was unmolested. This says something about the value of plenty of rest, but I'm not sure what. The crew were unfailingly polite to us from then on, and the Marine NCO in charge of training officially and obsequiously asked if we might share some of our knowledge with his people. He'd "heard somewhere" that we had "better than average" unarmed combat training. He said it with a straight face, too. We showed them a few tricks as a professional courtesy, and the Marines were solidly on our side from then on.

We jumped through to Earth, stopped not at all, but went right across the system to Earth Jump Point Five to Alsace. Fifteen days transit, then pop across another 36 lightyears.

The UN Star Nation of Alsace is the 11 Leo Minoris system. It's interesting. The primary is a G8, slightly larger but cooler than Sol, gradually coming off the main sequence into subgianthood, to be followed by a stint as a red giant. We can probably only inhabit the planet for another ten thousand years or so. And there's this tiny red dwarf companion orbiting at 800 million kilometers that is fun to watch. You'd think that not being able to stay for long (in an astronomical sense) would make the system less than desirable, but no one worries about the impending deadline. Well, they have time to do something about it.

We were there two days and managed some ground time, as the ship had a call in orbit anyway. One of our encounters was quite amusing. The three of us "Blazers" left the usual mobile assault/marine/specialist/seconded army haunts, along with Monty and two of his buddies, and traveled a slight distance. There was no way we were going to swill with vacuum sucking spacer pukes, so we found what we thought was a quiet bar to sample the local beer and wine, which was in order good and so-so. The Alsatians should probably not be allowed to run distilleries, though.

We thought it was a quiet bar. For some reason, Alsatians have an obsession with sexual orientation. They don't discriminate and will gladly insult anyone's preference. I knew mine, wasn't bothered by it and cared less what people said about me. Deni thought I was a charming rogue, one or two other women I'd had torrid flings with claimed I was a male dynamo (exercise increases endurance . . . what can I say?) and I didn't worry about the opinions of people I wasn't trying to meet horizontally.

As with most Freeholders, Tyler had made excursions to explore her sexuality. Despite everything else about her, she was timid in her personal encounters and had blushed and stammered while the three of us were discussing our experiences one bored night aboard ship. She definitely preferred men. Her only encounter with a woman up until then had been with a UNPF Space Force tech aboard ship. We ribbed her about getting more pussy than we had and she'd flushed red as she smiled. She was a late bloomer, and that was as fair game for jokes as anything else. That was among friends, though, not strangers.

One of the Alsatian Army troops, not realizing our language skills, made a comment behind her back, involving mention of her haircut, the typical body-hairlessness of Freeholders, her height and his greater height. There were howls of laughter and Tyler glowed infrared. I was about to put a restraining arm on her, when she turned and went to town.

Alsace is .82 gees. Grainne is 1.18. She was in peak condition. The joker came over her head and into the bartop through two of his buddies. The fight started. Being good soldiers, we backed her up. Being Operatives, we did so with great skill. Being slightly drunk, we did so with an excess of enthusiasm. Being wiser than most, we made no effort to resist when the Gendarmerie arrived.

Monty's friends acquitted themselves quite well, too, right up to the point where he slugged a cop.

Less than a div later, we were dragged out of the local hoosegow (where a couple of local bullyboys had received a lesson in manners, also) and delivered to the landing field. The UN Landing Officer and the local top cop and the army's honchos gathered around to roundly roast us. "Where are the rest of these hoodlums?" the soldier asked.

When the LO patiently explained that only three FMF Blazers were aboard and that we were they, he looked confused. When the local arresting officer confirmed that he'd dragged in the three of us, the three Marines and twenty-two local soldiers, the colonel there for her men and women looked as if she'd melt from shame. Tyler was tiny, and Frank and I are not on the particularly large size. Even with the Marines along, the mass ratio was impressive.

At this point, the arresting officer mentioned our passivity to his apprehension and our manners then suggested that perhaps the soldiers had had a brawl and we'd merely been caught up in the festivities. To avoid paperwork and international inquiries, all parties agreed. I suppose it didn't hurt that we had called the officier "M'sieur Constable" in our best accents throughout the incident, answered all questions truthfully and even addressed the receptionist as "Ma'meselle." I'd even managed to make them believe that Monty's swing had been an enthusiastic accident.

There was a brief dressing down for us and the Marines who'd been carousing at another bar, then we boarded the shuttle. The LO was a Marine lieutenant, and he punched my arm and winked as we filed by. I grinned and winked back, promising with that gesture that he'd pay for the bruise he gave me. It had been no love-tap, as he was using it as an excuse to make a point.

The only thing that bothered me about the whole incident was that we didn't get to see much of the town. I still haven't.

Chersonesus was settled by Greeks from Earth. It has Member status in the Colonial Alliance. It orbits a star that has no name, only catalog numbers, because it's barely visible from Earth. It was chosen for settlement because its distance and less than prime (though still adequate) characteristics meant that the major commercial and governmental powers didn't want it, as opposed to my home of Grainne which was settled due to distance and lots of resources to exploit by a rich national conglomerate. Chersonesus is 37 light years to Galactic North of Sol, slightly inward toward the hub and less than 6 lightyears from Arcturus, which is a brilliant amber jewel in its night sky. Its only jump point links through Alsace. The primary is a K2 spectroscopic binary, and both stars orbit a common center of gravity in a tight, fast orbit. My brief didn't tell me whether or not they were close enough to swap stellar material and gas, so I was eager to see it for myself. The light appears to human eye to be as bright as "normal" Sunlight (most do—the eye can't handle the output of a star at any reasonable distance, so uses only what it needs), with a yellow-orange tinge to things. UV is quite a bit lower and the Earth plants are engineered to handle that. The people are paler than one would expect from a predominantly Mediterranean stock, of course. Heavy element wise, the system is lower than Earth normal, but high enough to make it easy to exploit with modern equipment. Chersonesus orbits its "Suns" at .69 AU, so it's just slightly cool. The tropics get about as warm as is typical, they're just a little smaller, and the polar caps a little larger. It's approximately Earth/Grainne sized but has a surface gravity of only .78. Even that is high, considering the elemental makeup of the system. But it would make us high G types inhumanly strong.

We orbited, took a plain but adequate commercial shuttle down and were waved right through customs. I tried to use my broken Greek (they have an odd accent after nearly 200 years of semi-isolation from Earth), but the customs officer was so helpfully polite. "Gohead, gohead," he said, waving us through and turning to the travelers behind us.

So we trotted outside, hoping to find some clues there. In moments, a drab but modern tan eight-seater pulled up and a Chersonesi soldier with two stripes said, "Fweeheld?"

"Freehold Forces Third Blazer Regiment, yes." I was relieved even if I didn't show it. He opened the back and we tossed in our huge bags, then took seats up front.

Most "civilized" people would have been terrified of his driving. It was under different societal rules than I was used to, but just as fast. After a few minutes, we were all comfortable with his weaving, darting convolutions through traffic. He kept up a rapid-fire guided tour as he drove, pointing this way and that at things we'd never see again. Still, it was friendly and fascinating and Frank snapped some photos for us.

Things were brisk at the Chersonesi base, Ionides Army Training Center. We were thrown in like numbers, assigned, aligned and forgotten about. It was a moral imperative to us not to be considered part of the background scenery however, so we took steps to correct that deplorable turn of events. The first morning, everyone knew there were three Blazers present.

The day started early at "Iodine," as we took to calling it. It was a play on the name and on the orange tinged light we had. It was a familiar wakeup, with lots of pushups and screaming. It was great to be home, even with the twin suns a bloody stellar duel on the horizon, unlike anything I'd seen before.

Tyler responded to an instructor's smartass question with a roared "NAI, LOCHIAS!" (yes, sergeant!) that blew his ears back. He'd asked for us to be loud, so there was nothing he could complain about . . . officially. He shortly found an excuse to drop her for pushups, his obvious intent being to break this little woman physically, then emotionally. Little did he know.

She dropped at his command, getting face into the mud in less than a second. There was almost a sonic boom as she descended. I snapped, "Kinoumai!" ("Move!") over my shoulder to clear the soldier behind me out of the way of my legs, and dropped also, as did Frank.

The instructor asked for fifty pushups. Allowing for the gravitational difference, we gave him sixty. Then we did twenty more for good measure. It seemed fair, as we only used each hand half the time. We counted them loudly in Greek, popped back up in unison, and snapped back to attention. We weren't sweating. Of course, it was cool by our standards. But we'd use it as a psych advantage.

Whenever an Operative was dropped for pushups, we *all* dropped. When required to run extra laps, we all did. We moved as a trio, and that evening arranged to bunk together, by the expedient of telling two of the three Chersonesi troops in my room to relocate. They left in a hurry. Moments later, an anthypolochangos (second lieutenant) came in and began to whine about us screwing up his orderly chart. I snarled. He ran, tail between legs. He returned with a staff sergeant. I spoke to the sergeant in reasonable tones.

"Archilochias," I said, "the three of us are a team. We must be in close proximity to continue our language and technical studies"—I indicated our comms and a stack of ramchips—"and to properly assess this course, which is our mission here. Also, as ranking member of this team, I need to have my troops where I can be responsible for their safety and discipline."

The sergeant agreed as to how I made sense, and I apologized to the officer for scaring him, which elicited a grin from the sergeant behind him. The lieutenant couldn't see it, of course. We assured him that we were quite comfortable with coed arrangements and that Tyler didn't mind the other male's presence and he shrugged and left, towing the lieutenant with him.

There was another row the next morning when we were first in formation. Or perhaps it was our method of egress from the building—we jumped. From the third floor. It was only seven meters from ledge to ground and the gravity was lower than we had trained in, but for some reason, despite the fact we would later practice landing from that height or better, they objected to us jumping the gun.

There was an amusing aside to this. Their Ranger course was also required of their combat rescue troops. Combat rescue troops anywhere are nuts, and no one is allowed to do more pushups than they. So when we dropped, they dropped with us.

Then the Special Forces candidates decided they didn't want to be showed up, so they started dropping with us, too. That put the Ranger students in a bit of a bind, and their instructors suggested they shouldn't be shown up. That just left the Alpine contingent, who weren't going to be left out of the fun . . .

It wound up with the entire training battalion pumping out a thousand or more pushups a day. The instructors couldn't really ask us *not* to do so, so they had to reduce the number they awarded just to have time to get in the training. The lesson here is: teamwork wins wars.

The course was decent, we would report back. The technical capabilities of their Ranger students were comparable to Mobile Assault, although their shooting was poorer, but above average. They were not as physically active, nor did they have the emphasis on unarmed combat.

A note on unarmed combat, as I haven't mentioned this before. There's a debate on the validity of unarmed combat in modern warfare, as it is little used and some see it as outdated. I disagree. The necessity of getting into your opponent's face and beating on him, while taking damage personally, is excellent psychological preparation and of great value. The physical aspects of the training are good for strength and flexibility. Also, "unlikely" to be needed in combat is still "possibly" needed. I think our emphasis on it is valid. I will admit to a preference for shooting the enemy at a distance. It is far more cost effective in damage, casualties and speed of resolution. Martial arts will never replace good shooting, but can complement it nicely.

The course was no real strain. We learned the differences between our equipment and found a couple of useful items to consider. I liked their rucksacks better than ours. Their field shelter was to beat all hell. It was a combination insulation mat, bivouac sleeping bag, inflatable one-soldier puptent and hammock. It worked anywhere, and was no bulkier than the bag and mat we carried. I was impressed.

We only got one weekend in town. I wish we'd had more. It started off slow but was eventually a lot of fun.

There was a surplus store near base, naturally. We wandered in there to look at knives and such, that being my moral weakness, before the civilians were awake and moving. And behind the cluttered cases of knives, they had one of the combination shelters on display, hanging from pillars. It was a practical thing, just too damned cool to pass up, so I grabbed one to add to my non-issue gear. Then I grabbed two more, figuring to make gifts of them to Deni and possibly my sister for her camping trips. The shopkeeper didn't seem to mind my broken Greek, as much money as I was spending. But what the hell else did I have to spend it on? It came down to liquor, women and anything I could use in the field. I'm a practical person. As there were no women handy, and booze was cheap, it may as well be field gear.

As we left, Frank said, "Geez, Ken, three hundred credits? And not even one of those knives?"

"I know of better blades," I said. "But these are really cool. Are we ready for a drink?"

He replied with a shrug, "Hey, it's your money. And what do you mean, 'Are we ready for a drink?' We're always ready for a drink."

Tyler pointed and said, "Wine, ho!"

So we sampled the local wine at a little brick bistro. It was rich and red, their soil having a favorable chemistry. The wine was, I mean. The bricks were rich and red, though I don't think the chemistry made them any better, just a nice color. The climate was pleasant. We sat outside, the object of strange looks for our foreign uniforms, and had a good time. Frank drank liters. He said, "I plan to save up my empties, cash them in for the recycle value, and when I'm done, I'll have enough money for a regenerated liver." There was something wrong with that logic, but it made sense at the time. I was drinking, too.

The local women were not bad. Though I only have a statistical universe of one to draw data from.

The next week, we marched through a parade and got to add Chersonesi Ranger wings to our uniforms. Then we packed up and prepared to ship out, on a commercial vessel. It had been a good six weeks.

I've always thought myself a decent writer. It seems others agreed. Based on our experiences and service time, we all got bumped one rank to Operative Corporal slightly ahead of the usual time in service. For leading a deployment, even a small one, I got a note in my file. It couldn't hurt at promotion time. I also wrote a glowing review of the combination shelter, and graciously donated one to the FMF field lab for testing. We adopted it on a trial basis shortly thereafter and it became standard. I was only doing my job. But it was nice to be thanked officially and credited for the discovery.

CHAPTER 4

Every new Operative gets assigned a tour on embassy duty. It gives us a chance to see other cultures and their militaries and practice some rudimentary skills, as all military attaches and their staff are assumed to be intelligence gatherers anyway. I was fortunate enough to get assigned to Caledonia, and had a great time.

First of all, Deni was there, too. When not on duty or filing reports, we had several free divs a week. You get one guess as to how we spent them, and the only detail you get is that those times were "scorching." We'd only seen each other a day here or a week there until now. Now we had five months together.

We had to pull guard duty, of course. It's not that bad. There's gate duty, which can be out in the weather, but weather doesn't bother me. There's duty inside both at terminals and roving, or at the loading dock inspecting shipments. Then we have someone at the door to check visitors. We rotated to all stations under supervision to get a good grounding, and read the SOPs and all relevant logs and histories.

We did this duty for three reasons. First, we *were* there as security as well as (in my case) a junior attaché. Second, it was great cover for our other activities. If people saw us on guard, they would not assume we were anything more. The professionals could figure us out, of course, but that made them work, which was the idea; work spent IDing us was work not spent elsewhere. When every embassy does similar things, it stretches the resources and limits other intel they acquire about you. Of course, it also limits what you yourself can acquire. No free lunch. Finally, and related, we were the best available, but were not perceived as more than the average. It wasn't admitted then and isn't common knowledge now that Operatives are assigned to embassies. We were identified as Blazers, and there are always a few Blazer qualified guards at embassies mixed in with the MA troops. Most threats would underestimate us. Once. Once would be enough.

Actually, duty at the little box out front was okay. It was molecularly surface treated black and green, bore our address and "Embassy, Freehold of Grainne" in silver and was attractive as only simple geometric designs can be. We worked in day shifts of a squad of twenty, fire teams of four, with teams taking turns on guard in the shack, patrolling the fence and lurking as backup and covering inside. The Squad Leader handled outside the building, Assistant inside with the supernumeraries as reserve and a second echelon. We all had the nanocircuit contact lenses with ghost images from the cameras. It takes getting used to, but we saw a lot more than civilians thought we did. The patrols had jump harnesses. They are only good for a few seconds of thrust, but they could be anywhere for backup in moments, albeit hindered by the harnesses after landing. A call would have the entire squad there in seconds, and a 20-troop squad of Mobile Assault and Blazers with a few Operatives added in is a better armed and more capable reaction force than what most militaries laughingly pass off as a platoon. Still, even with it being friendly territory, well-secured and with no threat warning, we felt the weight of it. We were our nation's presence and first line of defense for all Residents who were in the system. And with other duties and a night shift, we were usually a bit less than optimal numbers. But all our Citizens are veterans, as are most of the staff, and there was local security from the host nation. This assumes one can trust the host nation. We could here, but couldn't assume that fact would always hold true.

That duty was so important, that we could not go outside the gate for anything. If we saw a vehicle accident (there were a couple), we had to ignore it, or rather, report the incident and observe only. We would have to let a local bleed to death on the walkway outside rather than leave post without relief and permission. After all, a staged or faked injury would be a great distraction, if it got the guards away.

Otherwise, we spent a lot of time checking out the capital of Skye and its restaurants and bars. We wore Blazer insignia, same as we do now, and joined the Mobile Assault troops who were the regular embassy detail in their pub crawls. A Freehold uniform and MA tabs is a guaranteed way to pick up chicks or dicks or both, depending on your preference or lack thereof. Someone wearing Blazer tabs may as well have "GET SEX HERE" written across the forehead. We also got a lot of free drinks, and made some good connections among the militaries from other embassies. There was a beautiful blonde Novaja Rossian sergeant I went a few rounds with, who filled me in on the unclassified portions of their relations while I filled her in with the obvious. I passed the data along anyway, just in case there was anything new. I shared some tricks she taught me with Deni, who returned the favor with a few things she learned from a Caledonian Royal Marine. I passed that data back the other way. All in all, it was most educational.

The Novajas and Caledonians put up with us gamely. The assorted Mtalis and Ramadanians were shocked numb by our "decadence." The others fell in between. The only exception was the Hirohito contingent, who invited a select few of us to their New Year's party that was a regular orgy. Redheads are unusual and highly regarded there, and Deni wound up as the centerpiece. It took her a couple of days to recover, but she was very enthusiastic about the experience, and recommended it to some of the other women in the embassy. I enjoyed my share, too, which involved three little second generation Japanese young ladies with remarkable flexibility and muscle control. That data I kept, but I did share my findings on the state of their embassy's security. It was so-so.

The ambassador at the time was Citizen Janine Maartens. Her assistant was Citizen Mark Webber. He was smaller and leaner than I, and his ancestry was more mixed and obvious than mine. It didn't affect him at all, as he had a solid psyche, but it did cause people to either underestimate him or try to intimidate him. I've never understood the need of people to do that. If you're good, you know it. If someone is better, you know it. Posturing won't change either one. If they really don't want you to know their capabilities, they'll stay quiet until you're overextended and then cut you off. Silly. None of the nations represented on Caledonia were at war, so why a dance over self-importance?

Citizen Webber gave me an excellent example of how to deal with such fools my first week there. I accompanied him to a meal at one of the nicer restaurants, to discuss some silliness with a UN dip from the European Union. He'd wanted to talk to Maartens. He got her assistant instead. He was annoyed, and Webber had to politely reassure him while brushing him off. That is an art. Really, though, we'd made it clear we were an independent system and didn't care what others thought. Continually rehashing it was annoying, though it did give us time to anticipate the pending war.

I was along unofficially as bodyguard. We don't let our Citizens wander around where they might get kidnapped or worse. We'd have to make examples of people if that happened, and we'd prefer to avoid that. Officially I was there as junior military attaché, not needed, but present at lunch before going elsewhere. I kept quiet and listened to the discussion, while watching for threats. Do you know how many potential threats are in a typical restaurant? I was hyperaware, and as we were seated, I made sure to get my back to a wall, facing the door, and checked pistol, extra magazines, sword, knife, dagger, grenades, retch gas and radio, all of it except my sword and pistol hidden inside my uniform. And this was in friendly territory. I understood now why we were assigned this duty. It developed a healthy paranoia.

Deputy Economics Advisor to the Ambassador to the Star Nation of Caledonia Ward McLachlan was pushy, as were all the other UN dips elsewhere, trying to get some kind of leverage over us. He shook hands with Webber, nodded to me as a mere formality and accompanied it with a sniff, and sat down first. As ordered, I said nothing and kept the insult from showing by looking around the Aristocrat Pub.

The decor was antique without being kitsch, with old news-papers, banners and select advertisements mounted on the walls. The paneling was real wood, as expected in remote systems, and was a decent mock of Earth cherrywood. I made another scan for threats and turned back around in time to order baked fish with white sauce and a chocolate cake dessert with all the extras.

McLachlan pretended I didn't exist. He was a weaselfaced, soft little troll and had a whiny voice. Not that there was anything wrong with the voice, just with his inflection and attitude. He had the classic neofeudalist blame-everyone-else-for-my-problems mindset. I detest it. It's gutless and pathetic. Don't whine to me that you'd be better off dead, because I'll give you the chance to compare.

Sadly, I couldn't bump him off here. All I could do was listen to his gripes about "concentrating money in the hands of the wealthy" (that's what makes them wealthy. They exist in every society. Deal with it) and "not giving the people their basic right to franchise" (we don't have elections in the Freehold because we don't need them. Do whatever the hell you want. If you actually hurt someone else, they'll sue. If you're crazy enough and rich enough to want to rule, we'll take your money and let you. What idiotic process makes it *easy* for people to run other people's lives?).

He wouldn't shut up about it, either. For an alleged economist, he seemed to avoid money, probably because he had no clue how to actually handle it, and concentrate on that soundbite that the Freehold denies people the "right" to vote. Again, why would anyone let morons of unproven ability have a say in the government?

I took notes from Webber. He was a genius. To Ward's unend-ing complaints, he replied, "It's interesting that your officials are elected to be representatives of the population, rather than chosen in a strict meritocratic fashion." I almost choked on my only glass of wine.

"Yes, isn't it?" replied McLachlan with a beaming smile. He'd missed the insult totally.

We turned our attention back to our meals, and it was halfway through dessert before the glimmer of awareness seeped into his brain. Moron. We didn't discuss any further UN hegemonic stupidity. He felt insulted at last, and dropped the issue. We finished in near silence, frostily said our goodbyes and left.

Within a week, we were in the Alsatian embassy as escorts for our ambassador, Citizen Maartens. We accompanied her gracefully, Captain Carvalho as senior was her official escort, and the rest of us milled around and socialized with the guards and attachés from other nations. We would be seeing much of each other that week, as it was Landing Festival in Caledonia.

The Alsatians in general strike me as snobbish. For example, while we were never seated at the head table at a function, it was a bit annoying to be considered background. And the correct etiquette in their culture is to ignore the servers, just pretend they don't exist. It strikes me as rude, but when in Rome and all that. I prefer to speak to the help when I can. One can acquire much additional intel that way.

The next night we visited Novaja Rossia, who prepared a wonderfully tart roast beef, pies, and heavy pastry. They drank vodka by the liter. The bread was black and heavy, the caviar black and salty and the beer black and bitter. I could barely move after it all. We toasted to them, they to us and both of us all around. It was considered rude to stay sober. I was very polite.

After that, the Prime Minister of Caledonia had us in for a real treat: curried yearling elk shanks and pears. He personally struck me as a rabbit, wincing and edging away from us military types, including his own troops. His cook however, was a genius. The creamed banana trifle was cloyingly sweet and refreshingly mild at the same time, and their beer was a fine ale. We toasted the Queen, the Crown Princess, the Royal Family, and the Royal Military. They didn't drink as much as the Novajas.

Things were tense late in the evening, presaging something interesting. Shortly, the Crown Princess arrived. Her guard detail looked picturesque in their archaic uniforms, but I recognized their motions and coordination as professional. They were not recruited for their looks alone. A receiving line was formed for the official personages, while we goon types stayed back and sized each other up as potential threats. There were definitely some competent people there among the uniforms, but unless someone could act harmless better than we, my compatriots and I were the deadliest creatures within reach. I didn't rule out the possibility of a good actor, though.

Crown Princess Annette is more sophisticated and wise than anyone has ever given her credit for in the press. She'll make a great queen someday. She made a point of spending a brief time in conversation with each of the Freeholders. I kept an eye out and followed her movements, and turned as she approached. As soon as we made eye contact, I bowed gallantly. As a foreign soldier under arms—we were all wearing swords and sidearms—I was not required to bow, but a courteous nod seemed appropriate as a diplomatic courtesy and I had orders to that effect.

"Your Highness," I said, smiling politely. She extended a hand and I shook it firmly but not excessively. She was sixteen of our years old or twenty-four standard, neatly built, attractive without being glamorous or overdone and very poised and controlled.

"Corporal . . . ?" she hinted.

"Chinran. Kenneth Chinran, Madam," I replied.

"It is 'corporal,' then?" she asked, leaning slightly closer, tilting her head and lowering her voice. "Not Operative?"

I kept my face straight, and replied, "Corporal will do, Madam."

"You aren't denying the other, though," she noted. This was a bit disconcerting. We stared for a few seconds, each gauging the other. She resumed, "Perhaps I should mention that I did an exchange tour with Second Mobile Assault Regiment. I hold a cornet's commission in aviation support."

I knew that. Apparently, she'd heard at least rumors. I made notes. I knew she knew I was making notes. And if she knew that . . .

Okay, that type of reasoning is silly. This was a hint, and I needed to decide if it was something for me to deal with or to relay higher up. "If you need the services of an Operative, Madam, I'm sure the Freehold could arrange it." This was dangerous, but I couldn't brush her off without looking like a junior level flunky, which I was, granted, but I wasn't going to look like one.

"If it ever becomes necessary, I'll keep that in mind . . . Corporal," she replied with a bare wink and emphasis on "Corporal."

Okay, so she knew, and wanted us to. I'd relay that.

She continued, less intensely, "And what do you think of the food?"

"Excellent, Madam," I replied. "The pear was an unexpected touch. I hope you'll be joining us later in the week?"

"I plan to. I admire the efficiency of your cooking," she said. It begged the question.

"Yes, Madam?" I replied.

"Because you use enough spice that the food cooks itself." She delivered it deadpan. We stared, waiting to see who would crack. I could have held longer, but this wasn't a negotiation. I laughed heartily.

We spoke for a few more seconds, then she said, "I must greet the other guests. Please enjoy the party."

"Than you, Madam," I said, bowing. "I will." A truly fascinating young woman.

The Ramadanians served a tasty lamb with mint sauce and sekanjabin to drink. Grape leaf salad and delicately seasoned rice added to it. Jellied rose petals for dessert was a new treat I'll never forget, and I buy it in boxloads whenever I can find it. It's great for scoring women, too. There was no alcohol of course, but the food was delicious.

We removed our boots as we entered the embassy of Hirohito. It wasn't required, but they were appreciative of our respect to their customs. The chefs were delighted to have an appreciative audience, and served the more daring of us smoked tuna and raw squid sashimi. Fantastic! The mere sight of dead animals made the effete snobs from Earth run for the restroom to heave. Rabbits. The sake was the best, too. For some odd reason, they served tequila in broad variety. Good tequila, not the stuff you buy in stores, ranks up there with Silver Birch and old Scottish Talisker. Really. That was a great subject of conversation that kept me distracted until it was time to leave. I got little intel.

In response, we had invited the lot over for good Freehold food. We served an appetizer of jalapeno mango-lime ice, vinegar steamed crab legs and spinach salad with asiago garlic dressing. After flat bread and crusty bread with herbed honey-butter, we started on the entrée: peppercorn and garlic crusted prime rib au jus, crisp and dark outside, red and juicy inside with chilied and gingered peaches, minted baby potatoes, and steamed fresh green beans with onion, mushroom and bacon crumbles. It was *real* beef, from a cow, not that vat raised stuff. A few were bothered by that, but the taste is worth it. The side dish was jalapeno chicken salad with lime wedges, and fresh cilantro and chili salsa with cheese stuffed into jalapeno shells. There was a side of satan pepper salsa for the adventuresome. We had rich red peppered ginger beer and garlic wine to wash it all down. The tears in their eyes I assume were of joy. We took a break with thick dark chocolate and sub-zero Silver Birch. Jhondo's Raspberry Mead with the vanilla bean and chocolate layered cheesecake was a hearty cap to it all.

By the end of the week, our "souvenir" photos of all the embassies yielded a wealth of intel. That everything would shortly change to account for them was irrelevant; our unofficial photos and observations also boosted the data. Each of us had at least once gotten "lost" while slightly drunk, and wandered into less public areas of the embassies and residences for a peek. It was all part of the game. I loved it. It was one of the most pleasant aspects of the job, while still holding a challenge.

I had mentioned the conversations with Princess Annette to the chain of command. Captain Carvalho took notes and nodded, thanked and dismissed me. It was the week after all the pomp that I got a message to meet with her. Carvalho informed me, "She wants to discuss Operative training and operations." He briefed me as to what I could and could not discuss, told me to do a good job, and sent me out.

I dressed in Class A, not mess dress, and was driven to Park Royal. Most of it is open to the public, but some sections are reserved. Those had been swept for bugs, I was sure, by the Lifeguards. It was possible her own people were spying, and that was assumed for intelligence sake. What we wanted was to avoid casual third parties from snooping.

I walked in through an amazing rose garden that must have more staff just to maintain it than most embassies. She was waiting, in uniform, near a thick hedge. "Operative Chinran," she greeted me, extending a hand.

I bowed briefly, shook hands, and replied, "Under these circumstances, yes, Madam," I replied.

"Cornet Stewart will suffice," she replied.

"Very well, ma'am," I agreed. We sat on a bench near a display of annuals in a riot of reds, yellows and violets, and led into the subject of covert operations.

"Have you had the opportunity to work with our SAS teams yet?" she asked.

"No, ma'am, but I'm eager to if we get the chance," I replied. I wasn't to discuss particular operations. We'd had very few real engagements, and didn't want anyone to consider our actual capabilities. "I did train with the Chersonesi at their ACAC," I replied.

"My brother James went there," she commented. I knew that. "What did you think of the course?"

This I could discuss. "Excellent technical training, sufficient rehearsal, adequate physical training, adequate shooting," I replied.

"Adequate," she noted. "You shoot more then?"

"More than our regular troops," I admitted.

"That's an expensive ammo budget," she said.

I said, "Cheaper than replacing troops, by any accounting."

"True." There was brief silence. "Tell me of your training. Your personal impressions, not the technical details."

I did, and she asked questions. Only twice did I have to say, "I'm sorry, Madam, but I cannot discuss that."

A lunch was brought, light sandwiches with hot mustard on the side for my benefit. I prefer peppers to mustard, but can eat anything.

Within two days there was a tabloid station with a load headlined, "PRINCESS ANNIE BEING COURTED BY FREEHOLD CORPORAL?" That wasn't good. Not only was I ribbed over it, we had to consider if it was just a snoopy cameraperson, or if there had been spying. Video would allow lipreading, and would give away our discussion. The picture of me was grainy, distant and from a bad angle fortunately. It's impossible to stop all photos, we simply try to minimize publicity. It revealed nothing that we weren't sure was already common knowledge in the spook community.

A week later I got tasked with an . . . interesting gig. I'm sure I'm not supposed to discuss it, but I don't see what it matters after all this time. Anyway, it's not hard to figure out and I'll leave the details hazy.

Captain Carvalho called me into his office. I reported and he asked, "Ken, can you handle another mission, late tonight?"

"Sure," I replied. He could order me, of course, but it wouldn't be necessary. I always volunteered.

"Good," he said. "We had an abrupt schedule change. You're going with me."

"Yes, sir," I agreed. Going where? I didn't ask, because I figured he'd tell me.

But first, we got dressed in local clothes, bought used by our Special Projects' network. We had false ID, local cash and a few accoutrements to make us blend in. "No weapons," he told me.

Wow. When Operatives don't carry weapons, it means things are *very* important. "Okay, sir," I agreed. This was definitely going to be a war story at some point.

Then he briefed me on what we were doing. "We're setting up a new cache of equipment for emergency response," he told me. "Most of the gear is already there. We're just adding a bit to it. You'll do the grunt work, I'll supervise and guard, and I'll help as needed. *Verstadt?*"

"*Oui,*" I agreed. He actually smiled. I think it was the first time I'd seen him do that.

"Good. Here's our gear. Sign here," he said, handing me a pad. I noted that it simply read, "Mission Essential Equipment Package Number X-247, Three Containers." I scrawled across the screen, he signed after me. There were no details as to content mentioned anywhere. The package was in three boxes. One was a crate that most likely contained four M-5 weapons and extra clips. The second was a commercial backpack stuffed full of what felt like local clothes, body armor and accessories, probably including some basic ID with holos of generic-looking blonds, brunets and redheads that would serve to get any Operative past most cursory checks while he arranged for better ones. And the third one . . .

I recognized the container. I'd dealt with them during training. It was a crated Q-36 Explosive, Special, Medium. They're designed to take out dams, headquarters, major transport junctions and similar targets.

I had just signed for a nuclear weapon.

Well, it was only a small one.

Out the back we went, me lugging the Q-36 and backpack, he with the weapon crate. We ducked through the trees that are carefully maintained on the Embassy grounds for their green prettiness and their effect as concealment. There, along the wall, leaned a ladder that been thoughtfully placed by one of the guards, who sat nearby with a carbine to ensure only we used it.

It was a warm, dry night, the air rather fresh. Despite the heavy load, I felt great physically, and bouncy-nervous from the mission. Carvalho climbed the ladder silently, the steps having been wrapped in tape to prevent clatter. I stretched out my ears and listened above the chitter of bugs and birds.

Car. Closing. Slowing. "Now," I heard and I tossed the backpack. He caught it and swung over. I dragged up the crated nuke and we muscled it across and down. Damned thing massed nearly fifty kilos with the shielding that reduced its trace, and was awkward to move.

"Hurry," he said, slipping down the wall with a thud. I scrambled over, dropped and rolled down the slight embankment into the drainage ditch behind the compound, getting scraped on the wall, an angry welt along my right arm. Then we had to clamber back up the other side, toss the gear into the trunk of a waiting ground car and pile in the back seat.

We'd scratched both the car and ourselves getting in. The driver, Sergeant Coonce, handed back a kit with bandages and disinfectant and we cleaned up the ones that showed actual blood. My arm was going to need nanos or else it would scab badly. "No sign of any pursuit," he said. He was one of the diplomatic drivers, trained to handle special circumstances.

"Good," Carvalho replied.

I don't know where we drove. I still don't. Not my worry. It was outside the capital about a local hour, in a remote spot. Some utility shed for power was our landmark. It was in a fenced off area. At the edge of that area was a treeline, then a farmer's field. We figured that treeline was safe from excavation until such time as the power grid underwent major changes. Any adjustment of property boundaries or easement access would register on our comms and to our staff tasked with such, and the cache would be relocated. For now, it would be here. And it might be here for fifty years. We had no plans to use the equipment in the immediate future. It's just something Operatives do wherever possible, so we have backup if we need it.

I did most of the digging, and it's not easy to do it with just a shovel and pick. I was soon sweaty and caked with dirt. I'd dig, flick the occasional bug off and occasionally sip at a bulb of "pop" I'd brought along that actually contained water. Soft drinks aren't good for one doing heavy work.

I was pondering the smell of the local earth, lower in minerals than what I was used to, when my spade struck something.

Carvalho said, "That's it. Now, find the lid."

I carefully scraped dirt away until I had a clear area about a meter square. It rose easily to my prying, and inside was similar packaging to what we carried. We replaced the older styled clothes and ID with the new kit, added the weapons to the one container already there, and topped it all off with the nuke. Or rather, bottomed it. We wanted that as deep as possible, even shielded as it was.

The hard part was covering everything back up. Dirt always mounds too high when replaced, then slumps as it compacts. Lacking power tools, we stomped it as hard as we could after each layer, and carefully replaced sod on top. This left us with a small pile of topsoil that we scattered around the area, trying hard not to damage local plants, trip over roots or get poked by branches. We were hurrying, because it was near dawn. We could see occasional flashes of gray against the black.

Coonce should be circling by soon, and since we only had shovels and one backpack to worry about now, we crawled to the road rather than risking him re-entering the access trail. He had to drive by twice, because there was some local wandering along behind him, refusing to pass even when he slowed down. He feigned a confused look, drove down to the next county road, came around the block and we jumped in.

Back at our compound, dawn well on its way, we timed our departure, rolled out of the slowed car through the passenger door, and he closed it with a burst of power and disappeared with the tools. We slipped through the trees, loving the dawn because the shadows would make us all but invisible, and were met by a ladder that mysteriously appeared from above.

Inside, showered, cleaned and dressed, we signed off on the comm that Item X-247 had been placed in secure storage.

No need to worry. We've never had trouble with Caledonia, and that package is still there.

But remember: if we ever *do* have problems, that package, and others like it, are still there.

It had to be related to the princess' interest that the Freehold got invited to send a team of "Operatives, or if Operatives are unavailable, an Embassy security detail" (sarcasm dripping from the screen) to a security exercise at Mountbatten Royal Space Force Base. Captain Carvalho called us in, warned us not to be caught being smartasses and sent us to have fun. Heeding his warning, we vowed not to get caught being smartasses.

We had a brief meeting with the exercise evaluators, who explained what we needed to know: comms would assess damage from photos of any area we attacked, and for safety reasons, we had to preface our activities over the commo systems with the phrase, "Exercise Transmission." They said a bunch of other stuff, too, but it wasn't important, so we didn't listen. We took the credchit ("bank card") they gave us, converted the amount of the budget to cash and returned it. They had no need to know what we were buying.

We got a car with most of it, along with enough parts to rig up six satchels of improvised explosive simulators and a couple of "missiles." I acquired a black-market weapon. (Sales are all registered, but for a small premium of 50%, one may buy a new pistol not far from the spaceport. They come in by the shipload, as they do anywhere the local rulers utter magic incantations to keep them out. Never let your religious beliefs get in the way of the law of supply and demand.) It was a decent one: an H&K A6 with two spare forty-round magazines. Our point here was to show that we used only locally procured assets. We expressed that we'd be ready for the exercise, and got a good day's sleep. That night, we hit the clubs and picked a few IDs from people's pockets. It doesn't take long to decode the PIN numbers from them and change a photo, and most people would assume they'd left the wallet somewhere and not panic. We did return one "lost" one to a sergeant who might notice his £500 missing, but the others were all low amounts. We'd return them after the fact. Deni wanted to keep the cash as our bonus. I said no.

We did nothing to them that Friday daytime. Why would we start off by being predictable? We waited until after normal duty hours, when everyone was getting ready for the weekend.

We had no trouble getting on base. We didn't expect to. Frank got hired two days before as a restaurant delivery driver and drove through the gate in his company shirt and hat, iridescent logo on the side of the vehicle, with a cheery wave to the gate guards. Tyler and I went under the fence at a remote part of the perimeter around noon, crawled through the brambles until we hit the perimeter road about "Six o'clock," then changed, cleaned up with wipes and became joggers with day packs. We crossed from there to the inner part of the base across the flight line, spending a few seconds pretending to be lovers for the benefit of a passing patrol. She's not a bad kisser, if awkwardly short for my taste. The car floated by, occupants grinning, and we smiled back. In another few moments we were near the central power plant. It had been a long day already, and we hadn't even got to work yet.

Shutting down a reactor is easy. Warming them up is hard. Our attack was obvious. We changed behind a loading ramp into uniforms bought at a surplus store, with me as a corporal, Tyler as a lance. There was an extra guard detail outside the plant, but no warnings of attack had come over the net yet, so they weren't really worried. The four of them were joking and goofing. We walked up with our packs and joined them.

"Hey, fellas," I said in my best Skye accent. "Worrup?"

One of them, a corporal, replied, "Norra bluhdy thing, mate. C'I 'elp ya?" (Okay, I'll use standard words from now on, because the accents were atrocious).

"Oh, we're just here to see Frank," I said. "He told me you blokes were stuck with your thumbs up your arses for the duration."

"Too bloody right we are," he agreed. "There's supposed to be five wannabe aggressors from the Freehold Embassy coming in," he said, eyes rolling in exaggerated disgust. "As if they're gonna wind up 'ere."

As he talked, I pulled bulbs of Loma Cola out of my pack. "Well, until you can have a beer, then," I said as I handed them over.

"Why! That's decent of you, chap!" he said. They passed them around, opened them and tipped the bulbs to us. We started to walk past. "Oh! You need to sign in," he said.

"No problem," I agreed. There was a roster tacked to the window with a scanner next to it, and we both swiped our cards and signed fake names. I signed mine with a sloppy, "U. R. Fuct," and as I expected, they didn't even check. Had they done so, I would have shrugged it off as a joke. Tyler signed too, and we headed inside.

We had no hassle at all. We nodded at a couple of techs while talking animatedly about power distribution, and they all assumed we belonged there. We had an unobstructed trip up the ladders and catwalks to the control room. That was the only place we had any challenge at all. We hid in the scaffolding at one side and changed shirts. They'd think four of us were here, when they figured it out at all.

The NCOIC was a burly, grizzled old sergeant. He cracked the door and looked as us suspiciously. I started with, "Evening, Sergeant. Leftenant Windle," as I flipped open my stolen ID pack to another card, "and this is Leftenant Rogers," I added, pointing at Tyler. "We've had an exercise warning and we thought we'd give you an 'eads up. Those bloody infiltrators are inside the fence already."

He checked the ID briefly. "Why didn't you call, Leftenant?" he asked.

A reasonable question deserves a reasonable answer. "They may have things tapped. Why let the buggers know we're going to pin them to the wall, eh?" I replied, and he chortled.

"Well, thanks, Leftenant," he said.

"No worries," I agreed. "Any chance of a gander at the plant while we're 'ere?" I asked.

"We really shouldn't at the moment," he said. "But give me a moment to clear it with the command post and I think we can, sir." He turned to his phone.

"I don't think that's necessary, Sergeant," I said. He turned to stare down the muzzle of the H&K.

"Bloody hell!" he replied as we pushed into the room. He recovered fast, and jumped for a warning button. So I shot him.

All we had were gooey simulation bullets, but they do hurt and he flinched. Before he recovered, Tyler was past me and pretzeled him to the ground. I didn't even see her snap on binders, but he was wearing them when she stepped back. His assistant was running toward me from the far side, and I had time to aim. I shot him in the belly and the balls and he didn't even put up a fight for some reason.

The sergeant had welts on his temple and neck and polymer stains on his shirt. I called it a kill and made a note into my comm as Tyler sprayed anesthetic down their throats. Couldn't have them yelling, after all.

This is why the FMF requires all soldiers to be armed at all times. A response is so much more effective if you actually have the tools to do something about the crisis.

We taped a note to the main monitor console that read, "This console has been destroyed by explosives. If you are reading this, you tripped another one as you came through the door. Please kiss your backside and consider yourself dead. NOTE: dead people do not call the command post to report that fact. Dead people do nothing but sit and bitch."

Tyler rigged a stun grenade on the door as our note suggested, and killed the troops' access to the comnet while I looked over the controls. They were similar enough to the consoles I trained on at Jefferson District Power Systems, and I killed the fuel flow and shut down the containment field.

Now we had to hurry. The guards outside would figure out

from the lights going off all around that something was wrong, and just might make the connection to those two friendly people in mufti. They'd be hard to argue with, especially after the Sparkle (a popular hallucinogen in the Freehold) that I'd laced the colas with kicked in. We changed shirts back to enlisted people, exited the control room, dropped down ladders, mostly avoiding the panicking crew, and headed for the front door.

We had one brief encounter that I used to spread further chaos. A corporal yelled at me, "What the hell happened to the controls?"

So I replied, "The controls are fine! I think we lost a bloody fuel feed on the second stage!" as we ran past. That would keep them busy looking in the wrong place.

We came out the front, sprinted across the street and through a parking lot to Hangar 1, and headed inside through the gathering crowd outside.

"What's going on?" and variations of it were all we heard. Tyler yelled, "Power fluctuation! We've got to get everything shut down before it comes back up, to prevent a surge and another failure!" It was pure BS, of course. Modern equipment is all protected against that, with delays on startup and comm lines to the power source. But it was believable to the ignorant, anyone who did know better would assume we were new troops who had our wires crossed and would be straightened out shortly, and it wouldn't hurt to do what we said, so they wouldn't be stopping us.

We ran down the corridor with our padded footsteps echoing off the sere walls, and tossed a couple of notices into the machine shop, the photo lab, and even into the hangar bay proper, under the nose of a Lionheart close-support vertol. They all read, "This is a 1 kilogram charge. Everything in a 30 meter radius must be run through the games comm to determine damage." We'd taken the offered transponders that simulated it directly to the comm, but added a few improvs so they wouldn't know how many charges we had. Yes, that information was supposed to be confidential to the referees, but let's be honest, they'd talk.

From there, we turned right into the front hallway, paused in the men's restroom (yes, segregated restrooms), to change into civvies again, and went out through the main doors (locked after hours, but you can always exit) and ran across another street, confident that we'd not been followed.

While we were doing this, Frank was having a ball.

He came zipping in and delivered a sandwich just before we took out the lights. As he left, he made use of the panic to run through the parking aprons around the hangars and drop "bombs" into the beds of a few trucks. They had triggers for both time and motion, and would start flashing a strobe and transponder to let people know they existed. He went right back out and grabbed another order, and came back to do it again. He made several runs that night. No one ever made the connection between the delivery truck and the bombs.

The power was out on his second run, and he was held at the gate for several minutes. He was just about to blow the gate and see what he could accomplish when they waved him through. This time, he detoured out to the end of the flightline, skipped past the warning lights and gates that blocked the road, and launched a home built "missile" at an incoming transport. A radio signal alerted the computer, and Landing Control was informed that the entire craft and occupants were casualties. He headed out and grabbed another order.

These pizzas were for the growing number of people in the Command Post and the surrounding offices. He had to stop and be searched four times, but his order was confirmed and delivered. They did not let him inside, but took it from him at the door at the top of the stairs to the basement. He made sure to tell them it was a special order and to be careful. On the way out, he left a couple of "mines" on the road. He had a quick meeting with Deni and Sergeant Coonce and swapped intel, then made yet another run. It was a busy night for him, and he made nearly £50 in tips.

Deni was being more down to earth. Specifically, she was crawling through mud at the edge of the base. The mud, the bugs, and the weeds, thorns and toxic plants were familiar, barring minor variations in planetary ecology. She managed to plant "charges" at the base of the fuel tanks, on the cryogenic fluid building, in one of the engine test cells (a flashbang which they wouldn't find for weeks. It was a souvenir for them), and around the edges of base housing. She then set up at the far end of the flightline from Frank, and caught a craft that was departing, with a laser designator. That caused the base security forces to respond in two different directions. Rather than stay around to admire her handiwork, she headed for the base comm center to raise more hell.

Sergeant Coonce was less subtle. He simply drove through the west gate. With no ID. At high speed. It took his pursuers some time to realize that he was ignoring all traffic niceties like signs, lights and roads. Then he led the security patrols around the base at a merry rate, crossed the flightline several times and caused several aborted launches while the computer calculated casualties for him. He turfed a few yards in base housing, ran through parking lots and across the parade field, and even crashed through the tennis courts. Since he didn't care about the car's survival, he was hard to predict. A large number of troops were busy chasing him at the moment Frank and Deni "brought down" the transports. Those troops scattered in several directions in a disorganized response, which left him to lose the last two pursuers, drive to the base hospital and wreak havoc there before adding to the carnage near operations. He drove and ran around planting "bombs" anywhere that looked interesting, and even got into the fire station after they were called out. He used a spare crew truck and rescue gear as cover to go back into the power station and bring it down a second time.

Back to us: Across the street from Hangar One was the headquarters building. The command post was in the basement, triple locked and ID required to enter. That was the obvious target, but we weren't falling for the obvious. Several other people in civvies were running in from all angles (that's one reason to choose after standard hours for an attack), and no one questioned us. Even our packs went unnoticed—others had comms, water bottles, and other accessories.

I turned and ran upstairs, avoiding the cameras and logs on the elevators. Tyler kept going through the building, out the other side and on to create more mayhem in the barracks area on her way to the control tower. My goal was an office on the third floor. It was easy to see, as this building had an emergency generator and it had kicked in already, so there was adequate light. I pulled a lock coder out of my ruck, which was bouncing in time to my steps, and managed to have it ready as I arrived at the door in question. I stuck it in the lock, told it to go, and hoped it worked. I could kick the door open, but that would make the rest of the op tougher.

The lock clicked, and I walked in. It was dark inside, and I let it stay that way. I retrieved the coder and closed the door, which bore a sign that read, "Brigadier Peter McAran, Wing Commander." I slipped behind a couch. It was a nice office—plush and nicely appointed, as they say. Real wood desk, leather chair, clean-smelling carpet with the wing logo stitched into it. I would be comfortable here, for as long as it took. Windows on only one wall, I noted with approval.

If I was correct, I wouldn't be waiting long. I was correct. Or rather, our intel had been.

Barely two segs had gone by before there were steps from the elevator, shuffling and rustling outside, and the door opened. "Come in, Ladies, Gentlemen," I heard the brigadier say. "I'll be right with you."

I waited just a moment while listening for my cue. That was it: They were all in the sitting area in front of me. I braced my feet, kicked the couch, and sent it tumbling into the legs of his escort. I stood, took aim, and began firing as I moved sideways. There were seven of them. Two of them were the Brigadier's security detail.

My weapon coughed twice, and yelps and shrieks rewarded me. In a second, I had the brigadier by the throat, kicked his feet from under him, and shackled him before he could put up much of a struggle. "You two are dead, so sit down and don't move," I ordered his security goons.

One dedicated bright boy didn't believe me and tried to stand, so I shot him in the forehead. His eyes unfocused and he went down. The other decided to take me seriously. I shackled them by their hands, back to back, and stuffed them against the wall. I now had their pistols, too.

Turning back, I said, "Good evening, Brigadier. I hope you don't mind if I join your tête-á-tête for the evening?" in syrupy tones.

"I apparently don't have a choice, do I, sir?" he replied.

"Not really," I said. "And please don't call me 'sir.' My parents are married."

He actually chuckled at that. Good. The others were looking absolutely murderous up to that point.

I heaved him into his swivel chair, pulled him away from the desk and lashed his bound hands to the bar in back. While I did that, another genius made a break for it. I swung my hands up, calmly took aim as he clutched at the doorplate, and caught him in the neck. He went down.

"Everyone lie face down, arms and legs spread," I ordered. The goat dance during survival training now made sense. I was alone against seven, well, four now, and would have to deal with it.

First I shackled their hands. Then I hobbled their feet so they could walk only in a shuffle. Then I searched them. Apparently, that was not regarded as proper.

Perhaps it was because I used FMF, that is to say, "real" rules. I *searched* them. I clutched crotches, ran fingers through hair, pulled off belts and shoes and tossed them into a heap, emptied out pockets. I was quick, thorough and professional. The only voiced complaints came when I searched the sole woman present, a Major Josephine Hardy, Base Public Affairs Officer. Predictably, the complaints came from the men.

"Is it really necessary to paw the lady, mister whatever-the-bloody-hell-your-name-is?" Colonel Popejoy, Air Base Group Commander asked.

"I'm not 'pawing the lady,'" I replied reasonably as I stuck a hand up her skirt. Lace panties, thigh stockings, no weapons. "I'm 'searching the major for anything that might be a threat,'" I explained as I ran hands around the waistband then clutched at her chest. "If I were to say, 'nice tits,' or, 'padded bra, what a shame,' that would indicate pawing. But since what I'm going to say is, 'I have no problem with the bra, Major, and don't find any weapons, but the stockings might be used to strangle me, so I'm going to have to have them,' it's just a search."

She replied with a faint flush of embarrassment, but gamely recovered with, "I don't normally do that without an intro- duction and dinner first, but I don't suppose I have a choice, do I?"

"No, lady," I replied. I snicked them with a knife and peeled them open to her ankles, then ripped the tattered remains off. Being a professional, I did *not* waste time sneaking a peak at her daintier regions. I had three other hostages to watch, and three non-corpses who might get up and walk. I pondered wooden stakes. Maybe you think I overreacted, but by sliding gently back and forth, one can slip stockings off the legs. Even shackled, a good yank to each would tear them loose and yield the equivalent of two meter-long elastic ropes.

The keys, pocketknives, tools, shoes (and laces), belts, and stock- ings all wound up dropped outside a window that opened onto the roof, along with comms. I sealed it again and turned back to my prisoners. Elapsed time, 200 seconds. The only weapons left to them were their bodies, a few books, and some commo cables I'd missed earlier. I ripped those last out of the walls and coiled them up. They'd be easy to fix after the fact, and disabled his controls now. I didn't really need updates as a "terrorist," as I was just trying to cause trouble. I'd be tied up here, and we weren't going to use radios much, except to jam and spread disinformation. "I won't cut out any implanted phones if you all agree not to use them," I said, waving the knife. "Deal?" They all nodded worried assent.

"What now?" the brigadier asked.

"Now we wait. Your people are in a hurry to stop things. Mine aren't," I said.

So we sat. I wouldn't let them talk to each other, and wasn't going to let them talk to me. That made it much harder for them to get any intelligence, other than my description and weapons. It was near an hour local time, more than thirty segs, before anyone figured out that the Brigadier hadn't been heard from nor yet come down to the CP, and called up to the office on the only line I'd left. I held the headset up for him. "Brigadier McAran," he answered. I kept the speaker on and my pistol to his head as the conversation started.

"Sir! We have more attacks across the base! What do you want us to do? Er, Exercise Transmission," someone screeched.

Carefully eyeballing my pistol, he replied, "Exercise Transmission. Give me a detailed sitrep, if you please, colonel," he replied.

"Exercise Transmission. It's all on your screen, sir. I expected you'd be in the command post by now."

"Exercise Transmission. I'm afraid I can't make it at the moment," he replied. "And my comm isn't showing that data. If you could send Data Systems Squadron to look at it, AND A SECURITY TEAM NOW! ONE TERRORIST—"

I cut him off by yanking the headset and shoving his chair over backwards. He hit his head and lay stunned while I spoke into the mic. "Now listen to me, 'colonel.' Exercise Transmission. This is the Committee for Utilizing Natural Terrain for Spiritualism," I said with a straight face. "We are holding your imperialist dogs hostage."

"Er . . . very well. And who are you, sir?" he asked. I heard hubbub behind him.

"I am the Great Druid of CUNTS," I replied. There was a moment's absolute silence.

"You've got to be bloody joking," was the reply.

"Exercise Transmission," I replied, according to their rules. "If you think I'm joking, I can start by killing Major Hardy."

There was more confusion. Eventually, I heard, "That won't be necessary, sir. And what does . . . your organization . . . want us to do?"

"Our list of demands will be revealed in due time. In the meantime, if you want to see your general alive again, it will cost you," I continued.

"And what will it cost us?" he inquired.

"CUNTS needs a thick, forty-five-centimeter Italian sausage," I said.

"A WHAT?" he asked.

"Pizza, you moron! From Ansatos," I said and slapped off the phone.

Nothing would happen for several minutes, I figured. I said to McAran, "Real World, sir. Do you need help?"

"If you could sit me back up, I'd appreciate it," he said, shaking off the dizzies. "You play rough, sir, er, Sergeant?"

"Not as rough as a real terrorist," I reminded him with a waggle of the pistol. I didn't answer his question.

"True."

There were chuckles at the exchange over the phone. "Was that improv, sergeant?" Major Hardy asked. She looked faintly embarrassed, probably at being amused in so crude a fashion. I actually looked her over now. About 25 by our reckoning, late 30s Earth years, neck length blonde hair. Her build was decent, and her eyes were brown but bright. No wedding ring. She must have been preparing for a date, as she was moderately made up. So her evening was shot to hell.

"I have a list of groups to use," I admitted. "It's always a better exercise with mischievous fun and misdirection mixed in."

" 'Better' for whom?" Popejoy asked.

"For me, of course," I said.

The phone rang again. "Yes?" I said as I answered it. The Brigadier wouldn't be speaking again.

"We'll order that pizza shortly. In the meantime, it would show good faith if you could release one of the hostages," he said. Step 1: try to negotiate.

"And why would I do a stupid thing like that?" I asked.

"Please, sir. People are scared—"

"They should be scared. CUNTS are not being allowed to act as nature demands," I said.

He strangled on that, then continued, "But if we are to give you something, we need something in return. Perhaps if Major Hardy could be released . . . ?"

"Why Major Hardy? She's a public affairs officer. I wouldn't want a professional speaker on camera saying bad things about CUNTS. I'm not even sure she knows anything about CUNTS." The look on Hardy's face indicated she was about to wet herself laughing.

"Sir, please . . . she's the only woman . . ."

"Ah, so that's it," I replied. "And what if I want to keep her here? Why is she more valuable to you as a woman? I thought she was just another officer. Yes, I think I will keep her here," I said as I scrawled a message on a notepad from the brigadier's desk. It read, "You are being abused, scream in pain, please." I showed it to her.

All of my "prisoners" were starting to get into the act. I held up the mic and she screamed to shatter wineglasses, with plenty of white noise that had to hurt her vocal cords. It was brilliant.

Into the ringing silence, I said, "This has been an Exercise Transmission," and disconnected.

They called right back. "Yes?" I said.

"Please, sir, we believe you. We'll have that pizza there in an hour," he said.

"Delivery time is twenty minutes. Send the driver right up with no delay," I demanded. "And that attempt to stall is going to cost you. The price for the Brigadier just went up. Make that two pizzas. And drinks. No diet drinks with that fake levosugar or I kill someone."

They conferred. "Very well, sir," they said. I disconnected.

We stared at each other. I went back to being a silent hardass. The CP called back twenty-five minutes later. "Yes?" I answered.

"The driver is on his way now," I was told.

"Good. He comes in alone, he goes out alone. Anyone tries anything funny, and I kill him along with the hostages here, as well as any of your goons who are in range of the bomb or the nerve agent," I said.

I heard outraged yells behind the speaker. I hadn't mentioned any bomb, so they hadn't thought to plan for it. They didn't need to—I didn't have one. But they should have considered it.

I heard rapid, frantic yells as they aborted whatever entry team had been preparing to come in shooting. They had less than five minutes, had told me the driver was coming, and couldn't stall now without making it obvious they were trying something.

I laughed at them and disconnected.

A knock on the door was followed by a loud voice saying, "Ansatos. I have a large, thick, hot, spicy sausage."

"Come on in, Frank," I said.

There were groans from my captives. They were utterly

dumbfounded at there being another one of us. The groans changed to smiles when we unshackled them and dished up pizza all around, with drinks. There were coffee and donuts for later. I made them feed the security detail though; I wasn't about to unshackle those gung ho clowns.

We made it clear that trying anything funny would get them shot and shackled and starved for the duration. Then Frank and I emptied out his pizza bag of tools and went to work on the Brigadier's safe, bypassing the primary lock and forcing his eyeballs up to the scanner, after reminding him that a real terrorist could gouge them out and use them before they cooled. He gave us no trouble.

We got a good photo of me sitting arm in arm with the Brigadier, big grins on our faces, although his was a bit forced, the safe open behind us, and the cover of a "MOST SECRET" document visible. They'd get that with my face blacked out. I'd keep a copy for bragging afterwards, then destroy it. Frank and I swapped updates, he left with the tools, the photos and McAran's hat as a souvenir, and the rest of us went back to waiting.

The next call had a different voice. "This is Major Malloy of the Security Squadron," he said. "I need to find out what your other demands are."

I knew he was planning something. "Where's that nice colonel I was talking to, Major? I'd much prefer to deal with him."

He paused before replying, "Colonel Cartwright is . . . indisposed. I'm afraid I'm in charge here now."

"Indisposed?" I replied. "Dear me, I hope he didn't ingest any psychoactives with the sandwich that was delivered one hour and twenty-three minutes ago."

Malloy squawked, swore, and disconnected.

I laughed at them again.

I spoke to the deputy center commander, who'd been reticent and calm for most of this. "Colonel Setzer, please consider yourself dead," I said. "Would you like the formality of me shooting you, or will you handle the simulation without it?"

"I think I can manage," he half smiled as he shrank back. He'd been observant, and was obviously still making notes. Clever man.

"Good."

We'd been at this four hours total when the newest corpse spoke. "Is there any way to get a latrine break?" he asked.

"Only if you can use the Brigadier's coffee pot," I replied.

I could see that the idea didn't appeal.

"Well, I will, then," I said. They stared at me dumbfounded as I put the pot on the ground behind the desk, sat on the spare chair, unhooked my pants, and began splashing into it. Their faces drained of color. It was the Brigadier's *coffee pot*. That was a sacred item on any base.

McAran said, "If I go next, Colonel, will that make it easier for you?"

The colonel looked ready to melt in embarassment. He was the only one who decided to hold it. Hardy excused herself to the corner, and I even decently turned away. She couldn't move from a squat without me reacting, anyway.

Of course, they did get me eventually. I was only one person, after all. My pocket beeped, and Tyler's voice said, "Watch it, Ken." We'd been saving the radios for necessity—the sooner we used them, the sooner they'd be jammed or used to track us.

I knew they were planning on coming in, and had to time my actions just right. I clicked back to acknowledge. "Brigadier, please come over to the couch," I said as I untied his hands from the chair again.

When the first faint rustles sounded through the windows, I sauntered over to the corner behind the Brigadier's desk. The others didn't notice it at first, but long silence had let them grow accustomed to the background noise so they noticed the difference. They tensed.

I Boosted. Everything quivered and focused, and I prepared to go balls out. The crash of the window breaking was my cue, and I ducked my head and clapped my ears. The actinic glare of a stun grenade punched me in the eyes, right through my lids and averted face, while the bang shook my brains in my head. My hair crackled from the static charge, but most of the neural effect was grounded by the desk. I had a couple of fingers tingling and a cold spot on my right heel.

But then I was up. A leap and a roll took me through the group of hostages, and I came up with an arm around Hardy. Always pick a female hostage—males are more reluctant to shoot in their direction.

I got three of the black-clad figures as they came through the window, then shot Popejoy, who was trying to help by jumping me. The newcomers spread out to get better angles at me, and I fired with impunity, while they held theirs. Then one of them made as to take a shot. I twisted and he got Hardy in the chest, just below my arm. She squealed and coughed and tried to swear. I dropped the "corpse," "killed" McAran and rolled away to come up in close quarters.

They hadn't expected that. With the pistol doing triple duty as a club and block, *I* charged *them*. I got one in the crotch hard enough to crack his cup, punched a female in both breasts hard enough to knock the wind out of her despite her body armor, fired off the rest of the magazine into two others, and yanked one down by the facemask until my knee smashed into his visor. He staggered back.

Then a blizzard of shots pummeled me cold. I went down still fighting.

I woke to a medic hovering over me. He was disheveled, and his helmet was next to me. "Are you okay, sir?" he asked.

I did a quick self-exam. "Other than bruises and rug burn, I'm fine," I assured him. The back of my scalp and between my shoulders would need nanos and local anesthetic; it was a mass of bruises.

"You are a crazy fucking bastard, sir," he said, shaking his head.

I was too light-headed to stand yet, so I stalled for time. "And how many of you are dead?" I asked.

"All seven hostages and five of twelve Entry Team members," he admitted. "And three others injured, for exercise purposes. One of those will need to be hospitalized real world for a bruised testicle."

"I must be slowing down in my old age," I replied.

"Cocky bastard, aren't you? Sir," he added.

"I think I've earned that right," I said. Damn, I hurt. I wasn't going to admit it, and I'd walk out unassisted in a few moments, but I hurt.

The debriefing was two days later, in the base theater. We showed them exactly what we'd done, none of which was particularly high-tech or difficult, and gave them a list of potential improvements. They were all sober, especially when the body count and property damage was assessed. We'd "killed" three hundred and forty-seven personnel, forty-six family members, "crashed" two incoming transports with another thousand plus people aboard, "destroyed" two shuttles, seven close support craft, tens of ground vehicles, hundreds of millions of pounds worth of equipment, and scrambled most of the comms and signal gear. (That was Tyler's doing, from the tower. Everything appeared to be working at first, so they'd never called up to find that the staff were trussed and gagged.) In all, we shut down the base for an entire day real world, for weeks as far as the exercise went.

There were five of us.

They didn't believe us.

Now, I've seen this before and since. The complaints are always that we "obviously are lying" about how few people there were, that we "broke the rules" of the exercise, that "the evaluators tell the aggressors exactly where everyone is to make it easy for them." Rabbits will come up with any excuse in the book rather than accept the three basic facts of the exercise, which are that 1) They're morons. B} They're ignorant, and iii: They're pathetically undertrained.

Don't get me wrong—there are always exceptional performers. But *as a whole*, most units stink. That's why they have huge casualties going in to an engagement—it takes time to shake down and learn to work as a good team. The whole point of such exercises is not to make the base look stupid, but to give them practice at dealing with events outside the expected norm. But they always take it as a personal affront, then try to deny the reality, and I don't know if they ever actually accept the lesson. But we'll keep trying. Even if they don't learn from such exercises, we do. We did. Look at us now.

The next stack of complaints was about our "recklessness." We should have warned them of the powerplant going down, in case they had problems with the backup generators at the hospital (which would have required generator testing that should have been done ahead of time and should always be current, and would have destroyed the whole element of surprise). We shouldn't have used hallucinogens because of the "danger" (Sparkle is sold commercially to any adult in the Freehold who wants to have an enhanced time. It is non-addictive, habit forming with repeated use only to those with weak and depressed personalities). We should have warned our targets that they'd need goggles against possible misaimed shots with my H&K. We shouldn't have gotten base housing involved because of the danger, or the flightline, or this, or that. Everyone seemed to think that they were exempt from attack due to their importance. We patiently tried to explain that that very importance *made* them targets. We were only partly successful. One lieutenant wanted us to "simulate" most of it, claiming that they would "act accordingly."

I told that officer that a placard on a soft drink machine marked, "Simulated unplugged," (as they'd done during the day Friday) was inadequate, and his people just weren't that good of actors. They were hitting the machine for drinks anyway. The whole point of such an exercise is to suffer the privations as one would in a real event.

The final review was in McAran's office. His unit commanders and the five of us met to do a detailed breakdown of what we'd seen. I won't bore you with it, but the beginning had a humorous note.

We were all greeted and seated. I asked my "victims" how they were doing, met Colonel Cartwright, who was very unhappy at being drugged with Sparkle, and made sure Major Hardy was okay after her experience of being nearly choked then shot in the chest. She seemed delighted by the whole affair, and urged the Brigadier to do more such training. Her only complaint seemed to be that she hadn't had a camera with her to record the whole event. I politely explained that any camera pointed in the direction of a "Blazer" would be vaporized, and the holder thereof also if we were rushed.

They served coffee, and started with me, as I was front row and right side. I don't like coffee, but we try to always be polite. I took a sip from the cup, decided it wasn't too hot, then took a gulp. McAran addressed me, "Corporal Chinran, how did you know I had the coffeepot cleaned since our little encounter the other day?" He had a nasty grin on his face.

I kept a bored look on my face and replied, "I didn't."

The looks on the faces of seven people in that room were priceless.

At the end, we shook hands all around and made nice. Major Hardy gave me a smile with a glint behind it. I don't know. I didn't have time to follow up then, and was nervous about the prospect of offending a foreign officer, and I still wonder. Was it just amusement and mannerism? Or was she hinting at a game of good kidnapper/bad kidnapper to be played out in a hotel suite?

Probably not. But it's a nice thought. And I need nice thoughts now.

Shortly before we left Caledonia, the Charles River flooded over its banks and threatened millions of hectares of crops and several towns. We volunteered as a gesture of international goodwill, and also got a look at their Home Guard troops, equivalent to our Professional Militias or Reserves. They were eager, fairly competent, and were good company in the wet and cold. It was quite an impressive flood, and it's no fault of the participants that they couldn't control it. Nature will always win. We spent a thirty day month getting soaked and chilled, then alternately baked in what passed for summer sun. All in all, I'd have to call it a good time and an educational peacetime deployment.

CHAPTER 5

Upon returning home and debriefing, I was promoted to Operative Sergeant and made team leader, and bumped to E-6. Likely, I'd stay Sergeant for some time, and get rate promotions based on time in service and technical proficiency. I wasn't worried. With space pay, jump pay, flight pay, demolition pay, the stipend we all got for being Operatives in the first place, the stipend for each language and skill we qualified for (I was qualified as a combat medic, combat marksman, combat engineer in construction and demolitions, translator in French, Russian, Greek and Spanish, intelligence specialist in security assessment, power and electrical systems specialist, welder with gas, arc, laser and electron beam, machinist, basic electronics technician, small arms repairer, heavy weapons crew, flight engineer (vertol and spaceboat), hazardous environment rescue specialist, perimeter defense security specialist, aircraft munitions specialist, explosive ordnance disposal specialist, and had master ratings in unarmed combat, small arms, support weapons, heavy weapons and vehicle operations), I figured I was earning enough to make even my father happy. Much of it counted as practical or elective credit toward the degree in Military Science I was working on. All I needed were a few courses in poli-sci, history and strategic calculus and

I'd be good to go. From there, I could go as far as regimental commander, with work.

That was before I learned the politics of the military. Every new troop has to do this, and I had actually been rather sheltered by the system so far, more concerned with the job than with the machinations behind it. That's generally a good thing, but those networks of friends and a good grasp of the unofficial military are what will get you ahead and help you do what's right for the service. It can also be used by self-serving assholes to get cushy jobs and bogus awards. That, of course, would never happen in our military, right?

I'll come back to that later.

Let's look at the key facts: we were a neutral nation with a small military. Until a decade before, the military had been mostly a joke. It handled a few rescues of idiotic sillyvilian pleasure craft, and was strictly a symbol of our statehood, despite the quality of the troops we had. We could hold off pirates, few that there were, maintain local order (very important and, defined by our constitution, it was our primary purpose), and tackle major terrorists that tried to get happy with us. If we needed real backup, we would have called the UN for force.

Then we'd declared ourselves a nation, not a colonial territory. Then we'd seceded from the UN, because we couldn't meet their "civil rights" criteria, and had no intention of doing so. Their definition of civil rights was what the Roman Legions gave their subjects—the right to complain, pray, and do nothing. We defined freedom as the right to be stupid. If you aren't allowed to ruin your life because of the "greater good of the whole," you aren't really free, you're a cog. But I digress.

With no UN support, we had to have a military that actually worked. First, we'd gotten better hardware. Then, we'd upped the standards for enlistment. Now we were working on increasing the size, but slowly, as we had no wish to sacrifice quality. Lastly, we wanted to ensure that everyone did a stint in a combat zone, for the experience.

That last being absolutely impossible for a neutral nation amidst an authoritarian hegemony. Who was going to attack us? Why would we go on the offensive? We had great troops, great equipment, great standards, and absolutely no way to ensure any of it.

Then, the year before I enlisted, Dyson had been made Marshal. He had strict notions of how we could get as good as we could without live-fire, and proceeded to institute those policies, despite the whining of the wannabes who really didn't want to be real soldiers.

Many of those whiners were still in service, even ten years after we seceded. Amazingly, we even had some in Special Warfare. I have no idea why someone joins SW and expects an easy time of it, but for some ludicrous reason, a few do. They took it upon themselves to commwhip every exercise and qualification they could, so as to sit, drink chocolate, and revel in the glory of their qualification badges. It bothered Marshal Dyson, and it bothered me, that their actions were identical to developing nation dictators and their Instant Colonel Syndrome—you know: where junior grade friends of the Faithless and Fearful Leader become commanders without doing anything to prove themselves.

They had to go. They'd done nothing actionable, and we needed the slots filled until we got competent personnel so they stayed in the interim, but their days were numbered. It took a few months for me to realize that I could have one of those slots, with a little patience, hard work and a few liters of spilled blood. The blood would be my own, spilled here and there in training exercises. The actual coup and assassinations would be bloodless and political.

Everyone in SW is in great shape. I'd actually come to terms with the fact that I'm a handsome son of a bitch in dress greens, no matter how goofy I look in battledress. I took it upon myself to be seen in greens off duty, or when on duty doing administrative work, so as to impress Captain Maron, the commanders of the units we were assigned to, and anyone on base who encountered me. Both my awards were placed, all my qualification badges were polished, and I cultivated a look of deep thought and alertness.

It worked. Maron was in the area late one day, as I prepped my team for our next exercise, and watched quietly as I spoke. We both knew we were aware of each other's presence, but pretended to continue business as usual. I had everyone's chameleon suits out, as we'd never used them in an exercise. I intended to fix that, and not because it was a good way to suck up, but because it needed done. We ran all the circuits through, tested them against a background screen and the local terrain of grass, buildings and parking apron, and I told everyone to put them away. I planned to brace our squad leader, Warrant Rutledge, to let me do a team run in a day or two. He was one of those who didn't see a need to do more than the basics. He thought of all this as "wasting time."

Once done, I told the troops to hang them in our bay area and dog off for the day. I turned, and there she was.

"Ken, how's things?"

"Just fine ma'am," I replied. SW troops never salute outside, and only on formal occasions inside. "You need to see me?"

She replied, "Tell me about today."

She'd seen what I'd done, but when your commander asks for a debrief, you give it. "I'm having my fireteam check all their gear. Today, the chameleons. I'll be arranging a field test as soon as I can, and meantime I'll be checking the exos, the jump harnesses, and all our environment gear. Our climbing and arctic equipment get regular workouts, but some of the other stuff is low use, so it needs at least a good exercise."

"Good thinking," she said. "But don't you think that would be better done at the squad or platoon level?"

"Yes, ma'am," I said. "But I don't have that authority."

She nodded. "Well, a warrant slot will open up eventually. Do you think you'd be prepared to take it?"

I quivered. That was not a casual offer, and the only acceptable answer (as if I'd give any other) was, "Absolutely, ma'am. If I'm qualified, I'll take it, if I'm not, I'll get qualified. But that's a way off. There's a lot of seniors who'll get a slot before I do, even allowing for rating jumps."

She nodded. "I'll put a word in for you. It doesn't hurt to think long term. Have a good evening, and let me know the results of your exercise. While you're at it, write up a plan for the procedure I can distribute to others."

"Yes, ma'am," I agreed. She nodded, turned and left.

The next morning, my comm relayed a "routine" message to

see the First Sergeant. Now, routine means it isn't life-and-death-skip-a-shower-and-get-here-because-we're-screwed. It doesn't mean to dawdle. I signed into the team bay of our squad room at two segs shy of three divs, and was at the First Sergeant's desk by three on the nose.

"Ken," he greeted me.

"Sergeant Jack," I said. "What can I help you with?" I was hoping it was good, but one always has the feeling that there's a problem waiting to screw one.

"Put these on," he said, handing me senior sergeant's chevrons. "The captain apologizes that she can't arrange a rate raise yet, but she'll be on it when she can."

"Thank you, First Sergeant," I said. "And please thank the captain for me." Wow. I resolved to see what command wanted out of me to push me higher. Money and power had heady appeal. Mostly the power.

I was a big hit with the junior troops and my friends that day, but did see a few disgruntled looks on others who disliked me bumping their positions, and figured where this was going. Rutledge didn't look amused and said so.

"Planning to replace me?" he asked, when I got back to the bay.

"No, sir," I said. "But sooner or later you'll promote or I'll get reassigned."

"You spend too much time worrying about prep and gear. That's my job," he said.

"That's everyone's job," I argued.

"Well, you just make sure you handle your team," he said. "I know my part."

Tense. I said, "Yes, sir," and made myself scarce. In actuality, I didn't want his job. I wanted to be me, not him. But he'd never believe that.

I followed up myself by drafting a letter of thanks to the captain. Always acknowledge the good. It makes people appreciate doing it, and helps them decide to do more. I mentioned Rutledge by name as my trainer and source of much of my knowledge. It was diplomatic. They might see it as window dressing. He might see it as sucking up. But at least I'd covered the issue.

I got tested on my new rank and alleged competence at once, and the fallout was shocking. We deployed to space aboard craft of 3rd Fleet (no, all these numbers are not coincidence. 3rd Fleet, 3rd Army, 3rd Mobile Legion, 3rd Mobile Assault Regiment and 3rd Special Warfare Regiment are all under one superior authority. We did do exercises elsewhere to rehearse for mass confusion, but by sticking together we created a well-oiled machine from practice . . . at least in theory) and split into five elements in order to conduct games.

So I took my team and prepared for a clandestine EVA to a target ship. For exercise purposes, we'd be attacking an intruding cruiser as it sat in port near a planetoid base. Actually, what we had was a derelict transport we'd gotten cheap. The engineers got to cobble it back together enough to mostly work as their part of the training, the bridge staff got to deal with the attendant problems of steering and commanding such a wreck, the rest of the crew got a creaky, groaning and banging ride with vacuum gear always at hand to stay in the right mindset while they jury-rigged defensive systems and things like working airlocks. Realism. With danger.

I got to blow it up. How can you beat a job like that?

I had Frank along, and Deni, and Barto Diaz and Eliot Christensen who'd been around for a year, and Gary Hulse, who was fresh from school and eager. Too eager, sometimes. I realized I'd matured about five percent when I looked at him.

We observed the mission start from the *Black Watch*, the heavily stealthed transport we were assigned to. Special Warfare has seven highly modified craft for clandestine delivery within occupied space, one for each Regiment and a spare, and a healthy chunk of our budget, all fitted for phase drive. They're stripped to make them as undetectable as possible, gunned enough to give us support to get in or out as is indicated and loaded with electronic toys and a shop full of low-mass, low-signature tools for Special Projects to use to build us assorted non-issue implements of destruction.

This would be the first time our squad had tackled a long EVA. One of the Operatives' most useful insertions is across space in naught but a suit. It's almost impossible to detect, and tricky enough that usually no one imagines anyone will attempt it in the first place. Even knowing to expect it, our own people would have a bitch of a time finding us.

What we planned was to come in from a stealth boat, EVA on sleds to within 20 kilometers, then use suit harnesses the rest of the way. Sensor image: none to speak of. Risk for errors: bloody high. And "error" would equal "death." There's not much room for it under the circumstances.

There are two things every Operative tries to carry in space. One is an emergency flare, in case one is lost during an exercise. The other is a grenade, in case one is lost in wartime. I know personally, intimately, with long practice what hypoxia is like. That doesn't mean I like it. If you can think of a colder (metaphysically), lonelier, more wretched death than to die slowly of suffocation surrounded by frigid points of stars and the searing blades of distant Iolight, I'd rather not hear about it. This was an exercise. It was also potentially lethal. We train as we fight—hardcore.

So, there I was with my team, ready to deploy from a boat. We greased each other up with a lubricant that makes it easier to squirm into a skintight suit. It's also been adapted as a surgical and sexual lubricant, but there was nothing sexy about the elastic mesh we donned, trust me. The goo was cold and slimy in the darkened bay. Not a thrill. Creepy, really. Hands helping get the small of your back and shoulders slick are not romantic in the slightest. It outgases to a powder with exposure to vacuum. Messy both ways.

We checked all our own gear. We checked all our buddy's gear. I buddied with Frank and we checked each other over. Carbine. Pistol. Sword. Knife. Cutting torch. Explosives. Comms and maps, keycodes and schedules. Smoke and flare. Emergency oxy bottle. Axe, used to rip through bulkheads and crack ports. Armor. Harnesses. Primary oxy bottles. Umbilicus for the sled's oxy supply. Sled. Emergency transponder. I did a quick check of everyone else's gear. If I sound paranoid and scared, it's because I was. Never mind my career; losing a person would be hell on my conscience. There were *not* going to be any screwups. Rutledge had grudgingly told me to do a good job as he doublechecked my checking. I'd agreed. We might have been a bit tense with each other, but neither of us wanted to succeed at the expense of lives. I wished him luck on his own insertion. We shook on it. He went to Second Team to see how Davis was doing. I ordered my team up.

We cycled through the lock, me first as leader, and hung on the outside by glued tethers which the boat engineer would detach later. There are no padeyes or other distortions on the skin of a stealth boat. Glued tethers are all we had, and I don't like them. I have this psychotic fear that the glue won't take. I prefer a mechanical lock. Yes, I know what the tensile strength of the bond is and what the chemistry of the glue is. I don't care. It's a phobia. As to the cycling, it was a bitch. Vac sleds are not designed to fit in personnel locks, and we don't use cargo bays on stealths because of the risk of a sensor image. It was one at a time, crowded and tangled with gear, near black with only a tiny glow tube to illuminate things. The image is fuzzy with your goggles' enhancement dialed up, and it shifts as the outer door opens and starlight and distant Iolight pour in, causing the goggles to polarize. The shadows are very sharp and dark.

Once we were all out, I waved hand signals and everyone mounted sleds. You have to strap your gear down, then yourself, with an old-style horsehitch to release as you thrust. We each thrusted in sequence, me first again, and took up a loose formation. I was leading. If my navigation was wrong, I'd die first. For an exercise, we could abort and use comm if we had to. If that happened, the shame and embarrassment would kill me. I didn't think about that at the time, as it was black and I was alone. I couldn't turn far enough on the sled to see behind me. I had blips on my visor that were intermittent even at this range; we were as low sig as we could get, but a good intel boat can home in on almost nothing. Our support boat would abort us if necessary, as long as we were still in its range. I didn't hear anything from them.

It went okay as an exercise. It simply lasted forever. We thrusted then floated in trajectory for almost ten divs—28 hours. Almost a full day. There was nothing to break the monotony except music—vid is too distracting. As we use an oxy-helium mix, the sound system has to compensate for atmospheric effects. I had an extensive library of tunes, from classical to scape to modern jazz and clash. I love music. I could barely listen to any of them. Tedium, boredom, hell. It was horrible. Nothing followed by nothing forever, while I clung to a metal frame. Harsh stars ahead, above, below, to the sides. I dozed in and out, watched the readouts for time and activity, and grew more fatigued the more I napped. The flavored goop in the food tube grew tiresome in short order. I made myself drink more water, as it's easy to dehydrate. You don't think about drinking in emgee for some psychological reason, just like in the cold.

We might arrive and find the other two teams hadn't made their missions, or had been discovered and left us hanging as targets. We might find the ship already "destroyed" by other factors, or moved out of orbit, even though intel said it would stay where it was. That would make us dead for the exercise, but dead for real if this were an actual mission. Six Operatives for a starship? A small price. Unless you're one of the Operatives. Why the hell had I chosen this job?

Nothing. Followed by still more nothing. I watched the scale tick off in my visor, wondering if it was actually working. Cursing it to move faster. Trying to avoid the nervous kicks and twitches one gets after hours of inactivity. I gripped the sled. It was my only company.

Finally, my nav system was telling me we were close, but I had no physical evidence of that. My hyperaware eyes finally saw a shadow occulting a star, though just barely, and I breathed a huge sigh. We would survive. Even if we failed the exercise, we would survive. I realized I hadn't peed from the tension. In fact, I hadn't gone in longer than I could recall. I vented liquid and felt better.

Then came the next stage. A signal chime in my right ear matched a flash on my visor, and I disconnected from the sled, switching to suit oxy. The barest practiced push would slowly separate me from the tubular frame, and my suit harness would take over. It's easy to shove too hard, which actually changes your trajectory considerably. You can miss the target by several hundred meters that way. A touch is all you need. "Below" me, the sled was braking with small shoves to a relative zero velocity. It wouldn't do for it to appear on sensors later, giving away the fact that we were present. These sleds would activate beacons and become an exercise for space rescue units; nothing was wasted. In a real war, of course, they'd be expended.

The suit thrusters kicked in, using compressed nitrogen to make bare corrections to the course. And no, it can't compensate for the shove that separates you from the sled. It handles your programmed trajectory only, not that of anything else around it. Sensors on a harness would be pricey, subject to detection, and incredibly inaccurate with so small an aperture.

We continued our apparent drift, even though it was a very precise orbit. For three more divs—2.8 hours each—nothing happened. The slight occultation I'd seen had been one tiny ship of the fleet in front of one irrelevant, distant star. We were within a div of our final time tick when I saw another, then another, then three more.

Suddenly, surreally, we were within the fleet. It was in a holding pattern near what would be a planetoid base, carved out by combat engineers to provide storage and rudimentary billeting space. They could build them on short notice and abandon them in seconds if the need arrived. They were referred to only as "rocks" because that's all they were. Not home, just a space equivalent of a windbreak or leanto. They'd be awfully glad for the use of that shortly, because the ships were about to go bye-bye. Sweat was pouring off me, and I adjusted my cooling slightly.

It was thrilling and bizarre. Here we were, surrounded by state of the art warships that could deliver enough ordnance to boil a planet, and we were too low mass and velocity to even register. We were drifting debris. Barring the astronomical odds of a repair crew or special courier, nothing would get near enough to affect us. Of course, if they had brought sensors up, they could refine us if they knew to look. Or they might get lucky and irradiate us with active search measures. The close in sensor systems are pretty potent. We were just as alone and endangered as we had been, yet I felt much safer, even amidst this "enemy."

Things got active after that, and I was grateful for it. I think everyone else was, too. The ships resolved themselves as black shapes against black space, the stars disappearing at the edges. A shifting, interrupted shape would be the fleet carrier, a huge framework designed as a stardrive to carry smaller craft. It stayed back from the battle, defended as well as could be by its systems, and a threat point. One team would be taking that out. That would leave much of the fleet casualtied as unrecoverable, forcing command to decide between abandoning crew or taking time to transfer them. Fleet carriers are not the best means of projecting power, but they're what we have, so we train accordingly.

Our target must be the shadow ahead. It was obviously a "cruiser," so unless there'd been a drastic shift, it was ours. Yes, we knew exactly where it was. Think of it as a sea fleet anchored offshore, awaiting orders. We were coming in from the sea with a good view, and would sink them in the shallows.

All at once, things started happening. The target filled half my view, then it was all I could see. Surface features began to resolve in starlight, and I picked out a good place to land. I waved my arms for attention, the tiny pinlights on my sleeves triggering indicators in the teams' visors. They watched as I lit a point with a milliwatt laser, just enough to be seen by someone looking hard. They and their comms grabbed the dot as a target, or they should have. I had no way to know.

Then I was close. I waited until I was sure I was going to slam into the hull then braked, the gas puffing in front of me. Inertia carried my legs forward as thrust slowed my torso—I'd left the leg section turned off for that reason. I was feet down, thrusted again with the lower jets and relaxed my knees. I felt my feet touch through the thin, insulated traction boots I wore, and collapsed, absorbing the momentum while grabbing a line from my waist.

I was down, and moved quickly to connect to a padeye, or any convenient point. I found said ring, set into the hull, and let the cable snap to it. I adjusted its retaining drum for minimal tension, just to keep the line out of my way, and looked around.

I counted four, panicked as to where number five was, and did a quick check. Me, Frank, Deni, Barto and Gary . . . no Eliot.

For just a moment, my head spun and I was lost. Then I clamped down on it. One of my troops was in trouble, and I had to help him now.

There was no point in a broadcast. The suit commo range is short. I would have to contact higher up and have the signal come down for him. It might blow the exercise, and that was still a consideration. Failing that test as well would hurt me. It may sound callous, but real world, I'd have to call him dead and move on. Here, I had to do the same for exercise purposes, while doing everything I could to find him for real. But there were no excuses. It would be a failure if we got discovered.

First, I touched helmets with Frank. "Anyone see him?" I shouted. We all touched helmets and inquired. No. He'd been last off, and had been slightly behind Deni. She'd last seen him some hours before. So he was in trajectory, and likely near us. Alive? Dead? We didn't know.

That settled, I opened a laser tightbeam to the nearest judge's ship, while Frank tried to locate a friendly ship for me. "Emergency—Three Zulu One," I said. "Casualty Casualty Casualty. Blazer Eliot Christensen missing in EVA. Believed to be on last trajectory Three Zulu One. Casualty casualty casualty."

"Emergency, acknowledged. SAR responding. Any further details?"

"Emergency—Three Zulu One. Christensen was sighted by team member after dismount from sleds."

"Emergency, acknowledged."

Frank clanked helmets and said, "Got a ship." Great. I could hook into their secure commo net through his maser antenna. I plugged and switched channels as I finished with Emergency.

"Emergency—Three Zulu One, acknowledged—break—Blue Force Command, Three Zulu One. Casualty Casualty Casualty. Report made to Emergency, holding, awaiting instructions."

A few moments later, just as I was about to repeat, I heard, "Blue Force Command, continue as best you can. SAR may ask for additional information. Good luck, and best wishes for recovery."

"Blue Force Command, Three Zulu One. Acknowledged." So that was that. I felt horribly sick and helpless, because I was. There was *nothing* I could do. Nor did I have any idea what had happened. Hypoxia? Blowout? Fell asleep, missed the alarm, missed the tick and was healthy but drifting? Suit harness failed and no thrust for corrections? Hit by a meteor (astronomically unlikely...but possible)? Fluke cardiac arrest? Alive? Dead?

So I quashed it all. There was nothing I could do. It was one of the things I'd trained for, but this was nothing like training. Except it *was* training, and might very well happen in the real world. The sweat from earlier was now a cold, greasy layer between me and the suit, even worse than the goop that had evaporated. I heaved a breath, held it and got my nerves under control. Continue with mission.

We were late, and we needed to move fast. I signaled with my hands, got waves of acknowledgement, and we started.

After that it was a frantic pace. We bounded aft in long, practiced strides, each taking a line for another. I led, waiting for the next troop—Gary—to arrive and fasten me to a new padeye, then leaping. I'd fasten, he'd jump, the next troop would repeat, and we flowed aft like a caterpillar, Frank as assistant at the rear.

There was the spot we wanted, and the caterpillar squeezed into a ball. We started laying out explosives to cut our entrance. This craft was an old lady, now used only for exercises. Despite that, she was lovingly maintained. After we blew the hole, the engineers would patch it and polish it until it would take scientific tools to determine where it had been cut. We joke about how one day, there will be just one square meter of surface that hasn't been replaced. And of course, the ship will blow a leak on the opposite side from there, on the newest section. Thinking that reminded me that Eliot might be out of oxygen. I clamped down on that again.

In short order, we had four sides marked with charges in a tapering rectangle, slight boosters at the corners, and us in a line behind a heavy shield much like a Roman scutum that had been folded up for insertion. We were gripping at line or padeye as we could reach. Everyone checked gear, squeezed hands to acknowledge readiness, Gary squeezed mine and I hit the stud.

We could hear the explosion through our suits, both from the contact with the hull, and through the nimbus of air and debris that engulfed us. I raised the shield, skidded forward and swung in. The shield went first, to prevent me getting cut on the raw edges across from me, and Gary shoved an identical one in the near side. I ricocheted, tangled with Gary, tumbled and came around in the compartment. Five meters square, two meters and a bit deep, plain bulkheads in our enhanced vision, merely a system access bay. It was empty. Good. I counted everyone by eye, four, not five. I listened through my feet, feeling normal ship vibrations and what was probably an alarm klaxon, rhythmic and persistent.

We moved to the hatch, repeated the squeeze, and triggered the emergency override—a hatch won't normally open in a compartment open to space. It popped open in front of us, and a roar of air evacuated the companionway behind it, billowing dust through the valve and around us. We swung it open and swarmed through. Remember that we were still in emgee.

It was a lit T intersection, and had three safety hatches around the T, as well as the one we'd come through and two others. There was no one here. One of those was a half-sized crawlway that accessed a main fuel line, and that was a target. I pointed to confirm, we still being silent, and Barto Diaz slapped a charge, cut his way through and went to work shutting it down. The rest of us moved out, forcing the hatches as we went, carbines ready. Barto was very somber. It was bad for all of us, but Eliot was his buddy.

Two hatches along, as lights failed, indicating Diaz had succeeded, we were ambushed. A Security Reaction Force poked out of cubbies, or rather, their weapons did. I saw flashes and leapt left, shoving off with my right foot so I tumbled. It was an immediate reaction, intended to make me harder to hit. It worked. I wasn't hit. I tossed a grenade sim by hand and followed it with a burst from the carbine, just to appear to be doing something. They were in secure positions, but we were better trained. We swapped fire and dodged around stanchions, inlets, anything that might provide cover.

We "lost" Frank to fire, we killed the ambush and moved on. At least we knew Frank was only an exercise casualty. But that was two down. I was getting a rough lesson in mortality, and prayed that Eliot was alive and just lost.

Shortly, we had another fuel feed down, and the crew was getting panicky. They had to see us on sensor by now, and automatic systems were trying to kill us. Those were basically shotgun mines set into the sides of passages, that were supposed to blow as we neared them. We used up a lot of ammo spraying suspicious-looking boxes, which also did more collateral damage to various systems. We'd brought plenty of ammo on purpose.

Eventually, we wound up in life support and engineering and shut the ship the rest of the way down. It was an example of how we could capture a ship and keep it mostly intact. Alternately, we could hold it for ransom. Or we could just blow it the hell up. That would shorten our lives somewhat. But we'd succeeded. The fleet command knew we could do what we'd claimed: get aboard enemy ships unseen and wreak havoc. We knew we could infiltrate over large distances and stay alive until we reached our target. It was a profound, exhilarating experience.

Except that we'd lost someone, and that put a damper on the joy at once.

As soon as we got the kill, I opened up and said, "Crew, I need commo, emergency."

"Ah, here, Sergeant," someone said, assuming my rank as he pointed at a connection terminal. I nodded, swam over, plugged in and identified myself to the bridge. I told them what I needed.

"That would be the lost EVA troop?" the commo tech asked.

"Yes," I said. "He's one of mine."

"He's been found," I heard, and before my relief could get started the, "I'm very sorry," hit me.

I felt nauseous, feverish, panicky. Spots were swimming in front of my eyes, but I needed to know. "What happened?"

"See oh two poisoning. They think the filtration medium was contaminated."

There was nothing I could have done about that. Everything had been checked, and Eliot had done his own final mark off. And not having any control over it made it worse for me. "Understood, thanks," I said, snapped my cable out, and turned. "Please, get me into gravity now. I'm sick." I wanted some kind of pressure on me before I heaved.

"Sergeant?" "Ken?" "Boss?" I heard.

"He didn't make it," I said.

All five of us wound up in sickbay, sedated and under .5 G to help us relax. It wasn't just Eliot's death; we'd been in space for almost two days. It's sheer murder on the body. I insisted that we wanted a shuttle to transfer us back, or a docking, and would not be EVAing across between ships. It was over-reaction on my part. Even if the system failed, the few seconds between ships wasn't a risk. But I was badly shaken and phobic.

Rutledge wrote the letter to his parents. I don't think I could have handled it. But we all served as pallbearers at his funeral. His parents were inconsolable and weeping, and we all had damp eyes from the experience. It's an honorable duty to bury a comrade. But it's not an easy one. It wasn't a relief, though it did put some finality on it. Odd, now, to think about a single death affecting me so. But every life and death is important.

I took leave, and Deni came with me. My parents had moved to a smaller place up in the Cairngorm Hills, with a beautiful view down into Westport to the south. Deni and I stared out across it for quite some time.

My sister Jackie was away at school, and tearing up the instructors over dramatics and presentation. I grinned. Good to know our tradition as troublemakers was secure. Deni and I had the run of the property while my parents were at work, and practiced our knots and lashings with the help of an antique four-poster bed. That was Deni's idea. Certainly a diversion, and fun. I prefer being able to wrestle, though. Besides, she was a sadistic, torturous bitch once she had me tied. But the endorphin rush was amazing. For a while, I didn't think about my mortality. Which is what was bothering me. Eliot was a friend, but not a close one. The fear I had was of being next.

Dinner the first night was still more awkward. All we could say was that a teammate had died in an EVA accident. My father wanted details.

"What type of equipment failure? I thought everything was redundant."

"It is. But some things are still susceptible to failure," I said. It was a subject I wasn't allowed to discuss, and didn't want to discuss.

"But how long were you out? There's nothing that would be lethal fast."

"I can't say," I said shortly.

"What do you mean?" my mother asked. "Don't you remember?"

"I mean it's protected information."

"Are they covering something up?" she prodded. They could really be overprotective, over-inquisitive and obnoxious, even well past my puberty. And there was no good lie I could tell. I was glancing at Deni now and then, my eyes pleading for help. She clearly had no idea how to address it, either.

"No, it was a predictable but rare accident, and nothing can be done about it," I said.

"But how could people not notice? He obviously stopped moving," my father asked.

"Sometimes we're still for long periods of time. And I can't discuss it."

"And there's usually convulsions associated with hypoxia," he persisted.

"I said I can't talk about it!" I snapped.

There was silence for a moment, until he said, "Ken, it sounds like someone above him is avoiding blame for screwing up. You might want to mention it through channels." His voice was quiet, calm, reasonable and concerned.

I said nothing. I just flushed and burned and gripped my fork.

Deni said, very softly, "Ken *was* his team leader. I was the last one to see Eliot alive. It was thoroughly investigated, and determined to be unavoidable. Life's like that sometimes, especially for Blazers."

There was more silence, until my mother said, "We're very sorry. But I do wish you could talk about it."

"So do I," I lied. Yes, Mom, I spend days cruising through space in a polymer skin for the privilege of blowing people's heads off and whisking away their breathing air so they flop like fish. Fun for the whole family. Wait until I get a chance to dig out that nuke I buried.

I was losing what connection I did have with my family. We had no common interests and no real feeling, it seemed.

The other three days were rather strained. I was glad when we were able to leave. Deni and I spent the last night in a hotel. I was glad I'd been vague about my schedule.

Once we were logged in, Deni asked, "How are you holding up, Ken?" She had that look with her head and eyebrow cocked. It was just inquisitive, but it was always so sexy on her.

Except right then. "I'll survive," I said. "But I'm going to be shaky on EVA until I get some courage back."

She nodded. "So let's not talk about it for a while. After you've lost some of the stress of the last three days we'll see."

"Yeah. Thanks," I said, and meant it. But I was still really screwed up. I'm glad for it now, and I owe Eliot thanks for teaching me about death. I was to see lots more.

I got promoted again later that year. I'd had the hoped for rate increase to E-7, but had figured I'd be a senior sergeant for some time, especially in light of Eliot. But it had been ruled an accident. As far as anyone could tell, all equipment inspections had been done. It had been a fluke. It absolved me of any blame, and our successful exercise had been credited to me. It didn't make me feel better, though.

With retirements and expansion, the FMF found space, and I was promoted to warrant leader and made a squad leader. It was often easier to get promoted in Special Warfare units, I'd found out, but this was still a decent deal even considering that. It wasn't unheard of or unrealistic; we won't let anyone become an officer without being a soldier first, but anyone with potential is promoted as fast as we can. I was officer material. I was second in my class at OLS. Two years of service had proven my abilities. There was no friction over this; Rutledge moved out of Special Warfare and became a lieutenant in intelligence.

"I'm not young anymore," he said. "I've done my time. Good luck, Ken. But do try to tone down the attitude, eh?"

"Will do, sir," I said. Well, I *did* try.

The standard squad arrangement is a senior sergeant as leader, sergeant as assistant, three fireteam leaders of corporal, assistants of senior specialist, and the rest privates. In actuality it would vary somewhat. Special Warfare units, however, are elite and small. We needed a certain number of ranks to fill slots, rank to go with the awesome responsibility we wielded by comparison, and enough rank to make us "respectable" to our contemporaries in other units. Besides, on a rank-per-damage-inflicted basis, we were on the low side anyway. So we filled our operational squads (as opposed to the backfill and training slots) with stripes. I was a warrant leader squad leader, with a senior sergeant as my assistant, three sergeants as fireteam leaders below them, and several junior troops who were Operative specialists or corporals. We had no Operative privates; by the time an Operative is trained, he's at least a specialist. I was warrant leader because I needed enough rank to operate on my own authority when attached to a larger unit. The same thing was true with other attached units, such as logistics and occasionally engineers. The rank may seem a little high for the position, but the pay we receive is comparable to others, we simply have more authority and responsibility to go with it. Fair trade, right?

Sorry. I'm not good at sarcasm.

It wasn't hard to fit into the slot. I found us lots of exercises, and got the troops used to me the hard way: I was a hardcase asshole bent on making their lives hell. Since I abused myself just as much, they could hardly complain without appearing to be non-hackers and wimps bitching about the world as it was.

I was still in 3rd Special Warfare Regiment, and still assigned as support for 3rd Mobile Assault Regiment. Whenever they or 3rd Legion got called to do light, fast forward deployment, we'd be along as eyes, ears, force multipliers and the enemy's worst nightmare. To my thinking, this was a better tasking than divisional or army level support, as it kept us where things were happening. It was harder to buff egos for a promotion, but would result in much better chances for decorations. Since the FMF is very stingy about giving out decorations, they count a lot toward promotion. It was a fair tradeoff, and lots of fun.

In the meantime, I had all my old friends to play with. Deni and Tyler were the only two women present, my old friend Frank was along, and we formed the core of the squad. I posted Frank as my assistant, gave Barto our first fireteam, and Deni was tasked as leader of the weapons team. With Adam Verani as second team leader, I had no concerns about the quality of my personnel; they were ass-kicking, hardcase killers who shot first and didn't bother asking questions later—answers weren't that important to them. They existed, as did I, to outthink, outfight, outmaneuver, and outgun anyone we were up against, and to keep score by the pile of bodies.

We were notorious, as we played by SW rules, not by anyone else's. Our first exercise, we were given a time and place to attack and told the rules of the game. I elected to stage a broken down civilian vehicle along the convoy route, just before the ambush area. Deni and Tyler could still pass as college girls, and they got the convoy bunched up and gathered around. When troops started to hear pinging in their helmets, and realized it was an attack, they grabbed the women and took them along into cover. At this point, my lovely ladies "killed" the headquarters squad with concealed pistols (two each and lots of spare magazines inside their autumn coats) and took the captain hostage. By the time his lieutenant figured out she was in charge, my flitting wraiths were popping up behind trucks to hose the occupants with fire, vanishing again to land on the hoods and glacis plates in front of the drivers, then to squirm into the equipment to plant mock charges. The pouring smoke and teargas, pops and bangs from simulators and blanks and the natural disorientation on top of psychoacoustic blasts was all the score we needed. The lieutenant never did get her remaining troops under orders, and we defeated them in detail. It was sweet.

Then came the complaints about us having troops out of uniform, which was against the rules. We had not attacked at the time and place we were told to. We shouldn't have stapled the captain's hat to our unit trophy wall, etc. It was just like the exercise on Caledonia, and I'd frankly expected better of our people.

Those complaints went nowhere, fortunately. The new doctrine was to play hard, fight hard and expect surprise at any moment. Marshal Dyson was wise enough to realize that troops get bored in garrison, and also get bored doing nothing but silly exercises. To that end, he instituted a bonus program. Troops who responded well in exercise got passes, extra leave, and bonus credits. They quickly became enthusiastic about responding, reacting, and stopping us. And then they started anticipating and planning responses ahead of time. The first time I actually got outflanked and shot up, I was chagrined at my failure, but equally elated at how our regular troops were progressing. They were reaching a level that few armies achieve in wartime, much less peace.

Captain Maron regretfully took a promotion to Commander of 2nd Mobile Assault Regiment and left Special Warfare. She was replaced by Captain Stig Erson, a former teacher at Officer Leadership School and fresh from Blazer Combat Air Control School. He was a hardass son of a bitch, and I loved him. We lived in the field, ran urban exercises through town with stiff penalties for getting seen, much less IDed by civilians. I drilled my people mercilessly, and they enthusiastically dreamed up new, even more impossible scenarios for us to deal with. We practiced our covert missions by sneaking into factories in local dress or shop uniform, planting simulated sabotage devices, and then having others sneak in to verify the "damage" and remove all evidence of the event.

It was arrogant of me (arrogance is when you can back it up, conceit is when you can't) to start thinking of Operatives, and me in particular, as gods of covert warfare. It wasn't long after that that I had an opportunity to prove so.

CHAPTER 6

Commander Naumann of 3rd MOB, mentioned previously, was exactly the type of thinker I was, and one of my role models. Dyson clearly had him pegged to get experience, move up, and take command of major units. He was barely twenty (thirty Earth years), but was in command of a regiment and heading up fast. He was a sheer genius at accomplishing outrageous feats with small forces and minimal gear. He knew his history, philosophy, weapons, tactics, and even his art and music. He would have made a marvelous Napoleonic Era colonel, except that he had no regard for fair play whatsoever. Imagine the Duke of Wellington crossed with a Viking marauder and you'll get the idea. He was a sociopathic killer who could masquerade as a gentleman when needed. It was much later I learned to hate his dispassion.

I knew him slightly from service, respected him, and was flattered when he decided I was perfect for a mission he dreamed up. He was forever thinking up missions and training people for them. Then when SHTF, someone would beg for a solution, he'd lay out the plan, it would be executed, and they'd stop bugging him about operating beyond his authority for a month or so.

He had a thing about terrorists. He was convinced we faced a threat, remote and detached as our system was. Many thought he was nuts, and ignored his obsession with a shake of the head.

"Madman Naumann," they called him. But he requested that Captain Erson maintain and improve our capabilities in that direction. Erson relayed that request to me, along with instructions to Special Projects to put a team at my disposal and ask none of the wrong type of questions. I got my people cracking on scenarios and languages and accents and everything else I could think of. Technically, I had more than a squad under my orders, and was thus a platoon leader.

Now, I hate terrorists. To me, anyone who attacks civilians in lieu of soldiers (collateral casualties do happen, but aren't an excuse to be abused) is a gutless turd. I don't care what the historians have to say about Lenin, the "Irish Republican Army" (which was neither Irish, Republican, nor an army), Hamas, al Qaeda, the Covenant of God, Free Canada, or any other group of thugs in history, or those running around now. They attack civilians to create terror, to force a government to yield. They do not attack politicians directly, or soldiers or cops. They attack civilians "because they have no choice" (and because their penises are too small for real fights and they lack the intelligence to stage real revolutions), and were and are, in fact, human fucking shit to be scooped up and flushed. I don't care how "noble" the cause is, how oppressed you feel you are, how "romantic" or "elegant" it is to shoot kids, blow up offices, destroy marketplaces, you will get naught but a bullet from me. If you want a fight, call me. That's why I'm here.

With that in mind, let me tell you about the mission we took against the Fruits of God. Yes, that's how their name translates. Feel free to snicker at the name. Don't snicker at their operations, because they like to throw big tantrums and blow people up. This is never their fault, of course. It's the fault of anyone who won't give them money, agree with their brand of extremism, and worship God in their fashion. Aren't you ashamed of yourself for causing so much anguish? No?

I was called in to Erson's office one morning, he said, "Hi, Ken, read this," and lit a screen without any further preamble. It was a report on the *Francolin*, a small liner registered out of Piedmonte and in service mostly between there and Novaja Rossia. It had been making an approach to orbit around Piedmonte when Fruit terrorists had jumped out of the passengers and seized it.

"I heard about this," I said. "What's our involvement?" It was tragic and disgusting but not in our area.

"Keep reading," he said shortly but not rudely.

I read. Further down were details that weren't yet on the news. It got uglier. According to witnesses, one of the passengers had begged Ali Muhammad Ghassan, their chief turd, to allow his daughter to be put off in a rescue ball. The passenger offered to stay voluntarily and give no resistance, if only they'd let his daughter off before initiating this plot.

Ghassan shot the daughter and stuffed her out the airlock. She was five years old by our reckoning. Then he shot the father and four other passengers. Jenny Marlin. Remember her. She was a young girl with a promising life ahead.

His point in doing this was that he didn't like the "infidel" influence that various nations (us among them, though we weren't named) had on the Ramadan system. Apparently, trade and exchange of ideas might lead true believers from the Path of Righteousness. I've always felt that if one is secure in one's ethics and morals, there's no threat from other philosophies. If one is not secure, one should seek out other ideas for consideration. Apparently, I lack the proper view to be a religious fanatic. Thank God, Goddess, Allah, Jehovah, Yaweh, Jave, Nature, Science or whatever.

Shortly after the incident, after much ranting and posturing, the politicians in Nuova Agrigento (the capital of Piedmonte) offered him free transit and freed the rest of his people. In exchange, he agreed to keep his activities elsewhere. In other words, they gave him a base.

I don't think words exist to express my loathing. No life form I could compare him to is disgusting enough to make my point. I won't even discuss the gutless slime who gave him more than the bullet in the neck he deserved.

Then I saw the key part: "Mister Marlin and his family were residents of the Freehold of Grainne." That made it our business.

"We're responding, then?" I asked.

"That depends," he replied. "Can you get to him without getting

IDed? Can we decide on a message that will convince them to leave us out of their squabbles?"

I'd have to think about that. "Probably," I said.

"Decide soon," he said, putting me on the spot. Could I handle the mission? Or should I be replaced with someone who could? Was the whole exercise pointless and counterterror operations not something we should bother with? It all came down to me.

"Yes, then," I said. "I'll need more intel, of course."

"You'll get it," he said.

It was felt among our Citizens that not responding would send the message that Freeholders could be treated like that in future incidents. The Citizen's Council spoke to Marshal Dyson. The Marshal spoke to the General Staff. They decided to contact Commander Naumann (as the pet thug and former Operative they could talk to at their level), and Naumann admitted that some exploratory operations toward combating terror had been made, outside the normal chain of command. He was cautioned again about exceeding his authority, the caution accompanied by a wink. Naumann expressed his guilt over the matter, then spoke to Erson and me. Then I spoke to the General Staff and the Marshal. That was a first for me.

I stood before those august ladies and men and gave my professional opinion that my "platoon" could find them, and express our extreme displeasure with their choice of targets. Captain Erson agreed that I was competent, even ideal to do this, and recommended me as the tool of our vengeance. It was decided that killing Ghassan would only strengthen the ardor of his followers. I agreed. I suggested that I would keep him alive, but had my own theories on how he should be handled, and would discuss them with Naumann and Erson so as to keep things official, but not involve the GS and the Marshal in case it was necessary to deny the incident. I said it quite casually, now that I look back on it. I didn't realize just how much I was leaving myself open for.

They all agreed, after some pointed inquiries that I didn't want to answer, and didn't. They hemmed and hawed and relented. I told Naumann and the Captain what I had planned. They agreed, chuckling. I was told to go forth and be a violent bastard, deliver a stern message, but not to kill the target. It was official, and I was to handle the operation from start to finish on my authority as commander of a roving unit. Heady stuff.

The first problem was how to infiltrate a squad (plus one team of Special Projects) into Nuova Agrigento without being IDed. The second was how to exfiltrate afterwards. The third was how to dispose of all evidence. The fourth and smallest detail was the hit itself. Killing isn't difficult. Not getting caught doing so is the hard part. We were at peace with Piedmonte and officially neutral and thus could not get caught assassinating anyone, no matter how badly they deserved it.

Special Projects provided each of us with three IDs. They were a mixed bag of legitimate and faked passports and visas from several different nations, all well-worn documents or rams so as to look old and used. We booked hotels ahead of time in various locations, and would plan to cancel some, use some and get new ones. It's expensive, but it makes it harder for the other side to plant bugs. Weapons we'd get on-site. Every embassy detail gets regular shipments of weapons under diplomatic pass. Freeholders are simply better at hiding them in transit and caching them insystem, if you recall. We would make a note, to be submitted after the fact, to replace the ones we'd use.

Some societies can get away with assassinations. It's a case of "We want you to know we did it as long as you can't prove it." It sends a message. Ours had to be better hidden. We needed the surviving terrorists (such a tragedy, that) to tell everyone how vicious we were, but not a hint that any government could even suspect against us, except for hearsay from the terrorists. We as a society had a political position to maintain.

I went in as a visiting political science major, made up in my best chair-warming, screen-watching getup. I actually have the ideal build for an Operative. Depending on dress and presentation, I can look like a skinny, wiry laborer; a slim academic; a lean, handsome businessman; a career military officer or administrator or a shaggy college punk. Huge vid show muscles and chiseled features are unnecessary and a hindrance. The sniveling geeks will be the death of you.

We took a week to trickle in from five different directions

under various covers while the intel gophers and Operatives in the embassy kept tabs as they could. They knew something was planned, but had no idea what. Nor would they ask. Just as I'd had some odd inquiries while working on Caledonia. I don't know what for to this day and will never ask. I know I performed the tasks in a satisfactory fashion, because there was no political fallout. It's all part of how we defend freedom, ensure peace, etc, etc. There were two other squads that were attached to the mission as decoys, an identical team heading in a totally different direction to play games with the Novaja Rossian army, and the rest flew in and out along our route, confusing people as to how many of us there were and what exactly we were doing.

First thing we had to do upon landing was find this anal pus pocket. We had an idea as to where to begin, but it still took quite a few days of surveillance and travel to find him. We had a basic profile, and added to it by the second, electronically and with human intelligence.

I loved Nuova Agrigento, or at least what I saw of it. It seemed to cascade off steep hills into a deep harbor. It was on a peninsula that turned into a mountain range inland, so was compact and crowded. Maybe "cozy" rather than "crowded." Snug little blocks of houses with small lots and deep terraces of flowers. They loved flowers here, and had colors found nowhere else, blues and purples predominating.

But further back were steep streets and narrow alleys around lifter landing pads. This was the industrial zone. It even had a railway, which will likely surprise some, but made sense with the size of the widening peninsula and tech base. It was an efficient way to transport materiel through hills. And around the pads, the railway and the truck accesses, were apartments, restaurants and warehouses where terrorists and regular, decent thugs and murderers could hide and stash weapons and loot. They spoke an Italian dialect predominantly, with some Greek and Romansch, but other languages were used around the docks, the lifter pads and the ports, as anywhere.

One of our disreputable embassy people was tracking an arms shipment. It wasn't really a surprise; we'd set it up ourselves. Since the Freehold allows any goods to be sold without silly inquiries, we're a popular source for dark elements. They never seem to catch on that just because we *allow* such sales doesn't mean we don't *track* such sales, so as to know who has what capabilities. This particular shipment was meeting a suspicious bunch of characters who wanted lots of Mobile Assault surplus gear that was ideal for penetrating ships and no questions asked about the sale. Not asked verbally, anyway. As I said, we generally knew who bought the stuff.

So Ghassan actually paid us a fair price for the equipment we used to track him, that we would recapture or destroy after we shoved a nuke up the asshole's rectum. Irony is sweet.

He was almost good, I'll give him that. Good at being a weasel. His safehouse wasn't where we first thought; that one was a decoy. It was an apartment above a warehouse. He would stop by there often, but I sent Gary, one of our best sneaks, in to do a recon while the guards played cards at night, and he reported it was just a cover. There was a shower, a bedroom and all the basics, but largely unused. "Dusty," he said. "And musty. I don't think that bed has been used in a month or more."

Ghassan was arriving, then departing out the back as a teamster on a cargo floater. Three kilometers away, it would stop at a traffic signal and he'd swing off, just like a cargo handler getting a ride home.

We didn't attack at once. What we wanted was a nice gathering of turds we could flush all at once, hopefully to clog the plumbing. At the same time, we needed to hit before things cooled down. It had to be an obvious response to that incident, in the minds of our targets. We'd eaten up most of a month already and we had to hit soon.

We got lucky. I'd picked a day by which we would attack even if no one else were present. Three days before that, we hit the jackpot. Something else was apparently in the works, as we'd deduced from the hardware he was buying, and it seemed he was doing an initial mass briefing. All day long, people trickled into this little house behind a strip of restaurants and bars.

I put the word out, and we kept it in view on all sides. Second Team watched outwards, looking for arrivals and security. That's a hell of a task, scanning the crowds with binox, comparing every face, sweating over the faces you can't see, straining to see who goes where without blowing your concealment, lying on rooftops in weather, which in this case was cold and wet. I didn't envy them that task, and had taken the easy one myself so as not to be worrying about it. I'd be worrying about it anyway, it was just easier from a distance and an intellectual basis rather than from the front.

We counted as they arrived, and knew this was the day to do it, assuming Flaming Asshole showed up. I sent people out for food and the rest of our gear and we eased closer, as leopards ease up on gazelles. By eight local at night (22-hour clock, 62 minutes per hour), I was in a building across the alley, that was abandoned and filthy and filled with cobwebs. It was perfect, I thought, as I brushed grit and sticky spider goo from my hair. By eleven, I was atop our target, having slipped over on a thin but strong board we use for bridging crevasses; it works on alleys, too. I had Team One with me, which included experienced elements of Team Two. I had the new kids watching for trouble outward as the rest of Team Two, and Team Three (nominally Weapons), moderately experienced, roving around, pretending to drink beer, eating pies and watching. My salty people were in close, and Eliot's replacement—Johnny the Squidboy, and don't ask about his nickname, as it involves a busty young lady, a squirt bottle of henna and a bar bet—was in with us to get experience.

Finally, there were twenty-three of them in the house. Now, most terrorists operate in small cells, so this was a bonanza. My team was utterly silent, and I was incredibly proud of them. This was a tricky op.

They had a woman. It was an important datum. Here they were, insisting that women should be veiled, barefoot and pregnant in the kitchen, speak only when spoken to by men and not interfere in affairs of state, business, etc. Yet they had one here. We'd had her on file, but only as a ladyfriend and cover. She was talking about techniques for smuggling explosives aboard ship. Clearly, she wasn't along as mere cover and sexual service, as their "beliefs" seemed to suggest she should be. I made note of it. We'd upgrade her threat level accordingly. As to their hypocrisy, it was likely that the rules didn't apply to them, being revolutionaries and all.

We were wearing assault armor, which is heavy ballistic padding with reinforcement and shields to prevent splinters and shrapnel. Our weapons were shotguns, loaded with special ammo that was a combination of impact stunners with neural shock cartridges, and coated with a substance that would act as a sedative also. You can never have too many backups.

It seemed like a good time to start. More might arrive, but we could deal with that. I clicked a code to my immediate flankers, Squidboy and Barto, to detain any new arrivals, double-clicked that we were starting, and hopped. I brought my feet together off the joists and fell through the ceiling.

Naturally, I dinged my shoulder on the polymer beam on the way down. It hurt, I ignored it. There were two of them in front of me, looking shocked and reaching for weapons. I double-tapped both and rolled on the ratty carpet, turning, getting the one behind me. I stood fast and cleared the room visually, behind the couch, a shot through a closet door before I swiped it open, and a quick poke into a hallway until I saw Frank and Barto in other rooms. Throughout the building, I could hear similar sounds, then descrambled bursts announced, "Bottom alpha clear," "Middle delta clear," "Middle beta clear," and through the entire building. The last two were "Out rear clear," and "Attic clear." They were last, to confirm both our safety and that all others had reported.

We dragged the limp forms into the kitchen of the restaurant, closed at this hour and for their own cover, and weren't any too gentle about it. Hey, these fuckers blew up civilians. They weren't soldiers, the conventions didn't apply, and I wanted them to remember that.

The kitchen was full of black polymer and polished metal tools that looked mean. I picked out the garbage separator by eye. Oh, to stuff them in piece by piece to be turned into industrial hydrocarbons. But no, at least a few pieces had to stay intact.

Ghassan wasn't hard to spot. I jabbed him with the antidote— yes, an old-fashioned needle. No sterility and not gentle about it, either. The stim hit him and he puked all over himself.

"Greetings, dogfucker," I said. He glowered at me and tried to get up. I smashed him back down with a kick to the knee.

He screamed. "Tell me," I continued, "why you hijacked the *Francolin*."

"I don't know what you're talking about," he replied. "Who the fu—"

Sigh. He insisted on the ritual. Very well. I used the weapon butt to smash his right hand into jelly, blood oozing under his nails and across the scarred white floor. He passed out, and we repeated the stim and the vomiting. His stomach had to be sore by now.

"Talk, or hurt. It doesn't matter to me," I said.

He tried to squirm, and I shattered his wrist. We did the stim one more time, and nothing came of his retching. He was crying in agony. I could empathize. Not sympathize. There wasn't enough suffering in the universe for this piece of filth.

"Why?" I asked.

"To . . . to show the infidel dogs that they cannot oppress the true people of God!" he muttered through his tears. Or something like that. Canned, unthinking hatred.

"So, to show disapproval of a government, you blew up a shipful of civilians and shot a little girl?"

"I didn't like it," he said. *Sure* he didn't. "But sacrifices are necessary in war. They died for a greater—" I shut him up with a shotgun butt to the jaw. He sprawled back, blood and a tooth flying from his mouth.

I'd expected this, but had hoped he'd be a little better than any other terrorist. No, he was just a piece of shit. It pissed me off, and I got angry. I shouldn't have, but it wasn't going to change the outcome much. I was furious, self-righteous, and at the time I enjoyed every moment of it.

"There were other children aboard the *Francolin*," I told him, as I dragged him up by the hair and slapped tape over his mouth. "Some of the civilians . . . and the children . . . came from the Freehold of Grainne, including Jenny Marlin. So they sent me to deliver a message."

All his people were now awake, and my boys and girls had them on their knees, cuffed, pistols at their heads, as these scum so delighted in doing to *their* captives. The difference was, we weren't doing it to compensate for lack of courage and small penises. We were doing it to scare the shit out of them. My nose told me it was working in at least one case. Gutless weasels.

I got to work on Ghassan. First, I pulled on heavy gloves. I didn't want my skin polluted with his blood, and this was definitely going to be bloody. I handed back the shotgun, and Tyler took it. I was going to use bare hands as there was a point to be made here. Actually, several points. I stuck him with another needle, this one full of shock stabilizer and another stimulant. We wanted him awake to appreciate this. I boosted for additional strength.

I put the boot in for several seconds, hard, augmented and accurately. I aimed for ribs, joints, nerve points. He was shrieking under the tape, and trying to shove it away with his tongue. Then I clicked open my knife.

I waved it centimeters from his eyes. He was still conscious, the pain having gone beyond the threshold of comprehension. He stared at the glittering tip and wet his pants.

The human body can take a lot of damage. He was hyped on stabilizers and stims. I was trained for trauma medicine. Suffice it to say that, in fifteen minutes, he resembled nothing so much as a butchered hog. All it took was the knife and some creative posing. He was still alive. Isn't modern medical technology wonderful?

He shrieked and screamed and passed out again. Several of his underlings spewed and choked, or simply fainted. Heck, even Tyler looked a bit queasy when I was done, and she knew what was coming and had once helped deal with a parachute drop gone bad.

I had promised he'd stay alive. He was a much better warning that way. A corpse is forgotten soon. A mutilated survivor is horrifying again and again. So I was very careful not to cut any major blood vessels that I didn't seal at once. But that wasn't much of a limit. People don't bleed out nearly as fast as vid would have one think.

Finally, I stood. He was a ruin underneath me. One trauma medic had taken him apart, others would have to put him back together.

"Here's the message from God, My Children," I said as I looked at his lackeys. They were the most terrified, bedraggled-looking bunch of punks I had ever seen, with good reason. Most of them had pissed and shit themselves and were showing signs of shock from sheer sensory overload. I peeled off the gloves and dropped them into a bag to take with us. No evidence we could carry would be left behind. Sprayed nanos would destroy most of our pheromones and any stray biological material after we departed. "If you *ever* fuck with a Freehold registry ship, or a foreign flag vessel with Freeholders on it, we *can* find you, we *will* find you and the results will be even less pleasant than this. You do not want to see me pissed off.

"Now," I added, "your grunting sodomite here is still alive, and will stay alive long enough for a trauma team to get to him." Squid held a phone up to one thug's ear and dialed. "Call for help," he ordered as he ripped off the gag.

The punk stuttered and jabbered but finally got across that a terrible accident had happened, and help was needed *right now!* We disconnected, and I strode along the line of them as John retaped his mouth.

"We can find all of you any time we like. This is a small sample of how we deal with our enemies. Given good skeletal surgeons and several years of anguish in regen, he'll eventually resemble something that might look like a human being in bad light. With no balls. Of course, he never had any to start with, if he kills children." Yes, I'd castrated him. It was symbolic, and brutal, and of great impression to the young men with him. Frequently, they fear that more than death.

I nodded, and in seconds, every right hand in the place was mashed into stew. As they tried to scream through their gags, we vanished.

Revolting? Why, yes, they were.

Oh, you mean us?

These people killed innocent children to show disapproval of a government. They couldn't even justify it as collateral damage, as the government officials in question weren't near their targets. Aiming for a politician would risk their own hides, and that was something Ghassan just didn't have the stomach for. Not until the doctors finished rebuilding him, anyway.

How do I justify it? Well, since then, no Freehold registry vessel has ever been targeted by terrorists. No foreign flag vessel frequented by Freeholders has been attacked by the Fruits, and the total number of such vessels targeted has dropped 85%. I stand by my results. As to his torture and suffering, he was entitled to no protection under the conventions, not being a soldier and not choosing military targets. Besides, as Ghassan told me, sacrifices are necessary in war. His suffering was for a greater good.

I hate terrorists.

Did it disturb me, you wonder? After all, I'd taken such glee in doing it.

I wake up at night sweating, hands itching until I get up and scrub them thoroughly. I can't look at a person confined medically, or a person in a regen tank, without thinking about the pain and fear that got them there, and how it might be inflicted, stroke by stroke, by me. I can't watch a cut up horror vid, although I never liked them before anyway, but now they make me sick. I have this compulsion to jump on a person with the slightest injury, do everything I can, take them to the hospital, assist in their therapy and follow them around for years. I can't do that, so I dwell on it in my thoughts, for every little injury I see. I even bandage birds' wings.

No, it doesn't affect me at all. And there *is* such a thing as a stupid question.

But I do take pride in the results. Terrorists then, entire armies now, quiver in fear at the repercussions of attacking the Freehold. No one dares mess with us, and I personally am a large part of the reason why. Others speak of their lives as "the ultimate price" for their homes. I figured years ago my life was forfeit for the training. If my home is at stake, I'll sacrifice my soul. Any Operative will. That's why we win. That's why we did win.

But we do have to live with ourselves afterwards.

JOURNEYMAN

CHAPTER 7

The civil war on Mtali was the first real shooting war the FMF was involved in. I was lucky or unlucky enough to be along for it, with most of my friends. Some people rave about how well it went. Others claim it was a screwup from the word go. The truth, in my opinion, lies somewhere between the two. Certainly it was a balls-up nightmare, but I can't honestly say it was any worse or better than any other conflict. And even if it was worse, you have to consider the environment:

Mtali was named after a scientist from the old Central African Union about three hundred years ago. That makes it older than many other colonies. It's in sad shape because there were richer claims closer to Earth, so it was put in trust by the UN. This made it useful to several groups bent on escaping Earth (a valid thing to do, granted), who each staked out a small territory where they could have religious freedom, meaning to most of them the right to oppress anyone wrong-thinking, which was anyone not of their particular delusion. A couple of centuries of expansion brought them into contact, and the fighting started, or, for several groups, continued its millennia long tradition.

Just so we're all on the same page of the script, let's cover the major groups on Mtali. First in my mind, are the Bahá'í pilgrims. They are peaceful, decent people, with a practical and inoffensive religion that prohibits alcohol and initiation of force. They do consider self-defense valid and reasonable. They are technical and educated and very decent people to know. I like them. I can't think of anything they could have done to deserve the fate of being among the rabble, but here they were, and they were paying for it.

Want an example? The week we landed, a 14-standard-year-old Bahá'í girl named Tahirah Rabbani was caught and "tried" by a Shiite (although I spell it without the "e") Mullah and his brave flock. The twelve of them gang-raped her, hung her up by her hair then lacerated her feet, leaving her to bleed to death. Her crime? Teaching the Bahá'í faith in their claimed territory. How can you argue with logic like that? The Bahá'í were the only people I felt sorry for on the whole worthless ball of mud.

So, onto the Shiits, or Shia. They were unchanged for five hundred years, and bore little resemblance to their 12th-century namesakes, who were not any relation I could discern. Regard-less of their books, their "clergy" held that being non-Shia was a crime worthy of death and dismemberment. Being close wasn't enough—the closer you were, the more obvious it was that one should know the "real" truth, and were obviously that much greater a sinner. To that end, they killed a few of their own periodically. That's the only good thing I could say about them. Their hygiene was minimal. If something wasn't useful for killing, they didn't care to study it. In fact, most of them were barely literate, but had memorized the Holy Quran (or at least the parts about kill-ing unbelievers and raping their women. I seem to have missed those verses in theology class). My opinion was that they were suffering a mineral deficiency in their diets—not enough elemental lead and tungsten. What do you call a Shiit armed with only a rifle and three grenades? A moderate.

The Sunni. They were better educated than the Shia, but still bent on eliminating "unbelievers" from the galaxy. As with the Shiit, odd that their "true faith" didn't resemble the original schismatic beliefs the sect originally had. The only good thing I can say about them is that they generally limited their attacks to either Shia, or real military targets of anyone else, thus mini-mizing civilian casualties. The running joke was that you could pick up their weapons as cheap surplus—never fired, dropped once.

The Sufi. Decent people, almost as nice as the Bahá'í. They and the Bahá'í had come here first as a partnership, both being poor, smaller sects. They were willing to engage in force, and did so to protect their borders and often their Bahá'í neighbors. The only bad thing one could say about them is that they were sometimes a bit too eager to prevent incidents by stomping potential threats. As those potential threats were Shiits and Sunnis, I couldn't hold too much against them. The Sufis ran a good military, had decent tech and capabilities, and held half the air and space facilities. What should be done about the problem of the Sufis killing Shia and Sunni out of hand? I don't see what your problem is.

The Amala. A newer, more recent offshoot of Islam, the Amala were trying to breed themselves into the majority. They were poor and starving and wretched, and would probably be better off dead. They were likely to achieve that, as the Shia hated them for breeding. Of course, the Shia hated everybody. The Amala were the least educated of the mostly dirt-stupid bunch, and paid for it. What do you call an Amala who can read at the level of a five-year-old? An intellectual.

The Believers. Technically, "The Faithful of the One True God," a Baptist offshoot, but don't tell that to either group. I don't blame the Baptists for wanting nothing to do with them. The Believers had come here to despise science and technology (using stardrive to do so), and were "creation science" nuts. Their take on the Biblical Deluge was that the Earth had been surrounded by a huge sphere of atmospheric ice. God had moved the Earth from a 360-day year to a 365-day year, thereby melting the ice and flooding the world. Where the water had gone afterwards they never explain. The lack of the ice after that had increased radiation levels, thus aging the bones of the dinosaurs, who'd all drowned in the Deluge, so as to make those bones appear millions of years old to delude non-believers. This had been simultaneously done on millions of planets to make them all look old. I don't even want to begin to psychoanalyze that. They used imported technology and weapons, while denying that the basic science behind that equipment existed. Harmless, except for a desire to shoot anything not Christian, and convert anything Christian to their one, true faith. Notice a trend here? Oh, and they had a thing about homosexuality. They could claim with a straight face that a gay-oriented bar in a city was the cause of floods, earthquakes and Signs and Portents in the heavens. Ironically, their founder, Frederick Felts, had eventually been raped and beaten to death while incarcerated for the crime of attacking a "baby killer" (a doctor who performs abortions). An acceptance and agreement with his illogic seemed to be a requirement of membership in the cult. The Colonial British wore red tunics so that blood wouldn't show and ruin the morale of the troops. The Believers wear uniforms with brown pants. Enough said.

Various legitimate but naïve sects of Christianity who'd moved here simply to live, then gotten stuck with the nutcases. I wasn't all that sorry for them—they bickered amongst themselves constantly in their "Christian Coalition," and spent more time debating the nature of God and the laws they should all live by than they did taking out the trash. If I'd ever wondered about the human race before, now was the time. How many Coalition troops does it take to change a light tube? Fifty. One to do it, and forty-nine to argue over the doctrine.

The Mowahhidoon, often called "Druze," which they don't like. They're a very old offshoot of Islam, but no longer Islamic. They keep the details of their religion secret. They don't marry outside the faith and don't accept converts. The only thing they were doing wrong was existing, as far as most of the other sects were concerned. Gods, what a world. How many Mowahhidoon are there? Enough.

The Zoroastrians. Another decent group. They were too few to be a real threat, even had they chosen to be, and too few to survive. They were taking the better part of valor and leaving the planet as they could, for UN owned orbitals and deep space habitats, or for safer homes. That wasn't good enough for their Shia and Believer neighbors, who shot at the remainder whenever the urge took them. The joke was unfair, but had an element of truth to it: have you heard about the Mtali Zoroastrian battle flag? A white circle on a white background.

That was it for major faiths. However, each faith had up to

fifty different factions within, of various political leanings, moral opinions on cooperation with others and within the group, etc. I won't bore you with that. Frankly, I'm not sure I understand it. It dealt with all those subtle and mystical things that might require you to kill your brother-in-law and rape your sister in order to save their souls. Important but complicated stuff. It's top secret. I wouldn't want to give you wrong info and have you kill someone who only deserved a beating.

Thank God and Goddess the Jews had been smart enough to stay away. I understand that it had briefly been considered by a joint Israeli-American Jewish group, who had seen the inevitable future and shied away, to settle relatively peacefully and reasonably on New Jerusalem. A practical people, the Jews. And of course, tiny Kuwait had sponsored the Ramadan colony and limited immigration to Muslims who didn't measure diplomacy in kilograms of explosive. I wonder why they had seen the pending strife that the system would fall into, while the UN political scientists hadn't?

Maybe it wasn't sheer poli-sci stupidity, although military science types like myself have always detested the self-imposed ignorance of our civilian counterparts in the field of human relations. It may have been bribery and lack of concern on the part of the Colonial Commission. I still bet the poli-scis had a hand in it, as they had in most of the failed "Republics" in Africa in the twentieth and twenty-first centuries, leading up to the Expansion off Earth.

So, into this ball of snakes had come the experts from the UN, decreeing that a solution must be found, and that solution must be peaceful in nature. As peaceful solutions are only possible with people inclined to be peaceful and reasonable, and as the groups in question were neither, that was a failure from the beginning. Being stubborn and conservative in its stupidity, the UN not only beat the dead horse, but tried to motivate it with speeches, then offered education and infrastructure to it. Financial aid was poured in, to promptly be used to smuggle in weapons and advisors to escalate the struggle. Then the benevolent protectors of the human future (sorry, I'll lay off the sarcasm) had brought in peacekeeping forces, oxymoron that that term is. As there was no peace, attempts to keep it were futile. That brought us up to our involvement.

We didn't tell anyone then, but a lot of people figured out afterwards, why we bothered. After all, we're a neutral star nation, and plan to stay that way. People come to us with money for our services, so what need have we to go elsewhere on imperialistic junkets? The happy, comfortable rich rarely have a need to squabble over leavings.

Well, think about what I mentioned earlier: we had wealth, independence, freedom, and were a huge drain on the UN for that reason. We were a threat to the accepted wisdom and status quo, by doing what they said was impossible and dehumanizing—to whit, being what we were. We were less than one percent their population. We had a military with first class training, and no realtime encounters to test ourselves or train us that extra crucial bit. So we sent a small contingent along to get that training and do live-fire tests of our prospective enemy. We needed a low intensity shooting war; we went to Mtali.

We were fortunate in a couple of regards. The mission commander was brigadier Charles Richard ("Ree Shard"), Third Mob was commanded by Naumann, who not only knew how to use Operatives, but was one himself. Frequently, the mission and skills of elite forces are unknown to the very officers expected to use them. Sad, but it's the norm. Even worse, those officers often aren't interested, as their goal is to generate good reports so as to get promoted. Naumann and I thought alike; we didn't care about reports, we just wanted to kill things. He defined our area of operations, we defined our own OPLANS, and he gave us the space and the support we needed to kill the factions' terrorists in huge numbers. Richard wanted the best results with the lowest friendly casualties, and listened to the advice of his subordinates about their particular fields of expertise.

The UNPF had been screwing up, as usual. Not because it was incompetent, although it was mostly trained to suppress urban insurrection, but because the politicians insisted on defining operations from up to twenty days away and without visiting the planet. They decreed that no hunt could be made for the upper ranks and organizers of the factions. Probably, that was because targeting foreign tics and dips would leave those gutless fucks open to retaliation.

They said no hunting. Our Citizens Council is made of sterner stuff. We hunted. We succeeded. What the UN took twelve Earth years to screw up militarily, or more accurately, masturbate up, we resolved in six Earth months. Cut off the heads of the hydra, it grows new heads. Cut out the heart, grill it and eat it, the heads die.

3rd Mobile Legion was tasked with holding the central district. That's ten thousand troops for two million residents. 3rd Mobile Assault Regiment, plus extra aviation support, held the capital, Attaturk. They did it by taking the city sector by sector and being ruthless. Anyone who faced them, died. They killed close to 15,000 Mtalis. Since the Mtalis and the UN had accounted for 300,000 over twelve Earth years, our count was far more humane, far more economical, and allowed the system to recover faster. They took each sector in turn, and exterminated the vermin.

While Mob pacified the city, Special Warfare Blazer Regiment probed, patrolled and secured the rural areas. While they did that, Black Ops ran reconnaissance and baited the factions. We'd go out in squads or even fireteams, dare them to attack us, then mash them to paste. If we felt it necessary (we usually did), we called in gunships, artillery and orbital strikes. We managed to keep collateral casualties to a minimum, too. But I'm ahead of myself.

The Citizens' Council and the Strategic Staff decided we needed the experience. They decided this would be the place to get it, despite the putrid taste of kissing the UN to accomplish it. They drew up a budget, a plan and the orders, then handed them down for us to do with as best we could.

I had advance notice of this little jaunt. Officially, I mean. I was told to get my squad ready and be prepared to operate in support of 3rd Mob *by ourselves* while the rest of the deployed force—about a third of the regiment—would support the Legion. An independent command, even if as an attached unit. I felt drunk for a couple of days. Then I sobered up, realizing people's lives depended on my every word as never before. Still, it was powerful.

There were plenty of hints that we were going. The Council discussed it. UN reps were invited to give us assessments and input on the war, excuse me, "engagement," and what was needed. That should have been enough for anyone. Then, everyone got told to check their gear top to bottom. Would you believe half or more of the Forces were surprised? Would you believe half or more of the people in elite combat units (Mobile Assault) were upset at the idea of leaving home? They even complained about how it would affect their sports, schools, etc. It made me wonder why they joined the military.

I made one very good decision. I hit Logistics early and ordered *everything* we might need, in triple quantities. Naumann signed from his end, Erson from his and I faced off with the bean counters.

I was told, "I don't care if you *do* have authorization for all this stuff, I am not letting this quantity of material go." That from a captain at Legion Logistics. Matt "Yankee" Blackman. An idiot controlled by his anger, who drank too much and was in crappy shape despite his burly physique. His office had the accoutrements of an officer from the First US Civil War, hence his affected nickname. "I have to maintain inventory, in case we get an order in."

"You have an order," I told him. "Right here. I need the stuff."

"And what if I get an inspection team in here? I won't have sufficient quantities on hand," he said.

"So you tell them it was drawn and show them the restock orders," I said. How stupid was this clown going to be?

"No," he said, shaking his head and screwing up his face. "I'm the word on logistics and I say 'no.'"

I did the only thing I could. I said, "Yes, sir," and left.

Then I went to Erson, who called up the chain. Then I went back over to Logistics. Blackman looked at me as I opened the door and said, "What the fuck do you want?" Then his phone beeped.

He stared at it, then at me, then at it. I said, "I think it's for you."

He snarled and turned the screen away from me. I heard him

say, "Legion Logistics, Captain Bla— Yes, sir . . . Yes, sir . . ." Then
he activated the hush field, but I'd seen what I needed to. He was
"Yes, sir"ing and nodding. As soon as he disconnected, he muttered to one of his NCOs, who nodded. Blackman disappeared
while the senior sergeant, Briggs was his name, took care of me.
He winked and smiled as I left.

Sure enough, a week later when the word came down to prepare, everyone hit logistics. All the savvy commanders had already
cleaned out every depot on the surface or in the Halo. What was
left over was dregs. The latecomers cleaned out what they could
get, threw tantrums when told the drain was so far back that the
manufacturers were backlogged and an emergency order couldn't
get them what they needed. Some few took advances against
budget, and in the case of one commander, a highly illegal but
effective loan against unit assets, to buy from civilian sources and
hope the budget would catch up. The rest paid out of pocket or
their troops did, or went without.

It was a bit shocking to me. Even with all our constant stressing
of the essentials, of never being short of critical materials, here
in the best military in space, people could get lazy and screw
up royally. Even here, I would have to fight my own system as
an enemy to get what I need. I thought about what would have
happened if I hadn't had gold collars like Naumann and Erson
willing to back me up. After we started fighting on Mtali, I thought
about it again and shivered. Even with all that prep, I was short
of what I needed. I would have been screwed if I hadn't had
good officers above me. And if it was that bad for us, what was
it like in the *bad* militaries?

The mess was repeated as we processed and deployed. It seems
as if everyone's family had an emergency come up around that
time, and that does happen. Murphy's Law. Also, minor issues
become emergencies when put under stress. Then there were
troops missing critical skills, or materials, or documents. Delay
after delay. My troops got through quickly, but we had to wait
for our support.

Eventually, we boarded our boats. It was a circus. Families,
friends, lovers, the media . . . we went in early, faces painted and
netted, tac helmets on. It made us look "gung ho." It also hid

our faces from prying eyes. We clattered up the ramps early, our gear already stowed except for our personal luggage. We lifted while everyone else was waving bye-bye, and spent our first div aboard ship swapping out crappy bunks in our billet for good ones from elsewhere. Also working fire extinguishers, better vid gear and anything that could be used as privacy screens. The poor bastards who came aboard last would have to use baling wire and strapping tape to hold their bunks together.

We started fighting the factions aboard the transports, by plotting. It's never too early to start winning a war. Brigadier Richard consulted with unit commanders, and we all gave input. The rest of them (except Erson and Naumann) tried to shut me out. Politics again. Certainly, I was an officer. I was a unit commander. I also was the youngest, newest one with the smallest unit, and an attached one, not a line unit. Never mind that I'd had more training than any six of the others. That wasn't a factor in their thinking.

So, they kept talking over me, and I let them. I'd played this before. The suggestions were good, no doubt. They lacked imagination, though. Get maps of the area, each from different groups so as to maintain objectivity. Study maps in detail. Review terrain. Get a political profile of the planet. Research background info of the friendly and enemy commanders. Teach history of the dispute (that was a *very* good idea, actually, and one that's often overlooked by junior officers). The problem was, all that would bore the troops.

After they wound down, and were looking at each other in smug satisfaction, Naumann addressed me. "You've been quiet so far, Warrant Chinran. Anything you think we may have overlooked?"

I could play politics, too. "I asked Captain Rutledge and Major Maron for advice, and put together a list with their help." I flipped up a screen on my comm and read, "Post rank charts of the various factions for the troops to study. Make sure the info is distributed to every hatch and bunkroom, all over the mess, and the latrine doors. We want to take the intelligence to the troops, not make them dig for it. That way it will seep in whether they want it to or not. Have the mess start serving local style meals to get everyone acclimated. Adjust the ship's gravity and environment for exercises, and have anyone who'll be doing local contact work on basic vocabulary. It'll make it easier to deal with the locals, and can be a good source of intel if they listen for key words. Do advanced language studies for the Blazers—my people already have primers on the four main languages—and offer it for any of the regular troops who want it. Use children's vids; they're easy to follow and impart basic vocabulary fast. Especially, use kid's books with myths and legends. It's the best way to gain insight into a people quickly. As far as equipment, have Documents print up some playing cards with pictures of the basic infantry, arty, armor and special purpose troop gear. Designate the royal cards after ranking officers, and list specs and numbers on the number cards. And if they're going to gamble anyway, create trivia cards so they can bet on who knows the answers."

There was a stunned silence for several seconds. Several officers looked sheepish, a few embarrassed. One or two grinned in appreciation and nodded, and a couple shot murderous glares at me, that I returned with bored but appraising locks to their eyes. They knew who'd be getting the points, the pips and the medals from this op.

The mission was entitled "Operation Restore Liberty" by the UN. Our part was dubbed "Operation Galactic Support." I swear that the first time I get to decide, I'll be honest with the troops and call the mission "Operation Goat Rope." Or maybe just "Operation Dogfuck." Yes, nothing ever goes as planned, but this hadn't really been planned. More precisely, every unit and political need had its own plan, which it assumed was The Plan. Everyone assumed they could pull enough strings to get what they wanted. Everyone got half. It was always the wrong half.

After twenty-one days and two hops, we arrived in the Mtali system. GRN 86 in Eridanus is a K0 with about 40% the luminosity of Sol. Our factory ship, FMS *Force*, and its destroyer escort peeled off for the meager planetoid belt. It would be hidden to everyone but its support crew and send us regular supplies that it created from raw materials and stellar output from 86. It didn't eliminate our logistics train, but it did reduce it immensely. I have to wonder why no one else has come up with a similar concept? Maybe because we lack capital ships and need such support? I think I prefer logistics insystem to dragging supplies for dreary parsecs, with the delay involved.

We cleaned out our bunkroom and headed for our assault boat. I did it as a ritual. Rituals comfort people and give them stability. From the rear of the compartment, each troop moved out into the companionway, flipping his (or her) mattress as he went. All locker doors were left open. All gear hatches open. When the compartment was empty, bare white and gray polymer panels and doors with dull mattresses, I went in and closed each opening personally, doing a final check. There wouldn't be a dust mote left in there unless it showed me authorization. We had everything we brought, there were no mistakes so far, and we were ready to land.

Then all we had to do was sit aboard our shuttle for a div while UN Space Control, Mtali got its thumbs out of its collective anus and gave us clearance. There were nervous conversations and card games in the stifling bay. At least it seemed stifling. There was adequate air flow and the temperature was 16 degrees, to allow for our clothing and armor. The dull background noise turned to cheers and battlecries as the clamps released us and we shoved off.

Down from orbit, bucking through the atmosphere. It read like a script. Officers maintained our calm, professional, "nothing to worry about" expressions to reassure the troops, while being terrified inside. Experienced troops cracked jokes to scare the newer ones so they could pretend not to be scared. The somewhat experienced ones nodded and agreed and grinned hugely to hide their fear. The new kids sassed back and boasted so as not to appear ready to wet their pants. It's a traditional illusion.

We were lucky. We were neither shot at, directed into a collision by bad control nor suffered any equipment malfunctions. Down we went, and when we hit the cloud level, sighs could be heard all around, the acts of earlier forgotten.

We all felt nervous again as we thudded down. Now we were in hostile territory, and not yet with weapons loaded. I planned to fix that ASAP. We rolled out quickly, our pilots understanding our concerns, and since they relied upon us as we did them, they gave us no hassle. We slowed, I rose, and as the ramp dropped I went out. It was sunny, warm and clear, with industrial and chemical odors in the air.

"Hot!" the pilot yelled. "Attack warning!"

We unassed in a hurry, skittering across the apron and diving into the green nearest us. It was thick and tangled and great concealment from whatever the hell was about to hit us.

It was a drainage sluice. The weeds were thick because it was boggy and wet. Slimy mud smeared across me, and warm, oily water splashed straight through the fabric of my uniform. I only noticed it after I felt my heart pounding enough to oscillate me on the ground.

There was nothing immediately in sight, so I pulled up my comm while transmitting, "Form in immediate teams with nearest troops, minimize movement, prepare for incoming threats."

A glance showed nothing nearby. What was the threat? Incoming kinetics to blow us to vapor? A terrorist somewhere getting off a shot? A real military assault with combined arms?

Nothing. Nothing on my comm, either. I sent out an inquiry, as water capillaried up to my neck. Nothing.

I don't know if it was the spaceport control having a wiseass joke at our expense, or if it was an attempt at pilot humor. He insisted he'd heard a warning, but he couldn't place the source. I intended to find out. A joke like that called for a retort.

"False alarm," I said in disgust. "Let's go get dry."

They followed me, Frank in the rear, and we sought some shade; the south temperate zone of Mtali gets quite bright. I found a convenient location near a maintenance building off the flight line, and we took a look at our gear. It was filthy, but only on the outside. Everything was wet, of course.

We were already armed with our basic weapons, but the extra squad equipment needed to be checked and prepped. While we did that, I had the teams take turns cleaning and inspecting their personal kits.

We had one brief, pleasant encounter with some of the departing Unos, as we took to calling them. A unit of US Marines came by, trudging on foot to their shuttle. Why they were slogging it and not on a vehicle I'm not sure, but I'd blame UN Logistics. They never were very reliable.

The Master Sergeant First Class in charge of eight troops was following their Field Officer (yes, they really do have fifteen enlisted ranks, and yes, they really do need an officer to authorize every operation), turned to face us, and grinned what he probably thought was a scary smile. He said, "So, you're here to fight the factions, hey?"

I matched his style and grinned a warface that would scare the dead. "No. We're here to *kill* the factions," I replied, slapping a clip home as I said so. He walked off shivering. We laughed.

Despite that, I made sure everything my troops and I had was inspected and solid. Weapon. Basic ammo load. Harness. Canteens. First aid kit. Tools. Tactical helmet and all vision choices—sonic, IR, visual, enhanced, magnification. Body armor. Blades . . . you can never have enough blades. I had my wakizashi, a short bolo, a dagger in my left boot, a heavy locking folder in my pocket and another on my gear, not to mention a folding multitool and a tiny one in another pocket. The knife was one of our first tools, and will always be one of the most important. I made sure everyone's blades were secure. We adjusted our optical sights for the .79 G and the odd magnetic field, which is nearly twenty degrees from the poles. Then we all checked our basic load of ammo for cracks, warps or other flaws.

I did all that as a precaution, assuming for safety's sake that the area was hostile and would remain that way. I was correct, it turned out. Professional paranoia scores another win. Once our heavy gear was ready, we formed up for airlift/convoy to the UN headquarters, which was for some odd reason not attached to the starport. This is what comes of letting diplomats and politicians with no military experience run your war plans.

At least the stark and sere compound, near the northern edge of town and easily reached by roads or air, had ringed perimeters and solid roadblocks and berms. I landed with half the unit as the other half brought vehicles, so as to clear our squad area ahead of time. The buildings were modern, basic and clean, far better than anything I expected in a combat zone. The chow hall was roomy, as were the theater, exchange, gym . . . I tried to decide if this was a war or a summer camp? The UN has the material and starlift capacity, but it struck me that being overly comfortable encouraged a long stay and lack of ardor in the fight. Best to move in, do the job and go home, not turn a developing nation (submerging, even) shithole into a parody of home.

The key to understanding the UNPF is to remember that they are all effectively reservists. A reserve unit needs some shake-down training and time before deploying on a mission, and so did they. In the case of reserves, it's that they only train a few days a month. With the UNPF, it's due to inadequate training and poor budgets.

Consider their "training": In basic, they shoot one string of "live" ammo with the charges reduced to near nothing. Beyond that, they shoot non-lethal weapons only once a year, and usu-ally simulate that with a machine. They fire a simulated string of "live" ammo every five Earth years, if they stay in that long. Their first aid and other support training is all done by watch-ing videos and answering true/false quizzes, which are corrected to 100%. If it isn't in the soldier's specific tasking, he gets either next to no training, or is denied training and told to "leave that to the experts." The infantry handles real weapons only once per month, and shoots only once per year.

Before deploying, all personnel shoot another "live" string, offi-cially. But commanders often skip that to avoid the adminwork, as every single round of ammo has to be accounted for. Since they don't allow people to possess weapons and account for them every time they go in or out, it seems redundant to count electrically fired cartridges that cannot be used as more than firecrackers without a weapon, but understanding the rationale of paranoid sheeple has never been my strong suit.

It shows in their chain of command—officers supervise every little task, they have constant roll calls and accountability and they have civilians and contractors handle cooking, maintenance and other support chores even in a combat zone. These are tech-nically noncombatants under the Mars Protocols, but accidents do happen. I consider those people braver than the troops; they have no weapons, little armor and only occasionally a single guard per detail.

The FMF has no noncombatant personnel. We shoot weekly or monthly, depending on unit. We use live ammo. Our training consists of going to the field and doing it. We constantly seek tougher challenges (such as Mtali) to increase the difficulty of that training. We issue our troops weapons in basic and, unless court-martialed and discharged, they keep them for life. Ammo is ordered by the truckload and dispensed by the kilogram, not by the round. I figured we'd outmatch them about ten to one. I was correct.

The biggest giveaway was when we met General Bruder. He seemed a bit on the slimy side. Not only that, he had a camera crew. Now, we have public affairs people, too, but this clown had a personal crew and a director to oversee the shots. Unbelievable. Especially as his acting resembled a tree, his face would jam an M-23, and his voice was a soft, whiny tenor to match his pale, sluglike body.

This wasn't a military operation; it was a PR circus. All it needed was ten clowns getting out of a little car. Then I saw his staff limousine. Yes, limousine. Naumann had a plain SPV-46 command car, armored and gunned. No flash. But then, Naumann has nothing he needs to prove.

I had a crawling feeling along my neck and shoulders. This couldn't be a serious operation. It had to be a dream, or a joke. Any second now, he'd smile, brace up, laugh and become a commander. Any second now. Any second. Now would be good.

It wasn't a dream. But it was a nightmare. Then it got worse. Someone panned the camera across the crowd. Across me.

I spun, getting my face out of view, slumping my shoulders to hide my posture, and flipped my visor down and my scarf up, as did my nearby squadmates. One of the crew came over to reassure me about permission forms and all that. I politely said, "Point a camera at me and I'll hack your throat open with a saw." He gibbered and left. So did I. This was no place for an Operative. It was no place for a soldier. It was no place for a real military.

Which was exactly why we were there.

CHAPTER 8

Nothing happened for three days. Nothing. We moved into our squad bay in the barracks, pinned our ghillies and cloaks up to create privacy screens, swept out the dust left by the last pigs and got moved in. We swapped damaged bunks for good ones on a late night scrounging mission, mostly from empty barracks, but Frank and Tyler couldn't resist the urge to sneak into an occupied hooch with troops drinking out front, hoist a mattress off a bunk with the sleeping soldier still snoring within the blankets, and swap frames underneath him. He'd wake up with a dry-rotted, squeaky, saggy bed and wonder what the hell had happened. But that was all the excitement we had.

It was tedious. Our weapons were loaded, our gear was ready, our vehicles maintained and primed. We had provisions, spoke the languages, knew as much as we could know without getting out there to look, and were required to stay where we were until we could have a scheduled briefing.

I suppose part of that was the fault of the FMF for having the gall to arrive on schedule. Or maybe we were being punished for the sin of being efficient. Either way, we had to wait for a briefing of all the things we already knew: factions, terminology, chain of command (although the briefing officer was under the mistaken impression that we took orders from the UN), emergency procedures, etc. We were told we'd be securing a warm sector against faction activity. Then we were told we'd be holding and reinforcing a secured area.

Finally, we went out to guard a retail strip plaza.

No, that is not a typo. They sent us, possibly the most lethal, brutal squad of professional killers in the system, out to guard a strip plaza. All of us. I could handle that job with three. My kids swore, I politely complained, Naumann sarcastically asked if they needed us to pick up any takeout while we were there, but it was a choice of guard the stores or do nothing.

Okay, it was a bit tougher than I expected. It did, in fact, call for all of us. Or all of *any* squad. Legion Infantry could have handled it. A squad of reserve Security Patrollers could have handled it. Even our base support personnel were more than adequate to the task. So we took it.

We did get a map. I did get to meet with the previous officer, a Belgian with good French and adequate English who was honest and forthcoming but seemed a bit frazzled.

"Mostly ground traffiique, not air," he said. "It was bizzee juring the eevenings, and on weekends, despite the relijious hollidays."

"How many people per hour?" I asked. It was a reasonable question.

"I am not sure."

Terrific. An unspecified variable. There were more of those. I took the map, drew up some basic response routes and stations for our vehicles, and drilled everyone on paper and on a comm simulation. I'd play it as it came when we got there.

Rather than run the half-day shifts from local midnight to local noon and vice versa, so everyone gets some daylight and is only half a day off schedule, the UN has a ridiculous "6 am to 6 pm" shift using a variation of Earth's 24-hour clock adapted to local requirements. It could have been worse; they'd started by using *Earth's* clock, which was nearly forty minutes different, so the shifts rotated around the local clock. While that was unpredictable for the locals at first (purely by coincidence), it kept everyone tired and off kilter. So the 6–6 schedule was adapted to the local day, but still meant one shift never saw daylight to speak of and one never saw night. The night shift wasn't worth much because of that, and even though they had an easier task (the stores were not open after local 10 pm for some cultural reason I never really grasped), they were a weak point we didn't need. We changed to our midnight/noon shifts. It was no big deal as far as scheduling went, because the place had been unguarded the last three days. Yet we were told it was a common hangout for weapons sales and exchanges. How? If there are troops guarding it even sporadically, dealers should move elsewhere.

I braced my troops and we laughed at the "make every effort to subdue militants with non-lethal weapons before calling for authorization to use lethal force." As we saw it, if anyone pulled a gun, we'd shoot them twenty times and have Orbital drop a bar on the corpse. Anyway, we didn't have non-lethal weapons. The UN had apparently forgotten that, or not asked, and we were not going to volunteer the info.

So, just before noon the next day we entered in teams through the narrow, cluttered alley and the broad front, and made a quick sweep from each end of the L-shaped facility to the corner. The corner was what I was interested in—they were serving lunch. It was a neat, well-kept little Indonesian place, and smelled great. I walked in the back door with Frank, as Adam and Kit hit the front and we gave it the once over. White, clean, cluttered with utensils, family employees running back and forth with dishes and fairly tight quarters. There was an auto shotgun behind the door, which I ignored; a person has a right to defend his business and it wasn't a long enough range weapon to pose a real threat to us. I did make sure they knew I'd seen it, and let them ponder how we were different from the Unos, who would have seized it mindlessly, because "guns in private hands are dangerous." The owner, short and skinny and absolutely cowed by my towering presence, gradually recovered from the shock as we strode through. We checked the kitchen for obvious threats before sliding through the counter and into a booth. We were joined by the rest of First Team shortly, and nearly filled the place; our rucks and gear over the seats made it a very tight fit. I kept two teams out patrolling the corner and rotated everyone through to eat.

Like many Freeholders, I have Indonesian ancestry. My maternal grandmother was second generation from Kalimantan, and I did recall some of what she taught me, as well as having recordings I'd reacquired to study once I started languages. I never thought I'd need it, and wasn't very good at understanding it, but I could memorize phrases and my pronunciation was okay. I ordered for everyone by holding up a wad of credits and saying in Indonesian, "Tolong disediakan gulai ayam untuk dua puluh orang dan air jeruk nipis untuk minumannya." ("Sweet chicken for twenty, lemonade to drink, please.")

The owner seemed surprised that I spoke his tongue, and I knew that would go into the stories about us. He said, "Boleh saja, mohon tunggu beberapa menit." ("Of course, people. It will be a few minutes.")

The server was the eldest daughter, probably sixteen Earth years old. She was cute, but lacked the doe-eyed innocence young adults should have. She didn't look abused, but she'd clearly seen enough violence acted out on the streets to make her tired and worn. We were polite, tipped well and treated her as a lady, not as a peasant wench. She and her family were probably some former Indonesian Muslim sect, similar to some of our founders, and likely as disillusioned by the idiotic squabbles as we were quickly becoming. I made it a point that we'd treat everyone as decent adult human beings unless and until they acted otherwise, in which case we'd deliver justice with large ordnance.

The food was good. The chicken was tender, juicy and had an untraditional piquant sweetness from some local fruits used in its preparation. The coconut and rice side dish was loaded with plump red peppers that brought tears of joy to my eyes and endorphins charging into my brain for a tactical nuclear engagement. I thanked the owner profusely and said I'd spread the word of his presence to our friends. He was all grins at having guests who appreciated good cooking, paid in real local cash, not Uno scrip or marks, and didn't hassle his daughter for favors she didn't want to share, or him about a basic weapon to protect his shop. It would go far toward making the area safe for us, and building neighborhood closeness that would keep factional bickering at a distance. We exchanged bows, I thanked him again and we policed up our own trash as we left. I spoke a note for record for other patrols into my comm.

After lunch, we resumed our check of the area. We stayed in fire teams, me with Team One, Frank with Team Two, Deni acting as third leader with Team Three (Weapons), as sniping wouldn't likely be needed, and she had the experience to handle that much authority. She was great at operations, but Frank had a bit more methodology for leadership. Being professionals, we all knew this and didn't stress over it.

We wandered around, eyeballing and using sensors on our Jeeves (General Use Vehicles) to spot anything resembling a weapon. It's harder than it sounds, because anything large and metal or ceramic, or complicated and electronic reads as a potential threat. We were busy. Additionally, anything with explosive residue would trigger, including anything that had been near a previous terrorist car bomb.

Our vehicles were in a clear area at the center of the parking lot, and we waved away anyone who got too close. If they drove by too slowly, Tyler or Kit would track them with a mean look and an M-23. They kept moving.

My first event was an attractive middle-aged woman, in a decent quality vehicle. She stopped, got out, and headed for one of the stores. My goggles were coded into the sensor web, and flashed bright red at her purse. I nodded at Neil, our new troop, and reminded him with gestures to let me lead and back me up.

We were close to her in a few long strides, and I asked, "English? Türkçe? Araybiay?" to get her attention and set us up.

She turned, looked frightened, and said, "I speak Turkish and I'm Sufi, sir, is there a problem?"

Neil moved around about three hundred mils, a safe five meters away. We now had good position to take her down, and no, I wasn't assuming a middle-aged mother in a Mercedes was harmless. From over my shoulder, Tyler had her covered with the heavy, if I threw myself flat. Actually, Tyler was good enough to shoot over my shoulder, and I trusted her that much.

"I need to see your purse, ma'am," I said as I took it from her with a firm grasp. She didn't have any wires or triggers to either my eye or the sensors, and wasn't clutching at it in fear, nor was her hand inside. It most likely wasn't a bomb, and I didn't want to waste time or personnel by jacking every threat spread-eagle on the pavement, so I took the risk of getting close.

She yielded reluctantly, holding onto the strap until I clutched at my Merrill with my right hand. At that point, she let me have it, and her face started working in what was likely fear of our reaction. I stepped back slightly as Neil took a low stance, ready to bear and shoot. The black leather purse was unfastened, and I opened it carefully. There was the usual civilian female junk, a sizeable but unsuspicious roll of currency and what looked like a Taurus snub 6mm pistol. Nothing else.

From my research, the Unos would consider the pistol a "military-style weapon" and seize it, plus likely loot the cash. They wouldn't harass or rape her in public, but such incidences were not unknown. Some of their national units are pretty savage. "What's with the pistol?" I asked.

She looked nervous and replied, "Uh, I carry cash for our business, sir. Please, just take it and don't hurt me." She'd obviously been rolled before.

"What business?"

"We're vehicle dealers, or my husband is," she replied.

Nodding, I handed it back. "Please don't take it out around our troops. If you see a threat, yell. It's safer if we have only the bad guys to worry about."

"Yes, sir!" she said, looking surprised and confused.

"Of course, if we're not around, do what you have to. Have a good day."

"Teşekkür, sőr," she thanked me, eyes wide. Neil dropped guard and walked off, I nodded, and she smiled dazedly and continued on her way.

For those of you confused, let me explain: as a legitimate businessperson, she needed to be able to defend herself against punks. Actually, everyone does. She was a prime target, however, with a nice vehicle and cash. Had I taken it, she'd just get another one in a few days, and do without food if need be to get one. When safety is a priority, other things must suffer. That would be no good for her family, wouldn't "get the weapon off the street" or any similar shitheadedness, since they were coming in by the transport load, and it wouldn't make us any safer. A pistol was unlikely to be used as a weapon against troops other than for assassinating clients of "hookers" (a derogatory term for sex industry workers used by those repressed enough to need them but pretending to disapprove of the idea), who should be more alert anyway, and which profile she didn't fit. Our body armor would stop such a round so well it wouldn't be noticed. And I'd hate to hear about her or her kids being robbed, raped, or shot or hijacked for the vehicle (which the factions did whenever they wanted fresh transport). Why bother taking it?

This was our routine for several days. It was boring most of the time, tense a few moments here and there, and we got decent food while making the locals happy with our presence. That corner plaza was *safe*. No one was getting robbed for gear, looted by those troops supposed to be "protecting" them, or shot or bombed by terrorists. We were actually accomplishing what the UN had promised and failed to deliver, by thinking rather than following text like mindless Uno automatons.

Then we hit local Friday. It got very interesting for a while.

First, we had a ground vehicle drive by that just lit the sensors. We quivered quietly alert, and waited to see what happened. I called a warning in case we needed air support, and we got into good positions without bunching up. It could be hard on a few private vehicles, should trouble materialize, but that was not my concern.

The vehicle was a ten-year-old Zil, rough-looking but intact. It was occupied by a driver, male, twentyish, and two other males and a female, also twentyish, young, lean, unremarkably dressed but with beards on them and a head scarf on her. Shia Muslim. Pardon the stereotype, but with the all the red on the vehicle's image, I pegged them as terrorists. Stereotypes exist because they are often true. It's a bad idea to rely on them, but a good idea to be advised by them.

Then they turned into the apron.

The sensors were starting to sort out the images as four probable rifles and a strong hint of explosives over a kilo. That was enough for me, and I wasn't waiting any longer. I said, "Go" into my mic and we rolled.

Neil and I sprinted across the lot, mindful of traffic, and took up positions ahead and to either side of the vehicle, so as to have clear shots at the occupants while being hard to run down. Geoff brought the second GUV over at high speed in low gear for maneuverability, and pulled up nose to nose as Tyler swung the heavy toward them, grinning a rictus that said, "I'd just *love* to splatter someone today, please make a threatening move, or any move at all, it doesn't matter to me."

Jay, Forest, Russell and Frank Number 2 from Second Team brought up the rear and the sides, leaving Frank and the second vehicle to cover us from the outer corner by the intersection, and the weapons team to cover both of us. It was a secure arrangement, and we had them pegged down. And damn, did they look scared about it.

Neil spoke better Arabic than I, as well as Hebrew, German, French, Mandarin, Aramaic and Sanskrit, of all things. He spoke clearly, precisely, and with all the force of a viper about to strike. "Get out of the car and lie face down on the ground. Make any sudden moves and you die."

I was worried about that explosive. They might have had it wired to go on a suicide switch. But it hadn't triggered on our remote detonator, which was designed to set such things off as soon as it could induce current in the arming circuits or hit the frequency used on a radio-armed device. And it wasn't a large mass, so it probably wasn't a car bomb, they had plenty small arms, so it probably wasn't a suicide mission, although they might try that as a "fuck you" gesture.

Luckily, they got out, slowly, and lay down. The fire was right out of them and we might have caught them on their first mission.

Carefully, we went through the car front to rear. We found four rifles, of which one was an FN WC. I find them overrated. Two were H&K Mod 96A1s and one was an ArmTech F-6. ArmTechs weren't common, but were a fascinating historical piece and well-made. I would keep that as a souvenir. There were three pistols, all S&W junk cheapies, and a Sufi military demolition block in the trunk which looked to be set up for use inside the plaza or some similar area. They'd violated Rule One: don't take unnecessary weapons that might give you away. They had no need of rifles to plant a charge. Or were they planning to shoot as well?

Neil questioned them one at a time, his hand occasionally straying to his belt, to caress the broad-bladed Viking style axe he favored in lieu of a sword. That dull gray chopper made them more nervous than the guns did. I stuck to the far side, listening for any whispers that might yield intel, since they didn't know I was fluent in the language also. No luck. The MO and dialect made them Shiits by my estimate, but they weren't talking.

We had instructions to be respectful of local religions. To that end, I let the woman keep her headscarf and had Tyler search her. I still had them stripped. When they started to fuss about the sin of being naked, Neil asked them about the sin of blowing up merchants and noncombatants. They steamed and kept quiet, except for the dainty feminine flower of Islam, who accused us of bestiality, compound incest and everything in between. I finally spoke, saying "Mohamed yunikku khinaaziir," ("Mohamed fucks pigs." Ungrammatical, I know.) while prodding her hard in the neck with a rifle muzzle. I was in no mood to be nice.

The search was needful. We found two more pistols and three grenades. Our chaste Muslim lady had a grenade hidden in a most unchaste fashion. I quelled the urge to make the obvious Freudian jokes, and we tossed clothes at them while calling for evac.

Would you believe the UN gave us a rash of shit over it? The arriving Intel Orificer shouted at me for "violating their rights" and "degrading them" by stripping them. We should not have laid hands on the woman. We should have shackled them and waited for "experts." He wanted the weapons for "Evidence," and then they'd be destroyed.

I didn't need his attitude. I have one of my own and it's quite enough. I shouldn't have argued back and made a scene in public, but I did. "Let me clue you in, Lieutenant," I said, a bit too loudly. "This is my op, and I make the rules here. Once they're signed over to you, you can interrogate them, or play pattycake, or watch pornos, or whatever the hell you want. But here, I—" I prodded him in the chest, hard, "am in," prod, "charge. You don't have to like it, but you can go screw a ripper for all the good it will do you to whine. I searched them, I found the weapons. You can keep the junk, I'm keeping the Armtech and the grenades for use."

"They aren't issue to your unit," he argued.

"Which is none of your business and how the hell would you know? The F-6 has an effective range of twelve hundred, twenty-three meters, muzzle energy of thirty-two sixty Newton-meters and a drop at three hundred meters of eighty-three millimeters. I like it. I'm keeping it. We can never have enough grenades. You have photos, you have my report, now take my prisoners and do your job. You may go now." From practical considerations and from relative chains of command, I outranked him, not that I gave a damn. He was wearing a *starched, tailored,* uniform, aftershave and a personal little pin on his collar proclaiming his support for the Equality Party in the upcoming European Federal Union election. I had no time for this clown.

He squawked and left and I knew we'd hear more about it later. I really *had* tried to be diplomatic. I was still young and cocky.

But first, we'd get a response from the clowns we'd tagged. I was partly expecting it, being suspicious about that possibility (any commander not suspicious about such issues doesn't deserve to command, or to live, and likely won't do either for long). I didn't expect the response we got.

Less than a day later, Saturday lunchtime, we got hit. We were taking turns munching sandwiches and watching, and I had Neil helping us with our Arabic. He suddenly cut off in mid sentence with a hollow gasp and a wide-eyed expression.

Then my brain noted the crack of hypersonic bullets. I said "Sniper!" loudly enough to be heard, without overdoing it—I'd be heard by my troops by ear and mic and wouldn't sound panicky. Then I dropped my sandwich and Boosted. It was less than half a second since the last of the shots and we were moving. Rather than dive for cover, we scattered in twenty, well, nineteen different directions.

I pulled up residual images on my visor, including a likely trajectory based on how Neil had been hit. It flashed probables to me in yellow, tagged the worst in red, and my eyeballs picked them out. Two gunmen, rooftop of the plaza.

Geoff informed me that he was driving around back, Kit on the gun, ready to support. Tyler was already on target and waiting for my orders, as I and others were between her and the targets.

"Adam, treat Neil. Tyler, stand by. Barto and Bryce around Grid Four and join Geoff. Team Two, stand to. Rest, rooftops."

I used first names, not tasks. I gave grid coordinates, not, "Around the south of the building." We knew who we were and where to go and I wasn't about to clue the enemy in more than I had to. So far, the response was great, but I was kicking myself for not having anticipated better. Still, we'd do what we could in response.

My vision steadied as my Combat NeuroStimulant Boost reached full force. I was flushed, sweaty, quivering with power, and running high from it, as well as normal adrenaline and endorphin response. A thought kept cycling through my head: "You dogfuckers are *mine!*" It was a strange, euphoric experience.

Then I reached the overhang of the plaza. The snipers had run off after a single shot each, and only one had hit. Rank amateurs, and I was keeping tabs on them as I could. Amateurs can be unpredictably dangerous, but will normally respond with basic human reactions once pinned. I'd been safe the entire run, and knew the risk would be greatest as I reached the roof.

The pillars supporting the overhang were polymer-concrete extrusions, with decorative six-centimeter wide grooves running their length. I grabbed two of the protrusions between grooves, and heaved, then got my feet splayed out, too. A second heave, fingers almost slipping despite my gloves, brought me to the top, and left me a meter of smooth sheeting to cross to reach the roof. I twisted and threw my body up, pushing off with my right foot, caught the bare ledge that existed between the pillar and the start of the roof, and arched again. I got my left boot toe over, then my left fingers, and drew myself up, rolling over.

There I was, lying on my right side, on top of my slung weapon, the hot, sticky roof compound gumming everything, bright Io or Sun or whatever they called it here disrupting my vision and glaring off my visor, and there was Sniper Number Two charging me. He'd seen he was blocked at the back, and was trying to find a hatch to go down and through a store, and here I was in front of him.

All I saw, however, was his rifle rising up toward me. I was scrabbling to my feet, still on my abraded and burned right side, glove stuck so tight to itself with the tarlike stuff that I wouldn't be able to shoot, and he was nearly on top of me. And that amateur move on his part saved my life.

Amateurs like to pose with weapons rather than use them. It's an icon, a symbol, an artificial penis. Professionals shoot and are done. Amateurs wave them around and chant, shoot into the air on camera with precisely the same naughty thrill as if masturbating, and this pathetic, illiterate corpse-to-be was trying to get as close as possible to intimidate me, scare me, thrill himself, and then wait a few seconds to shoot. His natural inferiority to everything with more self-esteem than a cockroach *demanded* that he see me cower in fear, and the overwhelming force facing him was forgotten.

I reached over my left shoulder, where my Eaves wakizashi was worn like a machete, and snapped it out of the breakaway scabbard. I swung it across, chopping off two of his left fingers as I chipped the fore end of that encroaching rifle and deflected it. He started to have that nauseous-pained look of someone who knows he's a victim, and I followed up. I heard shots toward the corner, and made note of that for later; there was nothing I could do about it now.

With the muzzle no longer pointing at me, I was able to take a fraction of a second to correct my grip, and my second swing caught him across the right forearm, nearly severing it. It wasn't cut totally, and flopped down like a broken branch as he started to scream. My backswing caught him above the hip, ended below the ribs, and he started spilling his guts, literally. I shimmied aside to avoid the roping gray snakes of his intestines, leaned to a sitting position and caught him by the collar as he bent forward, screaming. I rolled and threw and his body tumbled off the parapet, trailing entrails. It made the same sound as a splatting egg as it hit the pavement and splashed an outline.

I staggered upright, saw more movement and went to unsling my carbine as I sought cover. The tar was still gumming my gloves and was stuck to the trigger and guard. I'd be stripping it later to clear the gunk off. I identified the movement as Andut, our host for lunch these many days. His torso protruded from a hatch, his shotgun was at his shoulder and a third sniper, who hadn't fired and I hadn't seen, was dead behind Deni, who had the second one dead in front of her. Her spotter, Joel, had also dropped a few rounds into that third idiot. He was well dead. All being clear, I finished what I'd initially intended to do, which was to lean over the edge still only a meter from me, and put a bullet through my target's skull. It splattered again. Good. I hate the idea of "dead" people shooting at me, and this would make sure that didn't happen. It's called an "insurance shot," and I'd learned it when hunting jackalopes back home.

Right then, a VG-9 Taranis vertol gunship dropped down, ready to give fire support, and four more of my kids came up in different locations. That was fast. I quickly waved them back to cover positions, not wanting any eager gunners to think Andut was one of the bad guys. He'd done a great job. Whether or not we could have handled the third one—he and Joel shot just about simultaneously—his response was quick, competent, and bespoke trust in us and a contempt for the factional killings. I wished I could find a proper way to thank him.

It came to me as I descended the ladder to his place, CNS fading in an afterglow not unlike sex, that I'd made my first kill, and done it hand-to-hand. It was a strange combination of power and loathing, backed up by chemical enhancement, that would be with me for some time.

We each thanked Andut for his support, and gratefully accepted the proffered pitchers of pineapple juice, which we downed straight, no glasses. I later did find a way to thank him as he deserved, by quietly spreading the word again about his place. Every Freeholder who could, and even a few of the UN troops, made it a point to eat there until they could handle no more of the broad variety of cuisine. He had holiday level sales for about a hundred local days, troops crammed into every corner, out the door, and even around back. Even now, he's a popular host with the remaining UN force, and has made a small fortune. He deserves it. People like him prevent terrorism and factional stupidity by their presence, and it takes more balls than most people have to stand up like that. He'd increased the odds of the factions targeting him.

With a fading pulse thrumming in my skull, I dictated a report while a squad of Mob arrived to back us up. A Bison vertol equipped for medevac had Neil, and he was stable and fine. The bullet had been high enough power to breach his armor, and had missed his heart by three centimeters, but it *had* missed. He was stabilized, the hole in his lung temporarily cauterized, and was expected to be healed in a few days.

After a while, I was able to be objective again, and decided we'd had enough acclimation. My people had responded flawlessly to the attack, we'd taken out the punks and even kept the perimeter secure while we did so. It was time to move on. I brought it up to Naumann.

"Oh, I agree," he said. "If I ran this, you'd be hunting these rabble across the globe until they wet their pants at a mention of your name. But the UN won't let us out of this area, and until they thin their numbers, there isn't anywhere convenient to relocate and get any fire, so we're stuck here."

"Dammit, Commander, we can handle this!" I complained. "They sit there and follow a book written by some bureaucrat on Earth, annoy people, accomplish nothing and get killed! In a week I've made my area so safe that business has doubled, killed three ter-rorists, captured four, seized seven small arms, a case of grenades, explosives, documents and a vehicle. That's better than some UN *companies* manage in a month of alleged patrolling, including the pistols and knives they claim as 'military' weapons."

"I know, Ken," he said. "I'm on your side, remember? But we can't. If I could, we would, but it's not just political, it's a reality. Until we can move the UN, nothing is going to change."

I decided to escalate things myself, if that's what it took. I would provoke these assholes into attacking us, so I'd have an excuse to squash them like shit beetles. In a red-tinged huff, I stormed over to the clinic. Neil was awake from surgery, and I was told he would be fine. I went in to see him, accompanied by a nurse.

"How're you doing, big guy?" I asked.

His voice was better than a croak, but not its usual soft bari-tone. "Could be better," he said. "I'll be okay."

The nurse spoke up, "The projectile was slowed to subsonic by his body armor, thus minimizing the wound channel. It missed the liver, heart and inferior vena cava, and there is little additional hemorrhaging. The pleura and lung were punctured cleanly, and sealed at once, minimizing pneumothorax. With a few days of bed rest, he should be fine for limited duty."

"Thank you, Leon," I said. Medics like to use first names, to develop rapport with their charges. It makes sense, and I go along with it. Especially as "Warrant Jester" sounds ridiculous.

Neil nodded and said, "There you go, boss. Can you manage without me for a few days?"

"That depends," I said. "We're going to be hunting. You're going to miss it."

"Well," he said, "I'll get out of here as soon as I can. I don't like watching vid and I don't want to miss any action."

"I'll talk to the doc," I said. "Rest up. You did a good job."

He snorted. "I got shot and laid down. You guys did the work."

I didn't talk to the doc. I talked to Naumann. Naumann talked to Neil and the doc. The doc screamed. We pulled "Best needs of the forces" on him.

The next morning, we drove to our area, following yet another randomly generated route to minimize attack, and relieved the night shift from 3rd Mob. Neil was atop one of our GUVs, manning the gun.

The regular staff and patrons of the plaza were shocked. Less than a day ago, he'd been carried out in a basket, wired and tubed and with full medical support. Now he was back, standing and crewing a heavy machinegun. They didn't need to know that he was under orders not to fire unless ordered to do so because he was doped to the teeth with painkillers and shock stabilizers. The doctor wasn't happy, but Naumann had agreed with me, and Neil was only too happy to get out of bed. The psych warfare value was too much to let go. Shoot us and die. We won't even take notice.

The corpse of my target was still on the apron roadway, well-bloated and stinking. No one had dared touch it, lest they annoy us. That was one indication of how well we were doing: their religious need to bury the body had been overcome by fear of us. Good.

It was almost shift change before a man came over, abjectly

meek and with downcast eyes. He was dressed in local style in an absolutely unremarkable business jelaba. "Please," he said in Arabic, barely meeting my eyes, "I would beg permission to remove the body. The family would like to see that he is buried in proper fashion." He was obviously afraid of being nabbed and interrogated himself, just for mentioning a link to the sniper.

So I changed the rules yet again. "You may remove the body. Be sure to leave any non-personal gear behind. I pray he will find the peace in death he couldn't find in life." I would *not* interrogate him, I decided. We were the good guys. We existed only to stop violence and were harmless to honest people. That was the effect we wanted.

CHAPTER 9

After much begging, pleading, cajoling, the UN decided we could tackle patrols in the city's Ta'izz Jadeed mostly Sunni section. They marked off an area for us, plugged us into their comm, and coordinated their support with ours. We made tours and patrols with them until we learned the situation.

No, not really.

They did carve a chunk of city out of the blocks of gray stone and concrete. Then they handed it to us and told us to take it, best wishes, thanks, suckers, and don't call us again. I got the idea they were only too happy to sign it over to us, and that it was not choice real estate. I was correct.

My efforts to find out which sects and factions occupied this area had come to naught. The only UN officer I could find who'd admitted to having been in the area shrugged at my questions and said, "Sheetheads of some kind. They're all the same." He was representative of the forces present and a key part of the problem, not the solution.

We went in cold.

So there we were, patrolling in our GUVs, plugged into our net for air and arty support, driving past shattered hulks of buildings and watching for threats. That was everything. About 20% of the buildings were bombed out, another 10% already abandoned, the rest populated by people who stepped gingerly along the street and shied from parked vehicles. They also shied from us. Even when we tried to buy lunch. There wouldn't be any PR effect here. They were afraid to consort with us lest it bite them in the neck later, and too intent on keeping alive day by day, second by second to worry about the future. It was a precarious existence, hoping for someone to brave the threats to spend money, so they got only local business and some precious little from those who worked elsewhere and couldn't afford to leave yet.

We had to park and dismount often. Bombed out buildings had slumped across the roads. The streets were narrow, winding lanes, flanked by stark buildings and rubble that created shadowed canyons that are a soldier's nightmare. We'd send one vehicle around the block another way, while we stayed with the other two until the first reached the far side of an obstacle. Its crew would spread out around it on foot to search for threats, while the team gunner would sit in the open back hatch, covering a rear arc so the vehicle gunner could eyeball the front. One detour was eight blocks. Every street in the area had a severe blockage or more, chunks of stone and concrete surrounding shattered skeletons of polymer and old steel, resembling so many crushed limbs with bones protruding. Grisly. This city was dead, and no one had figured it out yet.

For right now, we were acting as infantry. I had other patrols around me from Mob and Legion, and we kept a steady flow of intel for safety and nervous chatter for comfort. The few breaks we took were for water and rats we'd brought along, and latrine breaks were behind anything that shielded our rears, taking turns to whip it out or squat and piss in the street while our buddies covered us from the front and the gunners scanned blank-staring windows from the rear.

Part of the fear people had of us might have been because a specialist named Kirby was with us, accompanied by his two assistants. The assistants were about 75 kilos each and 2.6 meters from nose to tip of tail. Trained military leopards. Great for sniffing threats both animated and fixed, great for hearing subtle whines and rustles that even AI sensors would neglect, and absolutely wonderful for scaring the shit out of people. Also, if we found someone who elected to flee, they could outdodge, outclimb and outrun him, and bring him down. While a barking dog can be surprising, we've had hundreds of thousands of years to get used to that sound. The snarl of a large cat is terrifying to the hindbrain. Kirby, Sphinx and Rasputin were effectively another fireteam as far as intel and fear factor went. I was glad to have them.

Despite all the damage, there were open shops in half the buildings, people walking around, staring at us in disgust as we urinated or defecated on their streets. They kept clear of us, but moved slowly and didn't reach quickly into vehicles or bags, lest they alarm us. The kids saw us coming and cleared out of the way, taking their balls, bats, paint and ropes with them. Older kids stood guard over them with rifles. They didn't treat us with the awe that healthy kids do, imagining soldiers as heroes like city safety workers or truck drivers, nor did they ask about the animals. We were a nasty that might kill them at any moment, should they get between us and a target. Or if we should decide they were acting threatening. Or if we wanted some fun. Inside of a few blocks, we had dour, bitter expressions on our own faces. It was contagious.

I was only too glad to hand control over to Sally Hayden and her squad of Mob at the end of the shift. I didn't envy her the shift that encompassed our first night (we'd started at midnight, come off at noon. So everyone knew we were new guys and had the day to plan what to do to us). We'd been first so we could get a good tour of the area in light and dark, and would soon take over the night like ghosts. Meantime, someone else had to be bait.

It went on like this for over a week, we taking the nights and sealing our barracks windows with black paint so we could sleep by day. There were sporadic shots at us that didn't yield many casualties but did wrack our nerves. There were car bombs and arson against the locals. Assassinations took place now and then. Pointless. What we needed to do and couldn't was just bomb the shithole into sand and let them start over. Though we might be able to. The UN and their sensitivity concerns were slowly pulling out, leaving us and a Novaja Rossian contingent on the far side of the planet for last.

Eventually, the odds caught up with us and my squad took fire. Along with the rest of our shift.

It was a quiet, late evening, still dusky, as we'd gotten there a bit early. We deliberately varied our shift changes to make things less predictable, and to ensure that we had a squad ready for backup and already in position.

We had good maps now, and I tapped my comm to generate a random patrol route. Everyone gathered around so to speak, even though none of us were within two meters of another and our sensors were dialed up to max to sniff for live explosives or weapons. With all the rubble and residue, it wasn't much help.

"We're going to swing around the west with a cross to the east at the lawyers' district and finish the first sweep at the blocks," I said, referring to a series of low, square apartment buildings. "Then we'll come back and crossover south of that, then dogleg through the market district back to our other point." I was using nicknames, acronym-laden speech and Spanish, even though we shouldn't be where anyone could hear us. It was the kind of area to inspire that type of paranoia.

It was barely sunset in the western sky, dark blue across the dome and with a faint fog settling in as we started off. The weather was calm and cool, about thirteen degrees. A good evening to patrol. Or at least a better than bad one.

We updated our maps regularly, so we had less need to detour, now. I was in the lead GUV, riding shotgun while Geoff drove. Crazy bastard always volunteered to drive. I had Tyler above me covering front with the heavy, and Neil sitting in the back hatch covering left. Second vehicle covered right and left, third vehicle covered rear and right. We actually could swing better firepower to the rear, which pleased me. We practiced dragontoothing— parking the vehicles in a zigzag so we have overlapping fields of fire—whenever we stopped, so if we needed to in an emergency, it would be a conditioned reflex.

It was a quiet, lulling evening. I hate those types. At the best, it dulls the senses. At the worst, it presages a pending attack. There was something definitely amiss. I took in the environment again. It was low buildings, ten floors or so. Squat, basic apartments built on cheap contract by some UN-connected contractor who'd built thousands of others in dozens of systems. We even had a few of the ugly things on Grainne, though we were getting rid of them as fast as possible.

Just at that moment, Rasputin growled, low and in irritation. Kirby said, "What's up, boy? What do you hear?" I leveled my M5 out the window and checked for the twentieth time that both bullet and grenade cartridges were loaded. I gave Kirby some time to translate from Leopard. Finally, he said, "He smells something, boss. All around, present, but nothing we have signals for. Not sure what it is. Sphinx isn't triggering, but seems kinda antsy."

I nodded even though he couldn't see me in the dark and crowded vehicle and said, "So we'll assume it's a general threat. Give them a treat." The buildings were now dark, with the windows black caves.

"Sure. Here boys, liver snacks!" His voice was followed by appreciative grumbles and the smacking sounds of carnivore jaws on processed meat.

As that happened, Geoff said, "Shit!" and slowed. I looked out through my visor and saw. Fresh damage, a crater and slumped buildings. Someone had cooked a car bomb. Spiffing. "I think I can make it," Geoff said.

"You just keep on thinking that, and stay here," I replied. I triggered my mike and said, "Frank, we're going around." He would lead, we'd dismount to cover, Deni would go second, we'd remount as Frank reached the far side to cover us, and come last as Deni reached halfway. I didn't need to say that, we all knew the drill. He would repeat the ping I was about to send to Control so they'd know what we were doing.

And it was right then that I heard fire. Then more. It came from two directions at once. Then a third. Dull thumps, sharp reports, the air-tugging Ba-ba-ba-ba-ba-BANG! of support weapons, all punctuated by the cacophonous crash of incoming arty. Who the hell could get arty through the interdiction batteries the UN had?

No time for that. I pinged a report to Control, not bothering with voice because everyone could hear it and the band was clogged with reports already. I heard a "SHHEEEEwhhhooooosh . . .

pause . . . WHAM!" that was too fucking close, and ordered, "Everyone out. Building to our right."

Then I bumped the door handle with my knee, rolled out onto hard, painful road and wet my pants.

Yes, I was scared, but that wasn't my motivation. I'd needed to go for some time, and modern hyper-velocity rounds will tear to sausage dense, liquid filled flesh. I wanted my abdomen as empty as possible in case of wounds. It would reduce the damage. If I needed to, I'd shit myself too. I would not be eating much even if there was time, and drinking in sips only. The skin irritation I'd fix later. My helmet said, "Three Zulu One—Control, unit approaching from your three hundred mil mark is friendly."

Around the side of the building behind and to our right came a squad of troops in three GUVs. Good. I could use some backup. It's awfully scary being an infantry bug while artillery swats around. The squad leader spoke in my helmet, "Seven Alfa Three. Glad to meet you."

"Seven Alfa Three, Three Zulu One," I replied.

There was a moment's pause as his comm translated that for him. He was being told we were a Blazer unit, Recon. He knew what that meant, even though no one listening would. Black Operations, pal.

He chuckled very briefly and replied, "*Very* glad to meet you, sir."

My brain caught up with my reflexes, then. I made an estimate of reports on the radio, explosive reports around me and small arms chatter. Some of it was coming from the buildings around us. Splashes of dust and rubble bit the road around us. Not good. This wasn't a probe, it was an attack in force. They must mean to use the confusion of the UN departures to distract us and over-whelm us. My brain zipped through tactical calc as it never had before, and I took it upon myself to make a command decision. Well, I was the only officer in the area.

"UP!" I shouted. I rounded up my squad by comm and eye, waved at all the nearby Mobsters, and indicated a building. I clicked a channel for the area, and ordered, "Inside, left, and up to the roof!" We dismounted in a hurry, flipping the encoding switches on the vehicles so no one could drive off without the hassle of bypassing the codes, which would take long enough for us to shoot them. I saw Deni pile out of the second GUV, tripping momentarily as she tangled in her carbine, which she was slinging, and her sniper's rifle, which she was porting for carry. Good girl. Joel was a step behind with ammo, scope and the smaller, close range marksman's rifle.

As our backup began moving in the indicated direction, I chivvied them along while shouting orders to my people. "No, LEFT!" I heard Tyler bellow. Someone had panicked and headed the wrong way. The right stairwell would be lethal, if the building were occupied.

Why, you ask? Because right handed shooters—the majority—need to advance stairs counterclockwise so as to have weapons pointed in the correct direction. It's even worse with projectile arms than it was in old castles where the sword arm needed to be free, which meant clockwise to avoid exposure. I'm told this is why old Earth castle stairs are all counterclockwise—the right-handed attacker must fight while exposed.

We got them through the narrow, dim corridors to the correct stairs and began advancing in pairs, with Frank and Neil in the lead. Tyler jammed the heavy up the middle and triggered an eardrum shattering burst to keep any bright boys clear. She hit something, as gouts of blood poured down amid the dust and rubble, very macabre. A squad weapon would have done just fine. The heavy was awe-inspiring. I had no idea how she handled it like that, as massive as it was and as small as she was. Kirby had the cats snarling their harsh killer cries. It served to scare the inhabitants further and urge our colleagues to move even faster.

As my kids advanced, they'd typically hit a foot and cripple the enemy, who'd applaud their marksmanship with a scream. One genius tried to poke his weapon through the railing and shoot down. Geoff shot him through the eye. At point blank range, the red mist was impressive. It also stank and I could taste the salty iron tang of it in my throat as we advanced.

I called HQ. Click— "Prime—Three Zulu One, moving to rooftops, suggest likewise. Have Seven Alfa Three with me. Request support soonest. Can hold for indeterminate time, but status may change."

There was little action currently, except for shooting the occasional wiggling wounded who'd not been sent to meet God yet, and since I believe in respecting local religions, we sped them along their journey. Most of the residents were wisely staying hidden. Anyway, it was a commercial building, not an apartment. Or it had been once. It seemed to be a refuge now.

The exec spoke in my ears. "Three Zulu One—Mob Two, movement endorsed, support as it happens, good hunting." That wasn't good. "As it happens" was a code phrase meaning roughly, "We are screwwwed and you're on your own for the foreseeable future." At least I knew it was an open party.

There was a clump of people at the top of the stairs. I shoved through and organized the squad, shouting back for the Mobsters to keep an eye out for laggards (ours) and targets (theirs). The roof hatch was locked, but a few rounds took care of that. We erupted in best assault formation, to a thankfully vacant roof. We dispersed and prepared positions.

Kirby and the animals stayed in the stairwell with five Mobsters. I wanted our rear covered for retreat, and there wasn't much the animals could do up here anyway. The rest of us prepared to render unto Caesar the things that were Caesar's, and to God the things that were God's, namely: the souls of his frothing followers.

Deni and Joel took a position in a drainage channel, soaking themselves through but getting a fine position to snipe from, with a generous opening to shoot through and thick concrete around and in front. Tyler set up near one corner and shouted for people to bring her materials for cover. She punctuated it with a burst at the advancing horde. Yes, "horde." From the north, it appeared. Not a wave, but tens of dodging figures who were obviously experienced at urban combat, and had artillery support at least. "I hate having lots of enemies. I never know which one to kill first." That was our joking motto. Very funny. Who had screwed up enough to let this happen?

It suddenly came to me that this hadn't been the brightest of redoubts. It was too fucking visible. On the other hand, staying on the ground meant lousy visibility and no position. On the other hand, underground was too much like going into a grave. On the other hand . . .

I noticed far too many people for my count. There were other Mobsters swarming up through the hatch while their buddies provided generous cover. That was good. But we were all massed. That was bad. I ordered, "Control—Three Zulu One. Link Seven Alfa Three to my comm. Break. Broadcast, elements within two hundred meters lateral. This is Three Zulu One, new arrivals pick another building so we have crossfire! And get your heavy and your support weapons on the corners. Your marksmen will do best on the south." I took a few seconds to look around and decide where to place people. We needed most on this side to stem the horde, but a few on other corners would help. The problem was, the other corners had no cover until we blasted a rooftop service building and dragged stuff from the floor below to build with. That meant splitting people up while we took fire.

It didn't work out too badly. Deni, meaning Joel doing the seeing while she did the shooting, had a clear view of the street and took out a mucky-muck in an armored car right through the plating. Some amateur thought of using an aircar as a shooting platform, and Donnie and Ross painted him across the adjoining building with a missile to gently let him know that that trick was old and stale. It got down to the business of our shooters versus theirs. Theirs had more combat time. Ours were just as willing to shoot, knowing survival depended on it, and were better shots.

A third building was reinforced from a VC-6 Bison that had been returning from some patrol or other, and we secured the area around us. I saw a cluster of enemies (translation: no one I knew) gathering in front of our second building, using vehicles as cover, and dialed up the rez to be sure they were enemies. They were. I leaned over and burped off four grenades and in moments they were cooked sausage. One of our compatriots returned the favor on their buddies in front of *our* building, and we waved acknowledgment at each other. A warning flashed in my visor, and I ducked, hoping everyone else's was working properly. Damned things will *always* fail when you need them most.

A farting roar shook the sky and made me cringe reflexively, then I grinned. The warning had heralded the sound of high-speed rotary cannon in large caliber, which meant our Hatchets had arrived, and nothing the enemy had could compete with that. This game was over, and thank you very much for playing, assholes. Welcome to modern warfare.

They knew that game, too, it seemed. A Hatchet was nailed with a vehicle-launched AA missile. It dropped out of view, but as I sneaked a peak I saw the pilot make a forced landing and take out the ADA vehicle. He landed *on* the ADA vehicle, while shooting a last burst into an oncoming APC. He hopped clear and was just into a building when the auto-destruct package took out all the enemy within the intersection. Still, they had an armored car, an APC, an AA equipped vehicle and three others I'd seen so far. This was not getting better.

We stayed there all night. The enemy were bringing up better weapons, and we were calling in ours. They took a few rooftops, and we had a tense time of sniper versus sniper. I was worried about Deni especially, and Tyler with her heavy, as they were prime targets. Deni was a demon, though. While hunkering down, I watched her. She breathed, went slack and squeezed. Utterly calm. Nothing could bother her when she was in shooting trance. The enemy were simply targets to her. Joel whispered targets to her, she shot them. She got one marksman right through his reticle. Of course, her rounds were somewhat more vigorous than his, and the hydrostatic shock turned him to goo from eyeball back to lower ribs. *That* was a psy war bombshell to his buddies, whose fire was a mere formality for several segs following, until someone convinced them to resume shooting. Tyler relocated to that side and hosed the top thoroughly, Neil and Barto and three Mobsters I didn't know and I lobbed a few dozen grenades over, set for two meter proximity burst, and Donnie slammed a missile into the top of their elevator shaft. The shrapnel from that was impressive.

For some reason, that rooftop was silent the rest of the night. Possibly because there wasn't one.

But we couldn't evacuate the wounded. I could hear one guy, lungshot, hacking deep, gooey wet coughs and shrieking in pain. The medics were near the middle, had laid their packs open so we could all grab bandages and painkillers and stims, and were frantically operating on the three serious casualties to keep them alive until we could get pulled out. I would have been terrified if I wasn't using every drop of adrenaline to keep me alert and moving.

My ears picked up something just as my visor flashed red, and I threw myself flat as an explosion blew the parapet next to me to dust. I was stung with tiny particles and slapped with the blast. It snatched at my breath. I'd wanted action, right? I was maturing at a hell of a rate through this.

Sensing a lull, I ran back to the rear of the elevator hatch. I'd designated that the latrine, and I had what felt like a turtle poking his head out of my ass. There was a young mobster squatting there, and she stiffened as I approached, almost as if she was about to pop to attention. "Relax, trooper," I said as I unbuckled and leaned against the wall. The drain trough around it was a perfect temporary sewer.

"Y-y-yes, sir," she acknowledged, and I saw she was shaking. Tears were streaming down her face. "Th-this is my first battle," she explained. "I'm s-sorry."

"Hell, it's a first for all of us," I said as I looked over. She might be twelve. Fourteen if she was young-looking. About the same age I was when I enlisted. "Fear isn't a problem. Crying isn't even a problem. Just do what you have to and keep yourself and your buddies alive," I counseled.

"Yes, sir," she nodded vigorously. Looking at my collar pips, she asked, "You're the Black Ops officer?"

"Warrant Leader, Black Ops Team Three," I agreed.

"So you're not scared," she said in presumption.

"Scared? I'm fucking terrified," I told her. That bothered her. "But it's all reflex. Remember your training, stick with your buddies, do as I tell you and you'll be as safe as you can be. I'm not itching to win any medals, sacrifice any troops, or do anything except keep us alive and kill as many religious freaks as I can in the process. I won't make you a hero, but I will get you home."

She grinned at that, tears running sideways on creases she shouldn't yet have at her age. "Thanks, Warrant," she said as she hoisted her pants and buckled them.

Morale boosted. Back to the war. Any of you prudes now understand the advantage of coed facilities? Battle, sex, and biological functions are intensely personal and strip away inhibitions. The best bonding takes place then. Besides, there's no time to have separate facilities in the midst of battle.

As I headed back to my south edge position, I passed the little tool hutch that was being used as our aid station. We had two serious wounded by then, one the lungshot guy and one with a leg pretty well shattered, but doped up on painkillers and shock stabilizers until she felt nothing. We had one dead.

The medics had tossed a shirt over his head to indicate his status (that's why they do that, not any ritual reason). There was also a Security Patrol armband draped across his chest. It had our flag, "MP" for "military police" (the standard designation for everyone to recognize) and a triple chevron to indicate a patrol leader. I looked quizzically at it. Where had an SP come from?

One of the medics turned and said, "That's mine, sir. My first skill was medic, but I'm now an SP. I was in the area, got separated, so I volunteered."

"Thanks, Trooper," I replied. "Why the brassard on his chest?" I asked as I nodded my head that way.

"Well, he's dead in battle," the sergeant explained. "Casualties in line of duty are supposed to be draped in the flag. We don't have any flags. But there's the embroidered one on my brassard. It's only a few centimeters, but . . ."

"It is a flag," I completed.

"Yes, sir," he agreed.

"That'll work," I acknowledged. I turned and ran.

The brief break had helped me relax and feel better. However, the battle had changed and it took me a few seconds to get back into the groove. I sought Deni. "How are you doing?" I asked between thunderous roars of her rifle. Yes, it was suppressed. It was just that powerful. An M-66 15 mm Precision Target Rifle has to be felt to be believed.

"Oh, fine," she said, with the barest of vacant smiles, that faded back to her slight pout that was designed to equalize pressure in her head and presaged another cacophonous BOOM! "I have sixteen rounds left. After that, I'll need some of Tyler's."

Wow. She'd been busy. Her basic load was sixty rounds. Forty-four fired meant forty-four freaks on their way to Paradise, in pieces.

Of course, I'd been asking how *she* was doing, not how her shooting went. That's just the type of woman she was. All business when it counted.

I heard Joel say, "Third building, top floor, fourth window low." They created code as they went, as any practiced team does. I scanned across and had just figured out where he was referring when Deni said, "Sight," squeezed and BOOM! Another wannabe was translated straight to heaven. Well and good. I moved on.

Frank had had Tyler move to another position. She was drawing too much attention. There'd been a minor mixup inside as someone tried to envelop us, but there'd only been five of them and the two leopards had enveloped *them* and torn them to bloody shreds. They were due steak and ice cream when we got back. They love steak and ice cream.

About 4 am local, we seemed to get control. The incoming artillery slowed. Our Hatchets had control of the air and didn't let go. The idiots opposing them, in badly reinforced air cars mounting missile tubes, were turned into blood-drenched polymer confetti. Some called it brave. I called it stupidity born of fanaticism.

As dawn became obvious, the fire quickly faded to nothing and stopped. We could see people moving about here and there, but none of them were armed. Typical of the type of warfare, I'd been taught. But at least my squad were okay. So was I. I had another thirty-one with me, of whom one was dead, two were critically wounded, four were minorly wounded, and all were tired, dazed and ravenous.

We were pulled off by VC-26 Hummingbird and taken back to the 'port. While the kids plowed into food, I headed for debriefing. None of us would be sleeping, though my troops might snatch a nap. The battle had shifted but was not over, and we were needed elsewhere. I hosed off and squeezed drugs both chemical and nano into my bloodstream to flush fatigue poisons and elevate my metabolism.

The base looked like a demolition zone. I'd heard we'd been hit, but hadn't known it was that hard. Buildings were crumbled, roofs collapsed, craters from mortar shells pocked the open areas. It was rather impressive. I grabbed what info I could and asked a couple of people.

Apparently, the battle was much more than the attack in the city. The factions were hitting us, the UN, several local installations, and even screwing with a few things in orbit. It was a serious push to get us off the planet.

They'd picked our sector of the base because of bad intelligence. They assumed that because of our low numbers and high mobility, that the Headquarters Battalion would be easy pickings. After all, they were rear echelon pukes, right? Recspecs, chaplains, key pushers and maintenance pukes. I got a warm fuzzy feeling at that thought, and I couldn't stop from grinning.

With anyone else's military, that would have been true. But we train *everyone* as infantry first, and all leadership schools, promotions and command slots depend at least fifty percent on one's ability in the basics, for exactly this reason. And we're *all* armed, *all* the time. On the occasions I chose to get my rocks off at the rec center, both I and the recspec had our armor and weapons in the corner. Pursuant to the Conventions, there are no weapons *in* medical facilities, but they are right outside. We don't have noncombatant medics, lawyers or chaplains; they carry rifles, too. Two hundred and twenty HQ personnel equals two hundred and twenty combat effective infantry. We also tried to rotate them through on basic patrols, so more than a few of them had at least a day or two of trigger time, and it's the first day that is the roughest.

So these poor, misguided, illiterate, prayer-chanting cavemen (Yes, I despised them. I said so already) stormed the fence with cutters, whilst their buddies lobbed shells. The idea was to pin our people down, march in, and have a mass orgy of looting and raping for the Mercy and Peace of God. Especially the raping. We used unmarried women (and men, but they didn't care about them) for sexual relief, and women as troops. That was sinful. Raping them to prove this was apparently acceptable to God, and would convince us to pull out.

Instead, the local yokels had run smack into all the traps our engineers had set around the perimeter. Since those traps were both against a real world threat and done for training everyone while we had a real world situation, there was an ungodly amount of wire, explosive, emplaced automatic systems, and pitfalls. As soon as word got out, our repressed support troops, eager to bag a body for record, enthusiastically took cover and gleefully returned a heavy volume of fire. Our replacement and training depot shills had swarmed to unpack their factory new guns and trucks, and dialed in a quite impressive counterbattery and support convoy, seeing as the guns had only been boresighted.

It had been a merry slaughter, but not the way the factions had intended.

We had a total of twelve dead, which was bothersomely high, but certainly on the low side considering the engagement. I counted fifty bearded freaks tangled in the wire, saw bits of ten others, and enough blast zones to account for another twenty. And that was only within sight of the gate. Most of our casualties were due to people being too enthusiastic in response and leaving themselves exposed.

That wasn't the end of the battle, however. Our sector had slacked off, probably due to the vicious response we put up. The northern sector of the capital was still a brutal, up close and personal tangle. Naumann did a datadump to my comm, I pulled it up on screen, and swore. Someone in Uno Intelligence had fucked the dog on this one, because as much hardware as I saw displayed didn't exist on the planet, according to them. It sure as hell existed in the real world, however.

The battle stretched north of the city, engulfing several strongpoints of various contingents, factions, units, all theoretically allies. This did help confirm that they were all on our side, because they were all taking fire. Of course, requiring your allies to die is a hell of a way to have them prove their earnest intentions.

On paper, the UN had sufficient modern counterbattery and interdiction units to suppress any local artillery stupid enough to fire. In reality, this was as much a joke as the rest of the UN.

Rather than choose the best tactical positions, they'd chosen to emplace guns where they'd do the least damage to the local environment, with consideration of the emotional well-being of the host culture, and where readily extractable by air assets in case of potential capture. That last really limited the range at which they could operate. I can understand not wanting the enemy to seize support weapons, so it was a limitation to work around, but I could think of better ways to prevent the enemy capturing pieces. Apparently, however, booby-trapping the munitions was a no-no, in case some luckless innocent native were to discover a cache as he just happened to poke around an abandoned artillery site in the middle of a battle, while walking his explosive-detection dog and carrying a machinegun, and "elevate the tube and slag the breech!" was not allowed without proper authority from above. The battery commanders were not allowed to be responsible for their own guns. They were allowed to extract the breechblock and exfiltrate with it to render the gun inoperable, but exfiltrating without specific orders to do so was a court martial offense. So it usually came down to abandoning the gun at the last second because of not having the authority to destroy it, and saving one's career at the expense of friendly casualties. This is what is known technically as a "giant group clusterfuck."

So, all the guns were in crappy positions, close to the city, exposed on rough terrain and could *only* be evacuated by aircraft. This meant they were rather hard to defend against mountain infantry. Several tubes had already been captured and were being used to shell parts of the city. As they were larger than most of the local howitzers, they had better range. The enemy were short-sighted, desperate religious freaks who nevertheless had a better mindset for fighting than the UN did, so they were using them well. As they'd had time to research this, their *own* arty was dialed in as support for the positions they'd captured. The captured positions all had good interdiction guns, to shoot down incoming fire. They were as solidly defended as before, just in enemy hands. A UN Mountain Infantry battalion, one of those that actually fought and reasonably well at that, was now pinned down as it tried to recover some of the emplaced guns.

Oh, did I mention that the UN satellite network was still giving us spurious and inaccurate data? Their transmissions were sporadic, their automatic grid coordinates were nonsensical, and it took ten segs ("27 minutes") to find someone with a paper map and compass to give us a good location on them.

Someone had to save those poor troops (or maybe his own career) using any means available. Luckily, whoever that was thought for just long enough to demand the best. I'll argue slightly with his comparison, as he teamed us up with a UN Special Unit. They're good at what they do, but they still have the fundamental flaw of being trained to fight a tactically inferior force. They *never* train for engagements against superior forces, as we do all the time. Still, we were all real soldiers, who rated our missions in terms of numbers of bodies piled up and wounded screaming, not in terms of smiles on the faces of villagers.

So I got called, I called my team, we grabbed our heavy gear, all smiles at the thought of getting to use it in a real battle, and all twisting guts at the thought of getting to use it in a real battle.

First, though, we had to have a briefing. This was a good thing. The briefing came down under orders from some general (the UN had far too many brass), who was in "operations" but somehow was off-planet in orbit, not on the ground where the work was being done. It was presented to us by a pretty boy captain who was in dress blues and obviously had never left the compound. This was a bad thing.

Obviously, the best way to present it would be a quick rundown on approach routes, air corridors, terrain, maps and equipment, hashed out between me and my UN counterpart, on the display in our helmets, with all our troops linked in to provide input, and pilots, arty, etc. placed subordinate to us and at our disposal. Naturally, this is the way we proceeded.

Your ass it was.

We sat in chairs and had the briefing. We sat in chairs while men and women died out in the mountains. We had a specially prepared briefing, with charts and tables and clever quotes from history (they thought the quotes were clever. Sun Tzu, Caesar and Clausewitz wouldn't have thought so. Hell, I didn't think so) and neat animations of how we'd overrun the enemy.

I couldn't help but notice that we didn't discuss commo. Or logistics. Or air support. Or chain of command. Somehow, the orders from the General (Furglen was his name) would get to us, and intelligence from us would get back to him, and he'd know what to do, relay that to us, and it would be in a timely enough fashion to make a rat's ass worth of difference to our operation.

Oh, did I say "our" operation? I'm sorry. I would have called this one "Operation Bend Over and Flinch." General Fucklen called *his* operation "Proud Panther." I'm told variously that the names are selected randomly by computer, or to reflect the important aspects of the mission. I still don't know. I don't think it matters. We didn't need an operation with a name. A frag order would have done, to be followed by proper supporting paperwork later. Naumann would have said, "Ken, get up on that mountain, find out what they need to get loose, do it if you can, call for backup if you need it. I'll have arty, aviation, infantry, and Blazers standing by for your call," and I would have left in fifty seconds. Of course, there's no glory unless there's a mission name for the news.

The only good part was that the UN unit commander and his Master Sergeant First Class looked as eager, nervous, and unimpressed as I felt. We met eyes a few times (we didn't get introduced other than to have our names announced), and shook our heads.

As soon as possible, I said, "Captain, I'd like to bring my team in on this briefing. Some of them have unique skills in mountain warfare and in alpine forest environments that could be relevant to this discussion."

He replied, "That's a good idea, Warrant Leader Rich, but due to security requirements, only command staff are being briefed at this time."

Only command staff. Never mind that I'd be telling my kids as soon as I left here, orders or no. Never mind that I had smuggled in a headset and was relaying to Deni. Never mind that we already knew the basics from gossip around the base and clear transmissions off the mountain, because commo security was a joke among the Unos. Forget that telling people what you need with sufficient lead time makes them better able to deal with a screwed up situation. We had "security" to think about. I didn't ask why, if it was so secret, we had a press release of the high points to issue to our respective nation's media.

We watched a battle plan on vid, wherein computer simulations representing the UN team and ourselves marauded across the hillside, took positions and rounded up enemy concentrations while the Mountain Division occupied positions until the "captured" artillery personnel could be relieved and replaced with others.

It was all very pretty. It was presented at the level of tactical understanding possessed by a ten-year-old. Ten Earth years.

Then we had an environmental assessment. Now, to me, a combat environmental assessment is "What terrain do I have to exploit, what resources are present, what weather can I expect?" This was not that. This was a detailed plan of all major local life forms and how we were to avoid damaging them excessively. Really. We were not to use lethal weapons or call for support unless the chance of hitting the enemy was "relevantly greater" than the risk of damaging the environment. I didn't even bother to comment on that stupid idea

Did you notice that the briefing assumed that the UN and we had identical gear and training?

Eventually, we got outside. We all stretched. We looked at each other and said nothing for several seconds. I finally broke the silence. "I'm Warrant Leader Ken Rich. This is Senior Sergeant Frank Walsh."

"Captain Glen Wilder," he said. "This is Master Sergeant First Class Petra Pandis."

"What do you know about how we operate, Captain?" I asked.

"Not much," he admitted. "You're very hush-hush, can go a lot of places, and do a lot of odd terrain training."

I nodded. This meant he knew more but didn't want to admit to intel, and knew less and wanted me to fill him in. "Our squad is twenty. Two fire teams of six with combination weapons and one support weapon each. One weapons squad with sniper team, anti-armor team and heavy machinegun. Frank and myself in charge. We'll be using exomusculature, body armor, jump harnesses and tactical helmets with four layer visual overlay on contact lenses."

"JAYsus!" he exclaimed. "That should about do it."

Then he continued, "I have two squads of eight, each with three buddy pairs and a support weapon pair, plus a squad leader. I've got a machinegun and antiarmor in a weapons' section, and myself and Petra. We'll be wearing powered assault armor."

I didn't want to tell him my opinion of that, yet. He was good, probably the best he could be with what he had, but what he had sucked for this type of work, and he didn't even know it.

"So let's gear up and meet at the flightline," I said.

"Roger that," he replied.

Frank had been over to deal with the UN over some minor details, I asked him for a download.

"Shit, boss, it can't get better than what we see, and that licks ass," he said as we strode to our vehicle.

"Tell me," I said.

"Well, you notice Pandis is fairly small?"

"Small, cute but alert-looking, yes," I agreed.

"Boss, they have lower physical requirements for women. And they don't require them to take muscle enhancers."

"In a special warfare unit?" I asked, my voice starting to take on a squeaky, cringing tone.

"Even here," he said as we climbed in. I waved the driver back to our tactical operations center on the far side of the base, inside our own perimeter. That distance told me what the UN, meaning "Earth," really thought of us, and that they'd only brought us in to make it a "multi-national" operation, without any regard or knowledge of our capabilities.

"Fuck me," I said.

"Worse," he said.

"Worse?" I asked. I was afraid to hear more.

"They have a precise quota of gender, orientation, race, nationality, education and social backgrounds for their troops. Whether the troops want it or not. So some of the troops we're going after are going to be idiots, some weaklings, some won't speak a language the translation programs are familiar with, or that have enough vocabulary, and some will not be trained for this at all."

"What shitlicking, dogfucking, bastard son of a goat came up with that?" I asked.

"It's their policy. The military cannot discriminate. It's bad for society to suggest that certain people are superior to others, and casualties are the small price you have to pay to maintain that equality."

"That illusion," I said.

"I have a unit roster," he said. "At least a few of them are disabled."

"God and Goddess, is *that* a possibility?"

"There are four paraplegics undergoing regen therapy in the artillery battery we're heading for first. They're designated as maintenance and support staff."

"They have fucking wheelchair ramps in a firebase?" I said, the cringe getting worse, the pucker factor about to kill me, and my guts churning with acid. Ohhhh shit. I grabbed my comm and logged in. I needed more info in a hurry. I tried to control my breathing; I didn't need a panic attack or to hyperventilate.

Yes, I knew the UN had civilian contractors, and less than optimal recruits. It never occurred to me in my worst fucking nightmares that they'd be so criminally irresponsible to stick people psychologically and physically unsuited for combat into firefights.

I reminded myself that this would be the last time I reminded myself that the UN regarded people as expendable units to be sacrificed to the greater glory of the human whole, to prove that "Everyone matters" and "Everyone counts."

Warfare is my venue, and if it bothers you to hear that most of you *don't* matter and *don't* count in the subject of warfare, then screw you. Call me an elitist, call me an asshole, call me George. You each have your place. A conference room with a screen full of programming or statistical or accounting figures is not mine. The middle of a war with unfriendly strangers shooting at you while bombs blow off and some asshole allegedly on your own side tries to screw you to death to win a medal is probably not yours. Come to think of it, I'm not sure I want to claim that one either. But we are different.

Keep in mind that while this was going on, people were still dying. We should have been en route at once, accepting that we would take a few casualties, to save them many casualties now and strategic position and more casualties later. That is what we're for. Instead, we'd had a conference. I tiredly gathered the team and everyone drugged up for the second fight of the day. No one complained. Good kids.

It actually wasn't as bad as Frank had braced me for. Policy or not, a Special Unit exists to fight, and stays alive by being good at it. They found ways to shuffle off the deadwood, and I was relatively happy with the group I met. They were a rogue's gallery, to be sure, but handled lethal weapons (as opposed to the non-lethal stuff most Unos were issued) with familiarity, and knew how to use their gear. That was a good sign to start with. And they were all English speakers, even if it was a second language. It doesn't matter what language a unit uses, but everyone needs to use the same one, and well enough to get across any basic combat data.

The flight line was dusty and crude, but had a decent runway. All the aprons were either basic concrete, or sectional polymer or even aluminum matting snapped together into sheets. The buildings were all knockdown frames. Despite the crudity, it was modern and complete. Which was a good thing, as we had to use a large lifter for this crowd.

In gear with full armor, helmets, exomusculature, chameleon suit, jump harness and weapons, the twenty of us scaled in at about 200 kilograms each. The twenty-four UN troops were in solid assault armor, which is a polyceramic crablike shell with a musculature, jump jets, weapons and mounts and an onboard microturbine generator plus fuel. The power supply needs more armor. They massed in at a hefty 450 kilograms or so each. So we broke fourteen tons total, just for us.

However, those suits are subject to failure. One cannot move inside one that's deadlined, so they had a five-person recovery section with extraction gear and a mini vertol. Then, they needed a security section for *that*, and to guard the craft when it was down, because they had to have support nearby, since the onboard fuel bunker was good for only about eight hours (one third of an Earth day).

We have variable power for the exos. Full power is as potent as the coffins our counterparts wore. Partial power would last us a day or more, and we could turn it off, humping on foot only, so as to use power only for our sensor gear. In an emergency, we dump the leg armor to move faster, and in dire need, can strip off the exo and abandon it. I suppose some people feel better inside a case, but I like to be able to *feel* my environment. Maybe I didn't play enough comm games growing up. Vid screens and handles don't seem real to me.

I had the feeling we were going to go crashing through the

brush, alerting everything within ten klicks to our presence, and accomplish very little. I was correct.

We slogged aboard, shook hands all around, Earth fashion. You use the right hand only and don't grab the forearm with the left. Everyone stared at Kirby, or rather, at Sphinx and Rasputin. They were in chameleon armor only. That was expensive enough as it was, being custom made for every animal. While leopards are bright, they can't control an exo, and let's face it, they don't need them. The effect of meeting growling, trained killers with commo gear and vid, dressed in armor that stopped clear of their burnished claws was intimidating to these experienced killers. I hoped it would be a bomb to our enemies.

Let me dispel a myth here: that we use the leopards and porpoises to plant explosives and then blow them up. No, we don't. Try thinking. These are not everyday zoo leopards or even wild ones. They are the product of generations of breeding for an animal that is stable, comfortable with people, able to take direction and can have an IQ as high as 115. They are far smarter than most people. Then we train them from birth. Each is a multimillion credit animal, raised to work with a particular person. They're as much soldiers as the rest of us, and we don't throw them away or even expose them lightly. My time with the cats was special, and they were as much my friends as Kit or Tyler. They are used where their senses and the fear factor will be of positive effect, and where we need a very stealthy infiltrator. Leopards are so good at that, in fact, that for a century they were thought near extinction because so few were seen. The leopard population was fine. They are simply that good at hiding. The porpoises serve a similar purpose in water.

We still had to await launch, while our people were getting smeared. The bird should have been hot and waiting, and rolled as we boarded, even before the ramp came up. Worse yet, it was a civilian contractor aircrew. The pilot came back, nodded and said, "I'm Werzel Nischalke. I'll be flying you." Sure, he looked dashing in his affected blue flight suit and customized helmet. Sure, he got paid for completion of the mission, and probably better than his military counterparts. He was probably very competent, I hoped. He was a brave son of a bitch to be over enemy territory in obvious civilian garb. Still, it chafes me to have someone I cannot dictate orders to in an emergency. There are times I need to be Ghengis Khan and brutally harsh in my discipline. Sillyvilians can refuse and pout. I don't like it.

But I was cordial. "Warrant Leader, FMF. Call me Rich," I said. It was good enough.

"Warrant Rich," he said. He at least knew enough to use the right abbreviated form. "Welcome aboard the *Peking Duck*."

I thought about that for a moment. "Plucked, stuffed and cooked to a crisp?" I asked him.

"Well, we're hoping not," he replied with a wry smile. Okay, he'd do. We shook hands and he jogged forward, after a cautious stare at the cats.

The flight engineer, also load toad and gunner, was his wife, Brenda. "Civilian doorgunner?" I asked her, incredulous. I could— have—seen that on Grainne, but in the UN?

"I was active duty until they riveted the slot. So I signed with Kelly United Services."

Well, that explained everything. I hated to think of the admin-work and hoops it took for her to handle lethal weapons as a civilian. Still, when in Rome. Though we weren't in Rome. We weren't on Earth, we weren't from Earth, yet we were using their rules. Yes, it was a screwed up war. But it was the only war we had. I shook her hand, gave her the benefit of the doubt, because one has to. There are only so many tasks you can handle, and if you try to second guess the other guy, you screw up your own job and get people killed. Possibly including yourself. I said, "Good luck," and turned back to my task.

The Unos and we eyed each other, assessing capabilities. They handled themselves well, looked nervous but with it under control, with just enough of a hint of eagerness on top to be reassuring. They were here to do a job, not be heroes. It didn't look too bad. Which of course meant things were going to suck. But then, things always suck for us. I noticed that neither they nor I spoke to the Landing Security Team who would keep the craft safe while we rumbled. We hoped. They did speak to their maintenance section, but there was no need for us to.

Everyone noticed the leopards. No one said a word. I was

amused and I bet Kirby was, too. Hopefully our enemies would be more than impressed.

The ramp whined up, the temperature rose five degrees, the turbines growled then howled and we were ready to roll. At last. The waiting is what I hate. Bring on the fire. I strapped to the port passenger bench, adjusted my comm to the intercom frequency and said, "Rich here, comm check."

"I check you, Rich. Loud and clear," Werzel said.

"Engineer, loud and clear," Brenda seconded from her own deck, monitors and weapon controls wrapped around her.

"Landing Security Team, loud and clear."

"Recovery Section, loud and clear."

"Twenty Fourth Special Unit, loud and clear," Wilder said, as his team shouted "Arruf!" Yeah, whatever.

"Loud and clear," I confirmed.

Nischalke lifted us smoothly and kept us plugged into the circuit so we could hear the flight operations. That was decent of him. As we rose over the trees at the end of the flightline, Brenda came on air and said, "Rich, can you have three of your people move to starboard for balance?"

"Three personnel to starboard side, check," I confirmed. Deni and Joel and Johnny Squid. I pointed, they nodded and moved. We got back to listening while the crew flew.

I wanted to start a few klicks back and dog in on foot, so as to be discreet. The needs of our lumbering bucketheads dictated we go in close. Screwup number one. Naumann and I both wanted our Hatchets on call for close support. The UN "denied" the request and said it would provide support as needed, but wanted us to be inconspicuous. Screwup number two. Being inconspicuous means not drawing attention to oneself until it hits the fan. It does not mean keeping oneself exposed and helpless.

The worst place we could have possibly landed would have been the flat valley floor beyond the hills east of town, in plain view of every surrounding piece of captured ordnance and all their backup guns on the ridge beyond that. We landed there. Screwup number three. Yes, we had some air support by that time, sort of. They had to "Determine the allegiance" of each position before counterattacking. If it shoots at me, it's hostile. I've never believed in "friendly fire." You shoot at me, I'll kill you regardless of your uniform. Yes, they eventually managed to suppress some of the fire from the second echelon. But there were support weapons in our targets that could see us from where we were, or be directed on target even if they were over the crest. It's called "indirect fire," and it's a new invention, only three thousand years old.

The idea behind this was to come in behind these units and surprise them. Forget surprise. It appears they were devious types who had access to binoculars. At every step, leadership assumed that "savage" equaled "stupid" and "incompetent." The three do not necessarily go together.

We did fly in by going around the hills, rather than through them. This took more time, but did keep us out of visual ID of our targets. It was the first smart move of the operation, even if it did delay us. Of course, there could be spotters elsewhere reporting our flight. When we took over operations from the UN, we'd remedy that. For now, we dealt with it.

The flight turned into a roller coaster ride as we hit the hills. We swooped, dove and twisted. No one heaved their guts, though I confess to being rather queasy, watching the metal grating of the deck warp slightly from the stress and shift in orientation. I was glad of the open hatches. The breeze felt good. I was happy yet again not to be wearing the lobster shells of our allies.

We couldn't see each others' faces, but they might as well have been mechanical themselves. The polymer and ceramic carapaces covered them totally, with attachment points for weapons and gear on the torso. The power-assist hydraulics ran through armored conduits behind each limb from the dome on the back that was the power source. Alongside it like bulky breathing apparatus were the jump jets, actually ducted turbines. Each jet set had an hour of fuel, assuming a full load. The troops could push to seventy-five minutes if they were less laden. The problem being that the bastards were *loud*. If they fired up, everyone within several kilometers would know. They'd also blow dust like you wouldn't believe. The surface of the suit could shift for different camouflage patterns or distortion effects. Their imaging systems were comparable to ours, except they would suffer a comm lag—

their system was run from base. Mine ran from a processor in my helmet, and I could ask for external links if I needed them. Any signal can be jammed or cracked, even if they dismissed the issue as unlikely.

Our body armor was soft if bulky and had the same surface chameleon effects as theirs, if needed. Under that, we wore our exomusculature, which was flat, bi-composition springs with compression controlled by mere amperage. We carried a battery to power it. Flying wasn't an option, but we were much quieter in movement and I personally could clear twenty meters in a running leap, even fully laden. Vertically, I'd practiced the technique until I could get my feet to five meters. I had all my basic weapons with me with extra ammo. My tac helmet and visor was supplemented by a full face shield for protection, and contact lenses with several microns of circuitry. I could see in whatever spectrum I wanted and plot my troops, any allied units and estimated enemy concentrations using my own network, not a centralized net like the UN used. I had access to our tacnet, but I would only do so if I needed additional system resources.

At least, being an air asset, the security detail and Brenda had real guns with real ammo, and none of that non-lethal crap. The maintenance section had the tools to peel someone out of the shell and a small lift platform to move one. Their weapons, of everyone here, were non-lethal.

Glen and I discussed our egress from the craft and potential maneuvers. I reviewed some of our tactics for him and we went over the little hard data we had and the maps. We were broken from our concentration by a change in impeller feel and engine pitch. Then we were descending fast. "Dropping in fifteen seconds," I heard. Neither Glen nor I had any say in the matter; it was between Nischalke and UN Control. I would have appreciated more notice.

"Lock and load, folks," I ordered. It was a private frequency. I was sure the UN had a regulation against loading weapons aboard a craft. I was equally sure I didn't give a damn. I had no idea what was outside.

Werzel counted us down from five seconds. At "One!" we airbraked hard but without jarring. The ramp was down at once and we took the lead because those clunky suits are not conducive to fast deployment. I also wanted to make sure the UN troops were impressed. Theoretically, Glen was in charge. But if I felt the need, I planned to start shouting orders. That works better if your allies are sufficiently confident to not question you.

I could have kissed my kids. Okay, Deni at least. The rest I'd buy beer for. I shouted, "GO!" and they were on the ground in a double perimeter in five seconds. They flew off the ramp, some bouncing straight down, others tucking headfirst into rolls. It was about a seven meter drop. That gymnast Geoff decided to do a pike somersault with a twist. Kirby stepped to the edge and waved the leopards over, who growled sullenly and leapt out. They all flickered as the chameleon circuits tried to turn transparent in air. The suits didn't quite succeed, but unless someone was watching closely, they'd see a blur at most. Upon landing, First Team went left, Second went right and Weapons formed the inner semicircle, ready to shoot through preplanned gaps in the formation. Deni just flowed past me with Joel a half pace to her left. They leaned far forward at the ramp and sprung off in flat arcs that carried them ten meters to land behind Second. Tyler and Rudy with the heavy, Donnie and Ross on anti-armor leapt the other way behind First. Glen's two squads and support elements lumbered out and took the front. They used the forward troop doors in addition to the ramp.

"Pony Three, 24th down and clear," he reported. I heard it echo, as we were using a common frequency, but it was also being relayed through our respective Controls.

"Prime—Lion One, 3rd Blazers on the ground and secure," I reported. "Prime" gave me both frequencies at once. The stupid call sign was a UN requirement. I'd picked a predator for obvious reasons. I was quite happy with "Three Zulu One," and all our people recognized that as "death with enthusiasm" when they heard it.

I could hear small arms fire on the ridge. Occasional mortar or light arty thumps and bangs punctuated the smaller stuff. We were in a hot zone, back in battle already. A third shiny star for my uniform. I could do without the honor. Behind me, the vertol lifted noisily away.

The terrain was hummocky with glacial moraine rock deposits and broad-bladed grass, varying from knee to waist height. Not bad. To my left (aircraft starboard: we'd come out the rear) and west was a hill that my map reported as 257 meters. The local equivalent of conifers started about a hundred meters up. Below that was more of the rock. There'd be lots of that rock on these low hills. It was basaltic and unremarkable.

Then my comm kicked in with other data. A transparent relief map appeared over my vision, and the location pips of my troops over that, with the UN showing as "enemy" until I designated their signal as "ally." Then they were repeated as pips over their helmets in my "real" view. The tactical sighting grid and reticle came up. Too much info! I deleted the "real" overlay; I knew where my people were, thank you. I didn't need sighting reticles for small arms. I stuck with eyes and map, with pips on the map. They were bright enough to see if I paid attention, dim enough to ignore when just watching.

"Overwatch advance," Glen ordered. A moment later, a cursor appeared on my map. Damn delay! It had gone through UN Control, Freehold Control, been stripped and encoded and cleared the protocols on my comm. "Prime—Pony Three, Lion One. If there's going to be a system delay, just tell me where to go. I can think faster than it can display." As I said so, I cut out the real time link.

"Lion One—Pony Three. Understood," he agreed. I had another motive—I didn't trust the UN Control. They might have a signal problem, or try to override my images with what they thought was important. That would only cause our systems to shut them out, which would leave me deaf. I wanted to talk to Glen directly. Control needs to be in the field, not some jackass at a console listening to another one in orbit.

We rolled forward and upwards toward our first target, listening for changes in the battle. Glen's first squad and our Team One advanced under Glen with all UN weapon elements. Then second and second with our Weapon Team moved around and through them, according to our agreed pattern. I sighted a good rock for cover, waited until the first movement was complete and ordered, "Element Two, advance." I rose lightly and pulled forward into a power-assisted lizard crawl that carried me thirty meters in fifteen seconds and never put me above the growth. It was fascinating to see my arms shift like moving grass from the chameleon effect, while my hands switched from green stem to straw stalk and earth brown.

As I took cover behind the rock and blended into it, I felt better. We were the highest tech bunch of killers on the planet facing a pack of illiterate grunting savages. Yes, it was bigoted. I didn't care. My vision rippled slightly as the map corrected, using my visual input (micro cameras on the sides of my goggles) to cross check against memory. Then I waited for the other element to advance. There was nothing to see while staying low and hidden, so I studied the rock and the dirt. At one side, a fat yellow bananaslug was rippling along a twig. They're not precisely slugs and do have eyes, albeit short sighted ones. But if it hadn't seen me, as close as it was, it was unlikely anyone above had.

Soon enough, Glen spoke and a wafting breeze of invisible wraiths floated past. I could tell the UN troops; they thumped as they landed. We were less massive and able to bend lower, so we danced across the grass tips while they jumped. I could occasionally spot Kirby, but the leopards were invisible, streamlined death at his word. I called the advance and clambered up a split in the rock, the ground grassy despite being near vertical for a couple of meters before sloping at a more reasonable rate.

At the tree line we split, they going south, us north. The plan was to clear two routes in, envelope the battery and then attack in two crossing directions with fire support. Once inside, we'd have the technological and tactical edge, as long as we were careful. Glen's team had non-lethal weapons clipped to their harnesses and ready for this, in case they hit friendlies. While it wasn't a bad idea under those circumstances (did I actually say that?), I intended for us to use lethal weapons. I'd bet on my people not to miss, and dead savages don't escape or attempt revenge.

So we regrouped and slipped away from each other, ghostly shifting patterns in the foliage. We'd only been at this a few minutes, and it was about an hour since we'd started. Pretty quick response by most standards, really. Hopefully, we'd take the battery, which would reduce fire on the others and disrupt their pattern. The Mountain troops would then be able to move more freely and we'd gain the upper hand.

Of course, meanwhile, the city was still being shelled, as were the Mountain troops. The firing was getting louder as we approached. I said, "Prime—Lion One, Control and Pony Three, make sure those friendlies are expecting us." I got two confirmations back. Good.

Glen called, "Lion One, stand by for support and movement—break—Control, Pony Three, fire mission. Artillery. Bunker. Troops in defense. Grid . . ." and coordinates followed. He'd found an outer perimeter. He'd hit it, we'd all move, and we'd start picking them off fast.

"PONY THREE AND LION ONE, SHOT. REPOrt impact," was the reply from UN Control, too damned loud until I corrected the volume. I clicked a confirmation and hunkered down.

And something niggled at me. The grid . . .

Right then it happened. Glen's response was, "Pony Three confirms, Contro-o-o-o—*shit*!"

Before I could inquire, my tac told me. A flash warned of incoming artillery. My comm jammed a demand into Control and came back with PARSON intel. It was about to hit our friends.

We'd forgotten that the enemy had UN equipment. Hell, *I'd* forgotten it. Someone had shut down the outgoing commo to the seized units from UN Control, but the UN had not sealed their end against intrusion. They'd been compromised from the beginning. My instinct to cut out of comm had saved us.

It suddenly all made sense. That Goddess-cursed network of theirs had been breached. The enemy (whichever faction it was) could eyeball the city. They could drag up intel on the UN. They could use their own maps against them. And the bastards had been sneaky enough to hold onto that ace card until now. They'd waited until we were in the trees where extraction would be harder. Worse, they'd diddled a program to shift the UN grid. Glen had called an artillery mission on himself.

By sheer luck, stupidity would save us. Had we deployed into the trees, they would have hit us at once and we'd all be targets. By using the approach we did, half the force was unsuspected.

While I was musing, the shell impacted near the mathematical center of the group. They were scattering. I didn't see any casualties on my visor, which was good. Their armor saved them. "PRIME—Pony Three, Lion One, you've been hacked!" I shouted. "Your grid coordinates cannot be trusted." Those smug grins at HQ had to be fading in a hurry, now, but that wouldn't stop these people from dying.

"GODDAMMIT!" I heard him shout, and others came through the frequency. "CEASE FIRE, CONTROL!" he yelled. It was drowned out by another impact. That one was not arty, but local mortar fire. Either a UN Mountain unit was helping with the mission, or had been defeated and its gear seized.

"Pony Three, this is Lion One, you're in our circuit," I said. He was stunned or scared and was going to get all his troops killed. I tried to help. "Control—Lion One, patch me through to UN Arty Control for this mission now!"

Five seconds later I heard, "Lion One—Control, you are patched. Go ahead with your transmission."

"Fire Control, this is Lion One, Pony Three's system is compromised. Cease fire. Do not fire on those coordinates. Say again, cease fire, cease fire. Stand by for correction." I slugged my best assessment to it and zipped it upstream. But we'd have to wait about thirty seconds to get any change of target . . . *if* the gun crews were worth a good damn.

We'd never know. What I heard in response was unbelievable, except that it was real. "Unit identified as Lion One, you are not cleared for this network. Request denied. Send requests through your chain of command."

I exploded. "UN Fire Control, Lion One, who in the dogfucking hell do you think connected me to you? Scrub that fire mission, you are killing your own troops!"

"Lion One, request denied. Clear this network," I was told. Then I heard dead air.

It was time to handle it ourselves, because no one else was going to. "Pony Three—Lion One, pull your people back to the last location we recorded," I told him. I couldn't load coordinates to him, because that would link me into their corrupted net. We'd have to do this the old fashioned way. Additionally, if I read that location off by number, it would *definitely* be intel for the enemy.

As it was, what I told him was only *probably* intel for them, if they had a recording (I was sure they did) and if they tracked back on it. That would take them a few seconds, however. It was just a numbered location to whoever was spoofing us, but it was a real place to we who'd been standing there. "Once there, offset yourself. Don't tell me where; I'll find you. And drop out of your net. They can't help you."

UN Control came over the air again, on that freq. Apparently, they could listen just fine, it was doing anything that was their hold up. "Pony Three, disregard that instruction. Stand by for mission revisions, to be transmitted soonest." Whoever it was was a rude REDF. That's an acronym for "Rear Echelon DogFucker," an admin puke who is technically in a combat slot because his blubbery ass sits at a comm. The polite term is "Console Commando" but I feel no need to moderate my statements regarding that one. He was no help.

There was nothing from Glen. He was truly screwed. If he stayed in the current link, he was compromised. If he didn't, he'd be court martialed, assuming he survived. That was a thin assumption. There were ground troops approaching now. And a light flashed. He'd lost someone.

Then he spoke, "Control—Pony Three. You can jail my ass when we're done. The net is compromised; I'm dropping out. Relay your instructions through Freehold Control. Out. Lion One, I'm clear." There was a moment's pause for breath. "If you and your people could see your way clear to saving our sorry asses, I'd appreciate it."

I replied, "Pony Three, you're not the sorry ass. Now do as I said—break—Tyler, suppressive fire on this mark," I lit a grid that seemed to me to be the source of a lot of mortar fire, "—break— Frank, take charge of Third and keep us covered as the BGs move—break—Second, swing over here" I lit another mark "and report as the friendlies fall past you—break—First, over here." I highlighted a spot behind and at an angle to Second Team, so we could have interlocking fields of fire and disengage by leapfrog. Weapons Team was actually off to our left, rather than behind and between. That was safer regarding their shooting, but less useful because they were further away. *C'est la guerre.*

I was just about to jump when my visor flashed a warning, and bullets splashed splinters from a nearby tree. Some enemy patrol had located *me* now. I spun, lobbed two grenades that way, turned back and jumped without bothering to determine casualties, if any; it wasn't that important. I skittered down the slope, trying desperately to keep my feet and dodge trees, and found a safer spot about 200 meters away. At least it seemed safer until another shell landed. It was far enough away not to injure, but close enough to slap me with the blast.

It wouldn't be even that safe for long. Little squirming red worms on my display showed probable enemies, and a lot of them. "Control—Lion One," I said. "If you could see *your* way clear, I could really use a CAC team to cover my exposed ass while I conduct this operation. Barring immediate response on that, I need some kind of fire support—mirror" (which tied in a second circuit) "—Frank, have someone talk to support and kill a few of these dots until we get more support or we run out of targets."

Let me say this again: heavy assault armor and jump harnesses are useless in trees. The signals created by our suits were well masked, but could still be located by an adequately equipped enemy, and this one was more than adequately equipped. We should have come in stripped, with weapons, sneaking on foot the last couple of klicks, but the UN had this fetish for techie toys that was going to get us all killed.

Our new problem was that we had no aircraft handy. Our Hatchets were still in town and the UN had called dibs anyway. They were not currently disposed to help us, as they were sulking.

But our aviation people have balls and boobs the size of basketballs. Our Hatchet pilots were *begging* for permission to join the party. Not only that, our arty folks gave less than a damn about counterbattery, and started dropping PGMs on the targets Frank's kids were designating. It may seem like overkill to drop a 100 kg shell on a single troop, but if it stops him from shooting, I'll take it. The Hatchets were en route and should be overhead in about 1000 seconds. That's a long time, but they were rearming and refueling. While taking fire, let me note.

Once surprise is gone, you want firepower, lots of it and

yesterday. The UN was still debating which thumb to stick up their asses, and I frankly didn't have time. Our allies were dying, and something had to be done now. We did it.

Major Jose Clavell with 3rd Mob Regimental Arty was a conniving little weasel, and I say that with the utmost respect. Using the data we had, the plotted positions of the UN guns and the reports of the Mountain Battalion troops' locations, he set up a fire mission that didn't quite target the UN guns (in case of survivors, and let's face it: we wanted those pieces back), but was certain to keep anyone in those positions ducking, scared and wetting their pants. His gunners were good, too, firing a time-on-target salvo of firecracker rounds so dense that no interdiction was going to have an appreciable effect on it. I understand the air got pretty thick inside a few of the crew compartments, but they were feeding shells to the autoloaders as fast as Logistics' drivers could get them there, and sat on mechanical problems. He dropped it on one position, then on another, then back, with just enough time for the enemy to think they might be safe, come out of their holes and get caught by the next wave. That still left the guns out of his range to worry about. But anytime I can get a 50% reduction in incoming fire, damn betcha I'll take it.

This finally gave our UN friends a chance to prove their own capabilities. They weren't too shabby. Not being plumbed into our commo, they had to verbally shout coordinates to Kit and Neil (whom Frank had handling it). They crawled and bounced around, taking hits but none of them critical. Whenever they took fire, they'd relay the location and keep moving, trusting that our arty and Tyler's heavy (also Barto's and Frank #2's. They'd swapped squad weapons for heavies. The exos meant we could carry bigger hardware, and we did) would be on target. They were fast, precise, got the job done and in a few hundred seconds we were back in control of the hillside.

That is when the armor came in useful. They could take numerous small arms hits and even a few heavier rounds and keep going. On the other hand, we wouldn't have needed it if we hadn't made so much noise coming in.

At that point, we used the gear as it was designed but not intended. The theory behind this stuff was to either sneak in or overpower inferior forces. However, they are built to take damage. We paired up, one of them with one of us, because they couldn't use commo. The spare UN troops formed a support squad and took orders from Deni.

The Hatchets arrived. Suddenly, the incoming fire lightened tremendously. There's nothing like large caliber cannon and plenty of bombs to dissuade the enemy. I don't know which batteries they were hitting, but whomever they picked decided to leave us alone.

Then we attacked. We crashed up that hill, dodging trees and making no effort to be quiet. The chameleons would hide us for a few critical moments, we were bounding in long, low leaps at close to 50 kph and shooting at anything that didn't look friendly. I almost killed a Mountain troop who'd taken a hit to the helmet and removed it. I was focusing for patterns and that bare head was not the pattern I'd expected. I kept ordering pairs and mixed teams to peel off after threats, adding Mountain troops to the mix with simple orders to join an element and shoot where told. We dwindled in number, but the weapons fire was different now. There was more of ours, less of theirs and cries of distress said we were smashing their domain. I peeled off a last group of Frank with Kit, Deni and Joel and two UN troops to handle a perimeter bunker complex that had been usurped. Pandis with Donnie and Ross and two of her people sought an enemy element in a hollow. That left Glen, Kirby, the leopards and me.

Glen and I rose and moved, clearing a downed timber and hiding behind its exposed earthy root ball. I checked my images, whispered, "Forward left, several troops, small arms," while pointing in that direction. It suddenly resolved as the edge of the clearing the battery was dug into, about a hundred meters away through dank foliage. Camouflage screens and targeting sensors showed easily. The guns were dug in and less obvious, spread across the area. The command track and a tent were the focus of activity, and where everyone appeared to be.

"Think we can handle that?" Glen asked. "Should we wait for backup?"

"Shock and surprise, fear and panic. They have no idea who's here. We've got these dogfuckers," I said. He nodded and grunted agreement. Nevertheless, I called Frank while I slid in fresh clips. I'd rather start a fight with one hundred rounds than seventeen.

"We're clear," he agreed. "Want us to guard the hole or come for backup?"

"Sweep the guns and have Deni shoot anything suspicious-looking," I told him. My voice was raspy. I took another sip of water from the tube at my chin. It was caked with dust so I got a mouthful of gritty mud, but it was wet. "Tyler, have our support element come around from the south and drop anything they can." I indicated on the map as I thought, then said, "Geoff, cover the north. We're going in the middle first, everyone else come in two ticks later. And don't leave any nasties behind." Then I called Control for a fire mission.

Kirby and company slid in behind us, the cats crouching atop the log. They understand the risk of bullets just fine. They also prefer height so they can see. It's how they operate, and anyone who works with them learns quickly not to argue with a leopard's tactics. It wastes your time and annoys the leopard. I could hear them panting when the fire slacked at brief intervals.

Glen rose with me, we jumped clear to minimize our targetability, then resumed long lopes. I enjoyed that aspect of the exo. Seven League Boots. Then I saw a cluster of troops and captives massing and kicked in the Boost.

We were all but invisible until it was too late, then we were on them. Three or four of them caught bare movement from the corners of their eyes, but it would do them no good. I braked my jump by drop kicking a tree and snapping my legs down. I smashed my hip against it as I landed but the armor took some of the blow and the Boost turned the pain to a ripple of secondary endorphin. I was chemically and mechanically enhanced, alert and in peak physical condition on a low gravity planet. My visor showed me everything in the universe and for a few seconds I was the God of War.

Up came my weapon and I snapped off shots as I panned across. Long practice paid off; I was attentive and not tunneling my vision. As each shot found its mark, I was already plotting the next. After three I twisted behind the tree to shoot from the other side before dropping for cover and firing twice more toward the nearest gun. I added a grenade to that, then twitched my feet and shifted three meters forward into the artificial meadow. Two more shots at targets by the generator and I rose as bodies were still falling. Seven troops were crumpling, three prisoners still standing, then throwing themselves down as they realized that rescue was here. The enemy couldn't shoot with us so close and the panic on their faces was a drug in itself. I'd jumped a bit too hard and was looking down at them from three meters instead of two.

Behind me, Kirby said, "Fight!" My henchman and my pet demons sprung like wisps past me. A flashbang exploded, then two more. We were ready for it and rolled through the concussion wave. More fire sounded from the perimeter, distinct and chosen shots as we took out the wanderers. Two heavy crashes announced Deni's handiwork. Overhead came the crackling of bursting antipersonnel rounds compliments of Major Clavell. They were too high to be a threat, but were a great distraction.

All the enemy before us could hear was the shrieking, snarling roar of leopards craving a kill, and all they could see were the flashing fangs and slashing claws with camouflaged ripples behind them. I stepped in with them and drew my sword.

Weapon in right hand over sword in left, as I'd practiced so often. I let my visor track with my weapon, the ghost images showing over the real view before me. Pilots have implants to handle that type of multiple input. I can do it without. A body rose to my left, screaming in panic and I chopped its jaw with a controlled snap that brought my arm right back. Two more shots splashed crimson from a target far too close. One beside it was at an awkward angle for a shot but in fine position for a roundhouse kick with hundreds of kilos of exomusculature behind it. The ribs shattered and it bent in half before crumpling. I shot and hacked and kicked across the clearing, then turned to do it again.

I looked around and saw nothing, just guns and trees and dirt and brush, reeking a salty, coppery, iron-tanged sharp propellant smell of death.

Two Operatives, two leopards and an SU ally. Fifty-seven dead soldiers whose only mistake was to be in the area we were assigned. Bodies clutched weapons or had thrown them away.

They lay in tangles, faces showing shock, agony or absolutely nothing, having died too fast to comprehend. Very few of them were alive. Conventions wouldn't matter; none of them would be alive by sunset.

Boost was fading, my vision in waves. I gasped for breath, and hearing the leopards pant, I looked them over. Claws and muzzles greasy red with blood. Blood in splashes that appeared to float in midair where it had landed on the chameleons. Very macabre. They heaved for breath themselves. Sphinx favored a paw that had gotten smashed against something, and had a nick that made his tail tip thrash angrily. That and my throbbing, burning hip were our only casualties.

"Son of a bitch!" Glen muttered, making it sound like a prayer. I faced him. He said, "I've never seen anyone move so fast. You bastards are terrifying." The grin on his face was a protective and hopeful one.

I smiled back the smile of a predator. "Lots of practice," I panted. He finally understood what I'd known my whole career: the swords, guns, grenades, sensors and armor were tools. There was only one weapon in this battle. That weapon was me.

With us prodding the succored captives, we set about restoring the unit to operation. "Mind you stay out of the net," I warned them.

"But how do we plot our fire?" the commander asked, looking unsure.

Did they teach the UN troops nothing? "Spotters," I told him.

Glen said, "I'll leave two observers here for that."

Mountain troops were trickling in, receiving orders slowly, as they had to be relayed from the UN to our control to me to Glen to the local commanders to issue. But we got them sent out to protect the perimeter, and we secured the battery.

I never again felt as I did for that too brief time as I mowed my enemies like wheat before the scythe. It was a heady, intoxicating potion that was addictive and disturbing. Pleading exhaustion, I let Glen and Frank handle the rest of the details, merely approving Frank's choices.

During the flight back I was a wreck. Two days of combat

with no sleep, running on drugs, adrenaline and Boost with a few sips of water and a couple of ration bars was a toll I can't describe. It's probably like running several marathons. Naumann called and said, "Hold your report, get some sleep. Well done." A "Well done" from him equates to a medal. He's hard to impress. I thanked him and didn't argue. I needed the sleep. My lullaby was artillery and turbines.

While I slept, the Sunni factions who'd seized the moment were put to flight. General Furglen was later awarded a medal for planning and leading the mission.

Do you know what the cause of the intel failure was that had caused the city to collapse? Someone, probably ten years old, backdoored the UN control signal and shut off the satellites. That was it. That let all those forces into place. As to our battle in the hills, someone real-timed Glen's movements and offset the UN network so as to show them further back than they were. Incoming fire intended for enemy targets splashed on their own troops. In typical "We aren't bigots, some of our biggest supporters are Mtalis" fashion, the UNPF assumed, *assumed*, that no one locally had the means and training to do that, and never doublechecked the coding. So a comm, a satellite dish, and a frequency analyzer killed our people and theirs because they didn't care enough to do the job properly. To say I was angry would be an understatement. Words don't exist for Naumann's frame of mind. He idly speculated on having us assassinate the UNPF comm unit, then made sure to insist it was only a thought. Good thing; we would have done it.

But my squad was blooded now, and I felt more confident than ever. Certainly, we'd taken a few terrorists from ambush and done a bit of infiltration, but that's not the same as face-to-face brutality. Not necessarily easier, just different. None of my people had flinched, none panicked, and all had good tallies of shooting. That said a lot about our training, and I made sure Naumann knew that. He was as happy as I was, and agreed that we should follow up as quickly as possible.

CHAPTER 10

Now, there's a fine line one must walk in guerilla warfare. On the one hand, one wants to be as ruthless as possible to terrify the enemy. On the other hand, needless civilian casualties will work against you by strengthening the resolve of the enemy, and driving those who are neutral into their camp out of fear. To make it more complicated, one must distinguish between those who are armed and friendly, those armed and opposed, those armed and neutral, and those who fit into more than one category. The unarmed may shortly be armed, or simply camouflaged belligerents. Since one moves clandestinely in these circles, none of the above described locals are likely to announce their intentions to you. They may also disbelieve your stated intentions.

In short, doing anything or nothing may get you killed, as the whim of blind luck calls it.

The UNPF had had twelve Earth years to screw things up. They'd made every mistake possible (and this isn't a condemnation in that regard. Given time, any possible mistake *will* be made). Some soldiers had been overly friendly to the natives and failed to impress the enemy. Some had snapped, slaughtered whole villages, thus driving friends and neutrals over to them. Some had done nothing, thus reducing the effectiveness of the campaign. It was what we call in polite circles a goat rope, though I use a different term.

I made an emergency demand for whatever intel we had, preferably from human sources. I drew cash, headed for the local bars in mufti (with a knife and pistol under the body armor I was wearing under my casual garb) and began asking careful questions. Tyler went the other way with Deni, and Neil did his own circumspect probing. I didn't send the two women together out of fear for their safety. I did wish to discourage any encounters that might reveal just how well trained they were. Besides, it was SOP for the UNPF, and we didn't want to stand out . . . yet.

I found the necessary minimum of intel on the factions, and by lubing a few UN officers at the club and nodding and listening to them bitch, I found who I needed to see next.

Not everyone associated with the UN is stupid, corrupt, or incompetent. That's merely the nature of the system they exist in. The personnel range from pathetic to exceptional, as everywhere. Our intel found the exceptional ones, and some of them turned out to be most conveniently located for our needs. UNPF Intelligence Branch had an observation and liaison point very close to the western edge of the border of 3 Sector, Division C, Area IV, just to our west. Don't bother looking for it on a map. I mean, it's there, it would just be a waste of time to look it up as it's not that important a fact. The fact that there were that many geographic sections should illustrate just how badly the people in charge needed to unscrew themselves. The reports looked good, the location was prime and targets were plentiful. I planned a visit, filed a mission statement and we headed out. I didn't call ahead. It's easier to beg forgiveness than to ask permission.

In lieu of tans, we arrived in basic black evening dress, so as to impress the locals with our savoir faire and social graces. It also made us look like one of the mercenary units. We deployed as a squad, and took all our gear with us. Cowboy, our lifter pilot, maneuvered us in for a slingshot landing and we hit the ropes. That got the locals gawking. As we peeled off our hats, the sight of Deni cradling her sniper's rifle and Tyler lugging the heavy, both with wide-eyed mean stares under their paint, gave the audience a quick lesson in feminine daintiness. The crowd parted as we swept toward the compound. I could hear an occasional whisper as we approached.

The building was a typical sprayed stone box with small, high windows. The UN builds them everywhere. It's as standard as the godsawful apartments they build. However, the block wall with razor wire and ditch was a new and decent defense against casual attacks and weapons, and the gate had real concrete pillars to stop vehicles. It looked promising.

Cowboy left, tracked by weapons. We'd passed IFF on the way in, our automatic response stated we were on mission profile and would discuss after landing, but these paranoids kept us in sight. Good. The local shift commander of the guard detail already had called into the main house. Better. The older man striding down the stairs I recognized from the file as Major Paxton, UNPF (ret). He was a veteran of the civil war on Chersonessus ten years before, was still healthy-looking, and was carrying a carbine slung and pointed down. I felt at home with these people.

"I'm Greg Paxton, the Liaison Officer," he said, stopping inside the antiquated iron gate. He seemed prepared to wait for me to take the cue, but I was ready.

"Pleased to meet you, sir. I'm Warrant Leader Jelling of the FMF. This is my squad. We're here to get a huge body count, drink a lot of beer and screw our brains out. I don't do adminwork, I don't deal with bureaucrats, and as far as anyone is concerned, I don't exist."

He smiled, then laughed. "Better get checked for testosterone poisoning, son," he said. "Right after we have a few beers." He signaled and the gate was opened.

As we filed past, still attracting stares from the locals, he said, "I won't ask you to disarm, but do please ensure you're safed."

I replied, "Sir, after dealing with the suzies back at the HQ, it will be a pleasure to comply with a reasonable request. My people are all professionals, and there will be no accidents. Or else."

He offered good beer. As every group on Mtali except the Sufis officially ban alcohol, it was off-planet beer. Alsatian, to be precise. It was cool and wet and crisp on the throat. We accepted one each. After that, we'd drink water. Only idiots boast of their booze consumption when they might need their reflexes.

His office was a working office. He had a Merrill subgun in the corner, a pistol at his waist and another on his desk in addition to his carbine. The walls were bare, the two shelves were crowded with rams and his desk was comm and clutter. He leaned back, raised his glass and said, "To dead assholes." It seemed like a good toast. We joined him.

"So what's up?" he asked after we had a couple of swallows.

"What's up is that my orders are to locate trouble by kicking around until it finds me. Then I will call down the wrath of God and Goddess from our support, and we'll shoot anything that moves and grenade anything that doesn't."

Nodding, he said, "You do realize that this area has the most factional violence in the form of assassinations, petty feuds and terrorism, don't you?"

"That was my intelligence finding, yes," I agreed. "That's why I'm here."

"I'd heard that all your exposure to vacuum killed brain cells," he said, mockingly. He knew who we were and the "vacuum" comment about our training said so, but not to any eavesdroppers. Good man.

"Yes, sir," I acknowledged, "but only the weak ones."

It actually didn't take long to drive the factions underground in 3 Sector. We went out and showed them modern, hi-tech brutality. They were fond of assassinations, so we gave them a taste of their own medicine, in gross violation of UN law. Paxton had set us up with pictures of the local leaders, who were known but stayed hidden, and we dug them out.

How, when satellites were useless for identifying against a pedestrian on the street? Well, a few UN marks or Freehold credits went a long way toward loosening tongues, especially when the (implied) alternative was to be ground into the dirt. We set out drones, not airborne but mounted high in the trees, and let them watch the outskirts for us.

Let me give you an example: Mister Alara bin Ali. Bin Ali had a boast of over twenty-three successful kills of tribal leaders and military officers. He was renowned as a local celebrity, and spoken of in hushed tones. So we outdid him.

He tried very hard not to fall into a pattern, but we were able to backtrack enough data to place the direction of his hideout, even though he often swung wide over several days before making a hit. It was easy, once we knew what to look for. He was sent after well-protected targets who openly spoke against the Sunni factions. There weren't many of those, and less every time he came to town. He was working his way through the list, and we were able to watch most of those targets on nanocameras.

We found him on his trip to kill a local shipper, and confirmed by letting him hit his target (hard on the target, I know, but he was not morally any better than his assassin), and then stalked him back to his hide. He came into the area, shimmied through a fence and across a courtyard, which was not guarded at that moment for some reason. We made a note of that. Those guards might need to be dealt with.

The next night, I sent Geoff and Frank#2, our two most athletic youngsters, to bin Ali's house. Or his son's house, thereafter. The security staff woke up in the morning to find bin Ali missing and two of their number dead and gutted with excruciating and horrified looks frozen on their dead features. The sleepers on either side, who were unharmed, discovered them. That sent a panic through the area.

Bin Ali was never seen again. He'd been killed, of course, and his body smuggled out. It was easier to move in sections. Then we loaded it aboard a departing shuttle and let the atmosphere cremate him on re-entry. No evidence to find.

We ghosted around the area with sensors. Whenever we found a bomb factory, we'd create an accident for it. We'd find convoys coming in and destroy them on the road, leaving some group or other without supplies. We occasionally snatched someone for intel and interrogated them. Unfortunately, most of them had heart attacks while being questioned. We did everything we could for them, but most of them died. Very sad.

We were doing a decent job of taking out faction leaders. Each one we bagged created a power struggle among his underlings for the privilege of being the next sphincter. That created internal stress that slowed their operations briefly.

But only briefly. The problem was, they kept blaming each other for these assassinations, accused each other of selling out those we captured alive, and running sorties against their perceived enemies. It was insulting to the extreme to us—the Muslim sects just assumed that we were harmless, being "infidels," and kept after each other. Provincial, egotistical little Paleolithic savages. As for the Feltsies, they were wimps. Long term, the Muslims were going to wipe them out, because they were willing to fight dirty and suicidally and the Feltsies weren't. They seemed to want an archaic stand up battle that they were never going to get, with Good and Evil led by angels and demons.

I reported the problem up through Naumann. He agreed with my assessment. "Yes, that's exactly the response it triggers," he said. "And part of the reason the UN hasn't accomplished anything. Open action has to be seen as nonpartisan, clandestine action is never perceived as it should be."

I replied, "Why hasn't someone said, 'They're right, you're wrong, sit down before we slit your throats'?"

"Who do we pick as 'right'?" he asked.

I said, "Well, the Sufis strike me as being the best combination of competent and decent. The Bahá'í are nicer people, but they're defensive minded only, and won't fight a proper battle."

"So team up with some Sufis," he told me. "I'll handle any flak."

I spoke to Paxton. He said, "I think I can arrange that." He nodded, sipped his coffee and leaned back. "Are you sure it's a good idea, though? I'm glad to see someone doing *something* concrete, but you might polarize the rest of them against you."

"You really think so?" I asked.

"I do."

"Good," I replied, grinning. Bring them on, I'd stuff them into holes.

Whenever we were back on base, we took the opportunity to go into town and drink beer, while listening for more intel and drinking beer. It was best done over a few beers. We'd get a lot of useful rumors, and the sooner the rumors were out, the better we could ID the speakers as potential suspects who knew more than they officially admitted. This included a lot of alleged "allies" and even a few UN officers.

There was also one payoff from the mountain battle. I'd been patient and philosophical, and it was all proven worthwhile when I caught a "No shit, there I was" story back in the corner of one favored hangout. It was too dim to see clearly, so I wandered back that way with my bulb.

The guy was saying "—so we get this call for support from this colonial jackass who doesn't even know what grid he's at on the map. I relay it to Battery C and they dropped it right on the X. It was a perfect shot. Perfect—"

He went on about some Novaja Rossian troops and how they hadn't been bright enough to know just how much manly power artillery packed, etc. I didn't like him. He wasn't a gunner, he was a REDF. He was more than willing to use their prowess to cadge drinks for himself, though. It only took a bit of listening to make me quite sure he was the same REDF who hadn't been able to grasp the concept that friendly fire is a contradiction in terms.

As an investment in research, I bought him a drink.

"Hey, that's good of you," he said. "I'm Joey Cotton."

"Walt Amparan," I replied with a nod. I didn't take the offered hand. "I'm a maintenance officer for the Hatchets."

He said, "Oh, those. Yes, not a bad craft, I'm told. Not as good as the Guardian, of course, but very good as far as colonial equipment goes. I'm the command artillery controller. Guy in charge." He thumbed his chest proudly.

"Really?" I said. "You're *the* guy to call for arty?"

"Well, daytime," he admitted. "I make the calls."

I sat back and let him drink and talk, occasionally nodding or grunting so he'd continue. There were a handful of newbies hanging around, but they changed regularly as the troops figured him out. There were no bar girls anywhere near him, and the server brought his drinks and left without waiting for a tip. That told me all I needed to know. He sprawled further and further back in the scarred vinyl booth he occupied, back to the door and oblivious. He might have seen a bit of combat . . . on vid. I picked holes in most of his stories, and frankly didn't care for the glamour of sitting in a chair watching people work. There's nothing wrong with that job. It has to be done, and it has as many stories as any other. But he wasn't talking about that job, he was talking about everyone else's, as if he were they. The crowd thinned and he kept talking. I sat patiently. I ignored the disgusted look from the bartender.

Cotton finally realized that we weren't being served any more, even with the lenient rules near base, which were in gross violation of most of the local laws.

"Well, I guess I should get back inside the gate. Possible terrorists, you know. Though I'm armed against that," he said with a conspiratorial wink. Jackass. Never admit that to a stranger.

"Let me walk with you," I said. "I need to take care of a couple of things."

"Sure," he agreed. He staggered upright and we wandered out, me waving to the bartender, who shook his head in distaste. He'd be in a better mood tomorrow, if Cotton came back to drink.

It was a bit foggy outside, just enough to dim visibility and dull noise. Perfect. I steered the staggering Cotton toward the gate and suggested a shortcut through an alley. It was that simple. Once inside the cluttered and narrow brick passage, I asked, "Any chance you recall a Special Unit two weeks ago? Needed fire support?"

"Oh, yeah," he agreed. "There was some mixup on coordinates."

"What happened?" I asked. I needed to know his side of the story, just to make sure.

"Oh, the goddam colonials couldn't get their location straight. Our people were getting pasted, and then some clown from their unit called in to try to shift the blame."

I could not believe he had *that* screwed up a recollection of the event. Or was it a fabrication?

"Any casualties?" I asked, trying to be conversational.

"Oh, a couple, I think," he said. "Happens. Those Special Unit guys are nuts, though. A few injuries don't even faze them— uuuugh." He cut off as I thumped him in the gut.

I'd heard enough. It's a good thing he was an ally. I gave him three good stiff hooks to the midriff, a toe to the shin to leave a bruise he could appreciate for the next month, then hit him on the right cheek hard enough to stun him and leave a nasty bruise on his eye, without quite knocking him unconscious.

He stumbled backwards, crashed into the wall and sat down

hard amid greasy garbage from a cafe. He vomited all over himself, thin and wet and stinking of beer and stomach acid. While his eyes glazed over and he gasped for breath, I said, "'Fire Control, this is Lion One, Pony Three's system is compromised, do not fire on those coordinates. Stand by for correction.'"

Then I applied a correction. I booted him moderately in the balls. "Next time I give you a correction," boot, "you relay the fucking data and try not to think," boot, "too hard. Got it," boot, "buddy?"

He gaped, writhed and fell flat on his back. Gasping, he whispered, "I'll have you in jail tomorrow, you son of a bitch!"

"And I'll slit your fucking throat before you kill anyone else," I rasped, with my best war face. I could tell he believed me.

I've found there's very few personnel problems that can't be resolved by a suitable application of a boot to the head. He could wake up here for all I cared. I went back to the barracks.

Paxton handled his part of our joint operation well. A Sufi unit arrived to discuss it the next day, right after we did. A dapper little colonel with the most gorgeously engraved Huglu carbine I'd ever seen came in, presented us with what I'm told was some excellent coffee, and sat at ease. He was slightly round faced and beamed smiles. A Colonel Kemal Cagri.

"Oo ar wiv e Freehild cotijen?" he asked as he offered a hand. I thought for a moment and translated, "You are with the Freehold Contingent?"

"I am," I replied, using his dialect of Turkish. "Would you do me the honor of letting me speak your language? I find it lovely to speak, and I need the practice for meeting your people. It's been some time." That's the diplomatic way of saying "Sir, your English sucks rocks. I'd rather translate from a language I know than from a patois I don't."

"Of course, Warrant Leader," he agreed. "While I'd like to practice English, it would make more sense for you to speak my language here, I believe." Good. He understood and wasn't offended. Of course, if I'd come out and said it, he would have been, as it would have impugned his skills. These are the important tricks that help win allies.

"Thank you, Colonel Cagri," I agreed with a slight nod and a hand on his wrist. They are even more casual about touching than we are. It makes most Earthies cringe.

I agreed that his people were the most deserving and trustworthy on the planet (true), and that it made sense to stop pretending and support them (true) and that I loved the idea of collaborating with them to do so (false. I'd rather have had the entire Special Warfare regiments and lots of air support).

"And what do you need from me?" he asked.

"A good squad of troops, well experienced and familiar with this sector," I said. I didn't say, "And who are willing to engage in a bloody slaughter." I would have insulted him by suggesting he had troops who felt otherwise.

Nodding, sipping coffee, smiling, he replied, "I think a squad from First Platoon Guards will do nicely. Come."

So we went outside, he called a loud verbal order, "First Platoon Guards! Fall In!" and his unit fell in from under trees, sunshades, their vehicles, and local kiosks. And they fell in *fast*. I was impressed. They were the image of "jump to it!" as they sprinted into the compound.

I couldn't believe what happened next, though. He shouted at them, "I need a squad of volunteers to accompany the UN and the Colonials on a mission. Squad sergeants, give me your best offers."

That sounds fair enough, right?

The troops broke formation and gathered around their squad leaders in a frantic panic. They were pulling stuff out of their pockets while covertly looking at each other, appraising the competition. What they were competing on, apparently, was who could come up with the biggest bribe. The squad leaders grabbed the proffered handfuls of notes, straightened them hurriedly, then tore across the field to the commander. He shuffled through the stacks, frowned, looked disgusted, then pointed at one squad leader. He turned back to me, smiled that broad beam, and said, "Fourth Squad is yours, Warrant Leader. Good hunting!"

The squad leader slumped his shoulders and sighed, saluted resignedly at Cagri's back and headed toward his people. The rest of the unit dispersed without any orders, and his squad, mostly kids around eighteen standard years, stood there with quivering lips and glazed eyes. The only universe they had for comparison was their own, and in that light, they thought themselves raped, abandoned and dead. Cagri apparently saw nothing wrong with how he'd operated. The graft was how he expected to be paid what he was due as a unit commander. We shook hands, bowed slightly, kissed cheeks and he was gone, the rest of his troops mounting up and skedaddling before they got dragged into this.

This was what I had to work with. And this was the elite of the planet. Triff. I started thinking at once of ways to turn this to the good.

Actually, I managed to come up with a few things. First, this group had had the poorest bribe (which they didn't get back, note), which meant they were either honest or incompetent. Hey, that's a 50/50 chance of a good thing. They hadn't run, which they could have. They came over at once at my signal. They would be native guides of at least moderate competency. And if all else failed, they could soak up bullets meant for the rest of us.

On the other hand, that soaking might not be necessary if they were worth a damn.

They stood at good attention while I eyed them, and my kids fell in behind me in best chained-killer pose. The locals looked impressed. They should be. Our gear was less than twenty years old, clean, in good repair and useful. Theirs was crap. Poorly made crap. Lowest bidder crap from shoddy materials. Abused by illiterates for twenty years crap. But it was uniform and in repair. I said to the squad leader, "Let me see your weapon."

He dropped his eyes, raised the weapon, cleared it, inspected it and handed it to me, just as if he were on parade. I snatched it as he thrust it at me, flipped it, checked the chamber and gave it a once over. Then I opened the receiver, pointed it skyward and examined the bore. Pitted from long use, rifling worn. This thing had seen a lot of rounds and not much cleaning. But it was clean now, even though it was too late to matter. I closed it and handed it back. In a glance, I reminded myself what the rest of their gear was like.

I dismissed my troops to embark. "Come with me," I told the

Sufi NCO, Sergeant Mahir Bolukbasi. He nodded and gave the order.

They marched adequately, too. Discipline was here, even if it had been abused like a third-rate escort and sold cheap. They'd do. I'd have them in shape by morning, I decided. I called ahead to Warrant Sirkot at 3rd MAR Logistics, our official source.

They boarded our vertols without question, though a couple of nervous looks indicated that at least some of them had never flown. But there were no complaints, even muttered. They awaited my orders before debarking at our flightline.

We got stares as we marched through the compound. First of all, we hardly ever march except on parade. Second of all, we were a mixed bunch. I took them to logistics section, marched them up the dock ramps and sought a roomy bay. The third one down fit my needs, being sparse on the floor and packed around the walls. I snapped orders again as I handed over a paper notebook. "Write your uniform sizes down, in centimeters, with your name. Then strip."

They wrote down the info, but there was muttering and head shaking at that last part. "STRIP!" I repeated. When nothing had happened after another ten seconds, I grabbed Bolukbasi, clicked open my pocketknife in front of his eyes, batted aside his attempt at a block—which impressed me; it had been quick—and peeled him out of his shirt the hard way.

They stripped in a hurry, looking ashamed. They were poorly fed, but wiry and well-scarred, and it was my turn to be impressed. These weren't cowards. They reluctantly came back to attention, shamefaced and flushed. I knew the basis of their embarrassment, even if I'll never understand it—there were women present. They have few women in the military, none in combat units, and they have this religious modesty thing.

They dressed fast when the logistics troops brought them uniforms. I put them in ours. They looked a lot more like soldiers. "Stuff all your gear in these sacks," I told them.

We hit the chow hall and filled everybody up with peppered beef, garlic and herb potatoes, steamed beans, cake, milk, coffee and sodas with ice cream for those who wanted it. They packed away food as if they hadn't seen it in days, and they may not have. Then I had them march to our barracks section and stuck them in an empty hooch.

They were intended for eight, packed with thirteen, but the Sufis were agog at wood floors, lockers, privacy screens and an attached latrine and shower with hot water. I showed them how to set the combinations for their lockers and said, "Rest. Be outside in formation at midnight," and left.

I cleared what I needed to with Naumann, who just laughed and said, "I know nothing."

Then I called Greg Paxton and told him what I planned. I called on a secure circuit, using one of our multiband scramblers. I'd left one with him. I didn't trust UN gear for this.

"Let me get this straight," he said. "You're going to rob our own people to get supplies?"

I replied, "You need them, they have them, they won't share them, so you take them."

He said, "Yes, but—" and I cut him off.

"We aren't going to hurt them, it'll be good practice for us, a good lesson for them and we'll get the stuff we need. If they're going to sell it black market to the factions and aren't going to use it themselves, they can't complain about not having it."

"That part's hard to argue with," he said.

"So I'll see you in a couple of days." I disconnected and went to get some sleep. It was going to be a long night.

It was also raining that night, which was awesome. I took it as a sign that we were going to succeed. The Sufis were waiting, at attention, with all their old gear over our uniforms, stoically letting the cold rain trickle through their clothes. Good discipline. "Leave that fossilized crap in your lockers," I told them. They hurried inside to comply, then came back, looking bothered. No one had any weapons except me, and I had only a pistol. We Freeholders had small toolkits and our tac visors.

"Follow us, quietly," I ordered.

The back of our compound has to have the fence replaced regularly. It appears that people bypass the sensor net and cut it to gain access. As this happens to the UN, too, they don't notice the repair crews. What they also don't notice is that ours are cut from the inside. We sneak out all the time to gather intel from the bars, smuggle equipment, get laid and find drugs and liquor. You know, the important things in war.

We snipped some slits in the fence and eased through. The Sufis followed us, being quite professionally quiet and experienced as they did so. Not bad. Our guards didn't notice us departing. It would be hard for them to notice us, as they were facing the other way and talking in loud voices. They would start paying attention again about ten seconds after we were clear. Professionals to the core. Of course, occasionally we'd slip past while they were watching, just for practice. It was practice for them and us.

Our target was a mere five hundred meters away, though we'd travel about ten kilometers to accomplish the mission. The UN 43rd Logistics Support Function's depot was on the far side of their compound, with plenty of outside fence. They may as well have given me the keys.

We used cover as it was, moving from building shadow to grass to trees and back. This was in part to assess how well our allies moved. I was impressed. The patter of rain kept our noise masked, as long as we didn't splash too much. They were very good light infantry, and clearly experienced scroungers. They'd just never had anything decent to scrounge before. That was about to change. And after this, they'd know where to go to get the stuff.

We stopped just beyond the illuminated circles from the compound's security lights. The dark slash of shadow edge, combined with the bulldozed ground gave us lots of muddy hiding places. I waited for everyone to settle in, with my people on perimeter and the Sufis inside. That way, we could keep an eye on them. We were unarmed except for me, so if we were discovered, I could legitimately claim it was a training mission and not mention the other actions we were trying to take. We'd keep our toolkits hidden.

We sat there, silently, watching for any movement. A pending night mission might dictate human presence, or someone might be catching up on adminwork. The security geeks might decide to hang out in the parking area to snooze, drink or just kill time. Never assume that because you have a schedule you know what's going on. There were two technical vehicles there, but a glance with IR proved they were cold. No traces of human passage remained, and a laser reflected off a window didn't jiggle from air currents against the glass. The stack of cargo pallets near a door was equally uninteresting.

It looked good. I gave it twenty local minutes. Nothing heard down there, and just as importantly, nothing heard from our allies. No shuffling, no exasperated sighs. We sat there and soaked, chilled and shivered. We could have brought cloaks, but those would have interfered with hearing, peripheral vision and been liable to catch on things, as well as bulking us out and swishing as they brushed. There are times a soldier just has to get wet.

"Stay here. Don't move," I told Bolukbasi. He nodded and stared in fascination. I turned and skipped down the hill. With me were Martin, Geoff, Frank#2, Johnny Squid and Tyler. I had a mix of experienced troops and newer ones, mostly on the small side. As I said, it was a training exercise.

The ground was lower on our side than the other, with a slimy ditch to negotiate. The oft-repaired fence before us was doubled, razor wired and had motion sensors. We'd go over them without triggering anything on the way in. The way out was a separate problem. As far as going in, we each Boosted. Geoff was the gymnast and was outrageously strong even by our standards. He'd been working out since he was three.

It was like a carnival ride. I dropped down into the ditch, stepped forward onto his waiting hands and jumped as he heaved me up. I tucked up tight to clear the wire, then straightened enough for the landing. A mere 3 meter fence was the toughest obstacle so far. There were reasons for that I'd discover later. Partly, it was because we were already inside an armed and marked perimeter. This fence was to stop petty pilferage. Well, there was nothing petty about what I had planned.

The others were over in short order. Geoff stepped back a measured distance, sprinted, bounded, came clear of the ground and soared over the wire.

Then his boot brushed it and he tumbled.

It wasn't too bad. He righted and landed staggering, wincing slightly. He'd be fine. But a centimeter lower and we'd have had to cut him loose.

There was no easy way across the parking area. It was flat fused dirt and well lit. So we ran for it, widely spread to make many little shadows rather than one large one. We flattened against the building, behind scattered pallets and under the two vehicles. Nothing happened. We hadn't expected anything, but caution is what keeps you alive.

I decided to start and shifted out of shadow. I walked casually up to the door, acting at this point as if I belonged there. You can confuse most people into ignoring you by pretending to be normal. You fit the pattern they expect, and you aren't questioned. If anyone saw me right now, they'd assume that anyone so brazen *must* have authorization. Really. It works. Frank#2 joined me with his electronics kit.

I felt eyes behind my back from our people. I had tense muscles as we slipped the locks. It wasn't hard. The doors opened outward, to facilitate moving stuff out on loaders. That meant the hinges were outside. All we had to do was scan for the sensors, convince them they were engaged, slip the hinge pins on one side and pull the doors away from them. Yes, they had multithousand credit security locks and doors that could be defeated with a pocket-knife applied to six fifty cent pins. Take a look next time you're somewhere "secure." It happens everywhere.

"Shit, problem," Frank said suddenly.

"What?" I asked.

"They put security pins in the hinges." Simple metal screws to stop someone from doing exactly what we were doing.

"Damn," I said, and dug for a silenced drill. We'd have to poke those out. That would leave us exposed a bit longer. Then we'd have to hide the holes.

The door came open. It was a tight squeeze, which was fine. I'd picked skinny people. Once we were in, I drew it as closed as it could get. No one driving by would suspect anything. At least, not enough to get out of a warm vehicle into cold rain.

Inside, we worked by torchlight. Most of what we wanted wasn't hard at all. The weapons we intended to steal were a pain. They were in heavy, secure vaults, the firing mechanisms stored separately and the whole mess inside a secured room. It took Frank#2 nearly another hour to convince the protocols to let us in, while I took low light photos of everything in sight. Finally, he succeeded in cracking it. "I can't delete the entry from the file," he said. "Sorry."

"No problem," I said. They'd have no idea who'd been here. That was the important part. We grabbed the rest of what we wanted and finished packaging it. We'd stacked the gear neatly by the door for our departure. It had taken longer than I expected. We didn't find replacement hinges, but we did find flush metal screws to hide the evidence of our entry.

"Clear?" I asked over my tac to Frank.

"Sure," he confirmed. We were as non-military as we could sound.

The exfiltration was quick. We opened the doors, I fixed the hinges while the others brought the gear out, we closed the doors and removed our bypass circuits on the sensors. We sprinted back and forth with our bundles, and Geoff and Martin heaved them over the fence. They might get muddy, but this was battle gear, so who cared? It would just break it in. Once done with two heavy loads each, we were tossed over ourselves. Geoff tossed Martin over, then stepped back and sprinted. With a clear run on packed ground and a lower target relatively, he cleared it with no trouble, only to land deep in the ditch. He needed help to pull loose, and was stuck until he suddenly came free with a squishing sound.

The Sufis were wide-eyed in wonder as we climbed back up, backs laden with presents. We all adjourned, near as silently as we'd approached, the difference being due to enthusiasm, and sought a quiet spot under some trees. We were close enough to have minimum risk of attack, far enough away for privacy. We sat down and divvied up the loot.

Every one of the Sufis got a new rifle, body armor, harness and pack, canteen pack, first aid kit, compass, position receiver, wet weather gear and shelter. It was more material wealth than most of them had seen in their lives, and they unconsciously scanned about for potential thieves, before realizing they were all thus equipped. "It's yours," I told them. "You can sell it or your old stuff when you get back. While you're with us, I expect you to maintain it and respect it. Steal from anyone and I'll kill you." They knew it was no idle threat, and I'd quashed the idea before it had even started. They knew who their friends were. "Tomorrow night we hunt," I told them. This time, they grinned without reservations.

The grins were the type I like: predatory.

CHAPTER 11

We moved out at once. We split up so we could do more damage. We had thirty-three troops as well as four spooks from the intel post and five mercs Greg said we could trust, for seven teams of six plus me. I made assignments, and put two or three Operatives on every team. We led, they provided extra eyes and firepower.

Geoff and I were teamed. I picked him because he was left after I'd paired everyone else, and because I'd not worked with him much. Greg came with us, and three Sufis: Sergeant Bolukbasi and two of his troops, Nafiz and Hayati, no last names.

Our first mission was intel. There was a lot of activity in this area. That required personnel, communications and equipment. The question was, where did the communications and other equipment come from?

The UN satellites weren't finding much. It was cloudy around here, with warm air from the sea south of us hitting cold air near the mountains. Additionally, it was foggy and misty due to the humidity and temperature swings. The UN's answer was to shrug and say, "No data." We decided to go look. There was a hollow in the hills where all kinds of stuff could hide.

It was a four day op. We were taken in a battered truck to blend in and wore civvies. In rough work clothes and my high

UV tan, I looked like a weathered laborer. My skin was a bit too smooth, but dust and a practiced squint took care of that. Geoff already had a narrow face and bushy black beard. It was his normal look.

We drove all day in dust and sun, the turbine stuttering occasionally. The air was thin though humid, as we were quite high, about 1000 meters. We arrived at our insertion point near nightfall. Our gear and weapons came out from under crates and we stepped into the dusk, as the molten primary quenched itself over the hills. The clouds writhed like snakes and created washes of shadow that turned into dark pools. Pretty planet. Too bad there were more assholes than mouths.

Geoff said, "This is about the alonest I've ever felt," as we plunged into the trees for cover.

"It's always like that," I said. "For me, anyway."

Greg said, "Maybe. It's good to be back, though." He'd gone slightly native, and liked this place. It takes all types, I guess. The Sufis were silent. This wasn't their native area, but they were still "local."

The woods were thick and tangled, which was great for cover but made progress slow. There were occasional dips in the ground and loose soil that made things treacherous. We were soaked in sweat and grimy with dirt, bugs, twigs and leaf scraps in short order. Branches snatched or sprung at us, roots and holes seized our boots and occasional disturbed animals would rise in our faces, causing us to freeze in place until we reswallowed our hearts.

I don't know if you've ever used night vision, but it's not what it appears on vid. Dark areas are just that—dark areas. They can be centimeters deep or sheer drops. The greater the enhancement, the poorer the image quality, by definition. I'd had years of practice. Geoff had a bit less. Greg was well-experienced, but a bit rusty. Our three locals were rank amateurs. We made slow progress.

Overhead came the sound of vertols. We stopped, even though the odds of them seeing us in this undergrowth were remote. The engine whine was familiar, and sounded as if the craft were on approach.

"Guardians," Geoff said. He was correct. "What the hell is the UN doing out here?"

Greg said, "If they're UN, I'm not on their list of people to inform. I also didn't hear about it from any of my local contacts."

Mahir Bolukbasi said, "I wasn't told. But they don't tell me much."

Interesting.

It was near dawn when we finally got over the ridge and angled down into the valley. There were no more aircraft flights, but there were the sounds of a base. "We'd better dig in," I said. And we'd better do it quickly. I'd forgotten how short dawn was on a planet with a rotation this fast.

We dug a pit and scattered the dirt broadly but carefully. A clump left atop a leaf would be a dead giveaway to an experienced tracker, with emphasis on the "dead." No, I'm not kidding. Experts learn to look for things like that. Their patrols would be familiar with this area and would notice the slightest irregularity. The site we'd picked for shelter was away from any signs of disturbance, including animal runs. The trick to recon is to not meet the enemy. All you want is intel.

After we dug, we covered it carefully with a folding mat we'd brought for the purpose, then local vegetation, not plucked, but rather dug to keep it fresh. Inside, we propped it up with a frame and some extra deadwood. It was a shallow pit we could shelter in and not be seen. We'd be in it until dark at least.

The day sucked. First it got muggy, and our sweat lingered in the pit. We stewed in our own juices until midday, with occasional sips of water the only thing remotely cool.

Then it rained. It always rains when you're in the field. It wasn't a particularly cold rain, but it pooled in our mansion until the sticks and frame were columns from a subterranean lake that ate away at the loam beneath them. We got no rest to speak of and spent all afternoon propping the roof by hand, in shifts, lest the roof slump and give us away. At least once we heard a patrol travel through the area, no more than a hundred meters away.

Near midday, before the rain, we had an attack, sort of. Geoff suddenly cursed in a whisper and started kicking at something.

People awoke, shifted and squinted through the dappled light. It appeared to me he was wrestling with his ankle while wearing a fur glove. As he didn't have fur gloves (at least not professionally; his social life is none of my business), I deduced it to be an animal. I snapped out my Eaves, carefully so as not to injure anyone with that wicked sharp edge, and slid the back alongside his arm. He grunted in pain, clenched tightly and held still as the blade rode over his thumb. Then I jabbed it into whatever it was. Or tried to. It chittered, jerked and scampered away, unhurt.

We all moved around for a look. It had been a pseudo-rabbit creature, small, white and gray with floppy ears. "Damned thing stabbed me with a thorn!" he said.

"Teeth," I said.

"Teeth and a thorn," he insisted. "It came in fighting."

"You were dreaming," I said.

"Like hell." He held up a long thorn with a broken base to illustrate. There was a puncture wound above his ankle.

"Likely broke while we were digging," I said, "and you rolled on it in the fight."

"I don't remember any thorn bushes," he said. He had a point. Neither did I.

I shrugged and bandaged him while Nafiz tried to no avail to locate the creature. It did have prehensile forepaws, I'd noticed. Possibly a tool user? I filed it for reference. We left Greg on watch and tried to go back to sleep, Geoff taking a painkiller. It wasn't a serious wound, but it was certainly a superficial mess.

At nightfall we crawled out, aching and tired and needing to piss like horses. We filled in the hole as best we could with deadwood, scattered additional greenery and planted our cover bushes on top. It wouldn't fool anyone who got a close look, but we planned to be gone before then.

We ate as we moved, chewing dried meat and combat rats. All trash went back into our small rucks. This was dangerous terrain.

We needed to get close enough to get photos, and not be seen in the process. I took point, Geoff and Greg were behind me with cameras, Geoff still limping slightly. I had to rely on our Sufi friends for rear guard. It's an indicator that I, the most paranoid and untrusting, self-centered and self-reliant asshole who ever lived, born of a culture of individualists, trusted them to do that.

We found a gully, rich with rotting leaves, that cascaded over roots and left micromeadows of silt behind. It had bugs and rodent analogs and lizard and snake analogs in profusion. It had a good view across the valley. We set up shop there.

There was something going on down there. Whoever it was had excellent light discipline, but there were still flashes periodically, as they lit something while moving or working. There were voices, the muted coughs of suppressed weapons in spates that were clearly due to a training range. We heard no aircraft, but there were several small clearings we couldn't see into that could hide them.

We lucked out at 0136 local time. A craft came in low and slow over the ridge and to our left and sought one of those small clearings. Greg and Geoff started shooting images. It was a Guardian. It was loaded with ferry tanks. It had munition racks with close support hardware of various kinds. It was ponderous as only a craft that is laden for charging rippers can be. Another followed it. Then two more. Then something else. Most of a wing flew in in a few segs.

That was enough. "Okay, let's go," I said.

"Shouldn't we find out who it is?" Geoff asked.

"No," I said. "It's not the UN. They have UN gear. So they've stolen it. We report back and the intel gophers and an armed assault force can handle the details. Let's squirm."

The trip back was boring but exhausting. Still, I felt good. We had intel. We were cracking this open. Soon, it would all tumble down around the factions and freedom would return. Yes, I was still naïve enough to believe that. Or maybe "idealistic" is more accurate. I knew how it would play out, I just didn't want to accept it.

Only I really didn't know how it would play out. I was to find out shortly, though.

Greg took his images, I took ours. We had a congratulatory toast with an Earth bourbon. Very interesting. I made a note to pick some up when I had a chance.

r   r   r

My report to Naumann didn't seem to take him by surprise. The bastard is so diabolically cunning he scares even me. But he accepted the report and the images from both Geoff and me, thanked us enthusiastically and bade me sit as he dismissed Geoff.

I looked the question at him and waited for a response.

"This is a perfect time to commence another mission," he told me, grinning.

"Yes?" I prompted. The grin looked like the kind I liked.

"We need an assessment of UN capabilities. That's why we're here. We need more intel on these backdoor sales or thefts. Recon and find out what you can," he told me.

"Sneak or methodology? Or just hack their files?" I asked.

He said, "I have intel hacking their files. We've got a lot. But there's much more obviously not in the net that we need. Go in personally and get photos."

"Can do," I replied. I was grinning myself now. This was going to be fun.

So I went back into the UN compound, alone, and disappeared. At night, with 90% of them asleep and 9% drunk and/or stupid, I dodged the woefully dispersed 1% who mattered and slid back into the logistics area.

I wandered through the bays and took low-light images of everything. I took an xceiver scanner and drank in the chips on the gear. The contents of every shelf, rack, pile and bin went into ram. Piles of camouflage netting and body armor had just arrived. I got them still in their shipping containers and on pallets. Even a container of UN Form 1, slang for "toilet paper," was imaged for file. It is a critical resource, after all.

When done, I exfiltrated and walked out the front gate, in a borrowed uniform, with a nod to the guards. That's just the kind of arrogant asshole I am.

I'd barely gotten enough sleep when my comm beeped. "Chin-ran," I answered.

"Naumann here. Please come over for a conference."

That was odd. We don't use the term conference, and if we did, Naumann wouldn't have any. He asks, you talk, he gives orders. "On my way," I replied.

I got dressed and walked over. It was, in fact, a conference. Some UN suit was there. I ignored him and reported to Naumann. This seemed to amuse the dip.

"You are Warrant Leader Jelling?" he asked.

Sure, good a name as any. "Yes, may I help you, Mister . . . ?"

"Larson. Andy Larson. I'm here from the Bureau of Defense's Office of Resource Security. We want to go over section three of your report," he said. That would be equipment. I assumed he wanted more details. I was floored when he said, "There's a lot of errors there."

"What 'errors'?" I asked.

"You didn't see any Guardians," he told me. It wasn't a question.

"Yes I did," I insisted. "At least six of them, all different. We have photos of four." Two other teams had also seen them in other locations.

"The photos were not assessed correctly."

What was he talking about? I persisted, "I saw four. My other people confirm those four. Two others were seen by squad members and confirmed. Those two and two of the ones I sighted were photographed. The profile is unmistakable. I can even tell you what the munition load was."

"The only Guardians on this or any planet are UN craft. We don't sell them to other governments, and we didn't have any there," he told me. "Nor do we have any unaccounted for." He was trying very hard to be firm with me. I don't push around worth a damn.

"Then someone stole or otherwise acquired a few," I said. "And there were Chevaliers from Alsace there, too. All kinds of stuff is overflying that area." That area, I recalled, where no satellite could get a good image due to "persistent cloud cover." I suddenly didn't doubt it. They didn't *want* photos of that area. They were setting something up to give control of a large chunk of the planet, if not all of it, to the Shia.

Oh, boy. Now, how did I convince him I'd had an epiphany about his viewpoint, without revealing my epiphany about the real issues? "Are you sure?" I asked to his disbelieving stare.

"Positive," he said.

I put on a dumb look. "It must have been some old S-96 cargo lifters then," I said. "But I was *sure*, really sure they were Guardians."

"No chance," he insisted.

Naumann played from my lead. "Well, Ken," he said, "the old S-96 general cargo series do have a similar profile. Our photo recon people could have been mistaken, too. Nighttime, fuzzy images . . ."

I nodded slowly and said, "I guess so." There is and never has been an S-96 series. He and I knew that. This clown was a pencil pusher who was just too happy to have us agree with him.

"Don't feel bad," Larson said. "Mistakes happen, and you did get some valuable data on terrain for us. In the long run, that's far more important than any mere equipment data."

I "Oh, of coursed" and made nice about data that could help revitalize, blah blah blah, until he left.

He backed out all smiles, we smiled back, we all bowed, then Naumann and I were alone. We whirled to face each other, locked eyes for about three seconds before he said, "Come with me." I followed. He unlocked a cabinet, grabbed stuff out of it and relocked it in a hurry. As we left, he spoke into his comm, "Logistics, Naumann. We have a shortage of generators right now . . . oh, yes we do. Don't let anyone tell you otherwise. I need a request order to borrow some from the UN. I need it in my system in one hundred seconds, timestamped for two days ago, early afternoon."

He didn't need to say anything else. His driver was waiting, an earnest young woman who slapped down her comm with a lesson on it, which was covering up the flat reader with the vid on it she'd really been watching, and had the turbine spinning by the time we jumped off the dock and landed next to the car. "UN Logistics," he said to her.

"Yes, Commander," she nodded as she slammed into gear. She drove quickly but with good control. Clearly, she'd been assigned here at least a few days.

"Just look around and keep quiet," he told me. "I want your input afterwards."

"Yes, sir," I agreed.

We pulled up in front of the 43rd Logistics Support Function. It was the exact old railside type building I'd been in last night, and we jogged up the steps as the driver stood to with her weapon. Our SOP was that anywhere outside our own perimeter was hostile. It seemed that it was several kinds of hostile. I hate political games.

Inside, we were met by eager young soldiers who really wanted to help. A shame we would be taking advantage of them.

"May I help you gentlemen?" asked one young corporal. He was about 22 Earth years, youthfully lanky and energetic. He tried not to stare at our slung carbines. I never got used to the idea of a military that's afraid of weapons.

"I hope so, Corporal," said Naumann, all smiles. "I'm Assault Commander Naumann. I came personally because this is important enough I don't want to get shuffled off. I'd hate to put you in the spot of being stuck between my troops and my messages and your boss." He was so friendly and sweet I wanted to puke. I didn't know he could act. On the other hand, he was an Operative, too.

The kid looked relieved even though he hadn't been stressed. It was that, "Oh, good, I can step back now" look. "Right this way, then," he said. We followed.

The carpet was nice here. Very nice. All the comms were brand new. Whatever budget problems afflicted the deployment, they weren't bothering Logistics. Maybe not suspicious, but something to keep an eye on.

"May I help you gentlemen?" asked the logistics commander, a Colonel Gaynard McCord, unknowingly mimicking his subordinate. Or maybe not unconscious. For all I know, they had a script.

Naumann spoke to him, I looked around more. Desks were new. Everyone I could see was wearing nice watches and jewelry. Money. Now that I knew to look for it, it was obvious. I tuned back in as the commander said, "It's possible, but I doubt it. I'll let Toby show you back there."

So we followed Corporal Toby (the UN uses names to "maintain morale." We use ranks to "maintain discipline." Guess which keeps you alive in war?) through the office section and into the back, which was the actual warehouse section. All military logistics buildings have this same basic layout. Toby punched in a code to unlock the door, without checking to see if we were watching. Naumann was, I kept rear guard. There was a sign that clearly said, "This door must be kept locked at all times." That was odd. Even more odd for this bunch was that they were actually abiding by that regulation.

So, if security was so important, why was this door locked and all the other doors beyond it wide open and untended? Let me rephrase that. The logistics yard had a gate guard. The yard was bare fused dirt, enclosed by fences. There wasn't any practical way to hop the fence while carrying stolen property. Okay, unless you were me. But this was daytime. The office up front was a gauntlet for intruders. Every partition inside was wide open from laziness or a desire to save time moving or both. So why bother locking this door? Answer: because they wanted to know when someone was coming through it.

Suddenly, I knew where the Guardians had come from. I knew where the factions' weapons and ammo were coming from. As Naumann kept Toby captivated in gesticulated conversation, I slipped aside and scanned a couple of aisles. Open aisles, not compacted rollouts.

Not six hours ago, I'd taken photos. There'd been pallets of camouflage netting, the big sections used to conceal vehicles and small structures. I looked. There were a lot less of them today. Tens less, maybe hundreds. It had been a huge pile, big enough to create tall shadows. It wasn't there now. Next to it had been heavy battlefield comms, the kind a unit uses to plug into a secure, multichannel satellite and air intel net like our PARSON network. Many of those were gone, too. No one issues hundreds of those in a day. I caught up to the others.

Toby sadly informed us they didn't have any spare generators. Hardly a surprise. We thanked him and left.

Naumann said nothing while we were driven back. Once in his office, he asked, "Well?"

"New carpets, new gear, nice luxuries on the staff. Large amounts of military gear missing since last night. No vehicles there now, so it's not that they were making up shortages for their units. Stuff is going missing, and that's a clearinghouse," I said.

"Can we prove it?" he asked.

"No," I admitted.

"No," he said. "It's all circumstantial, and we may be mistaken—"

"No, we're not," I said.

"We're not," he continued. "But unless we can prove it, it's irrelevant. And even if we can, who would we prove it to?"

That was a damned good question.

"Who can we trust?" he asked.

"None of them," I said. There wasn't even any need to think about that answer.

"I'll let Richard know, at least," he said. "Maybe some rumors will make them slack off. Or maybe we'll find a link."

While he handled his stuff, I called Greg. "Get a visit from the tooth fairy?" I asked.

"Funny you should mention that," he said. "I guess our recon was wrong." The look on his face said he didn't believe it, either.

"So it seems," I said. "Well, I'll come out later today and we can see where we went wrong." We swapped a few pleasantries and disconnected.

The "final" assessment we came up with was still an incomplete one, but it told us everything we needed to know. The military at various levels were supporting certain factions in given areas out of personal reasons. The military as a whole, meaning the Bureau of Defense civilian force under UN guidance, was supporting the Shia. Why, I have no idea. Sufis I could see, but the Shia? Maybe somebody knew where the body was buried and was using it for leverage. The Union of Federal Government Employees was supporting a Marxian sect of the Sunni from political reasons. The UN Embassy was supporting the Sufis, as were we and some of the UN intelligence agencies. Three or four religious "charities" on planet were supporting the Felts Believers wackos. Everyone had an axe to grind and the system was so full of holes that anyone with a credit could get illicit, controlled merchandise.

In other words, the Law of Supply and Demand continued to work, despite any simpering do-gooder idiocy. The factions wanted to kill each other. To do this, they would swap money for weapons. Nothing was going to stop that. Out of professional paranoia, we checked our own stocks. Mostly, they agreed. The few discrepancies were either combat-lossed equipment or a few personal incidents that were tactically unimportant even if they did call for disciplinary action. Apparently, some of the Freehold based mercenary companies were providing "security" for various towns and infrastructure. A majority of them are veterans of the FMF. It appeared they were calling in favors from friends for additional supplies. Dealable with, and understandable. But we'd have to assume that anyone we fought had decent quality hardware and plenty of ammo. Which we already knew. Of course, the UN politicians kept insisting the elephant was a rope, a tree, or a kazoo.

CHAPTER 12

Many of us flipped out on Mtali. I wasn't the first.

Maybe "flipped out" is the wrong term. I didn't go insane. I did get outraged, furious, angry beyond words at the waste and stupidity of the human race. I became convinced of my own superiority to the point where I no longer thought of the locals as a combination of poor and/or stupid, but as less than human, filthy animals to be exterminated.

The UN was posing in the cities for PR shots for the "stability" they'd brought. Meanwhile, we got stuck with every nasty, gritty real military mission. They were all the same—some group of assholes would shoot up a school bus to "punish" that faction for blowing up a church, who'd done that in retaliation for someone spitting on someone else. With the Muslims, it went back to who was the proper heir of Muhammad some 2000 years ago. With the Christian Coalition, it went back to which version of scripture was correct and whether God was a trinity or a sole deity. With the Feltsies, it was still a debate over whether "fags" should be castrated or just killed, "adulterous" women stoned or simply exiled, and nonbelievers killed or only beaten. We and the few real UN troops left would go in and separate them like scratching children, and it would start all over again. It was tiresome.

The trigger for me was a call we got regarding an Amala village.

It seems that some locals lost contact with the village and went to ascertain the situation. When they got there, they puked at what they saw and called the Unos. The Unos heaved their guts and called us to join the party. We got rather ill, too.

The village was a razed, smoking ruin. It takes a petty child to raze a village. All the rude huts were torched, every possession destroyed or defiled and the occupants were missing. It wasn't hard to figure out where they were. There was a roughly filled and mounded pit behind one of the hovels. The first responders had started digging, then called for help.

I stared into that hole, dark and earthy and filled with the disgusting stench of rotten flesh. Local and imported Earth refuse eaters were turning the bodies into a gooey, slimy slush of indistinct blobs melding together. But I could see enough to make me choke vomit, and I've eaten things and seen things that would gag a maggot.

The bottommost corpses were adult men, all with severe wounds. They'd fought and died. Above them were the women, growing younger as the depth grew shallower, until the topmost of them was around ten Earth years. The tattered clothing told me all I needed to know. They'd been raped and worse. Some of the violations were out of Jack the Ripper's legend, and bespoke a mind gifted in its sickness. And above all those, in decreasing age, were the children.

They'd killed the adult males, who were a threat. They'd raped and tortured and slowly killed the women, who culturally and spiritually were far less so. And they'd made the children watch, made them learn about death and terror and hatred for . . . how long? Until at last they'd shot the kids one by one, from oldest down to youngest.

What horror had those smallest experienced, knowing only that dreadful things were happening to everyone they knew, to the people on whom they depended for everything in the world? And what had they felt, watching their playmates one by one, kneel, cry and die? Watching and hearing the crack of a pistol, seeing the convulsion of the body, the splattering of brains and face, the slump into a quickly filling hole? Had they understood that they'd be next?

I was revolted beyond anything I can describe. Then I was revolted worse to find I understood the logic. It was logic based on flawed postulates, and proceeded without compassion or conscience to an end I could not condone. But it was a logic. I knew I wanted to use that same exact logic to hunt down the perpetrators and end this atrocity, and I hated myself for that.

I turned to Naumann, and he said nothing while I got my mouth clear enough of saliva and bile to speak. "Boss," I rasped, "we are going hunting. I don't want to answer any questions, and I don't want to file any reports."

He looked back at me, face unmoved but stiff, and said, "Assets are at your disposal, Warrant Leader."

I planned the operation. I executed the operation. I used one squad: mine. The whole operation was pure psych warfare. And it worked. It was unpleasant, like surgery on a child, but necessary, I thought. I've never liked that "greater good" crap, because it's too easy to slip down the slope to Marxian or Fascist oppression and find yourself justifying it as right.

"Unpleasant" isn't a strong enough word. It almost put me in the giggle ward, and still bothers me after everything that's happened since.

I knowingly violated rule one: I made us stand out. We got into black uniforms. We stayed in blacks. From head to toe, our gear was black. No matter the terrain or the daylight. I wanted them to know who we were. We planned to sow terror on a scale even these lice pickers would shiver at, and the mere sight of a figure in black would make them shit their pants.

We hit hard. Our first target was the village that logic and forensics said was responsible for this atrocity. We landed far back in the woods and hiked in.

The vertol hovered low, and we rappelled slowly through the impeller wash, rather than using the barely controlled fall of fast-roping. I hit first, took three large steps and sought cover behind a tree. Kirby was with us, and his two assistants slowed him. Leopards can't rappel. I stayed attentive with finger on trigger, just as a precaution. No, there were no threats here, but I couldn't know that and needed to get into the right mindset at once. The right mindset is "paranoid."

Those woods were thick. About like heavy second-growth on Grainne or Earth. Lush enough, considering the overall climate, tangled and green and dense enough for great concealment and muting of sound. We found game paths and beaten areas, slipping through them with practiced ease. We avoided the few "roads" that were mere rutted trails, and the places where children obviously played under fallen trees or in cozy glens. It took most of the morning to move ten kilometers, and we were well-drenched with sweat by the time we stopped for a light lunch, taking turns and watching for locals.

We let lunch settle for a while. Once we were ready and rested, we wriggled the last kilometer.

It wasn't much of a village. The huts were built with polymer panels and corrugated sheet metal roofs, but they were still huts. There was electricity of a sort, furnished by a solar generator with nuclear backup. I doubted they ran that often, as they couldn't afford the uranium nor the service charge. There were no village roads to speak of, merely dead grass with occasional boards over puddles. Hell of a way to live. In this day and age even.

Twenty huts. About eighty inhabitants, twenty of them mature males. One support weapon there, and about ten men with archaic rifles. I mean ancient—they were magazine in front of trigger assembly type weapons.

At my order, everyone triggered Boost. Then we rose as one and swarmed them.

We went in *fast*. At a Boosted sprint, I covered fifty meters in about eight seconds, in gear and across rough terrain. I wasn't seen until it was too late. The two men I'd picked were jabbering away, and spun just as I arrived and clocked them with a stun baton.

They'd only seen a black figure. I had no features for them to discern. This was good. I'd be staying hidden while the others finished the task.

"Black Ghosts," I heard muttered in awe as my people rounded them up.

"*Why aren't these filthy, stinking hovels in flames? Why haven't these whores been raped yet*?" I shouted. Barto got a good closeup of my face on camera as I stormed in.

The women of the village whimpered. No one noticed that we were speaking in Arabic. Frank turned to me and said, "Sir, I wasn't sure, and . . ." he trailed off. Good act.

"I've told you how many times?" I continued. "*First* we torch the hovels, we rape the whores next because it's sexier by firelight, *then* we chop the children to bits, shove our barrels down the throats of the men and splatter them, then waste the whores as we leave!"

"Yes, sir!" he snapped, looking properly cowed.

I said, "Well, we're short on time. Go round up the brats."

And there was the cue. A young father with huge balls opened his trap and said, "You *filth*! At least let the children go. They didn't do anything."

"They're Shia. That makes them the enemy, and they die." I punctuated by smashing the butt of my carbine into his cheek and salaaming him to the ground. He went down, blood splashing. Barto moved in to get some good photos. We had these peasants convinced we did this for pleasure.

"Do the headman last," I ordered, while stamping around. I was acting like a tin-plated little dictator. Well, some claim I am. "And his whore. Let them enjoy the show."

"Son of a *dog*!" that worthy called, identifying himself.

"WHERE ARE THOSE BRATS?" I roared. I turned back to him and said, "If I kill you for the deaths of your neighbors, the brats will grow up wanting revenge. If I kill them, you'll do worse than you have already. So you all die. Easy solution. No Shia, no Shia problem." I had a sick grin on my face and bright eyes while I said it.

The kid I'd belted struggled to his feet. "How can you kill children, you fucker?" he asked. "They did nothing!"

"Why didn't you think of that before you killed the Amala babies?" I asked. "They were worthy of your hate, so why should mine be different?"

At that, one of the mothers burst into wailing tears. Barto got her on video. She was stricken. They seriously believed that we'd watch this later, laughing and eating popcorn.

The kids were released from the hut just then, and came shriek-ing, running toward their mothers, who bundled them close and hugged them, bawling as their offspring did. Their faces were colorless and lifeless. They knew death when they saw it, and they saw their own staring at them. Several fell to their knees and began praying, some to Allah, some to me. They called me "Lord."

Then the men got into it. The headman broke ranks and came forward, bowing to the ground. His skinny old knees were rat-tling like cold teeth. "*Please*, Lord!" he began. "I beg you! Show mercy on our children! Kill me, hurt me, do as you will, but not the children!"

I remained aloof, waiting for him to offer the bargain. If I did, it would smack of setup. So I waited. He groveled at my feet.

"I confess before Allah that we murdered innocents!" he said. It was muffled in the dirt, but we got it in ram, and that was good intel. "I confess that we helped the Revenants—" (one of their factions)—"I confess that we did so of our own will. Before Allah, we have sinned. All praise be to Allah!"

He ran on as I stormed around, shouting orders, rounding them all up in a tight group, the better to make them feel like sheep at the slaughter.

Then was when he did it. I had been running out of delays and was worried about my next move. He caught his cue just in time. "*Please*, Lord!" he begged me, hands clasped in supplication.

"What do you expect from me? Mercy?" I demanded. "Why?"

"We are not worthy," he moaned, shaking his head. "I freely offer my life for the sins of my people. And those of my wife and family and all the men, but spare the children and their mothers, I beg you!" The other adults were nodding and leaning toward me, hands clasped.

"Why now the courage?" I asked, quietly.

"Before Allah I am shamed!" he replied. "I should have obeyed the scriptures. I let my anger and fear rule my actions, and not Allah's will. But I offer our lives as penance, and pray that Allah will cause you to spare our children, that our village will continue."

"I think he means it, boss," Kirby said. The growling leopards were sending the children through the roof. I was glad I'd thought of bringing them.

I hesitated, strode around him, and finally stood in front of him. Gently, I lofted my boot toe under his chin. "Stand," I said.

He staggered to his feet, weeping so loudly he could barely speak or hear.

"Now," I said, "I don't like you. I don't like *any* of you. My job is to bring peace. And in death there is peace." I leaned in close and locked eyes with him. "I'd rather just wipe this *whole fucking district* off the map with a nuke. But that's not up to me." I pulled back, to emphasize the point.

He knew deep inside that he was doomed, and everyone with him. Perfect. Now to give faint hope. "But if I don't have to come back here . . . perhaps I can convince my commander to let some of you live."

A smile of hope started to cross his lips. I quashed it. "I said 'maybe.'" I said, and he dropped back into the depths. "He's a hard man. But we have many villages to visit. We will visit them all, of course, but some are less trouble than others."

"We will never be trouble for you, Lord!" he assured me, fast and stuttering. "None have—"

"Shut up," I said. He did. "There are to be no, none, zero, no killings of anyone. If you need to punish a criminal, you lock them up and call us first. We want this district quiet, and we'll do whatever it takes to accomplish that."

"Yes, Lord, thank you, Lord!" he replied.

"*One* dead child, and I kill you all. And I *want* to kill you all, so don't even think it," I insisted, moving in close again. I'd eaten raw garlic that morning, on purpose. He tried not to flinch as I breathed it in his face.

"Yes, Lord!" he nodded.

"Allah has spoken to you. And he speaks to me, too. If any are harmed, I will know."

"Yes, Lord! Allah is merciful! We know that Allah is the true God. We thank him for interceding and softening your heart!"

"None will attack you. If they do, you call us. *We* will take care of it." I gave him a grin that was far from friendly, and he quailed. He couldn't even speak, just nodded.

They were all wailing and praying at that. I walked over to the group, and pulled out the mouthy one, who was bleeding and groggy but tracking, and two others. Proper stage presence kept all eyes on me as the squad began to fade into the woods. To punctuate my speech, I pointed my carbine at the head of the newest babe, perhaps a week old, snuggling against its mother's breast. The mother began to cry again. "If I come back, I start here and work up to oldest. Fair enough?"

The rest of the team had slipped away as the village nodded and shivered and agreed, and I turned to walk off. "We'll take these three—" I indicated who I meant—"back to our base for questioning. Perhaps they can live if the commander is generous, and if they speak readily."

There were sighs at that. Everyone knew the tough young men of the village would never talk over military matters, and would die. I hadn't threatened the children if they were silent, so everyone knew in their guts the men were dead.

I disappeared into the trees, driving the prisoners ahead of me, doing my unconscious best to seem a shadow. I faded from their view, but could hear the mutterings again of "Black Ghosts." They thought us supernatural and inhuman.

So, to drive the point home, we traveled at a trot. The squad fell in with me within a few paces, and we ran. The path was familiar, clear on our tacs, and we made good time. Our poor, undernourished peasants couldn't hack the speed. After 10 km, they were collapsing from sheer exhaustion. That too, was planned. We ran that regularly. We were well fed and rested. We were buzzing from Boost.

"Leave them," I said. "We don't need them. There's better intel elsewhere."

"Shoot them?" Neil asked, following my cue.

"No, just leave them. Why waste ammo?" I replied. We kept running, and left them to wander back slowly and tell of how we *ran* through the deep woods, and were barely bothered by the exertion, while they could not keep the pace. More image for us.

We managed to cow most of the villages into outright fear. Occasionally, we would be able to identify particular troublemakers who operated in small cells. When we did, we shot them like rats where we found them. Some disappeared in their sleep, often from inside their own homes and were never seen again. We moved across the province in swaths, visiting villages, promising, threatening, being sociable as called for. Everyone knew of the Black Ghosts. Everyone knew they were omnipotent killers who didn't answer to the UN. No lawyers or bureaucrats to restrain them, the Black Ghosts were judge and executioner, with no jury. Even villages that had no connection to the fighting panicked when they saw us, wondering what they could have done to deserve a visit. A few facts around us permeated the haze, and it came to be understood that we took no action against minor squabbles or peaceful farmers, but were impartial killers of anyone partaking in organized fighting. No one dared defy us, or question our authority.

It worked fine for nearly a month. We stormed village after village. Some cowed readily into submission. We were not merely death, we were inhuman. Their superstition did the work. Some villages we found were led by fanatical leaders or terrified into collaborating with local bullies. In those we delivered justice, carrot and sticked them into acquiescing and made note to follow up later. Some we subjected to punitive action—we'd leave people rifles for hunting and defense, but took any support weapons and killed a few as object lessons.

It got much quieter. Fighting dropped more than 90% in that month. We'd shown these peasants that there were people out there more ruthless and callous than they, with technology they didn't even realize existed.

Then we came to, well, I'm not going to name the village. Better that it never have existed. They'd boated upriver and wiped out a village for "polluting" their water with their pagan waste, etc. It was a typical "DEATH TO FANATICS!" incident. These people revolted me.

I often wonder why people settle some of the desolate holes they do, or bother with rat mazes like Earth at all. I'll never question why people live in Landing District on Mtali. It was all lush and green and pretty, and had a pristine cleanness to it. I wondered how such nut jobs could live here and maintain their mindset. It was the type of place to put me at ease.

The village was a fishery. It was beautiful. Thick, humid mist, redolent with the smell of rich earth and a slight bite of decaying fish, dark green leaves dipping into waters as smooth as oil, and small frame houses on stilts against flooding, that seemed to fit perfectly into a cluster for a photo. I could retire in such a pastoral place.

Then I'd get bored and install a weapons range and resort hotel and casino. The spaceport would go over there, and the boat tours . . .

Not for me to live in, but it was gorgeous just the same.

We'd seen it on a river patrol, wearing standard Blazer green for the environment, and heading upstream fast. We took our intel photos (we took photos of *everything*. My squad alone took over two million during our tour) and kept going. Now we were coming back.

There were no roads; this place was reachable only by boat, as it had steep bluffs behind it and swamp upstream. So we came in from the edge of the swamp. It would be that much more surprising to them.

It was different from the "back" or land side. The backs of the houses were ragged and dilapidated. Trash was piled around; they were too lazy to even toss it in the river. Everything was filthy and worn out.

I will never understand what compelled people to do this. The Travelers, Mennonites and Seekers I've met eschew technology on religious grounds, but are clean, hardworking and industrious. They are peaceful, love what they do (okay, so Deni hated it. Note that they let her leave) and are a delight to meet. These sects on the other hand seemed to take religion as an excuse to be filthy animals. I suppose you get out of it what you put into it.

We swarmed in amid the huts and jacked them up. It was becoming a routine for us. That was likely my first mistake.

As we rounded them up, they started berating and trying to shove us. One brave fool grabbed the muzzle of Martin's weapon and tried to pull it away. Martin, being surprised, shot him in reflex as he pulled the weapon back.

The splash of gore was unbelievable. The local had grasped the top of the receiver and under the grenade launcher. As a result, were enraged, self-righteous and murderous. I couldn't let them survive.

I tried. The deputy, likely the fat bastard's son from the look of him, turned defiantly and said, "We shall kill ten infidels for every outrage you have committed."

"Then I'll kill you all," I replied.

"Allah will not allow it. ALLAHU AKBAR!" he shouted and charged. I dropped him.

There was nothing doing. They had sold out, they felt no remorse, and were more than willing to do so again. From a local view, I could kill the adults, resettle the children, and be done. From a strategic view, if I let any survive, I would be admitting that I was less than the ultimate justice. That would weaken my previous efforts. The children would remember, and when they grew up they'd seek out vengeance and the cycle would continue. And the body count these sick scum had already racked up was revolting.

"Kill them all," I rasped quietly, punctuating it with a shot. It was the hardest, most degrading, most horrifying thing I'd ever done.

I wanted not to look, but had to, to ensure my aim. And because it was my responsibility . . . I started with the children.

Eighty-seven lives as an object lesson to save thousands over the next few years, tens of thousands long term in this district, hundreds of thousands or millions over the course of the future of this planet. Sound logical? Then *you* point a rifle at a three-year-old and pull the trigger.

I felt as if I were dreaming, floating . . . my head spun as if drunk or fatigued. All I could hear, all I could see was the cough of bullets and the splats of impact. The logic was inescapable.

Sometimes, logic is a barbed stick up your ass.

I was crying, tears gushing down my cheeks as I blubbered like a . . . well, a child, after we finished. We turned silently and strode back out as Johnny Squid and Geoff torched the buildings. We needed to leave for our safety and our sanity. We could not *not* follow through with the killing, or our reputation as superhuman phantasms would be ruined. We had to be so ruthless, so above humanity, that no one would dare ever ask, "What if we don't the muzzle was aimed right at his heart. The hypervelocity slug hit the pressurized, fluid-filled sac and burst it. Blood gouted front and back and the man gurgled and died.

It was a signal to his buddies, who all tried to attack or run for weapons. Three of them actually held their own children hostage, knives at throats. I ordered, "Deni! Joel! Take them now!" Three shots coughed and three heads exploded. The children screamed and ran, but were rounded up by Second Team at the perimeter.

The shrieks and squawls went on as Deni took Weapons around to check the other houses. Someone shot back at her. He missed her but got Rudy. The shot tore fabric from his sleeve and caught him a nick. Donnie yelled at them to drop and thumped four grenades through the plywood walls of the source. The resulting explosions were impressive, a continual string of bangs.

This wasn't surgery, it was butchery. Two more had tried to reach a boat. Barto sawed the stern off with his squad weapon. One of the idiots drew a pistol. Barto cut him down, too and the burst continued into his buddy.

We finally got them into a group, but it was too late. We'd lost our superhuman effect with a minor wound and a struggle. I didn't realize it at that moment, but it was at the back of my brain, warning me that something had gone dreadfully awry.

"Who's in charge?" I asked.

"I am, defiler of pigs," a fat, bald, bearded man shouted. "May Allah visit you a thousand deaths."

"If your friends hadn't been stupid, they'd still be alive. Their suicide is not my problem." And with that statement it got worse; I'd tried to justify myself. I was human to them.

Negotiations got nowhere. The headman frothed louder with every response. "I shall return Allah's vengeance upon six villages for what you have done today!"

I did what I should have done at his first act of defiance, under the circumstances. I shot him. A sadistic part of me made me aim right through his throat and blow his spine out the back, so his head tumbled free ahead of a crimson gush.

"Who's next?" I asked. Then it hit me.

They weren't crying in anguish. They weren't begging. They

do as they say?" But if someone called our bluff, as these people had . . . we *had* to follow through.

We were perhaps a hundred meters into the forest when it hit me. I swayed, blotches in front of my eyes, pulse hammering in my ears, and leaned forward in the mud, on all fours, just in time to *hhuuurrrrllll.* I puked, puked again, mouth wide, and heaved on empty space and abused muscles. I had to have cleared not just my stomach, but my upper intestines. I strangled on saliva and bile and acid and rolled sideways in a paroxysm of coughing. It left me weak, dizzy, and flushed with endorphins. Hands helped me up, and not a word was said. I don't recall who; I barely remember it at all.

The vertol arrived and we exfiltrated silently. Not a word, not a sound. We just stared at each other, unmoving. The crew knew better than to ask, fortunately, and left us to ourselves. The thousand meter stares in our eyes must have been enough. They checked that Rudy was bandaged, nodded and moved forward.

Back at base, I checked in, debriefed as factually and simply as I could to Naumann directly, and asked if I could be excused. He squeezed my shoulder and told me that unofficially we would not be called for a couple of days. "Best I can do," he said. "Now go get some rest, or whatever you need. Any hassle, come see me. Or call. But Ken?"

"Yes, sir?" I replied, looking over my shoulder as I was already leaving.

"Keep it on base and with our people," he ordered.

I nodded and kept walking.

Violence often gets the hormones going. I'd been busy, and Deni and I were curfewed from each other for the obvious reason of being on a mission. I needed sex badly, but I had no desire at *all* for human company.

I wound up in the Rec Center. We'd had to put it off limits to Earthies, and thus to all Unos, because they loved the idea of free sex, were all repressed, frequently carried diseases, and were asocial wretches. Besides, our specialists were professional ladies and men, but that didn't mean they *liked* having sex with people who might only shower once a week.

I cleaned up well in the shower, washing psychic stench off with the real filth, blood, grime, black paint, clogged pores, dead skin . . . let's face it, I was a mess. Just that helped me feel a bit better, perhaps three percent.

I was embarrassed, ashamed, hurt . . . words can't describe it. I spoke to the sergeant in charge in quiet tones. She matched them. Professional all the way. That helped.

"How can we help you, Warrant?" she asked.

"Stress," I told her honestly. "I need sex, but I don't want human company . . . I need . . ." I couldn't go on. What I needed was a person to *use* as a tool. But I couldn't say that.

She nodded in understanding to my silence. "We can do that. Do you prefer a specific companion?"

"No," I replied.

"Female, I presume?" she clarified.

I nodded.

She put an arm on mine gently, and it wasn't offensive to be touched by a caring human being. Nor did she recoil in revulsion at touching me. "Room Three," she almost whispered. "Give me a few seconds to set her up."

I wandered down the hall, slowly, trying not to think. At the sound of her clearing her throat, I turned to see her nod and point. I nodded once in reply, curtly, and opened the door.

The recspec inside was young, beautiful, and exuded energy. Most people wouldn't have noticed, as she was a well-trained actress and kept it tightly controlled for my benefit. I'm a professional observer, however, and caught the glimmer. She was naked, said nothing, and looked at me as I dropped my robe. It wasn't an inquisitive gaze, she was just looking, to follow my cue. She had the clear, bright eyes of someone who has yet to be spoiled by life, supple skin, and an unusual curve to her. Very nice. She lay back and spread her legs as I approached, arms reaching for me. She was already lubricated. I got the idea I wasn't the first troop to have had a reaction like this.

After three thrusts, I had her turn over. Then we tried sitting. Nothing. I had a raging fire of hormonal energy, but any attempt at sex was sheer mental torture. I dropped off the bed, onto the floor, and leaned back against the wall. It was cold, the industrial carpet spiky on my buttocks, and I sat, head between knees and with my arms wrapped around. I began crying again, sobs wringing from me in anguish, and I swallowed acid again.

She slid easily down next to me, cautiously wrapped an arm around me, and just sat there, a presence. It helped. Shortly, my slow thoughts figured out that I could get that from friends. I gripped her arm back, stood carefully, and walked out, grabbing my weapon as I went. I forgot the robe. I forgot my uniform. I shrugged inwardly. I could get it tomorrow.

Casual nudity doesn't bother most Freeholders, and sure as hell doesn't bother Operatives, but I passed a visiting Uno contingent, and there were gasps, giggles, and the usual immature reactions to the human form. No wonder they're sexually repressed. The voices drifted out of hearing as I approached our barracks.

Deni was in her cubby, and said nothing, just gathered me up and sat with me. After long sobs—both of us—she handed over a bottle. It was some Earth rotgut. The bottle said "Old Number 7 Tennis Shoes Whiskey" or some such. She swigged, handed it over, and I took a gulp. Yep. About right for cleaning rifle bores. Gah. The discomfort of drinking it seemed a fitting, if minor, penance.

I was too caught up in myself to notice the first crash. I did notice the figure rebounding off the wall and stumbling into a heap across from me as the lightweight door clattered again.

It was Frank. He was bombed out of his skull on a similar bottle, I think it was "Tucker's Green" or something.

"Dammit, boss, what in the fuck are we doing here?" he cried. Literally cried; there were tears streaming down his face. They matched mine. And Deni's. Before I could reply, he upended the bottle and took an unhealthy swig.

"Trying to make a difference," I said. I didn't believe it. Nor could I say, "To learn how to be hard-hearted killers in case we face Earth."

"Fuck the little savages!" he said. "Just fucking fuck the fuckers!" He chugged again.

"Yeah," I agreed, not being rational or reasonable enough for intellectual debate. In any case, I didn't care. And yet I did. I felt Deni squeeze my hand. She was usually quiet, and beyond words now.

"I can't do this anymore!" Frank said.

"I'm praying we don't have to," I said. I really was. There was no way, *no way* I could do that again.

Frank's only response was to tilt the bottle and chug. "Maybe I'll wake up and not rememberrrr," he slurred. "Or maybe I zhust won't wake up a' all."

He passed out shortly after that. We'd been drinking buddies since Chersonessus. I knew his capacity. He'd had most of that bottle fresh.

Deni dragged a blanket off her bed and wrapped it around his shoulders, patting his cheek very softly. He flinched in his sleep.

I don't remember her dragging me back to my slot and putting me in bed, but she did.

CHAPTER 13

It seemed I hadn't closed my eyes when I heard, "Extraction mission. Emergency." It was Naumann.

I jerked awake. "Huh? Wha? Commander?" I stuttered as I writhed out of the sheets. "Where's Combat Rescue?" I asked, grabbing my comm.

"That's who you're extracting," he replied.

"Shit. Yes, sir. On it." Thank the deities I don't suffer from hangovers. The clock said I'd slept about a div. Less than three hours for those using "standard" time.

He debriefed me while I yanked on a jumpsuit. While Ops isn't tasked with combat rescue, we can provide support for it if need be. We were handy, so we got the gig.

What had happened was that an intel bird had gone down, with a crew of eight. Our Combat Rescue, backed up by UN close support, had gone in to get them. On the way out, the rescue bird had been hit, and hard-landed. Not unheard of. Another transport had come out, escorted, and the gutless Uno flying had reported it as "too hot" and tried to return to base. *He* had been shot down. The escort bird had a braver pilot; he stayed orbiting and called for backup. We had two other rescue squads. Both were otherwise engaged. Black Ops Squads One and Two over at Legion were split on suppression patrols, leaving only a team of each. We were mostly complete, we got the call.

I zapped the message to the team, announced, "Rescue Mission. Us. Real. Now. Small arms, explosives, grenades. Airfac. Bird hot and ready—break—all ops, Three Zulu One. I need six bodies to round out my squad. Rescue mission. Real. Now. First come gets the glory." Rudy was still (just!) on sick list. Donnie and Ross were over at the starport checking on arriving equipment for us. They wouldn't be back in time. The other three would go with Frank to extract the downed UN transport pilot. It was better than he deserved. I grabbed a bottle of electrolyte soda and chugged it as I ran, using it to wash down neural stims.

The commander's current driver was waiting at my door. I hopped in and he burned for the airfac. We were there in one hundred seconds. You have to love Operatives; my team was there within another forty, and others began arriving immediately, sprinting across the concrete to join the party. I grabbed the first three bodies, all from Squad One, and got them aboard. The late arrivals groused only slightly, two of them manned the guns on the escort vertol, and the rest threw gear at us.

"Barto, Geoff, you're medical. Check the kits," I ordered. "Bryce, Frank Two, you're on doors, and Tyler, you're ropemaster." My glance took in something. "Tyler, I said small arms," I reminded her.

She slapped the receiver cover on the weapon. "The Emm Forty Two *is* a small arm, sir," she replied with a grin. Bloodthirsty bitch. She'd given up the Heavy, but was lugging a dismounted vehicle weapon instead. Gods forbid she not have autofire and lots of ammo. I shrugged. Technically, she was correct. If she wanted to tote it, I knew better than to argue. It wouldn't slow her down. I was curious as to how she'd gotten hold of one on a few seconds notice, but that wasn't important right now.

We were airborne in short order, to hearty waves from members of squads One and Two, and sorted gear as we went, scaring the hell out of the crew by leaving the doors open and hanging gear on the rails. Operatives are not bothered by altitude. Actually, Operatives aren't bothered by much of anything environmental. We distributed extra ammo, explosives, and armor, and prepped ropes. We had twice as many gloves as we needed. Good. Better than not enough. Behind us were the support vertol and the empty one for the casualties.

We weren't totally familiar with UN craft, but transport vertols are transport vertols. The flight engineer refamiliarized us with the lasers on the doors as we flew. No, they aren't actually lasers. With the UN's love of cute acronyms, they were billed as "Light Aircraft Support Rotary Cannon." The C is silent. Idiots. While he did that, I chatted with the pilot.

"Warrant Leader Three Zulu One, commanding. Here's the plan," I said as soon as I plugged into the intercom. "You ever done insertions for recon?" I reached through the tangle of bodies for my drop armor.

"Yes, sir," he replied. Firm. Assured. I liked this guy.

"Good. We're inserting behind wherever the hell the attackers are," I said. We'd been informed that the first one had landed near a small convoy, and been brought down by their ADA. That should localize most of them. I was waiting on a map and a sitrep to bring me up to speed. "We'll flush them. Our gunners and the escort will pin them from the other side. As soon as we're through, we'll meet up with our team on the ground. We load the wounded, we load us, we bail out, we destroy the evidence, we call Thor in to clean up the area."

"Think it'll go that smoothly, Warrant Leader?" he asked me.

"Shit, no," I replied with a disgusted tone. I checked my armor. Cup, thighs, greaves all snug. I whipped out my compact and applied a dainty brown and black formal makeup effect, with green highlights.

"Good," he said. "I hate optimists. And uh . . . I'm sorry Thoensen skipped out on your guys earlier." He sounded embarrassed.

In response, I asked, "You gonna stick with us when it gets hot?"

"Yes, sir," he replied.

"Good enough."

A few seconds later, we had our commo patch from the air control bird, and in a few segs, we came within hearing range of the grounded team's transmissions direct. "This is Three Zulu One," I said. "I'll respond to Rescue or Evac, but I'll be using Three Zulu One. It's what I'm familiar with. Rescue Two, got it?"

"Yes, sir. Three Zulu One," I heard Warrant Jack Carpenter, commanding Rescue Two, reply. He was healthy. Good. I hate to lose friends. He sounded reassured that it was us and not the UN, and I kept the firm, positive, calm, bullshit-doesn't-bother-me demeanor going to keep the others relaxed. As relaxed as one can be while taking gobs of incoming fire. It was fucking hot down there. Well, it's only scary from the air. We were dodging and twisting against the occasional heavier round.

On the intercom I asked, "What's your name, Pilot?"

"Volokhonsky, Oleg," he replied. Russian. I thought I'd heard an accent there.

"Okay, Oleg, I want to swing around to the pip I just lit in your visor, and we'll hit the ropes there. You'll land immediately, five hundred mils across. Doesn't have to be a perfect line, but as close to the opposite side of the circle as you can manage. Don't flinch, because we'll be driving them straight at you. Trust your doorgunners. They're good." Everyone was in the circuit, as I believe in keeping my people informed. "Hand the copilot and flight engineer your weapons, medics," I ordered. "Extra firepower and all that."

"We aren't trained on small arms," the flight engineer replied to that. "Sorry."

First snag. I replied, "Well, haven't you shot—" *one for rec-reation?* I had been about to ask. But no, Earth didn't *allow* people to practice with weapons. They might be unstable and kill someone. Earth killers had to use poison, explosive, crashed vehicles, or blunt instruments. After all, why would anyone need to practice with weapons?

They likely had drilled with the usual non-lethal UN stuff, but in that case, I really didn't want to hand them hardware. The first rule of non-lethal weapons is to shoot anything in front and sort the bodies out later. The difference being between unconscious bodies their way and bodies with gaping holes our way.

I had started shooting when I was four. It's second nature to me.

"Screw it," I said. It was that time. We were over the grid I'd marked and incoming metal was making itself known. "Bank us. Oleg, I need you down ten meters . . . down two . . . Hold for my signal." I looked down through a dark green tangle of forest. Those branches all looked spiky, arachnoid, or otherwise bothersome. Well, it's only scary for the five seconds of drop.

I took a look around to confirm it was really where I wanted to rope. It wasn't, but it was likely the best location tactically, regardless of what I wanted. I leaned way out, head under the fuselage to be sure. There was a slight rise that matched the map. From there were soft rills paralleling the road. We'd take them.

"Ropes!" I snapped.

Tyler and Deni kicked out the rope bags, checked their rings, and nodded.

Had I mentioned how crowded it was in there? We were asshole to elbow. I mean we were hanging out the sides, grabbing the door rails ourselves. Tree armor is bulky.

"GO!" I shouted. Tyler threw herself into space, Deni went out the other side, and we humped across the deck of the craft like metallic caterpillars until we reached the doors.

Then I was over the edge, and going *down*! Face first, rope rattling against the ring, sliding smoothly through my gloved hands and getting warm. I twisted hand over hand, swung sideways, got legs down, and didn't slow at all. Actually, I slipped and accelerated. The highest twigs scritched in a blur across my visor, ripped at my gear, poked at me and then the heavy limbs thumped against my legs. I tumbled, steadied, tumbled again.

Then I spun in a hurry and crashed into the ground, jarring my brain. I hadn't seen the surface through the shadows, and it was closer than I had thought. I hit the release, and ran for the nearest cover, as I was on that tall, rocky ridge, perhaps four meters above average ground level. Spiffing. "Oleg, Three Zulu One, GO!" I remembered to shout, and all four ropes began coiling and thumping down through the trees as he released them. His craft dopplered away as he went to deliver Frank and our three backups.

I moved quickly, while triggering Boost. Someone was taking potshots at me, and was far too close. Actually, there's no incoming fire that isn't too close, on reflection. I had jarred my left ankle and knee and they hurt. Every step pinched a fold of thigh between the cup and thigh armor, and I shrieked hoarsely over the clattering polymer. The gloves were hot from friction, and that friction was starting to burn through. I'd have to lose them quickly, as I could smell the sickening smell of burning leather and knew that my skin would be next. That, and I couldn't handle weapons properly with those thick palms. Amazing how fast things always go to hell.

I dove into a depression, grabbed the right glove by the tip of its middle finger with my teeth and ripped it loose while singeing my lip. It was that hot. The palm was smoldering. I had come down *fast*. I grabbed my weapon from my chest, stripped off the other glove and began to unsnap the armor. It fell in an articulated heap, and I dropped a small charge from my belt on it. It would destroy the armor and create a distraction when I moved, which would be now. One cannot stay still for long in a firefight, or one tends to stay still permanently. I gave my shredded thigh a brief, tender rub with my fingers and stood, keeping behind that ridge.

I shot three grenades toward where I guessed the fire had come from, then ran. I took a second to glance at my display, and swore. "Open squad channel, Goddess fuck me, what's *wrong*, Martin?" I asked. He was showing as wounded. He was our Combat Air Controller for the support craft, and I needed him. Hell, I needed everyone. Behind me, the demolition charge on my armor boomed loudly.

"Cracked my ankle," he replied. "I can move slowly. Don't worry about it."

"Says you. Barto, stay with him. Tyler, lay down some fire and let's move! Neil, cover for Martin and clear some of these armored vehicles out," I ordered, highlighting an area on the map that was showing as rather hot and with no friendlies nearby. His dot winked and headed for the woods edge.

Tyler was already laying down fire. I could hear the distinctive sound of an M-42 chewing dirt, wood, and unidentified other things to my right. Then I saw the enemy convoy, or at least its cargo vehicles, ahead.

Or what remained of the vehicles, I decided as I ducked again. They'd been hit pretty hard. Still, it doesn't hurt to be sure. I fed the rest of the grenade clip at them, using the sight to estimate best trajectory, and fired a few bursts as I shifted to the cover of another clumpy tree to put a new clip in. I wasn't the only one with that idea. The wrecked vehicles were exploding into polymer and metal confetti from the impact of perhaps ten clips of grenades. The stink of ammonia, fuel, scorched polymer, burning magnesium, bugs in the earth, rotten foliage . . . it reeked, let's just leave it at that.

But that had the desired effect. The enemy stopped paying attention to the downed crews. Some few of them ran as fast as and as far as they could away from us. That wasn't very far. As they entered the clear area, Carpenter and his people hit them, and two brutal hoses of fire lashed out from our crashed vertol, over the downed party's heads. People seem to assume that a craft once down is helpless. That depends on various factors. This one might not fly again, but the crew had unlatched the door guns and were propping them across dead trunks. Not the most accurate base, but good enough for this. The UN doesn't believe in arming evac vertols, relying instead on the red cross logo to protect them, so we didn't have a third cannon, but two seemed to be enough. The enemy hesitated and died, dove for cover, or otherwise ignored us. We began to circle wide around them. I heard the distinctive sound of a Hatchet element overhead, then the pleasing sound of enemy armor being mulched. A quick listen on his frequency let me hear Neil's singsong control voice chanting, " . . . confirmed on the ADA, Katanas. Target Two is an IAV with rapid fire cannon, eight zero meters north of your previous target, five five meters west . . . and that's a splash. Target three is a . . ." I stopped listening. He was doing his job.

Frank pinged for attention and said, "We have our recovery, we're landing." I pinged back without speaking.

Volokhonsky had balls. At Frank's suggestion, he dropped *between* the casualties and the enemy, using himself as shield. Not quite what I wanted or had asked for, as it increased the risk of damage to what would be the savior of us all. But it did offer more cover for the extractees. The rescue bird was landing behind him from my point of view, on the far side of them.

"Ops, turn in. We're going through the BGs," I said, for I could see that they were still sniping at our people. The only way to stop that was to keep them occupied. Well, it's only scary while they're actually shooting at you.

"Leapfrog by team. Er, new guys are in third team, everyone else buckle down," I ordered. I'd forgotten to tell the replacements what team they should be in, and they'd been too eager to ask. Luckily, all the missing personnel were from Weapons. Just as well. "One!" I hissed loudly, and leaned between the trees to lay down suppression. I caught movement at the right range and direction, and put a few rounds and a grenade right on the spot. "Two!" I said after a timed five seconds on my visor display, and rolled sideways around a protruding root. I had to wait my turn, but didn't feel like being an easy target in the meantime. "THREE!" I snapped, and moved.

I rolled sideways, got into lizard crawl, and advanced behind another hummock. I stood in a crouch, hopped over the top and skittered into the next depression while shooting, threw myself low and banged my chin on the ground. It burned and hurt and stunned me for a moment. "One!" I ordered as I shook it off. Damn, that hurt. "Stagger position for best advance, Two," I said as I refreshed clips and laid down more fire. Second fire team formed a rough skirmish line behind the best available cover. "Stagger out, Three," I said next, then took a good position behind a tangled bush to my right.

We were close now, and these bastards were panicking. They had heavy fire from aircraft and evacuees on one side, heavy fire from us on the other, and they were stuck spread and naked. "Boarding!" I heard Jack inform me.

"Boarding, acknojjed!" I replied. We'd been on the ground all of one hundred and fifty seconds, according to my tac. I felt as if I'd run a marathon.

The escort vertol made a pass along the road, guns laying a swath of tracer that did resemble a laser, or at least a vid game version of a laser. Small munitions shattered some of the remaining vehicles. Now it would get interesting. We would be going through the wreckage, as we didn't have time to go around. Well, it's only scary while you're doing it. "Through the middle, by team!" I ordered, and braced myself. "Oleg, Frank, keep this spot clear of fire, no matter what happens!" I ordered, and lit the map for him.

"Acknohleged!" he replied. His accent got thicker under stress. A ping from Frank echoed Oleg.

"ONE!" I yelled. They sprinted through, weapons tucked and firing, as the vertols and we poured fire on both sides. They made it through and hit the ground, and then fire started pouring over them from the vertol.

"Oleg, Three Zulu One, CEASE THAT FIRE!" I shouted. It was already lifting. The flight engineer had apparently manned the unfamiliar gun while Bryce helped hoist casualties, and had gotten eager. Luckily, no one was hurt that I could tell. "TWO!" I followed up while the enemy was still confused. Team One shot the hell out of my right, we shot up the left as Two ran between them. That's the way muzzles naturally point for right handed shooters. We practice things like that until everyone knows what to do and it's almost instinctive. Then Two was through. "THREE-EEE!" I screamed as I dodged and ran through smoking, twisted wreckage that clawed at me, protruding pieces of damaged vehicle frames and shells, cratered and pocked earth and corrosive air burning my lungs. I was aiming about five meters in front of myself and poured out an entire clip. I shifted my point of aim as Tyler hopped in from the side and she ripped off the rest of the drum in the 42. Then we were through.

We were through! I yelled, "Control, Three Zulu One, FIRE SUPPORT!" and the Hatchets made another pass behind us, Neil guiding them within meters of us. Oleg brought the vertol around tail to us, and both door guns proceeded to dump money and ammo behind us. We retreated leapfrog through the tall grass around the roadway, shooting as we went, although I didn't think there was much left of that convoy. Call it a target of opportunity. They'd picked the wrong people to screw with.

Then we were scrambling aboard, metal rungs and steps hard under our feet and against our hips and shins. Someone got hit as we did, and slumped as something spattered me. I helped shove the limp form ahead of me. Everyone clicked a signal as they got inside, and in seconds my tac showed them all aboard one aircraft or another. "OLEG, LIFT!" I demanded. It came in stereo, as I was still transmitting, and had just coded back into the onboard net. He relayed to the other two craft, and we all rose ponderously over the trees, wind and impeller wash and dust and twigs pelting us through the doors. It was still cramped.

"Control, Three Zulu One," I shouted into my mic. "Thor! Thor! Thor!" I lit the coordinates and sent them, even though they were already in the database. It never hurts to be sure. Then I turned. The casualty was Neil. Head shot through the visor. Dead. Shit.

"Thor confirms target," I heard back from Control, then a few seconds later, "Thor confirms fire." Then the now distant site erupted in a brilliant flash as metal bars homed in on the remains of the convoy at 7 km/sec.

"They were friendlies," Oleg rasped in my ear.

"What?" I replied.

"They were Christian Coalition fighters. We didn't get the advisory until after we lifted just now. I guess our control didn't relay to yours in time."

I had just enough presence of mind to drop the clips from my weapon, then I turned and started smashing it against the bulkhead. There was profanity under my screams, but the noise was all that came through. I was absolutely fucking berserk. I mashed a finger and didn't care. Pieces of ultratough polymer broke off the stock and I didn't care. Dents appeared in the bulkhead, and I didn't fucking care. I didn't dare think about how many people had died in the last two days because of bureaucratic fuckups and human stupidity, because I knew *exactly* how many it was, and didn't want to think about it, because . . .

I was wrestled down to the deck. A noise in my ears resolved as Oleg shouting, asking what was wrong. Deni was trying to talk to him through the din, Tyler and Kit were holding me down, and Tyler was screaming into my ear over the roar of the craft and the slipstream. "Boss, either you calm down or I will trank your ass right here and *carry* you off when we get back!" I finally heard.

"Shit," was all I could think to say. Through a red haze of CNS afterglow and fading adrenaline and hyperventilation my thoughts became rational again. Someone had screwed up a target along the line, and before a correction could be made, we'd lost three craft and a few people, and they'd lost a convoy and a lot of people. Great. Thrilling.

But it wasn't over yet. Oleg called again. "We're overrmass," he said.

"How?" I replied. I came back to rationality because it was the only way to stay alive.

"Impeller damage. We're going in if we can't lohwer mass. Two zero zero kilos might do it. What can we lose?" he asked.

I dragged Neil's soggy form toward the door, stuffed hand grenades and demo blocks into his gear, and looped four weapons around him by their straps. I gripped a grenade tab, kissed his battered helmet and rolled him over the lip. "Fire in the hole!" I yelled. Five seconds later, a boom slapped at us. Hell of a way for an Operative to be disposed of, but I knew he'd support the mission. Too bad we hadn't been able to support him.

"Noht enough," Oleg said. I could almost see his head shaking. "Ze bearings are starting to gall," he explained. I could feel it. The ride was getting rougher and noisier as we went. The craft might stay airborne . . . if we were lighter. I looked around for things to dump, like our own considerable mass, the gear, the rescue kit . . .

"Toss the winch," I said, and the flight engineer reached down with a wrench to twist the lugs loose. I tossed out a couple more weapons, after rigging grenades to them. No need to leave anything the enemy could use. Two more harness rigs followed them, and the winch.

"We're steady for now," Oleg said, "but it won't last. We can't make it back unless we're stripped . . . and I'm not sure then."

Let's face it: it *always* sucks to be us. "How are the other craft?" I asked.

"Fine," he said. "A few scratches." That was a miracle by itself. "But we can't land here," he said needlessly.

"Rescue Two, Three Zulu One," I said to get Jack into this.

"Go, Ken," he replied.

"Strip mass out of that lifter. Dead over the side, extraneous gear, rucks, harnesses, damaged weapons, and destroy it all. Soonest, and get back to me," I ordered. We weren't quite sure who was in charge now, so I took it.

Losing mass was a tough call. On the one hand, if we didn't, we'd go down and need another extraction. That might be a no-hitch proposition. Or, we might land in the middle of one of hundreds of little disputes and make a big one. This was a hot area. If we lost too much gear and went in anyway, we wouldn't have enough to hold off attackers until rescue did get there. No right answer.

"Oleg, what's the available mass rating on the rescue bird?" I asked.

He conferred with the other pilot. "Three hundred kilos," he replied.

"Bullshit, what's the real figure?" I asked again. Damned thing had to be nut to butt to be that full. Well, it was going to get even more crowded.

"Almost a thousand," he admitted. "No margin."

"Good. Get all the altitude you can, have him come to starboard, lateral by five meters and as close below as is safe, then a bit closer," I said.

"What do you have planned?" Frank asked.

"Insanity," I admitted. It couldn't be called anything else.

Once the other craft pulled in and both were hovering, I leaned out. Jack stuck his head out below me, perhaps twenty-five meters away, and waved back. I tossed a rope and watched it coil lazily down toward him. He reached way out, snagged it, and made it fast to the skid.

If this bird couldn't take the mass, we'd just transfer a bit. "Operatives, down the rope," I said, and made a flamboyant gesture of confidence I didn't feel. Ten people with basic gear would be close to 1000 kilos, no margin.

Deni and Tyler had already donned gloves. They snapped rings to the rope and dropped over, Tyler's face betraying the barest fear. It was the first time I'd ever seen it visible in her. Deni was as imperturbable as ever; her face rarely showed anything. Frank and the pickups from Squad One followed them down. Then four more. Bringing up the rear, I snapped on a ring, leaned over the side, and dropped.

That was when the firing from the ground started. Rounds cracked past my head and banged into the vertols. "START

MOVING!" I shouted into my mic, hoping to God and Goddess they'd move in something approaching unison. I felt moderate thrust, and breeze pulled at me. They shifted unevenly, and suddenly I was over the rescue vertol's intakes, staring down at a blurry, whirling hell that waited to grind me and cook me if the rope snapped. Then I was over empty space, staring at cold, hard ground under cold, hard, wickedly pointed limbs that would skewer me if the rope snapped. I kept descending. It was only twenty five-meters, after all. Only. Have you ever descended twenty-five meters on a ten millimeter rope, attached by a ten millimeter titanium alloy ring, suspended several hundred meters over a thick forest full of unfriendly strangers whacking rounds off at you while heartless wind whistles coldly past you? I don't recommend it as a treat.

Oleg's engineer, I never got his name, started shooting back, and I was in a crossfire of tracers. It was a brown pants moment. The rounds from below floated lazily up in gentle arcs, to seemingly accelerate and snap by. The rope slackened and I dropped lower and could hear the howling intakes below me. "OLEG, TIGHTEN UP!" I said, voice reedy and tenor with fear, hoping my mic would pick it up over the background noise.

Apparently it did. The rope became taut again, quickly, and made a *thrum* sound as it did so. I felt it stretch, and hoped it wouldn't part. I slid down as quickly as I could, and felt something tug at my foot.

Then I was grabbing the door channel on the other vertol and being held by strong, friendly hands. Jack reached out and unlatched the shackle. It would have been faster to cut the rope, but modern rappelling ropes are woven with a molecular fiber that doesn't cut. It is safer most of the time, but this wasn't most of the time.

But he got it free in only a second, and we kept moving, with me sitting on the hatch sill, feet on the step rail. Jack looped a bungee cord around me as an ersatz safety line. Oleg took the lead with us flying behind and below as backup. His altitude dropped steadily, but it looked as if we were going to make it, crammed in like a city transit capsule with litters under us.

We did. Everyone relaxed as we entered Controlled Territory, and again as we neared the base. They had our ground crew and the emergency vehicles ready, but the latter weren't really needed. We flew straight in to the landing pad, settled, and began dragging casualties out to the waiting ambulances. The vertols began spooling down.

As they did so, a *screeeeee!* announced the catastrophic failure of the main impeller bearings on Oleg's craft. We'd made it down with less than twenty seconds to spare. I will dispense with the joke about the difference between pilots and their craft being that the craft stop whining after landing.

CHAPTER 14

Dear Mr. and Ms Hallowell,

"It is with deep regret I record this message to inform you of your son Neil's death during an operation here on Mtali.

"A major attack had our forces split and occupied in several places at once. One of the combat rescue teams that had gone in to recover a pilot was pinned down and stranded, and we were called to assist in the extraction. Neil was very enthusiastic, as always, and was one of the first to arrive at the Air Facility.

"We were flown to the area and roped to the ground. While Neil was one of our youngest troops, he was very competent, and did a commendable job of supporting our approach to the site. With our senior Combat Air Controller wounded, he took over and directed our support aircraft to provide cover fire both as our craft landed, and as we extracted with the casualties and stranded soldiers. He was instrumental in recovering the rescue unit and their charges, and we would have had a much rougher time without him.

"As we loaded casualties and boarded the craft for extraction, he personally provided cover fire for the victims. As he boarded, last to do so along with myself, he was hit and died instantly.

"It hurts me to say that his body cannot be returned. It was destroyed in an explosion during the extraction. I have enclosed all his personal effects from his quarters, along with the hand-written thanks of everyone involved in the mission. We truly could not have done it without him. While his death affects all of us in the Blazer Detachment here on Mtali, we are proud of the fact that several other lives were saved due to his competence and bravery. We hope you will be, also.

"I have enclosed contact information for VetSupport, a group that assists families of dead and wounded veterans. Additionally, if you need help, do not hesitate to contact me. I owe him as much as anyone does, both for this mission, and for many operations before it. I consider it a privilege to have led a soldier of his caliber. I have recommended him for a Purple Heart and a Soldier's Medal. With luck, they will be approved shortly. I regret that mere awards are all I can offer.

"Sincerely,

"Warrant Leader Kenneth Murdock, Third Blazer Regiment, deployed to Mtali. Comm, time and date, send soonest. Note to attach the two items scanning . . . now."

"Accepted. Two attachments physically mailed to same recipient."

It was the first such letter I had to write. I hoped it would be the last, because it was gut wrenching. If I had any idea then of what I know now . . . And I couldn't even admit that he wasn't a Blazer, but an Operative. It hurt.

I'm not really that religious. I attended services during training because it was a social event and broke up the austere life I was leading. I go on occasion with friends. It's rare for me to bother on my own. But the events of the last two days demanded I talk to someone who wasn't in my chain of command, who could be trusted not to tell anyone that I was twitch, over the edge, and about to go nuts with a rifle and a list of officers, and who would understand the sheer hell I was in.

Think about it. I'd committed what was technically a war crime: murder of civilians. That it was strategically necessary and would save other lives was not enough of a counter argument for my soul. I'd seen people who hated each other so bitterly over stupid ethical points that they'd do what I'd done and be glad of it. I'd seen alleged allies shoot at me while I wiped them off the planet. I'd seen a coward run out to save his own life, while other, braver troops died in his place. And the worst thing about that last one was that I could see myself doing it. I was scared. I was more terrified than I'd ever been in my life, and I was wondering when I'd crack and bail out, getting people killed. People like Deni.

Which meant I was admitting feelings for her, not just based on steamy sex and a wicked mind. Which was a potential disaster with her in my squad, and there was no way to avoid it. Personal liaisons are legal, as long as not in chain of command. We hadn't done anything while I was in her chain of command, but had before and it carried over. Expecting people *not* to become friends or lovers with those they serve with is stupid and unrealistic, but there are risks, and here was one.

This was no longer an honorable war for me. It was as filthy and obscene as it was to the locals, and I understood why it had gone on so long. There just wasn't any way to stop. I hated most of the local groups with a passion so bright it burned. Yet, one-on-one, I felt for them as I would for anyone. They were *people*, and deserved decent lives. But name any group and I could explain why the logical solution was to shoot the lot of them and be done with it. And part of me, a growing part, craved to do just that.

Priests are normally very relaxed and wait for you to bring problems out, thus dealing with them on your terms. I don't know how bad I looked, but my gaze must have still been promising slaughter, because he bounced to his feet and came over as I walked in the door.

"Come, son," he said. "Sit, please. I'll get you some tea."

"I don't want any tea," I replied. Actually, I did. But I wanted attention, I wanted to fight, and that was as good an excuse as any. I craved, needed someone to feel sorry for me, but couldn't ask . . . doing so was a "weakness" that I would never admit to. And I knew that was a contradiction. So I played hard. It was an act, but I enjoyed it, in angry, infrared thoughts.

"But I do," he said. He was of average height, slim, pale-skinned by our standards, and had his rusty hair and beard roped in neo-Norse braids. One earring in topaz matched his eyes, and they weren't afraid of me, weren't bothered by my radiating hatred, weren't the slightest bit perturbed. If I went nuts, I could literally rip him to pieces with my hands without Boost, and he knew it and still wasn't worried.

And that calmed me. At once. I still was full of rage and confusion and hate and even apathy, odd as that seems, but I dropped down in intensity maybe ten percent, and breathed a deep draft of air. It was thicker air than back home, a bit oppressive, but it still helped.

"Rough out there?" he asked, conversationally.

He knew it was. He knew at least on paper how insane it was. That lighthearted, casual sentence made a mockery of the whole situation, and wasn't insulting. It was hysterical. I laughed.

"Yeah, just a bit," I agreed. I slumped back in the hammock chair, relaxed a bit more, and wondered what was next.

"We got a bit of excitement here that first week," he told me. Of course I knew. "I think I may even have killed someone. I know that's what we're here for, but I'm supposed to help people resolve problems in this world, not send them on ahead to talk to the Lord and Lady. It . . . bothered me. And I'll never know if it was the same bother you guys feel, the first time. You know that's why you're here. For me it just sort of happened. All I can hope is that I don't have to find out if it's easier the second time."

I had to stop and think about that. I could count my kills, and they all took a piece out of me. But that was my job, and I'd prepared my entire career to be a killer. Here was a man whose job was to keep me sane after killing, so I could kill more. Heck of a dichotomy, that.

"It's not easier ever," I said. The chair was holding me up. I was limp in it and didn't care to move. He was sort of in my view, but so was the cracked ceiling and the wall behind him.

Nodding, he said, "I suppose that's healthy. At least the shrinks tell me that. On the other hand, they try to quantify the soul. To me, every soul is different in some ways, and so alike in others."

"I don't think anyone has the problems I do," I said, and realized he'd tricked me into talking.

"Maybe, maybe not," he said noncommittally. "Of course, it

depends on the person just how bad the problem seems. To a baby, not being able to reach a bottle and blanket is a disaster. To us, missing a meal is a minor annoyance."

I had to wonder if he'd snuck a view at my file and mentioned babies on purpose, or if it was chance. I suddenly didn't want to talk again.

He kept talking. "Self doubt is the bad one. One can go over and over how things could have been different, and it's true, they could. But they aren't, and won't change. All we can do is learn from the experience and move on. If it's good, be glad it happened and not sad that it's over. If it's bad, be glad that it's over, not sad that it happened."

I nodded. It made sense, and I knew it, but it wasn't very comforting. "Will it ever be over, though? That is what I don't want to ask, in case the answer is 'no.'" I surprised myself with that. I'm not sure why, but I did.

He offered a non sequitur. "There're kids downtown, twelve standard years old, eight of ours, who are tossing explosives at our people. And not on duty, but in bars. One got a UN aid worker, not even a noncombatant support, but an aid worker, with a grenade last week. Young boy, but a threat. And hard to shoot, because we're conditioned to protect the young. That faction, Sunni, I think, are using that perceived innocence as a weapon. To me, that's a sin of the worst kind, and that this boy doesn't know he's being manipulated makes it worse."

"The only practical solution is to shoot him," I said.

"I agree," the priest said. "Much like a rabid dog. Or a ripper trying to claw through the cab of your car and eat you. The worst thing you can do is get emotionally involved, because that's what makes it painful."

"It's impossible not to get involved," I told him. Oh, how I knew that.

Nodding, he said, "A jaded soul is a dangerous one. And you're right. That's why I'm here. I help make killing easier for people."

He'd hinted at that earlier, and it sank in now. "How do you feel about that?" I asked.

Shrugging, he replied, "It's my job, and I knew it when I took it.

I try to concentrate on how our people feel, pray for our enemies, and hope that no one takes the war personally. The feuds are what keeps it going. But if I worry more about the locals than our people, I won't be helping ours."

He was right. My purpose in being here was to learn to kill our current allies, in case they became a threat. It was to keep my people alive, so they could fight that threat. It was to stop the locals from killing each other, to save them from themselves, without dictating terms to them.

No, that was the politicians' job.

Dammit.

I stood and left, mumbling on my way out. I had a whole new set of ethics to consider. It didn't make me feel better, but confusion was at least an anesthetic. And so was that godsawful Earth whiskey.

The war was going well, as wars go, but we realistically weren't a large enough force to change things. We could maintain a district, but not the entire planet. With the UN withdrawing, it got worse.

Then the UN finished pulling out, militarily at least. Their State people still thought we worked for them. On the plus side, we did less fighting. On the minus side, we did less fighting. All the areas we'd pacified started smoldering again, and it looked as if it might turn even uglier than it had been.

I have no idea what happened, but something pissed Naumann off. I've never seen him that angry, before or since. The man is coldly and professionally sociopathic in his duty. Nothing fazes him. But something did.

It was about a week after that screwed up extraction that I got a call from him. "Ken," he said, "get your people ready, we're going hunting."

And we did. Aviation flew non-stop CAP. We hunted in town and nearby on rotating shifts. Infantry did flying squads as support. Arty fired. The factory ship *Force* could barely keep up with demand for munitions.

We bombed, shot, gunned, and smashed everything that dared fight. The Sunni and Shia sent out hundreds of suicide fighters, the Feltsies sent their best brown pants, and we assisted them to Allah and Yave. It took only a few days for the entire capital and surrounding area to learn that any fighting got them dispassionately slaughtered by us.

Then Naumann called in the leaders, with the threat that any group too cowardly to send reps would be summarily eliminated. It was a crass, humiliating insult, and they didn't dare call his bluff, because he wasn't.

He sat them down at a table, started talks, and shot anyone who argued until he got Muslim and Christian to agree to simply not kill each other anymore. They thought him beyond mad.

Then he required they agree to police their own factions, and prevent incidents before they happened, or punish them immediately afterwards.

Luckily, the UN was too political to do anything, because they could by rights have had him mindwiped for the authority he was usurping. At our end, Richard stood back and let him do it. I don't know if Richard was afraid of Naumann, or if they were playing good guy/bad guy. All I know is that a mere commander started dishing out orders to every Freehold unit in the system, demanding and getting assistance from the Novaja Rossians and the remaining UN forces and kicking every ass that got in his way. I thought I was bad when angry. I had nothing on him.

It was a warning of things to come. I didn't realize the significance at the time.

In a few days, there was peace. It was peace born of terror. No one wanted to offend us, because we would wipe out entire towns in response. They talked, they agreed, they stopped.

Then we had to leave.

The factions resumed their mindless slaughter in less than six weeks.

CHAPTER 15

We returned home. We got a heroes' welcome from those who follow such things, and were forgotten in three days. That didn't bother me. At least I told myself that. I got a couple of medals, one for that insane "rescue" I wanted to forget and the other for the ridge battle. I stuck them on my greens and forgot about them. Most of us got bumped in pay, and were ordered to write up our experiences both technical and personal, so they could become part of the training doctrine.

It took some time to unwind from the hair trigger I was wrapped around. Everyone else was like that, too. I think we had it worse, though. We'd had the most face to face with the enemy. We'd seen the most fire.

It showed in us. We'd snap and snarl at each other over petty maintenance issues. Then we'd apologize and drink ourselves blind. Deni wanted to try Sparkle, never having tried an hallucinogen. I took some with her and we both went through an agony of nightmares. I don't recommend it for anyone who's recently seen anything disturbing. It seems to carry over, much as it would in a dream, I suppose.

The only good thing about returning was being able to take leave. Deni and I headed for the nearest hotel first, and spent four days wrapped around each other, craving comfort and touch and sex with someone else who understood the coarse edge we were riding. We talked about going home to visit, but it didn't seem like the kind of thing we were comfortable with, so we made calls and sent letters and begged off, pleading stress and schedule. It disappointed our families, mine more than hers, as hers were still uncomfortable with the idea of military service. If they had any idea of the body count she'd racked up they'd scream. It was better for us, though.

My sister did sneak out to visit us from school with her boyfriend Chuck. It was a shock. She was grown up. I just can't think of her as mature and sexually active. She's my little sister.

She was perceptive, and Chuck seemed to understand why we were so edgy. We treated them to dinner, which they were grateful for. They packed away their salmon. Deni had elk and I had venison, but my enthusiasm for the subtleties of food wasn't there. I mean, it was wonderful to eat real food again, but other things were keeping my mind busy.

By the end of dinner, I'd come around slightly. The looks Jackie and Chuck kept giving each other were amusing, and I sent them on their way. "G'night, Squirt," I said, just like old times.

"Jacqueline, please! Kennie," she said, exasperated and mocking in return.

"Kennie?" asked Deni with a smile and an eyebrow.

"Alright, I concede," I said.

It was different from what it had been, but it was home.

We returned to base and got back into training to keep our minds from moping. Counterterrorism was our gig, and we had a full schedule of activities and techniques relevant to the upcoming Olympics to worry about. I spent all day and night rehearsing entry techniques, reading reports, studying maps and conferring with Special Projects. There were two other squads assigned the same duty, and we trained against each other with the third team assessing the other two. We had our own Public Affairs officer, a Captain Hidochi, who was neat and cute and capable of distracting any reporter from the filthy thugs behind her, who knew our operations so well that she could bullshit anything important into a full screen story that would fascinate the masses and bear no resemblance to reality whatsoever, and make petty details more exciting than the real work.

We didn't really expect any problems with the Games, but we prepped as if we did. We had only three months to get our edge back.

Westport was the host city, and there were tens of thousands of athletes, support staff, and news whores planetside with more arriving constantly. Numerous reservists and Private Militias were making money as security, and the private agencies were all booked as security escorts. The bars and entertainers in and around Westport were making a killing. I wondered if I'd have time to swing by home, but was there anything there for me?

A week before the Games, we got a mission call. I was surprised. I was nervous. I was ready to kick ass. I was disgusted at the prospect.

It seems some terrorists never learn. This wasn't the Fruits, this was the anti-royal Marxian extremists from Caledonia, the Common People's Action Group. They'd tangled with one Operative before—Rowan Moran. They now were to meet with a whole squad. Masochists.

I got the call, scrambled the squad, and headed for Westport, posthaste and with all gear, as I read the brief. Their hostage was one Caledonian equestrienne, Annette Stewart. You recall her. Princess? Military background? Their plan as stated was to have several "political prisoners" (read, "gutless shit who should have been flushed, not incarcerated") released and taken off-planet (off Caledonia. We don't hold prisoners in the Freehold), or they'd kill her. Simple enough. Rather boring, actually. The last time I'd played terrorist for a field exercise, I'd demanded steaks, beer and the best female blowjob artist on base, to do me while she wore the general's uniform. At least be original with your demands. It keeps the CTs guessing.

We landed and drove nondescript ground vans to the district where we were pretty sure they had her while we prepped our gear. I got briefed. She'd elected to play tourist the week before, and do some riding at the ranches in the area also. Busy week. She planned to follow that with the Olympics. If I had her figured correctly, she would still plan to, assuming we got her out intact.

We drove up and debarked inside the cordon, and Naumann and I had to deal with politics.

"This is Warrant Leader Kenneth Chinran," he introduced as I approached. "Warrant Chinran, Sir David Carstairs, Caledonian Ministry of State."

I reached to shake hands in Caledonian style. He did so, but reluctantly. There was a definite sniff of disdain as he looked at me. He turned, eyes still on me, and said, "Commander Naumann, I understood you were bringing in your best team? I was expecting . . . someone of higher rank."

Naumann looked the way I felt. This clown obviously hadn't read his own nation's report on our training mission. Still, that spoke well for my personal cover. Naumann said, "Warrant Chinran is as good as they come, recently returned from Mtali, has a rested, fully-trained and battle-tested squad that took almost no casualties in the densest combat, is one of our counterterror experts and has met the princess personally. That's an edge I think we can use."

At least he had the decency to admit his error. He looked surprised and impressed, gripped my hand tighter and said, "I apologize, Warrant Leader Chinran. It seems you are the right person for the job."

"I don't look the part, sir," I replied. "Which can be a good thing by itself."

"Quite," he agreed. "So, how do we proceed?"

"First, I need all the intelligence I can get and my support team needs to set up their comm post. After that, I'll let you know."

Naumann had his comm people come in. They're not assigned to us except during our activities. I'd rather have a dedicated team, but we lack the funds and personnel. But they're good enough, I trust them.

Next was to find intel. We couldn't just go in shooting.

The area was filled with the usual traffic both on ground and in the air. Terrorists like that because they think it gives them more children to hide behind. I like it because it lets them think that. We started overflights in unmarked cars and in flight harnesses, carrying sensor suites that were the equal of anything on the battlefield, but tuned for this type of work. Four of our vertols flew higher up. That was expected, and unless these cretins objected, I planned to fly them ten divs a day.

Of the millions of images we took in various parts of the spectrum, the filters in the comms pulled a few hundred for us to look at. Those were matched against what records we do have of people and rated according to threat level. It would be easier if we kept people under constant orders and forced them to live in barracks, but then, so would everything. You work with what you have. We recorded every broadcast in the area, and flew solo flyers through the streets looking for telltales of a laser that a signal could ride on.

The first suspect was stunned senseless when a team of Operatives dragged him off the street and into a van. A few quick questions and checks proved him to be a local artist who was not likely to be helping terrorists. Still, he'd been in the right area taking images and making notes. We apologized, offered him a good view and a nice dinner if he came with us to ensure his silence, and he agreed. He'd get a "good" view for a civilian: what we wanted him to see and nothing else.

Skanda Nashold, the CPAG's local goon, repeated his demands while we were searching. Carstairs wanted to negotiate with him. I've always believed in negotiating with terrorists. I give them the choice of a bullet through the face during the engagement, or a bullet through the neck afterwards. Carstairs had less practical ideas, of course. Naumann played nanny and reassured him that we really did know what we were doing and that it might take time to achieve a resolution, but the princess was safe as long as we were under deadline and didn't push too hard where they could notice it.

It was 1 div, after most clubs closed and things started getting quiet, when we got a break. One of the pictures pulled showed a man in a building window with low-light binoculars. He was constantly scanning the streets around the area. A check showed there was a laser operating intermittently. We tracked that to its destination. Shortly, the snitch was face down on the floor while Tyler jammed a carbine into his spine and whispered sweet nothings to him. "There's nothing to stop me from killing you," "There's nothing I'd rather do more," and similar comments. She got enough of his voice on file so we could hopefully fool his buddies into thinking he was still secure. Then she brought him down.

Now, there are strict rules of decency where warfare is concerned. On Mtali, we went out of our way to abide by them until the endgame. Prisoners were decently treated (we did "encourage" a few to talk, but no permanent marks were left), wounded were treated, and civilians were kept as far out of the line of fire as possible. This makes sense for several reasons: first, so the enemy has reason to reciprocate, second, so as to reduce civilian fear of invaders, third, because it's the decent thing to do.

These rules, of course, apply to civilians, enemy troops, and the wounded. Note that terrorists aren't on that list. Most counter-terror teams aren't overly concerned with how our prey fare. As far as Freehold law, the thugs are welcome to file suit against the government and/or the Operative, and see how far they get in Citizens' Court; typically, nowhere. I had no name, my unit didn't exist, no one had seen a thing. I like that advantage.

So, we dragged this sorry waste of breathing air into the van, slammed him against the framework, and encouraged him to talk. I shook him and banged him until he was almost vomiting from dizziness, screamed into his ear something to the effect of, "I'm going to jam your dick into a meatgrinder and feed the sausage to my dog," and kneed him in the gonads a few dozen times. Several full-body slaps across the face, a few punches, fingers into the gut, boots into the knees and shins, and a burst of blanks fired off close enough to his right ear to cause hearing damage and disorientation got him in the right frame of mind: bewildered, terrified, and unable to track.

He was stubborn and wouldn't talk. However, I could see the "meatgrinder" comment hit him. The word was out in the terrorist community, and I was glad to know that. But he was too stupid to talk. I stepped up to stage two: I actually asked him questions.

"Who are you? How many? Names of the rest of you? How are you positioned in the room?" I punctuated the questions with more slams into the frame.

No, I wasn't going to dismember him, fun as it would have

been. We might need him to answer more questions later. I
kept varying the attacks, preventing him from getting used to
any particular pain, and avoiding permanent injury, although
his bruises would mark him for months. I paused for about a
second, said, "Well?" and when he didn't sing went right back
to it. The idea is to give them no respite, no break in which to
collect their thoughts, and eventually you override self-control
and the unconscious begins answering you to avoid the pain.
If they have time to think, they'll fabricate a story to make you
happy, whether it's true or not; so you keep pounding without
pause until they answer. It's a skill. Don't ask me where I learned
it, just accept that I have done so.

I bent his fingers until they almost broke, twisted his wrists and
shoulders, grabbed one of our tools and teased his face with it.
The tool in question was a tiny, spiked wheel used for laying out
stitching by old-fashioned hand sewers. Applied gently, it can be
very tingly and actually erotic. Applied a little harder, it punctures
the skin and hits nerves. The face is *very* sensitive.

I could see him starting to break, so I tore his clothes open and
ran it over his scrotum and up his belly and chest. That almost
feels like being gutted. The tool is polished alloy and *looks* like a
surgical tool too if you keep it moving too fast for a good image.
It leaves a trail of punctures that weep surface blood. That did
it. He named names, gave me an accurate if stuttered map of the
suite, and begged me to stop. I kept rolling it over him, leaving
long, bleeding, red welts and demanded more and more information as it glittered in the glare from the spotlights. Occasionally
I'd place my palm in front of his nose, smack it, and jam his head
back into the frame. He'd wince, loll his head, straighten up and
insist he was telling me everything he knew. And I believed him,
but I'll take any opportunity to cause a terrorist pain.

In no more than five segs I had all the information I needed. I
dropped the limp form to the bed of the van, turned, and headed
out to plot and scheme. Behind me I heard Carstairs say, "Well,
he's certainly . . . forthright."

First, we had to wait yet again. We had to gently let slip that
we knew where they were. Naumann handled that end while I
listened. Nashold ranted and screamed.

After he wound down, Naumann said, "Sir, you must know how this is played. Of course we're trying to find you. After all, we don't want innocent people hurt."

"If I don't see bystanders on the street, I will shoot this bitch," Nashold insisted.

"We hope you won't do that, sir. But at least by knowing where you are, we can arrange a proper pickup of the princess, and yourself when you wish to leave." He was so reasonable and bumpkinlike. We didn't mean to break your rules. We're sorry we outthought you. Sorry, sorry.

"We will make our own travel arrangements," he said. "And we'll take this Stewart bitch with us."

"We really wish you wouldn't."

"You can't stop us. The people have the power, now. Once we show the universe that—" and off he went, masturbating again. As long as he was ranting, he wasn't shooting, so we let him.

Meanwhile, I walked to our support van and spoke to the Special Projects sergeant, Danielle Clancy. "Danni," I said, "I need civilian clothes with camouflaged integral armor, ID and accessories, vid and a transceiver they can't detect."

The best thing about being considered yokel colonists is that we can do outrageous things to catch people off guard and not be suspected. I was about to play on that.

Shortly, I was garbed and ready. I had a microburst transceiver buried just below the skin, which would appear as a typical hi-tech executive implant phone to a scan. I hoped. It would rip out easily and leave only a painful, bloody wound. Of course, they might just stab through it if I got caught. It transmitted in scrambled bursts when triggered, and only for a few microseconds at a time. I had contact lenses in that were molecular scale cameras with inductance circuits to the "phone." It was several hundred thousand credits worth of hardware, which we hoped was still secret at that time.

Meanwhile my team was sneaking into the building as housekeepers and support staff, their weapons being delivered in service vehicles.

On the whole, a hotel room wasn't a bad place for the terrorists to use. It had a good, clear field of fire. They obviously had staked out rooms on other sides to keep an eye on things. It was easy to watch the halls for infiltrators. And most importantly, the money tied up in all those rooms, as well as the cost of fixing any damage, would make both the owners and the underwriters nervous about vacating the premises and having us storm it.

Of course, any professional could think of a lot better places to use. In fact, a true professional never takes hostages, and certainly not on enemy soil. These punks were conniving but not particularly intelligent. The only risk we faced was being eyeballed by one of their spotters. There was no real risk. Except, of course, the value of the hostage. They'd pinned everything on that. But that also meant they would have to think twice about killing her. They could wound her and make it impossible for her to compete, but killing her would not help their case. On the other hand, these shitheads were insane idiots to start with.

The tech crew started listening for any signals transmitted inside the hotel, including phones. The hotel was advised to monitor all room to room calls. We wanted to confirm the little data we'd gotten from our capture, and ascertain that his cover was still good as his faked voice went out on schedule and in response to hails. The squad snuck in and started flowing up the access corridors and quietly cutting their way through walls to stay out of the corridors. The guests from those rooms were being housed in suites elsewhere, under guard of Blazers but with all the amenities. A couple of people with pending appointments groused slightly, but agreed to go along with the program out of decency. Despite the damage we were doing, the publicity from this would more than pay for the damage, which these non-capitalists would never have thought of but the hotel owner had. A true capitalist ghoul will sell his own intestines to the sharks. It would take most of a day, but they'd get into position.

It would have been easier just to evacuate the hotel, but that would have told them we were planning something, and their spotters would of course refuse to leave, and then we'd have a situation. As I said, it came down to the fact that these freaks were out of their sideshows and would *not* react rationally.

I spent a while outside in the gusty wind, in a Commerce

Boulevard suit, outside the military cordon, watching through binox. I'd shake my head periodically and say something to my assistant, Frank, who was dressed likewise and armed with a phone and a comm. He kept dictating notes. I got on my phone at one point and paced around while gesticulating. I looked every inch the harried young executive. Shortly, we went inside "again."

Inside, I hung out with the manager in his glassed office, talking and looking bothered. Eventually, I shrugged and muttered and headed upstairs. Management was going to have a word with the troublesome guests.

Taking a breath, I knocked on the door.

Nashold answered, yanking it open. "Who the fuck are you?" he asked. Mannerly.

"I'm Amiso Coruna, the hotel general manager. I need to discuss your situation," I said. He stared up and down at me, took in the suit, and looked confused. "Wait here," he said.

A few moments later, after loud voices spoke back and forth, I was invited in. More accurately, the door opened, I was dragged in with fingers painfully in my biceps and a Merrill Model 66K submachinegun jammed into my right nostril. It wasn't too hard to appear scared. Nashold spoke to me. "What the fuck do you want, Mister Manager?"

"Please, sir, no guns are necessary," I said. They eased off about five percent. "I'm very sorry," I continued, "but your presence here is disruptive to the other guests. The owner has asked me to relay his regrets and inform you that must leave—" I paused for a moment as they howled with laughter. I made a second scan of the room, and saw the princess over by the left wall. Her eyes flicked recognition, then went dull again. She twisted in what was to me a nod, but would be just a shift to anyone else. Perfect. The one concern was that she would break my cover. I'd been fairly sure she would follow my lead, but I was facing the risk of a small-caliber lobotomy.

As the laughter died down, I continued, "We will be happy to refund the balance of your payment, and furnish you with a free three-night stay, good anytime except the week before and after Landing Day."

The laughter resumed. It stopped at a signal from Nashold, and he said, "You are one stupid dogfucker, Mister Manager." He turned and added, "Toss him over there. He can be another sandbag if we have a shootout." He turned back. "Always useful to have an expendable hostage to prove we mean business."

They did frisk me, well enough I could have asked for a date by the time they were done. I had ID, scuffed and worn, so as to look authentic. Many infiltrators have been caught because they used pristine ID. I also had a watch, a phone, and the usual executive toys. They took them all. I'd hoped to have the watch at least, so I wouldn't need time ticks through the implanted phone. They didn't notice that my suit and other clothing were constructed of ballistic cloth. It wouldn't stop me from dying, but nothing they had would get through both sides of it and me and have enough energy left to do permanent injury to the princess. Yes, I was expendable. I looked suitably scared. Was I scared?

What do you think?

But I'd gotten a good look at four faces and knew who they were. That was a start. I'd get more info as this went on. Below, Frank and Deni were watching it all. Frank would direct, Deni would lead the assault. I had no concern about her shooting. Terrorist assholes were about to become dead terrorist assholes.

It was hard not to get more scared as I sat there. We were nearing midday, and I was glad I'd eaten beforehand, because I was unlikely to be fed here. Sure enough, the goon on duty, Damon Melchi, brought a sandwich for the princess, which he placed on a napkin atop the vid so she could pull at it with her teeth while still shackled. I was ignored.

"Any lunch for me?" I asked.

"Shut the fuck up."

It seemed I'd been correct again. That was good.

After she finished eating, I spoke. "I'm not sure I approve of royalty," I said softly but clearly.

"Oh?" the princess replied. "And why is that?"

"Frankly, if you weren't considered more valuable than anyone else, we wouldn't be here," I said, sounding put upon.

"I'm quite sure you have wealthy elites here who are targets for this sort of thing," she said, playing off my lead and sounding miffed. Good.

"Yes, but at least here—"

"Shut up or I'll crack your teeth, Mister Manager. And you too, rich bitch," Melchi said. He was the worst kind of enemy: a true believer. I'd have to make sure he died first.

We resumed our silence. Melchi was replaced by Todd Mellars a bit later. He was a rough-looking punk with a bulbous, bald skull and eyes too deep and too close together. He was fat over little muscle and clearly about as bright as a typical cockroach. Apologies to anyone's pet cockroach I may have insulted. Melchi crashed out on a bed.

Waiting is especially hard when some asshole with no penis keeps pointing the muzzle of a weapon at your eye, your ear, up your nose. I think this sack of fertilizer got off sexually on it. He'd pace the room, sigh, look at his watch, then come over and caress my face with it before threatening me with the muzzle again. I vowed that if he survived the initial assault, I'd kill him myself.

Midafternoon, the princess was taken to the restroom. Mellars went along. I'm sure he watched. He was that kind of pervert. I was left guarded by Melchi.

After another hour I said, "I need to use the restroom."

"Go right ahead," Mellars said. "The carpet will soak it up." That grin of his said he was definitely some kind of pervert.

I could have wet myself. It's not as if it bothers me. But I wasn't going to give him the satisfaction. Anyway, I'd only asked to gauge his pliability. Absolutely every detail was going firsthand down to my people. I'd get the warning that night, I hoped. The deadline was "9 am" tomorrow, which they agreed with some embarrassment was 3:50 divs. They really hadn't done their field research. This is why they'd been screwing around for fifty years and gotten nowhere except dead.

I had a slow-release pill in me that kept me awake. It didn't feel very good, especially without regular water and food, but it *did* keep me awake. Acid in my stomach and sour taste in my mouth went with bladder pressure, a quivering colon, aching spine and numb wrists to remind me of how easy it would be for me to die in this escapade.

Just after the 6 div time tick, the princess was fed another sandwich for dinner. When nothing was done for me, she said, "I really think it would be appropriate to feed our other guest, rather than giving me the royal treatment."

It was a slam of an insult. Nashold was in the room, and snarled, then admitted that she had a point. Not that he said anything, but he did indicate that I should be served a sandwich and a sack of juice with a straw.

"Thank you, Princess," I said.

"You're welcome," she replied.

"Shut the fuck up, both of you," Nashold said. It seemed to be a typical response of the movement. But I was taken to the bathroom afterwards. Two of them uncuffed me and recuffed me in front so I could pee. I'm guessing they didn't want to help me as they had the princess. She was still getting the royal treatment.

The first transmission came in with the midnight time tick. "Construction done for the evening. Everyone dog off and go home." So we knew who all of them were and where they were. Not that it would matter. Any we didn't kill in this room would get theirs later, but it's so much neater to do them all at once.

Almost a div later, everyone at their lowest ebbs in the middle of the night, I heard, "Okay, flip the breaker and let's see if it works."

I waited for the message that would announce the attack. I triggered Boost for the metabolic increase, in case of injury. "It works," I heard. I tensed slightly, shifted imperceptibly, and dove.

I got my cuffs high and over the princess' head, grabbing her in a bear hug, almost a romantic embrace, head to toe. We landed in the corner of wall and floor behind the vid, her wedged in, me on top. I didn't kiss her on purpose, but we did crack our teeth together hard enough to sting. Our weight landed on my shackled wrists and drove the metal bands into my bones. That hurt. No, it was excruciating. Pain lanced up my arms, my fingers tingled and went numb, and I heard bones grind in my wrists.

I thought I'd jumped at the wrong cue and was about to die for my effort. It was just my subjective time stretching out. All three goons present had woken or spun toward me, and were still trying to figure out what had happened, when the wall behind them exploded. Light akin to a nuke flashed through the room. A *bang!* shattered the picture frames and my ears. My nerves tingled and made me convulse. The dazzle and ringing took over, and there were *ugh!*ing coughs as the goons were accurately riddled with fire, the wet eggshell-cracking and slapping noises telling me they were being hit in heads and throats.

After that was anticlimactic. My people shot those three, rounded the rest up and shot them each at the base of the skull, and that was that.

As soon as I heard Deni shout, "CLEAR!" I rolled free, disentangling myself from the princess. "Captain Stewart," I said, offering a hand for her shoulder and helping her upright. Or at least I tried to. I shrieked in a very unmanly and unkiller-like fashion as she fell back. Hey, screw you. It *hurt*. Yes, I said "captain." She'd been promoted.

"Operative Chinran," she replied, as brightly as she could through her haggard outside. "I am grateful for your response."

"My pleasure, Madam," I replied, as Tyler moved in to check her for wounds. Barto uncuffed me and numbed my wrists with both topical and deep-penetrating local anesthetics.

"How are you, boss?" Deni asked me. There was an undertone that wasn't professional, and told me she was going to be very passionate later as she sympathized with the injuries and called me a "crazy, stupid adrenaline junkie" in six languages.

"Did you shoot me?" I asked. My senses were coming back from the ear-ringing and roiling purple dazzle of the flashbang. I could smell propellant, explosive residue, the shit and blood smell of dead terrorist assholes and the dust of shattered walls. I was dusty and rumpled, as was the princess. The team looked like bakers, they were so caked in white dust from cutting the walls. They smelled like wrestlers. We don't make any half-assed messes in Black Ops. When we trash a place, we are thorough.

"No, but I'm thinking about it," she replied with a half-mock smile.

"Then I'm fine for now. Good shooting."

The princess was in great shape, other than a loose tooth that matched mine, and we adjourned outside to take care of the details. We each donned body armor, or rather, my people put us into body armor, our hands being largely useless. We took a stained service elevator down with one team, while the other two teams each took different routes. Even now, we weren't ruling out a suicidal idiot or a marksman. Though I was floating in that endorphin stage from fading Boost and wasn't paying much attention. I chided myself and came back to ground.

We regrouped in the empty lobby, and Barto commed out to make sure everyone was in place. Hidden from the view of most civilians were another squad, all snipers, who had a very good view of the area, by eyeball, comm, sky-lifted cameras and assorted other sensors. If a mosquito tried to bite the princess, someone was designated to blow it away. I didn't envy them the task. It calls for exacting precision and frantic alertness. Sort of like the task I'd handled already. Around the area, another squad was patrolling in vehicles in civilian clothes, backed up by a Security Patrol platoon and Westport City Safety. Outside the glass doors we were approaching, yet another squad, Blazers, were tasked to be brutal killers if anything came close, and to throw themselves on grenades if necessary. It may not have looked there was much going on to the casual viewer, and that was on purpose. But trust me, that lady was *safe*. Our reputation was at stake and nothing was going to be allowed to wreck it.

The word came back that we were clear, and we trooped through the atrium and outside, Deni and Bryce holding doors for us. Even with the small crowd we'd allowed, of military, government and a select few reporters we could trust not to get in the way of a shot, the cheer was enthused and loud. Annette settled for a smile and slow bow, not waving. That let spectators know she was okay, and couldn't be misinterpreted as a reflexive move from an attack by anyone. Professional at both her tasks, that lady was, and is. She'll make one hell of a queen.

Carstairs was about to wet his pants. The muted gunfire and flashbangs had scared him. We came out, me as the "manager" alongside the princess, with the team around me in masks. There were lots of pictures. Luckily, besides my cover ID protecting me, I was pretty ragged-looking. It wouldn't affect my security. The Princess took almost all the attention, and I just had to look sweaty, scared and worn out. When someone finally got around to sticking a camera in my face, I caught lots of shadow over my eyes, rasped my voice as much as I could without it being obvious and said, "I'm just glad it's over. I really don't want to talk right now." They left me alone and no one ever was the wiser. But if you track down the video of that event, you'll see me. It may be one of five photographs since I enlisted, and the only unofficial one I'm aware of.

When all was said and done, Malcolm Allender, the one who provided the answers, was encouraged to leave the system rapidly. Then we announced in the press that he'd been crucial in finding the data we needed. A week later, he was hit. Unfortunately, the bomb took out three other people. Very sad. I keep hoping these jerks will learn to be accurate and efficient.

Naumann knew my capabilities and had for some time. Erson got to handle all the files that came down to the unit. Richard had his own report on me. The Citizens' Council wanted to make sure I was thanked properly for the task I'd accomplished, even though they didn't know who precisely I was. I was doomed. Before I could refuse and run screaming, they'd slapped lieutenant pips on my collar. I was taken away from my personal squad and put in charge of Counterterror Operations, which became a specific platoon rather than three individual squads. It was an odd platoon. I had three squads of Operatives, two of Blazers, the sniper squad, a Special Projects squad, a maintenance section and our own SPs to secure any cordons we needed. Captain Hidochi and her staff of fast talkers were attached to us. I still got to play some, but I did more adminwork and couldn't hang off buildings with my friends. If it weren't for the honor, I'd have told them to stick it.

Yes, it was a great career move. Yes, it made me more promotable. Yes, it was a challenge. No, I didn't care for it. It lasted about a month. What happened next changed human history, though I didn't really pay attention to the significance at the time.

MASTER

CHAPTER 16

It was a routine morning at my new task, tens of rams, books, loads and charts to examine right after a morning run and a rappelling exercise, when I got a call to see Commander Naumann at my convenience. That meant as soon as possible, so I checked my uniform for obvious damage—he wouldn't care about a bit of dust—and went over to the HQ building.

He was up front talking to his people, rather than back in his office. "Kenneth," he greeted me as he looked up, "let's talk." He waved at his office and headed that way. He walks as fast as I do.

He closed the door. His security fields were already active. That made me realize this was not a routine matter. I wasn't in trouble for anything that I knew of, and a quick memory scan confirmed I'd done nothing that I need be ashamed of, so I had to wonder what this was about.

He got right to the point. "What do you know about the situation with Earth?" he asked me.

I replied, "They don't like us being a nation rather than a colony, resent that we chose to bow out of the UN, and are terrified that we might be a precedent for others to follow. They've been like that since we declared independence, which is six years now."

Nodding, he asked, "What do you think of the UNPF as a combat force?"

297

I snorted.

When I said nothing else, he said, "That's a conceited assumption and you know it. Try again."

"They outnumber us a hundred to one. Their production is less efficient but has a larger base. They have more of everything. If they ever got around to funding it as they should, their military would defeat ours in a stand-up battle," I said. "We'd inflict casualties at a ratio of ten to one, but that wouldn't stop them if they really meant it. I'm not aware of them ever committing full resources to a conflict."

Nodding, he said, "I expect that last item to change in the near future."

"Really," I replied. It wasn't a question, more of a questioning acknowledgement. If Naumann told me we were swapping camouflage for pink tutus, I'd assume he had a valid logic behind it. So I waited for enlightenment.

He didn't offer it right then. Instead, he asked, "How would we defeat the UNPF under such circumstances?"

I pondered for a moment. We have kicked around every possible conflict with every nation there is. So I dredged up the data on the UN as a whole and let it percolate for a few seconds. "Earth is the key," I said. "Any threat would politically originate on Earth. The Extrasolar members don't care enough to start a war."

"Earth is eighty nations," he said. "Can you be more specific?"

"Why?" I asked rhetorically. "It's one system. Any political move would originate in the North American States, the European Federation or the Greater Asian Union. The halfway industrial nations would jump on board to show their importance, and the rest don't matter worth a damn."

"So how would we defeat them?" he asked again.

"We'd have to keep them busy with disruptions to the infrastructure and political processes, so they couldn't commit full resources here," I said. I had a creepy feeling he would be sending me to do recon on Earth when this discussion was over.

"Very good," he said. "We'd have to be in place ahead of time, of course. Sending a unit in after the fact would be inefficient and complicated."

"Well, yes," I agreed. Yes, this was going to be a sucky recon in Developing Nation hellholes.

He handed me a case full of rams. Not one, but a case. "Figure out what it would take to train an Ops team to handle it. Here's ideas on what techniques the operation might use to achieve sufficient disruption. I wouldn't expect we have more than a year to prepare. The budget isn't much yet, but I'll try to wangle more."

"This is official?" I asked. I knew the answer, but I wanted confirmation. In the case were captain's insignia. That was fast.

"This is through me," he said. "I've told Dyson. No one else knows. No one else needs to know. Don't ask about the budget."

Something about that bothered me, and I said, "You do realize that the Constitution requires fifty percent of military forces by type and equipment to be Reserve, and you are forming an unauthorized Freehold unit?" It was a rhetorical question. Of course he knew.

"Actually, you're forming it," he said. "We'd both be taken down on this one." He didn't grin.

I said, "Yes, Sir, Is There Anything Else, Sir?" and got out of there with minimal small talk.

I had been wrong. The rat bastard was planning to send me to *live* on Earth until we had such a war, and fight it from behind, with no support and in violation of every law and treaty. I'd wanted a challenge, I had one. Be careful what you wish for.

I hoped he'd included lubricant in the plans. I hate getting dryfucked.

CHAPTER 17

You might think I picked the best, brightest, most physically perfect specimens to form the team. It's logical and reasonable. And wrong. I wanted punks. Thugs. Non-regulation, obnoxious assholes. The kind of person who would cheerfully face off the entire military bureaucracy, and dare them to put him or her in front of a firing squad. Anyone can be trained to be physically well above average, if they have the will. It requires guts and intelligence and a certain amount of sheer stupidity to deliberately buck the system and get noticed. I'd have to weed through them, certainly, but attitude was first. With that in mind, I didn't even bother looking at Soldier Performance Evaluations. The system changes every few years, but basically, within three cycles, the new system winds up being a mutual admiration society. Whether it's numbered 1–5, 1–10 or lettered, it becomes politically impossible to rate a troop honestly. Everyone must be considered "The exception. Consistently sets the standards for others." It's silly. At least we require a promotion board as well. The UNPF bases it strictly off the reports, so no one is ever deemed inadequate for the task.

I didn't limit myself to Black Ops, Blazers, Special Projects, or even Mobile Assault. I looked through *everybody's* file, from the Marshal down to the newest recruit awaiting training. Then I had to look through reserve files, too. That would be a bitch. Reserve forces are under control of District Councils, not the Freehold Council. It keeps our government honest. Half the military doesn't answer to the Citizens' Council. There'd have to be some personnel swaps if I could find any reservists willing to go.

After I'd gone through for attitude and brains, I looked at disciplinary records, then at physical scores. In truth, I'd take as many as I could get. In practice, I had limited funds and time. The better-trained and skilled they were to start with, the easier it would be. I whittled it down to 300, and decided I could do interviews from there. And I'd have to hurry on some of them.

I hopped out to Maygida Base, and found Engineer Kimbo Randall as he was on his way out the gate. Test scores off the chart; excellent PT scores (by normal criteria); master rating in small arms; expert in unarmed combat; recreational parachutist, spaceboater and climber; first class troop in his specialty, which was utilities for an engineering unit, and they were getting rid of him because they didn't like his arrogant attitude. He was only thirteen. You have to give youth the chance to develop before you crush them. I'd give him that chance.

He was a cocky bastard. I caught up with him as he was out-processing at base personnel. He was walking back to his car and as he grabbed more adminwork and headed back inside, some By-The-Book asshole senior sergeant started in on him.

"Excuse me, you need to move that car. There's a half div parking limit for guests only," he said.

"I've only been here three segs," Randall replied.

"No you haven't," Sergeant BTB replied. "It was here at three divs this morning, and it's still here." This guy was getting soft and out of shape, and apparently had nothing better to do than harass over technicalities people who clearly were working.

"I left and came back," Randall snapped and kept walking.

"No you didn't."

He whirled at that. "Are you calling me a liar, dogfucker?" He jumped into the NCOs face and looked ready to go to town.

Oh, I loved this kid.

Sergeant Flabby started to bluster. "Who are you and what unit are you with, soldier?"

"I'm Kimbo Randall, and as of the moment I sign this," he said as he shook the adminwork in Softy's face, "I'm a civilian, so fuck you, suck me and get the hell out of my face!" he shouted back. Passionate, but untrained. I would train him. He would be molded as I saw fit and the killer within would surface. Time to step in.

"I'll handle this, Sergeant," I said as I approached. He saluted, nodded and made to hang around and watch. I stared at him until he decided to split. "Engineer Randall," I said.

"That's Mr. Randall, to you, Captain," he replied, sounding bitter.

"It's Engineer Sergeant Randall, if you want to stay in," I corrected.

"Huh?" he said. I'd confused his worldview.

"If you want to stay in, I can arrange it. Interested?" I said casually.

Had he been sophisticated, he would have held out to see what I was offering and see if the deal would sweeten any. It wouldn't, but it never hurts to check.

Instead, he looked ready to blow me. Patriotic and dedicated, too stubborn and stupid to know when to quit, passionately defensive of his honor and ability and proud of his service.

Only an idiot would get rid of this kid. I needed more people to fill in as Special Projects techs, and he seemed to fit the bill. I wasn't disappointed.

There were names I recognized on the list of course—most of the qualifying personnel were Operatives or Blazers. Some of those still surprised me, though. For example, Sergeant Irina Aleksandrovna Belinitsky, my old Bitch of an instructor. She was only two years my senior and had transferred to reserve after her second tour. The question was, could I get her back?

She'd be great, too. She spoke Russian of course. Also Spanish, German, Hebrew and Greek. Her accents were excellent. She had experience at five different embassies and had done several covert intel missions. She could act as an instructor. Her primary training had been as an interpreter and general spook. She'd be reliable and flexible and would make a great squad or platoon leader, if I could get her.

So I called her. She answered the phone with, "Hello?" She stared, and appeared to recognize me after a few seconds, probably from a file photo—instructors like to keep track of former students, at least in Special Warfare. She added, "Hey, ya little prick! They made *you* a captain? They must be desperate. What's up?"

I grinned back. "I need an obnoxious bitch. I thought of you. And I want to screw you."

She snorted. "All men want to screw me. What are you offering?"

"You back on active duty, covert mission," I said, trying to be evasive but informative. I'd not practiced.

"And when do you screw me?" she mocked.

"When you die." It was just too good a straight line to pass up; I love double entendres.

She laughed loudly. "Tell me more."

"Fly out here," I said.

"Buy me a ticket."

I rounded up the usual suspects—Deni, Frank, Barto and Tyler. I'd worked with them. I knew their capabilities. I ran them through my program as a doublecheck, but it was a formality. They came through clear and they'd want the challenge.

Flights were booked, lodging arranged, a few cover stories and falsified orders issued. A lot of people were arriving in a short period of time, and it was bound to create rumors. So I assisted. We were forming a new team for counterterror only. We were creating a new, tougher training program and these were the brains behind it. We were planning another mission to Mtali. We'd made First Contact with aliens and were sending a force to accompany the diplomats. We planned to boost our military budget by sending out teams to train mercenaries and local troops elsewhere. Each story was either very believable and wrong, or so totally outrageous as to be laughed at. Meanwhile, the people I'd called arrived, were bedded down, and added to the rumors from their ignorance, which was taken as deliberate evasion by the yackers.

I called everyone to an empty briefing room. It was used for pilot briefings, and the Air Ops Building staff looked a bit bemused.

A couple of them tried to hang around to hear, but this was none of their business, and we ushered them unceremoniously out. The doors were barred, the security field activated, and we got to business.

I climbed the two steps to the podium and stood relaxed. "I am Operative Captain Kenneth Chinran," I announced without using a mic. Raw voice can be so much more attention getting. "Some of you know me. Some of you know each other from Blazer or Black Ops. The rest of you are new to Spec Warfare.

"I don't care where you came from. As of today, you're Operatives. We're in a hurry, and we'll bring everyone up to speed asap. There'll be refresher courses, and a *lot* of training. In fact, you ain't *never* seen training the likes of what you are going to see here.

"Now, I don't care where you came from. I'll be making assignments as I see fit. If I put a Legion sergeant over a Blazer corporal, I'd better not hear a *word* about how the sergeant isn't 'qualified' to give orders. Because I am going to *make* the sergeant qualified. Everyone understand that? Say, 'Yes, sir.'"

"Yes, sir!" was the ragged response.

"IS THAT CLEAR?"

"YES, SIR!" the responding roar shook the podium.

"Your relationships are your own, if you have friends here, but if you think it'll get in the way of duty, I recommend parting as friends now. And any relationships only exist in the rare off-duty moments you'll have. Both of them, to be precise. Because we are going to be training.

"As to our mission," I said. "We'll be going clandestine as no one has ever gone before. No uniforms, nothing identifiable, strictly cash and not much of it, few if any weapons. No one is even going to suspect who we are. We will be the sweetest, most loveable bunch of dedicated young professionals and laborers anyone has ever seen . . . right up to the point where we fuck them in the ass with a sandpaper and barbed wire dildo lubed with hot sauce and hydrochloric acid." I waited for the shrieks and laughs to die down.

"I can't say more than that until much later. Don't plan on having any outside contact about this for the next two years. If you have family, any move to the area is at your expense. We just can't admit that anything is going on. And you'll have only a few days notice to tell them you'll be going, when we do. And they still won't know where. It sucks, I know," I said over protests, "but we have to be utterly covert on this.

"I can't tell you what our objective is, except that it's essential, challenging, and nothing you can ever talk about afterwards. You're going to be tired, hurt, dirty, ignored, unappreciated and generally taken for granted—"

"How's that different from life now?" someone shouted. I could have kissed him. The laughs made it clear no one thought of those as problems.

"Just don't expect things to change," I said. "I wish I could fill you all in. Just take it that this is the ultimate challenge, and after it is over, you'll have all the war stories you'll ever need and a few credits for beer." There were more chuckles.

"I'll be in my office all afternoon. Each of you will stop by and tell me 'yes' or 'no.' If 'no,' we'll slide you out again immediately. If 'yes,' we start training tomorrow, early. That's all."

Deni was not the first one in. I think she wanted to be, but was afraid of any appearance of favoritism after my statements on relationships.

She saluted, and after I returned it said, "I'm a 'yes' on the mission."

"Good," I said. I'd assumed so.

"I assume we won't be seeing each other socially?"

"Afraid not," I said. And I'd hate that. I took a long look at her. She was just 16 of our years, 24 standard, at her peak and incredible. Face, body, skin, everything flawless and proportioned. She knew it and knew how to use it. A bit too visible for an Operative, but Earth's definitions of beauty were different. She was also a first class actress. That recalled to me a game we'd played the other night that had left us flushed, weak and unable to move. I shoved those thoughts away.

"Well, we've been there before," she said. "So count me in on the mission." She saluted before we could say any more.

I returned her salute and she left. It took some seconds to calm myself enough to continue.

Next in was Cecil Tanaka. I'd grabbed him for his language skills, degree in chemistry and experience in plastic and metal fabrication. He'd done all kinds of improv work in orbital construction. He was a combat vet from Mtali. Highly rated by my criteria. I wasn't sure I could convince him to stay, though.

After he reported, I sat him down at ease. He obviously had things he wanted to talk about. He sprawled in the old stuffed chair I'd acquired in lieu of the issue chairs, which are just right for grilling a derelict recruit and no fun for professionals.

"Can you give any more details on duration or location, sir?" he asked.

I shook my head. "I have no idea myself. It's a potential threat issue," I said. "We may stand down in a month or two. We may disappear at any time. We may all die."

He scowled slightly. "Thing is," he said, "I want to help you, sir. But I have a family. I can't just leave them without a word, possibly never go back and abandon them to the fates."

"I know," I agreed. "And you aren't the only one in that situation."

"*Any* clue?" he asked.

Damn, I wanted to tell him. He was so good at what he did, and we could use him. But there couldn't be a suggestion of a rumor of a leak of a hint. "I can't," I said.

He scowled deeper. I could tell he was agonizing over it.

"Let me make this easy . . . well, less complicated for you," I said.

"Okay."

"If your family is important to you, which is a good thing, then put them first. You've done your duty and more, you can serve honorably here, and if it ever happens to be something we can talk about, you can tell them you were selected but had to refuse." I hated to let him go, but I didn't want to destroy his family and if there was a chance of it bothering him, it could blow an operation. This is no criticism of him. He was a damned good soldier and a damned good man. I needed something just a little different. Someone more psychotic.

"I guess so," he said. "Well, thanks for the invite, sir. And good hunting." He left without ceremony.

I whittled 293 down to 240 that afternoon. I would take no more than 200, and perhaps a few less. So I had 40 spares I could cripple in training. It sounds callous, but one has to do real human tests of techniques to get a good assessment. And that causes casualties. Also, I'd found out since I'd sent out the invites that three of them had been on Earth. Anyone who'd been on Earth in a military or diplomatic capacity would have a photo on file, and likely DNA, too. Their intelligence services are paranoid on the subject. I couldn't use those people. However, since I couldn't mention "Earth" in any fashion, they'd simply have to flunk out in training and be sent away. Get the idea of how "fair" this was going to be?

Then, there were the gender ratios. 15% of the Forces are female and only 3% of Special Warfare. I was running around 25% with my current selections. I *had* to have women on Earth to help maintain cover. Large groups of single men are a red flag to an investigator. "Couples" and single women are necessary cover. I couldn't lower my standards, but I had to keep as many women as possible.

But I wasn't done yet. I had a list of people I needed to speak to regarding our training.

Senior Sergeant Ryan Mercer was a recreational skydiver. He had three hundred and nineteen military jumps, four of them technically combat jumps, and four *thousand* and more civilian jumps. So I made him team jumpmaster. "Ryan, I want everyone qualified in a week," I told him, "and that includes suicide drops." I was referring to a High Altitude, Very Low Opening jump. One pops the canopy about three seconds from pending impact. If there's a mistake . . .

Alternately, it refers to exiting a nape of the earth aircraft and only having three seconds to deploy and hit. Both are very useful in our line of work. Both require expertise and precision.

"A *week*?"

"Ten days," I confirmed. "They're all yours, and take anyone you need as jumpmasters."

He frowned, wrinkled his brow, and said, "It means five jumps a day, every day, starting tomorrow."

"We have pilots, we have the craft. Get to it," I encouraged.

"Yes, sir. I'll have you a schedule this afternoon."

Then I called in Roger Smith and Tracy Liu. They were my master climber and fitness instructor, respectively. "In less than a month, everyone must be able to scale a standard building wall," I told them. "Get to it."

Rappelling, small arms, unarmed combat, demolitions most especially, everything we already did, the new people had to be brought up to speed on and the veterans refreshed. Everyone had to be ready as soon as possible for us to deploy. Political situations change rapidly and we couldn't count on plenty of training time. If we happened to have it, we'd use it, but in the meantime, we had to hit it hard. My job was to get everyone *thinking* like Operatives. That was a task by itself, and not one I could delegate.

The next morning, we met in the mothballed hangar that we would be cleaning out and calling our own. It wasn't the ideal building, security speaking, but it was roomy, cold, drafty, dusty, and otherwise perfect for creating a training environment. They were all in formation when I strode in, and I cut it short. Very short.

"Bugünün lisanı Türkçe. Bütün faaliyetler Türkçe olarak yapılacak ve başka bir dil kullanan herkese kusturucu gaz verilecek. Derhal başlayın." I said. (*"The language of the day is Turkish. All activities will be conducted in Turkish, and anyone using another language will be retch gassed. Get to it."*)

A couple of people muttered to the effect of, "What the heck did he say?" and were immediately spritzed by the current squad leaders, all of whom were Operatives or Blazers and fluent in Mtali Turkish. The victims shouted and complained and were roughed up further until they took the hint. They looked *mean* after that.

Could they actually learn a language in a day? Goddess, no. The intent of this was to get them used to observing in unfamiliar surroundings. They'd have to pay attention to body language, hints, and goings on, and that would make them better at gathering intelligence for their own survival and the team's. When the newcomers were dragged out to an empty field, and after mowing it flat shown how to fold and pack a parachute, while the lecture was in Turkish, you'd better *believe* they paid attention. There was a lot of hands on from the instructors Mercer had drafted—my goal *was* to keep them alive, after all, but they looked rather pale as they were herded onto the railings of a VC-6 jump trainer.

They all made it down alive. Then a few got gassed for cursing in English. *C'est la guerre.*

The next morning, I said, "*Hoy es el dia de Español. Usando qualquier otra lenguaje resultara en el uso de lacrimogena en la cara. Additionalmente, considera que desde ahora en adelante, su brazo derecha como descompuesto.*" (Same requirements as the day before, with, "Additionally, consider your right arm to be useless," tacked on.) *That* would keep them bothered. They were learning in a hurry not to assume anything. We used every language commonly available, including sign languages of different types. After realizing that I hadn't prohibited it, several people started carrying translation programs so they could at least hear. Eventually, everyone did. I made them train blind, with aural nerves blocked, with limbs either blocked neurally or simply on their own responsibility as unuseable. Anyone can be clever and competent when fully capable. A more important assessment is how well one operates when stressed from injury, lack of sleep, hunger, when in a strange environment of shifting rules. This was no minor risk like losing a squad. *Any* mistake on this op would kill all of us and possibly destroy our home. The training got rough.

We ran through basic combat skills and PT as fast as we could, and gave everyone already qualified refresher training. And yes, I included myself in all of this. I'd been stuck behind a desk planning this, and many of my basic skills like diving and such had had only the formal bimonthly reviews. I needed the refreshers.

We learned how to drive vehicles, and how to wreck them. It might be that we'd be chased on Earth, but a vehicle on manual is a weapon, too. We not only used simulators, but also brought in old vehicles from unit salvages, wrecks from insurance agencies that Senior Sergeant Kimbo Randall (yes, I promoted him again) and his tech crew rebuilt into useable shape as many times as they could, and crashed them from all angles. We even (at what I decided was an acceptable security risk) got a few new ones from manufacturers and insurers, under the pretext of doing "survivability tests" for diplomatic vehicles. They were as eager as we to see real-world results (as opposed to simulations) and made furious notes as we saw just how much damage different vehicles could take from different directions. We used all kinds, but the substantial presence of Earth vehicles got a few of the more astute troops nodding thoughtfully.

Kimbo was a genius. We have no vehicle autocontrol modules in the Freehold, but everything we'd handle on Earth would. There're only a handful of planets where the traffic density is high enough to justify them. He found a few on Caledonia, shipped them in, and had his people practice assembling duplicates from parts, wiring them in, testing them, then building bypass circuits from parts found in hobby and electronic stores. They did it multiple ways on various budgets and with various qualities of tools. Then they'd put six functional vehicles together from every ten we wrecked, and hand them to us to smash again. The spare parts from the destroyed cars he used for training the Special Projects squads in the manufacture of knives, swords, cartridge firearms, and other improvised weapons.

We followed that with vehicle chase and surveillance training. For that, we went on the streets. Jefferson is nowhere near as large or crowded as our target cities on Earth would be, but there's no autocontrol. It would actually be a decently complicated sim, if different. We started with training in observation and surveillance of our own people, then of strangers who likely wouldn't notice, moved up to executives and Citizens who should notice anything suspicious, then back to Operatives who were looking for tails. We got everyone trained to a level I was happy with in a fairly short time.

Combat driving was tougher. We needed to learn as much as we could before playing games, because wrecks would cost us money here, and get us killed there. We had to do it, though. You train by doing a chase late at night when it's quiet, then at slower times of the day, then during rush times. Sooner or later, there is going to be a crash. No question. We had a bogus insurance company set up to pay claims, relying on prompt and generous settlements to dissuade questions. We'd still have to justify a few payouts to the chain of command, though.

I had my own driving test, administered by Reza Asadourian, who had been a diplomatic driver on Novaja Rossia, which had some of the most offensive drivers anywhere. He devised tests that were truly unique. In my case, he had me follow one of his deputies at rush. The bastard waited until I had lunch on my lap as I circled downtown waiting, then told me I had a target and to pursue.

The food hit my lap and oozed and burned into my pants. I nailed the throttle and brought the crappy electric ground car up to speed. We were rehearsing worst-case scenarios, and that meant Earth type vehicles. You ever try weaving through heavy traffic in a kid's toy, chasing a high performance vehicle while dinner soaks your crotch? Without causing a wreck? On a tight schedule, and without being IDed by the prey or called out by City Safety because a thousand other drivers are complaining and swearing out charges?

I taught a few subjects myself as well, and proctored a few tests to ensure things were progressing. All of us already qualified or with practical experience were trained on the curricula, then took the rest out for exams after training. It was a group gestalt, everyone learning from everyone else. The technical experts from the schools and the Special Projects people were hit hardest. We sucked their brains dry.

We started on reconnaissance and infiltration of dwellings. That was tougher here than it would be on Earth, which was one bright spot in this nightmare. Think about it: On Earth, people "mind their own business" and "wait for the authorities to handle it." They just assume that someone else will deal with a problem, unless it has specifically been laid on their plate. We don't have that option. If someone sees a problem here, they deal with it. Whoever is closest takes the job, because there is no "authority" to do so. You look out for your neighbors because you want them to look out for you.

Consider that when breaking into an apartment for a sneak and peek. You don't belong there. The locals will notice you. If you do anything untoward, they'll come looking and be armed while doing so. They might call city safety for backup but you can't count on it. It might simply be the business end of a shotgun that comes for you. Now: get into that apartment, find the intel you've been asked for and get out without anyone noticing. Then, to make it tougher, do it again a week later. Then we started stealing stuff and returning it later, with apologetic letters about our "kleptomaniac" brothers or sisters, who were sorry and needed help. Then we started doing it at night in occupied dwellings whilst the occupants slept unaware. Then occupied dwellings in the daytime whilst the occupants were awake . . .

Okay, I'm kidding about the daytime. But you believed it, didn't you? We might have to actually do a daytime job at some point, so we practiced what we could. I'd name a residence, tell the students to get info, and give them a time frame, either short or shorter. They'd fake uniforms of delivery companies, food delivery people or whatever, and try to bring me at least the number and ages of residents and approximate value of contents, etc. I was training a pack of professional thieves, even more so than Operatives already are.

We added theft from and of cars and finally, major business offices, which were on the lookout for industrial/commercial espionage and had been known to arrange "accidents" from time to time. Eventually, I even staged a few raids on secure military offices, requiring them to start naked, since that was socially possible on Grainne, and precluded them hiding assets among clothes.

Learning to break and enter isn't hard. Almost any reasonably intelligent person can do so. What's hard is the right mindset, avoiding the fear of getting caught, which is what leads most people to screw up and get caught. As we'd be risking our lives, our mission and (though most didn't know it yet) our homes, we had to be cold and unshakeable.

I set up much of that myself. It was good training for me, too. I chose residences, dug up ID on the occupants, then sent Operatives in to confirm. I enjoyed that. I'd sit well away, well concealed, watching as they eased up to the residence, then hopped in a window or picked the lock. If challenged, they were "friends," or "maintenance" or some other innocuous cover. They'd offer fake ID and continue as if they belonged there, which is one of the key traits of a professional.

Afterwards, they'd come to me. "What do you have?" I'd ask.

I'd be told, "Occupant is a female, approximately eighteen years old. Long red hair, pale skin, green eyes. Likes bright makeup in a variety of styles. Clothing tastes run toward neofunk and dash. Employed by Critical Business Services in reception and referral, approximate income, twenty thousand credits annually. One pet parrot, small aquarium. Likes Italian cuisine. Exercises frequently and takes dance lessons, rides—"

"What kind of dance?" I'd ask.

"Er, jazz and ballroom. Rides a bike in lieu of driving. Prefers men as partners . . ." and on it would go.

I'd have them report on every facet possible, and grill them on anything they didn't mention, to see if they'd noticed those facts too. "Where does she shop for groceries? Clothes? Entertainment? What net provider does she use? What net chatgroups? When does she sleep?" Some of this required making inferences from other data. They had to get inside a subject's mind in only a very short time.

We took turns at different activities, but after two months we went out to run a small exercise on strict combat tactics. It was great cover of our actual activities, good training for them as a group and a chance to see how they interacted and handled stress. We convoyed out the old fashioned way: trucks on the road.

It was a day long trip from Maygida to the deep valleys north of Mirror Lake, so we went out for dinner as a unit for the first time. It wasn't much—a buffet style steak and chicken place with a few odds like kangaroo, buffalo, ostrich, alligator and hippopotamus, but it was hot, fresh and free. None of my kids would say "no," or I'd discuss with them the practical aspects of the Scavenging and Procurement Military Technical Specialty. We pulled off the road and parked on the grass, truck after truck being convoyed in, a security detail left behind until the first squads finished and relieved them. We piled through the door into the prefab building and across the red tiled floor.

The cashier looked nervous, even though she wouldn't be the one cooking. Our line ran out the door and would obviously fill every table. "So, what can I get you?" she asked, sounding unsure.

Tyler's a clown. "Meat," she said, pointing at a menu item at random.

"The kilo hippo filet?" the girl asked. "How would you like that cooked?"

"Sure, why not?" Tyler replied, grinning.

While the girl was trying to decide how to reply, Kimbo cut in. Tyler should have taken lessons. "Enough of that," he said. "We want a buffalo, medium rare. Milk it first, then shoot it. A truckload of salad, another of baked potatoes and a drum of sour cream. Start dealing it at the front and keep going until we say we're done." He pushed past Tyler in the tight confines of the railed alley and headed for a seat while I doubled over laughing. Efficient. Rude, but efficient.

The poor girl really looked bothered, as did one of the cooks, leaning over from the grill. I said, "Just start cooking anything. Someone will eat it. Make the portions large and don't worry about excess. We're hungry." It seemed to clarify things for them, and they jumped to it.

Three days later we headed back in. I'd seen enough. Three days may not sound like much, but we slept not at all and were on foot and moving for most of it. There were a few people who couldn't handle the stress and talked too much. I'd ease them out over the next several days.

Shortly after that, I had to admit that we would be on Earth for part of this. While I'd like to not tell anyone, we would be going there and had to fit in. That's easier if you have time to prepare, naturally. Especially for small details like body hair. Most of us remove it. Most Earthies have pelts like apes. Everyone had to flush out nanos or stop shaving.

I went into excruciating detail over our cover. It would only get better as we got practice, but I wanted the beginning to be as flawless as possible as a confidence builder. We pored over maps and tourism guides, local documentaries and entertainment vids. We ate foods local to the areas in question. Everyone took languages from tutors we brought in. I even found five culturalists who were transplanted Earth "citizens." We met with them all day for a few days to refine our accents and usage of slang.

For North America, we hired one Kendra Pacelli. She'd escaped from the UN as a political refugee, and she'd been a UNPF logistics sergeant. I had reservations about a veteran possibly making our cover, and she was astute enough I think she did. But if she did she kept the knowledge to herself, not even telling the two reservists she was involved with, who were carefully and quietly debriefed to determine if she'd leaked. Not a word.

There was nothing easy about this. I had to use people who'd never been on Earth, and I had to ensure they would fit in once they got there. I had to have cut outs, ID and ways to stay in contact set up ahead of time in virgin territory.

One major problem was maintaining contact. The only ways to send messages were by ship or by relayed radio. One was impractical—I couldn't get hard copies or rams to ship crews we could trust to be loyal on a regular basis without falling into a pattern that would blow cover. Transmissions were not possible at all. I'd need a "licensed" transmitter, a license to use that much power, and even with a directional antenna or a coherent beam, there'd be signal leakage. No joy. Nevermind that I'd be transmitting to Freehold registry ships about to jump.

What we could use was the free mail servers on the nets. Those were all tracked by the UN security agencies, but we would only be using each one once. We came up with a list for me to setup at my end for transmission, and they'd be checked automatically at the other end. Another list was those I'd receive on. The messages would have to be encoded into innocuous, plain language messages that wouldn't trigger the security protocols, and each address would only be used once. There was no need to memorize them—I carried them in a comm as a data file. The servers I worked on a strict rotation, and could in fact use whichever was most convenient. It was only the prefix address that would be awkward to memorize: we had to use combinations that sounded normal or at worst as mass-mail "spam" headers, and weren't recently in use. Even if discovered, there'd be no incriminating messages, as all that would be sent in response would be comments like, "Sounds good (or, 'I hope not'). Hope things are well. Stay in touch, my friend." It would be hard to prove espionage over that. Not that the concern was them proving it on us, we were concerned that any agent not be able to prove to his buttonpushing superiors that it was suspicious. As long as the bureaucracy wasn't spooked, we'd be fine. If they got antsy, they'd provide money to do a search for us. As with any war, this was a logistical fight; without properly assigned resources, they'd lose.

We developed a backup plan whereby we actually hid data within the message, by masking the relevant words with an algorithm I memorized. We hoped it wouldn't come down to that. There was also the likely chance that all contact would be lost. "If that happens," Naumann told me, "you continue to gather data, send what you can, and decide on your authority as an independent command what to do. If you can, hurt them enough to make them back off, at least for a while. If that's not possible or won't help us significantly, then evacuate your people off Earth, try to get back here if you can and help us directly. Otherwise, head for a neutral or friendly foreign power and fight a political and clandestine war. But don't give up."

Now, aren't orders like that reassuring? The only thing he didn't add was, "Tuck your head firmly between your legs and kiss your ass goodbye."

We agreed that I might be able to pull a favor from Princess Annette under such circumstances, that Novaja Rossia would probably give us refugee status, and that I should wait a couple of Earth years before going on a smash and destroy. If it came down to that last, we were to leave testimony of our existence and reason for doing so, and hurt them as badly as we could. That of course meant we would die.

The biggest apparent stumbling block is the implanted ID chips everyone on Earth has. The stated purpose of these is to locate missing persons. As very few people actually go missing, it's economically ridiculous. A secondary purpose is to track criminals. Still economically ridiculous. It also has the side effect of making it virtually impossible for dissidents to hold meetings, stage riots, etc, without being located. That is the truly valuable purpose to a society. "Only criminals are afraid to be seen," they say. I can't argue with the logic. I can argue that it is absolutely dehumanizing to do it. I mean, if people generally are so inclined to crime, it is a natural human event, no? If people wish to rebel, you should be asking what's wrong with the society. The monitoring reeks.

Very minor surgery or makeup would get us past the recognition circuits in the cameras. Even if they did spec us, we'd show up as "null, not on file." That wouldn't be noticed, as machines make mistakes all the time. But if we showed as a null *and* the implant didn't read, that would get a reaction. One or the other was necessary. They wouldn't see a pattern on us to arouse suspicion until we bent them over and did them Black Ops style. But walking down the street had just become an issue to deal with.

If we had chips, it was statistically very safe for us. While officially the cameras and the chips and the AI programs and cops watching them stop crime or track down those who would damage the fruits of society, the reality is different. *If* a camera is looking your way, *if* it catches you in the act, *if* an AI or cop is watching and recognizes what you are doing, then you might get a ticket in the mail. If you have connections or money, nothing will happen. If you can bribe or extort the crookedest cops in human space, nothing will happen. If you ignore it, it can be literally hundreds of violations later that anything is done. Only if it's a severe crime will anyone be sent after you, and even then, it has to be pretty severe for them to waste money on a trial. Usually, they'll just lock you in a stinking holding pen for a day or two, feed you revolting food, make you pay outrageous amounts for the "courtesy" of having your vehicle impounded and home searched and valuables stolen, then drop the charges and let you go because they still have a weak case without testimony or a basis for the action.

So we had little to worry about, as we'd be utterly nondescript. We'd toe every line, smile as we did so, and give no reason to be questioned. It would be awful.

But how to find two hundred chips without killing two hundred unattached, uncommitted people and replacing them? That was my problem. Although I'd do that if I had to.

Actually, I didn't need that many. We'd keep most of the team "hidden" for the duration, meaning "Away from observation." As long as they weren't in a large public venue or a metropolitan downtown, they wouldn't be seen by cameras. Unless someone is reported missing or wanted, the chips aren't tracked outside the cities. So we'd keep them in safehouses or rural areas and minimize the risk. I'd want at least two people per detachment to have good cover, and go from there. I'd have to decide as we went if it would be safer to find more chips, or if the risk of someone being discovered would make it inadvisable. Also, we would cover a lot of our most exposed people with petty criminal records. That would make them part of the scenery, and less suspect as infiltrators. It doesn't pay to be too squeaky clean.

My initial training plans had to change, based in part on the culturalists' input. I'd been pushing physical arts for combat insertions. I realized that was not entirely appropriate. Certainly, some of our people would be jumping, climbing, shooting and otherwise acting as soldiers, but most of us would be acting as local nerds. We dug up the files we needed and started studying bookkeeping, accounting, procedures and protocols. We all had in depth briefings in law, because there were so many things we took for granted that were restricted on Earth. They actually required government certification to operate a normal vehicle, obtain industrial tools and materials, even to get basic medicines. No wonder the place was a screwed up nightmare. Then there were the taxes and fees to pay for this. They even taxed shit. Not directly, but there was a tax on the water and sewer service, even though a theoretically private company handled the task. Yes, they recycled it for minerals, energy and fertilizer, just as we do. Yes, they then sold it. So why tax it? Apparently, just because they could. There was even a news load where some mouthpiece for policy recommended a tax on something, I didn't catch what, on the grounds that "it's one of the few things not yet taxed for revenue." In other words, "gee, we haven't screwed anyone over this so far, let's start now!"

The only historical parallel I could find was to ancient prisons, where the incarceree or his family were required to pay for the privilege of being abused under guard instead of killed outright. Never in my worst nightmares in training had I foreseen being dragged down because I didn't fill out the enemy's admin properly. Nor will I bore you with the petty details. It went on for weeks, every layer of stupidity revealing another. We'd have to wangle supplies, tools, everything we needed clandestinely and illegally, hide the operation and existence thereof, and especially any residue. We were going to need to build lots of heavy weapons on site while appearing to do nothing.

It was, quite literally, to be an infiltration into a prison, then the instigation of the largest prison riot in history.

Eventually, we were gigged to go. Everyone was trained to a level I considered acceptable if not ideal, the little gear we would take was ready, the administrative details like wills and such done. Time to kiss the world goodbye and hope it would still be here upon return. The only minor detail left was how to slip 200 people into a societal prison without being seen. That wasn't solely my problem. I'd been working on it for weeks with the Special Projects people. I truly love those devious, scrounging little bastards. Give one of them cr500 and a morning and he'll bring you five fake IDs, employment and banking histories for each and a couple of bombs. It's a talent.

Meantime, as a unit bonding ritual I planned a feast for everyone. We were looking at what might be our last decent meal in life. It would certainly be our last meal at home for a couple of years. I spent some Residents' fees to set the team up right.

One of the best places I've found to eat is not one of the headliners in town. In fact, it's reached through an alley. Phill's Mediterranean Grill doesn't advertise. Word of mouth keeps the place packed and a line waiting that sometimes extends out the alley into the street. They don't take reservations. I called Phill. He answered, round faced and sweaty under his traditional chef's hat, spatula in hand. He's the best kind of restaurateur, who does a goodly amount of the work himself, from setup to cooking to cleanup. "Ken!" he said. "It's been what? A year?"

"About that. How are things?"

"Busy," he said.

"Busy is good. Can you do me a favor on reservations?"

"Sure," he agreed. I'm on the special list. I did him a favor once and he's been very good to me since. And I really appreciate it. Good food always counts highly with me. He paid me off for the favor (heck, I did it for fun. He doesn't owe me, and he knows it. He's just a good guy) years ago. But he keeps paying.

"I need to bring an entire unit in. Two hundred people."

"TWO HUNDRED?" he asked, goggling. "I can barely seat

that many." The camera followed him while he turned and stirred food.

"I need them all there at once, not spread out. Can we do it?" I asked.

"I guess I can close around six that day and let you in at seven, then reopen as you start to leave," he said, nodding.

"Thanks, Phill. It'll be worth your while. How's Ioday night?"

"Okay," he agreed. "Will the time work for you?"

"Works fine. Thanks. See you then," I said.

"Bye," he said and went back to cooking.

Most of the kids had never been to Phill's. They were in for a treat. He starts at the bottom with chicken, lamb or beef marinated and roasted or skewered and kabobed with pickled beans and vegetables, seasoned rice, feta and peppers washed down with sekanjabin or strawberry daiquiris, and goes all the way up to lobster drowned in wine or whole fresh roasted lamb shanks with cilantro and pepper. Fish, crabs, occasional duck or pheasant are there, too. The servings are generous, the food is never less than excellent and usually perfect, the prices very reasonable and the service can't be beat.

As I walked in, here came the service. Kirsten is young, energetic and lovely. She smiles lots, pays attention to the customers, and was wearing an outfit that made her easy to find and guaranteed her attention. It was black, had no back and not much front, a skirt short enough to be a tube top and lots of her tanned, toned skin, tattoos, liquid brown eyes and blonde hair. She wore little jewelry. She didn't need it. "Hey!" she said. "You're just in time. I'm leaving in two weeks."

"Oh?" I said. "Where?"

"Basic training. I enlisted."

"To do what?" I asked.

"Jump Point Traffic Controller," she said. Apparently, she was even brighter than she looked. That's no skate job.

"Good luck," I said. I didn't want to talk further; I had a cover to keep. She nodded thanks and started the menus coming as people trickled in. I ogled her. She was well worth ogling. Slimmer than most but nicely proportioned. Perfect for reminding most of the men and a few of the women why we should do our jobs and come back—to protect people like her.

I had portabella mushroom ravioli, pork souvlaki and a bean salad to warm up, then the lamb shanks with the herbed potatoes. We plowed through enough food for twice our number, buried a few cakes and pies for dessert, and paid attention to the show. Kirsten's enough to trigger fantasies, but Dagmar...

Dagmar does traditional belly dancing in untraditional costumes. She's an Amazon elf—thin and tall, taller than I. Her garish costume of scarlet and yellow chiffon, lace and silk revealed most of her when she moved, covered her legs when she stood still. But when she stood still it was usually to flex and roll her abdominal muscles, first up and down, then left and right. Those would be the only part of her that moved when she did that, except for her breasts, heaving from exertion, while the beads on the edges of her outfit jingled in perfect waves. Men watching her get instant hints as to what *else* she might be able to do with muscle control like that, and start groaning. I find her exciting myself, and I have to laugh at the way otherwise totally controlled people melt in her presence.

The next performer was Dave Frieman. Luckily, he didn't have to try to compete with her looks. His hook is his deep, strong voice and guitar strumming that looks chaotic but is very controlled. He started off with his traditional, "Hi, I'm Dave and I'm a musician," to which the regulars reply, "Hi, Dave," just like at a 12-Step meeting. It gets funnier after that. Most of my kids seemed to be sophisticated enough to get traditional music, and some of them really enjoyed it. He even moved a few of his recordings.

When we were done, I peeled off Cr6000 in cash for Phill, added a grand for Kirsten and her two assistants for carrying the load and slipped Dave two hundred and Dagmar five hundred from the unit, as well as all the individual tips she was getting. She bowed, hugged me and left a sweaty imprint I could smell all night, then passed the money back to her drummers and bouzouki player.

After that, we started leaving in small groups. Yes, it was fairly obvious to a trained observer that we were military. But I wanted to at least try to hide the fact that we were out as a unit. As we drifted, it could be just a party for a retirement or anniversary. If we all moved as a unit, it would be obvious that something was up.

I had booked everyone rooms at various inns, from the Hilton to the Bon Place to the Crown. Basic rooms, but at nice hotels. I'd let everyone draw a thousand for the evening, to gamble, drink, dance and pay for some of the best escorts in town, and made sure to call several of those escorts to let them know to expect some business. I hired one myself; Isabella is a very flexible and exotically dark young lady with quite a repertoire. She left exhausted; I had a lot of frustration to burn off. I don't dance anymore unless I have to but I did check around the clubs to make sure there weren't any major problems. The only minor problem was a pickpocket who tried to lift a wallet from one of my kids, who caught the pressure, turned and flattened him against the wall with his nose mashed to paste. Sergeant Dixon suggested that he wouldn't press a case if the wannabe freelance Marxian would slink off and get his nose fixed quietly, City Safety decided that any claims would be handled without their assistance, and we all left that area post haste.

Our night of revelry cost the Freehold Residents Cr340,000 for my two hundred killers. Considering our training budget, it was about a day's expense. I hope you who live here won't begrudge us a little relief from the most intense training ever devised. In the end, you got your money's worth.

CHAPTER 18

The infiltration was a bitch. Two hundred Operatives. Even with good cover, that's a lot of insertions and a lot of room for error. And one error would be all it would take.

I decided to go in in four stages. First would be our twenty-six solo sleepers. They were going in "legitimately" with various jobs for Earth employers or as contractors to Earth employers. I just wish we could have gotten more in that way. They trickled in on commercial flights, with passports that proudly stated "Freehold of Grainne." Actually, our "passports" aren't really such. We have no government agency in charge of such things. So the standard document is purchased from one of our national banks, then after being matched with your photo and thumbprint (we don't require DNA, retinae or any other crap), you take it to be officially recognized by a Citizen. It causes some hassle with certain other governments, notably those on a certain planet with a name that starts with "E" and ends in "arth." Suspicious bunch. Even sworn ID doesn't make them happy.

There were no repercussions three months after they'd trickled in. That meant I would go next, along with my Continent Element Leaders and our assistants, using the best false ID we could find. After us would come 114 others, with fifty to come later in what would amount to a combat insertion.

At least I got to travel in comfort. I had only a crappy ID right now, that of an Earth businessman who we'd blackmailed into going along with our program. Seemed he owed a bunch of taxes on Earth, and had a substantial smuggling operation going. Neither of those is of interest to the Freehold, except that it was handy leverage to swap with him. He might eventually get homesick, but he only had to stay out of sight for the duration of my trip, because I would swap ID again once I got there. After that, if he dared show up, any fallout would be on him. We didn't tell him that yet. It might be useful later.

I went first to Breakout Station, Jump Point One. It's the direct route to Earth. "He" was booked on a berth aboard Earth TranSpace's *Shining Star*. It docked directly, no transport needed, and I would simply swim in like a moderately experienced civilian and hand over my ticket. So the theory went, anyway.

I had four days to kill at Breakout, first. I'd never had the chance to actually look around, even after seven trips through it. I decided to be a tourist. It would help me relax.

I shouldn't have bothered.

There are bad parts of the Freehold. The cheaper docks and inner passages of Breakout are some of those parts. It comes with the relaxed society.

There's always stuff being smuggled through our system. It seems odd, but follow: We don't care what comes in, so there's no need to hide manifests, or even bother with manifests. However, a lot of stuff is shipped through without ever officially entering our system. Much of that is illegal either at source or destination. So the shippers thereof like to keep a low profile. Meanwhile, various national police agencies are set up to watch for them. There are paid informants looking for info to sell to the highest bidder. Blackmail, extortion and murder are quite common here, "common" meaning about 3% as bad as in major Earth cities. I looked around me, compared that to what I could expect, and shivered.

Then, there are the itinerants. There are stranded spacers looking for work, layabouts who drink, smoke or wire themselves into bankruptcy then grab another menial job to get a few more credits to repeat the process, refugees from elsewhere who've heard about how great the Freehold is and move, without planning what to do when they get to the Land of Milk and Honey. They become said layabouts; petty criminals if they weren't already; cheap sex workers, some of them not checked for diseases at system entry because they never officially entered, who aren't very good and bring down both the price and average quality throughout the station; or they become beggars and whine about how unfair it is they were taken in for free with no questions asked but not given all the benefits of the systems they were trying to escape. It's really not worth leaving the official public levels, no matter how much they may cost. It's an example of how one gets what one pays for, on an asymptotic scale. Believe me when I say the bottom end isn't worth it.

Also remember that any station has stray rats and cats and we don't have health inspectors for restaurants. Every dive is "Certified," but unless you know who certified them, it simply means they paid some money to someone. Raw capitalism on the edge of society is not for the beginning tourist. I went back to my pricey and paid-for suite near the surface and stayed there until ship call.

Somewhere, the dice were tossed and came up in my favor. I swam aboard unchallenged and unbothered, other than having to show my ID to the crewman on duty. I scanned clean and headed aft.

My stateroom was inboard down a passageway lined with plain gray polymer. It was just big enough for a single bunk with emergency harness, an emgee shower stall and toilet and a comm. The comm was a joke. Being Earth-based, it was free. Being Earth-based, its access was crap. Nothing "objectionable," "dangerous," "malicious," etc. is allowed. On paper, the UN has free speech. It's subject to "sensible" limitations. So as long as you don't say anything nasty about other races, religions, creeds, the political party currently running the show, figures with enough political clout to complain, anything to do with rebellion, anything unpleasant about a government agent or agency, anything to do with weapons, explosives, hazardous chemicals, keypass forgery, comm cracking or encryption decoding, among others, you can say, print, or broadcast anything you want, subject to licensing agreements with your service provider, the UN Communications Authority and any UN agency that decides it has jurisdiction over you.

Hell, that was everything I'd based my life on. I couldn't say a damned thing.

The "entertainment" available on this terminal wasn't, so I played mind games, using it as a chance to rehearse the Evasion and Escape techniques to stop one from going mad as a POW, which I just might need. That task was made tougher because the bed really was comfortable, and easier because the food was about average for Earth, or slightly better than combat rations served amid greasy, smoking, flyblown bodies. Luckily, it was only one day to jump and ten days to Earth orbit. I stayed quiet and pretended to work in my cabin. That was normal for Earthies, so no one noticed. Nor did they notice the few packages of civilized food I'd brought with me. They'd be my last for a long time or forever.

I'd been surprised that Immigration wasn't taken care of as soon as we entered Sol System. It wasn't taken care of in orbit, either. No, every habitat and each major port on Earth each have their own Immigration office, where one would suffice if placed right. I won't complain. We exploited that weakness to slip a few people in.

So I transshipped to a shuttle, also clean and neat if old, with gee couches at least ten years out of date. The ride down was professional if a bit bumpy. We mated with the service tube and I stood. The gravity was a bit low. The air was rather thick and pungent, but I decided it would improve once I got out. I joined the shuffling heel-to-toe throng and made my way out. Directly ahead was my first gauntlet. I took a deep breath of thick, strong air and walked forward, smiling as a returning resident should.

I was near the front of the pack and handed over my perfectly forged North American passport to the nearest agent. At least I hoped it was perfectly forged. There wasn't anywhere I could escape if caught. I ran my right hand and its implanted ID chip past the scanner. No beeps or lights. Good.

I nodded as the agent took my booklet. He glanced inside and said, "Hello, Mister Lesce. How was your trip?" It was a formality, and a test.

I replied, "Trip was okay, I guess. I'm just glad to be down."

"Yeah, there's nowhere like Earth," he said, flipping pages and touching every fourth or fifth to light up the coding for a closer look.

Thank God and Goddess for that, I thought. "No, there isn't," I said.

"Anything to declare?" he asked.

"Nope. I never do," I replied.

"I see that," he said, nodding but with a slight frown. Shit, now would *not* be a good time for them to decide to investigate. A good smuggler would have brought gifts through now and then, and occasionally paid a duty. Not this idiot. We'd caught him and we weren't even concerned about the issue. Earth was going to get him sooner or later.

"Well, welcome home," my warder said.

"Thanks," I replied noncommittally, while grabbing my passport and leaving quickly.

I knew I was on Earth as soon as I entered the terminal. I started seeing porkers.

Now, I know some people have weight problems. Fine. Ten kilos, twenty, even twenty five over "norm" is not uncommon, and not necessarily unhealthy. Some people can't exercise, some have hormonal issues, it happens. My fetish is for lean, powerful women, but I've seen some very attractive women who were rounder and soft. Well and good. Some few people exceed that for debilitating medical problems, and it's more common in emgee habitats where exercise is damned near impossible. You can see that they are either ill, or that they have a functioning musculature underneath the excess mass acquired from environmental factors.

On Earth, you find brontosauri. Beached whales. Gastropods. Self-propelled stomachs. We're talking fifty, a hundred, even two hundred kilos overweight. It is obscene. They're huge, they're ponderous, and the body's systems simply can't keep up with the strain—they reek of ketones and other aromatics that are fermenting inside them. The fabric it takes to clothe one of them would build enough tents for an entire Bedouin village.

It's worse: they're considered to be "differently abled." That's a bullshit word that means "*dis*abled." They can't do what most people can (like fit through doors), so they get exemptions. They're given priority parking so they don't "strain" themselves, thereby getting less exercise than they do already. They get wheelchairs, and powered ones at that, so they don't even have to work their flabby arms. Businesses have to provide special chairs for them to sit on, because regular ones break. They need taller chairs, because they can't heave themselves up out of regular seating.

There was a whole family of them sitting in the first restaurant outside the gate. Their problem was obvious: they were slopping like pigs. I spend close to three Earth hours a day at hard exercise, carry massive amounts of stuff constantly and move around on foot most of the day. *I* could not eat at a sitting what the poor little kid sentenced to live in this family was shoveling into his gut. His gut, I might add, that he had to reach over to get to the food. His gut that caused him to throw his shoulders back and bend his spine to maintain balance. He wasn't yet six Earth years, and his life was ruined. The only "medical" problem I could see here was that they hadn't had their jaws wired shut.

The myth is that it's a "genetic" disorder, and we should feel sorry for these poor, sick people. Well, I don't and I'll tell you why. You find them virtually only on Earth. Specifically, in North America. If it were truly genetic, you'd find them localized to one specific isolated group, and North America is a hodgepodge of immigrants from elsewhere. Or else it would be universal—we have millions of people of North American extraction in the Freehold. We don't have even one percent of the blubber-laden hippos I saw on Earth. So it's not genetic, it's cultural. It's true of the best-fed, best-gadgeted, laziest society on the planet. They are disgusting slugbodies because the only exercise they get is feeding their chops. The best thing the environmentalists could do would be to make them lumber on treadmills to reduce their mass and generate electrical power. Sweating off a few gallons of aromatic hydrocarbons would increase their lifespans, too.

I looked at a man, if you could call it that, packing away just for lunch more calories than Deni and I together would consume after an assault exercise with full gear, and wanted to heave at the sight of his pallid, quivering, bucolic slushpile of a corpse.

I could render him down for enough fat for a hundred liters of soap and a few hundred old-style tallow candles. His skin would make drumheads for an entire percussion section of an orchestra. Never mind the Bedouin village; I've seen regimental headquarters based out of tents smaller than his pants. My sick mind had a momentary vision of him and his roly-poly wife slapping meat as they bumped uglies, if they could get close enough to actually mate, and I turned away, feeling ill. That was how my trip started. It went downhill from there.

I joined a seething morass of drab, wretched humanity who were all buttoned and tied and zipped into shapeless clothes, and headed for the outside. A bare flicker of my eyes to keep alert to my surroundings brought home to me the overwhelming sameness of everyone. Similar modes of dress, makeup, accoutrements, shoes, reading material and expression. It was like one of those bad movies where a hive intelligence takes over and controls everyone, only here it was an *un*intelligence. The dull looks betrayed little intellect, and those few who had any were no doubt hiding it.

Before I realized, I was outside. A deep breath did not help. I don't know how anyone figures the atmosphere of Earth is safe to breathe, because it's revolting. Air should have a bare tang of ozone after a storm, the hint of flowers and trees later, the rich odor of warm, healthy soil, and maybe a suggestion of nearby human activity.

What I got was a lungful of crap. There were particulates, from what I'm not sure, since IC engines have been banned for centuries and even turbines are restricted. Maybe it was just dust churned up by the herd. I restrained myself from coughing although my lungs burned. The stench of industry and city was obscene. The sky was murky, and it wasn't from fog. Note that this is despite the massive pollution control regulations they have.

I found a public phone and called for a reservation at a sleep cheap. It wasn't that hard to find a phone at the spaceport. Elsewhere, it could be a bitch. It was assumed that everyone carried a personal phone, at least in North America. It's only because you can't take electronics aboard craft or into government buildings that they have public ones handy.

I took a cab. I had to. Despite the megablocks of huge scrapers and habitat buildings on Earth, the ports are kept separate, just as they are anywhere. So my first intrusion was fairly normal in that regard. The cab (automatic, no driver) pulled out, locked into the pattern and cruised to the highway, then sped up and headed for town. Then I was trying not to gawk like a yokel.

Jefferson is near two million people. It's the third largest single city on Grainne, though the sprawl along the west coast and around the bay where Jefferson is are populous but broad. Taniville, our largest, is almost five million with suburbs. Washington-Baltimore is near ten million people. I knew it intellectually, but it was still a shock to see. Greater New York was near seventy million, and I could only wonder what it looked like.

Ahead of me, buildings rose from the sky. It wasn't that murky, I decided, just hazy. But the buildings were huge blocks. Close to 400 meters square or more, some close to 1000 meters tall, they were squat and blocky, unlike the delicate spires in Jefferson. They were simply storage boxes for population. But they were impressive. I lost count at twenty as the cab took the long curve toward the wretched hive.

I was glad most of our ops would be outside those edifices. It was too damned easy to block them off. And in fact, that would be one of our tactics for the battle. We'd block people in and drive them into panicking. Then they'd commit random destruction for us. I made a lot of mental notes as I traveled.

Soon enough, the Sun set behind me. It was a rather boring sunset. Sure, the sky darkened and got pinkish in the west, but there was none of the brilliant blues and violets, the scorching ruddy oranges and radiant yellow clouds we get. And that star is just dull and yellow. I see why our first settlers were so enthused, despite the higher gravity and more variable seasons. Or maybe because of them. Our climate is more vigorous, more exciting, more vital than Earth's.

The cab pulled off the highway, switched to a local controller and slid into the pack of vehicles on the streets. They moved in synchronized blocks, bare centimeters apart on the main thoroughfares. I understood why they had the control systems they did. No human could handle that crush of vehicles efficiently. So when we took out that control, it would be an instant block to escape. We'd have them bottled up.

I was thinking that it couldn't be this easy. No one would make a system that was so vulnerable to attack. Then my training caught back up with me. This was just a larger scale, but people are still idiots when taken in quantity. This wasn't going to be a hard job at all.

The buildings out here were older, smaller, no more than three or four per 160 meter block. The blocks here were still based on the old "mile," which is a bit more than 1600 meters. so major blocks are a mile, the ones in between are 0.1 miles. All my studying was roaring through my brain. It was as if I were split in two—one of me present, the other watching the vid and analyzing.

So I looked at these buildings, mostly with attached rather than floating signs, the signs of various types—self lit, remote lit, holographic, translucent—and often at odds with building architecture. It was a slightly older area. I saw my hotel and got my bag ready.

The cab pulled over and stopped. I got out and was under an awning. There was a security guard there, and he was one of the elite; he was armed. He had a stun baton and a single-shot stickyweb gun. His physique and mental acuity made his proficiency subject to debate, but it was one more reminder of the weird place I was. The message here was "You're not safe, you need protection. But that protection can't be competent or armed, because it might threaten someone. We don't trust him, even though he's here to protect you." I just nodded at him, he nodded back, and I walked inside.

He was the only person visible on the premises. I checked in automatically, was issued a slip with a keycode, and went to my room. It was a box with a bed and a shelf, the everpresent comm with minimal net access, a small bathroom stall that was adequate and sanitary but hardly pleasant. That was it. No window, no features. I slipped out of my shoes, lay down on the bed, and left my bag at hand. I would need to nap now so I could be up early for my appointment.

CHAPTER 19

Citizen Ambassador Janine Maartens had wangled the slot on Earth. That was good for me for several reasons—personal knowledge of the person, she had good capabilities, was practical and would be easier to beg, cajole and/or threaten for the things I'd need.

Her office was done in earthtones again, warm and pleasant and soft. It was a nice suite, spacious but with enough seating for functions. Her comm was properly secured, I noted with approval, and the door was locked. I was sitting on her couch when she walked into her office, the door in front of me and between me and the desk. "Good morning, Citizen," I cheerfully said.

She whirled, reaching for her pistol while yelping in surprise. "God and Goddess, Chinran, don't do that again!" she snapped as she recognized me, while lowering her posture. "How the blazes did you get in here?"

"Professional secret, ma'am," I told her. The security was pretty good. I'd almost given up and used the rear service gate, but had finally slipped in. They almost caught me, too. That wouldn't have been too problematical; I knew the Operatives assigned there, after all, as well as several of the others. Then again, that was part of the reason I'd snuck in. I didn't need rumors of my presence floating around.

Shaking her head, she said, "You are really something. What exactly, I'm not sure. Now, what's going on?"

"I can't tell you exactly. But is my exchange ready?"

"Yes, he is," she said. "Shall we do this here and now then?"

"I'd appreciate it," I agreed.

She called in the staff physician, who didn't know me, was told to forget I existed, and to forget the whole morning while he was at it. Also along was a defector.

Theodore Marquette was about my size and looks, which was a help. He'd hinted in the right places that he didn't like the system he lived under, and wanted out. Arrangements were made. He would leave Earth for the Freehold, then to Caledonia, while I took his place.

He sat down silently, as he'd been ordered, and the doc pulled his implant locator, sterilized the case of the tiny black bead, and inserted it into my hand. I forewent the anesthesia as a psychological ploy. It hurt intensely, but the expressions on their faces as my expression didn't twitch gave me the opening I needed. The surgeon left at once, and I turned to Marquette.

I said, "I want you to remember that if you let this slip, the UN will be after you as much as after me. As a defector involved in espionage, you can imagine how angry they'll be."

He nodded. The government-as-the-omnipresent-deity mindset was still with him. He'd be some months losing it, and I was confident he'd say nothing in the interim. It was if . . . when . . . the war started that there might be a risk. That's why we'd arranged him a job in a remote habitat of Caledonia. It paid well, was away from anyone likely to notice, would help him feel secure, and made it hard for him to talk.

With little else to say, we slipped him enough cash to make him nervous all over again, and shoved him out to depart with a courier who was another Operative. We'd use a lot of Operatives and Blazers for this job, but only certain ones would be staying behind.

I turned back to Maartens and said, "You'll understand in a few months, Citizen. I'm sorry I can't be more informative than that."

"I'll deal with it, 'Mister Marquette,'" she said with a wry smile.

"I'll have the rest of your profile changed accordingly in a few weeks. Try not to get arrested between now and then."

"Count on it, ma'am," I said. "And here's a shopping list. You'll be contacted as indicated on the codes. Please use this hardcopy and do not file it elsewhere. It stays in your code case for destruction if threatened."

"Very well. Anything else, sir?" she asked in half humor, half bother.

"That's it. I'll be leaving now. Could you make sure I have an unobstructed trip to the loading door?"

"Since it will get you out of my hair faster, yes," she said.

I left.

That night, I stayed in Marquette's apartment. His neighbors, as with everybody, took no notice. It was almost impossible to be noticed here. Even if people did see something suspicious, they were so afraid of either revenge when you got out of jail after a week or two (why bother detaining people if you aren't going to either rehabilitate them or keep them away from society?) or that the cops would pick on *them* for some violation that they'd not complain. You could be loud, rude, violent, even reckless with fire or vehicles and not a word was said. It was downright dangerous on Earth. I was lucky he had a "nice" apartment. And I was lucky they wouldn't notice my long absences. This was looking easier all the time. All I had to do was keep quiet until everyone was here, and get to work.

I couldn't speak highly of the apartment. It was allegedly a "pretty nice" area, he'd told us. Either he had screwed up standards, or North America did. "Pretty nice" apartments don't reek of garbage and urine in the elevators. Any holes punched in the walls should be repaired so as not to show. Insects and other pests should be rare. The appliances should be less than 20 years old and the plumbing should deliver fresh, clear water without texture and flush everything away the first time.

I could have called him to ask. He was still at the Embassy, but would be moved out in a day or two. I'd feel safer then. Meantime, it wasn't an important enough issue to call about. The call might be traced. Besides, I'm an Operative. I've slept worse places.

The rest of the advance party of the North American section slipped in over the next few days. Each day, I would stop at a library or café and check that day's prearranged comm address for messages. Tyler checked in as a returning college student. The actual student from Eastern Capital University on Grainne had been offered a chance to do geological studies at a remote site, and was whisked off after a note to her parents not to expect her. Tyler had a duplicate chip and had made clandestine flight arrangements. It was another case of risk. Her family didn't expect her home or to call often, the government had no reason to expect her on Earth, but also no reason to look for her or notice the discrepancy.

Frank showed up a couple of days later. He was replacing a single businessman who we had made politely but firmly disappear with more offers of money and unsubtle threats. Our intel gophers were trying to quietly change at least the images on file, if not retinae and DNA. That was another mixed problem. DNA on file would make us safer in the interim. It would also make us easier to track if our cover was blown.

A mass-mail spam came in, with hidden codes that announced the arrival of Irina Belinitsky in the Russian Alliance of the European Federal Union. Pao Chan arrived in United China in the Greater Asian Union and checked in. Sylvestre Vargas reported from Rio de Janeiro in the Estados Unidos de Sudamerica. Peter Hathaway mailed from Johannesburg in the Commonwealth of African States. My old training buddy Tom Parker pinged me from Melbourne, Australasian Republic. All my commanders were in place in a month, the rest would follow. I knew only the real names of those personnel, would never know their covers. I could at most betray one squad if caught, and after we got established and split up, I'd be able to betray only four individuals.

Being on Earth was only the first step. We needed to set up legitimate lifestyles to blend in, so we could move around and acquire more assets. Certainly, I had a stack of anonymous cash cards I could use. If I got caught, those would get me arrested. With a job and business, I could accomplish much more than as a parasite.

The experts will tell you that Earth has two classes—the rulers and the ruled. That's not quite true. There is a middle class. It's small, hard to get into and harder to remain a member of, but it puts one above the peasants, yielding a better character of treatment from thugs and wardens, and attracts much less notice than the upper class. Our goal was to be average. In plainness there is privacy.

Several of us were setting up a personal warehousing business in the suburbs of Washington. It gave us jobs, a home and hopefully invisibility. Other teams were scattered about with other covers. I liked this one, because with a few keystrokes, we could define a rental unit as "occupied," and any investigator would have to get another warrant in order to search it. It might only slow them down a few minutes, but wars are won on those few minutes. Stuff could be "stolen" or "abandoned" and put to use by us, with some level of deniability if found. As we'd be bringing in a lot of stuff, it was nearly ideal. Search us and find nothing. It was all elsewhere. We even officially rented space to ourselves at both our facility and others, leaving nothing incriminating in those.

I looked at our home to be in Winchester, Virginia. It wasn't much. The outside was graffitied with the illiterate scribbles that are the street gang equivalent of animals pissing to mark their territory. The myth is that they're "codes," but our cryptologists have analyzed them and come up blank. They're just the pathetic scrawls of illiterate fucking punks with no respect for anything including themselves. They weren't even particularly artistic; they were just vandalism. A perfect cover for us.

The building was no real style. It was blocky, and had been a warehouse or office or other nameless creature in its previous life. It would be a warehouse again now.

What we had planned would have been impossible ten years before. Until very recently, it had been the case that eight multinational and about fifty regional corporations ran almost the entire infrastructure of North America and Europe, and eventually all of Earth. It had started in the 20th/21st centuries, with encroaching bureaucracy making it increasingly hard for small businesses to operate. With crystal clear antilogic, the neofeudalists ("Democrats," they were called at the time) demanded even more government standards and bureaucracy to "control the corporate interests." Each succeeding addition to the adminwork made it that much harder for a small enterprise, until there were contractors to handle taxes for them, payroll (because wages are taxed and special deductions are taken out and the employer then taxed again. I aced strategic calculus and this idiocy makes my head hurt), employee issues, hiring, dismissal, inventory (which is also taxed), regulation compliance . . . It took either ten employees full-time to handle the crap for a "small" business, or ten contracted personnel or offices. This of course meant no small operation could succeed. All the companies providing that contracted support eventually were absorbed into the conglomerates themselves, and conspired to make it even harder for independent businesses.

Then they went after the family-owned businesses, who did everything themselves, by cranking up the number of audits and size of penalties. The few thousand marks one would be fined for a sub-par electrical connection, for example, wasn't even a blip to one of the sub-sub-sub-sub-corporations of Citi, for example, but would utterly break a family operation. For some reason, despite the procrustean "equality" the neofeudalists pushed, these fines were not put on a sliding scale as were taxes and rates. After all, that small operation was a "corporate interest" and had to be reined in. An Us vs. Them siege-state mentality existed to claim that workers were the pure, sweet holders of civilization, and those who employed them were ravening ghouls. This mindset was encouraged by "unions" (akin to our professional guilds, except that membership was mandatory and they themselves swung huge political influence and investment portfolios to boost their income, which they justified as "diversifying assets"), and made things even worse. Small operations and individuals were thus made the enemies of success, and blindly went along to hobble themselves further and widen the gap.

Enough of the history of human insanity. That had been, and still mostly was the condition of Earth economics. No wonder nothing gets done on time and their products are pure shit.

Recently, however, a tiny counterswing pushed the notion that small development was good for a nation. They didn't point fingers at the Freehold, but we were clearly the ideal, although they'd never get rid of the government standards that of course had to exist in any moral, modern, progressive, right-thinking society, but perhaps with proper encouragement from the government these small businesses could create a few jobs here and there where nothing else was working, on an experimental basis, of course. They even offered loans to that effect, loans that were necessary, considering the massive overhead of dealing with bureaucrats who found such things offensive to good order. I didn't want to think about the internal wars between the bureaucrats trying to enable business and those trying to suppress it. I was surprised they weren't taking out assassinations on each other. Then I read about "workplace violence" and I wondered if it weren't happening. Either that, or being a less than totally dominated slave allowed the psyche to reach a level of discontent that resulted in oscillations that ended only with a stabbing spree.

God and Goddess, this place was a shithole.

My predecessor (Marquette) had, at our suggestion, started the necessary paperwork to create such an independent business entity. We would use that as a cover, and the entire loan amount would be used to run the business. It was accepted that it might legitimately take a loss for up to three years before showing a profit, at which time if we weren't a review would be conducted to determine if we had the right to try for two more years. That would be enough time for us to either conduct our mission, evacuate, or infiltrate deeper. I could only imagine how discovery of us would "prove" the danger of private business and thus smash any future hope of anyone escaping the utopia of working for the government or a multi-quadrillion mark megacorp.

The initial inspections had been done, the plans approved, and we got to work. "Doug" (Kimbo) had his lists ready, and called in the contract construction crews to build our warehousing operation. While that happened visibly, underneath we went out to acquire tools legal and illegal, parts and supplies, and prepare to work beneath, between and behind the official work. It took twelve weeks, with me sitting in "Marquette's" apartment, still fearing discovery by his neighbors. I needn't have worried. The mindset on Earth was as I said; not to talk to anyone one didn't have to, not to interact with neighbors lest one find a flaw and report you to the government, not to question anything. I found this out first hand, when a robbery took place in broad daylight in a convenience store.

Two punks came running out to alarm squawks, carrying illegally imported knives, and took off down the street, climbing into a car and rolling off. They didn't even try to hurry. I watched from afar, wondering when anyone was going to stop them. No one did. I heard mutters of "Where's the cops?" "Why aren't they stopping that?" and similar comments, as if it was up to someone else to deal with the problem. I wondered if these people expected someone to "do something" about the problem of unwiped anuses. I decided I didn't want to know.

But ironically, it did make me feel safer in my current location.

We called our contractors to rough everything in. They were paid by a combination of government grants, government loans, investment capital from "my" savings, and, for the important parts, cash in untraceable low value cards. The initial building inspection, which was actually the third, there having been a "preinspection" and a "starting inspection," took place without us present, the general contractor explaining everything. That way, we couldn't be questioned. Everything was official, and to question us would require that the inspector find fault with the plans that were already approved by his department. That does happen. However, the contractor dealt with this often and had his own lawyers to keep the inspectors honest and him employed. My presence wouldn't help and could hurt.

Eventually, that work was finished. We then moved in and did our own share of work, which was technically illegal. We had things we didn't want anyone to see until later, however. Kimbo supervised. He didn't enjoy it, but he got it done. Then we had to face our own ordeal.

The building inspector arrived at ten. I was glad to see him. Really. Mister Gerry Hanaka, Winchester City Building Inspection Division, was unremarkable. He wore a better than average suit, was neat and clean, slim enough but with the soggy muscle and pallid skin typical on Earth, and carried a small doccase as well as a comm. I stood and shook hands and he said, "Mister Marquette?"

"Yes, I am," I said. "Where should we start?"

"Oh, I already looked at the outside," he said. "There's a couple of cracks in the foundation you need to seal, but they aren't serious." He was a helpful type. I wasn't yet sure if that was good or bad. Deni handed him coffee and a pastry, and smiled just enough to hint that bribes other than cash might be available, if called for.

Kimbo went with us as facility engineer, and I'd ordered him to speak only when spoken to. Yes, I trusted him, but this was my op. We started on the ground floor and worked our way up. Hanaka was quite observant, and glanced around. "What's the length on those bolts?" he asked, pointing at the floor studding that supported the dividing walls.

"Hunnerd fi'ty millimeter," Kimbo replied. "Want me to pull one?"

"No, that's fine," Hanaka replied. He kept walking, ticking off notes. Occasionally, he'd ask a question, and Kimbo or I would give him the correct answer, studied from the same reference he carried.

"Is your vehicle door in compliance with Ninety-Seven Dash R?" He asked, indicating the rollup door tenants would drive through to unload.

"Impact resistance rating Z, channel material three millimeters, double sensor beams, self-resetting code box, double rack mechanism, emergency release on each side, " I said, smiling with faint smugness. That was better than code by one level on each requirement. "I take my customers' safety seriously."

Hanaka smiled back. We were making his job easy, and that had scored us points. Now to put him to use. "Everything looks good down here," he said. "Let's see your upstairs." He indicated the freight elevator, and checked it over. He might or might not ask to see inside before we were done, but it was all squeaky clean, too.

"Certainly," I said. "Although we aren't finished up there yet," I admitted.

"Not finished?" he asked. "What are you still doing?"

"Oh, the document storage is done," I said as we entered the elevator. "But we're still working on the back half, which will be offices and a break room. That's why the front office is so cluttered." The front office was "cluttered" only by the standards of a sergeant instructor. He looked faintly impressed yet again.

We wandered around upstairs. There was some rough framing, which we'd left on purpose so he could see how sturdy it was—and it was. We were serious about the job. "Offices here and here, break room over here," I said, indicating a larger area. "Restroom here, we already have the fittings in, and that back there will be closed off," I said, pointing at the back half.

He frowned just barely. I made a signal behind my back to Kimbo, who said, "Uh, boss, I need to get back down for that dolly delivery."

"Go ahead, Doug," I said. He departed, leaving me alone with Hanaka. Bribes are always offered alone, so both parties can deny their existence.

Hanaka continued, "I normally do my inspection after everything is done. Walt handled the preliminary last month."

"I am sorry," I said. "It's taken a bit longer than I expected. We had delays getting good materials."

He looked around again. Everything in sight, from nails and bolts to tools, was neatly stacked on workbenches or in corners, wireless power receivers all grounded, everything name-brand and at least one grade better than code called for.

"I understand," he said. "But you should have called and rescheduled."

"I am sorry," I said again, with an embarrassed look. "But is everything okay so far?"

"It's fine," he agreed. "First class work. I don't see this level of care very often."

"Doug's very good at what he does," I said. "He keeps all the codes on file and tries to anticipate updates, so we stay ahead. It's actually cheaper in the long run, and a few saved marks is not worth an accident."

"So true," he agreed. And it is true, even if the regulations take megabytes. Rational people impose such standards on themselves.

People disinclined to be rational sneak around them anyway, in the same way I was about to for my own reasons.

"Is there some kind of clearance we can get, for Doug to finish up? It would save both of us a lot of time, and you can see that he isn't cutting corners."

He hemmed and hawed for just a few moments that there wasn't any official way to do so, then admitted that unofficially, *unofficially* of course, he could see that we were earnest. Five hundred marks later, in an anonymous cash card, he said, "Tell me honestly what's going in up here?"

"Just the office, the break room, and a couple of beds," I said. "There will be a fire escape. You know how it is—work late, and not want to walk out on the streets. I really don't want my employees to worry about that."

He agreed that that was a responsible idea, and hinted that he wouldn't notice it during the annual inspections, meaning that the bribe was good and he saw no reason for a recurring kickback. The five hundred covered his small risk in ignoring it, he would be happy with that because our stated purpose, while technically illegal, was based on good motives.

He left a few minutes later, and we were good to go.

Of course, there might be changes to regulations and other problems in the future. Hopefully, we'd be here two years at most.

Two years. It wasn't a thrilling prospect.

Do you have any idea how much it costs to maintain a good cover? We had twenty Operatives hidden in various parts of the building, but only five with good enough ID to work. We five had to feed all twenty, hide that outrageous amount of food from the authorities, plot our targets for our eventual mission and still work our cover jobs.

Then there were little things. Everyone in the modern parts of Earth, and certainly in North America, has a phone attached to them like a bad smell. They chatter half the day, meaningless but time-wasting babble. We had to do likewise, while never mentioning anything suspicious and sounding as if we were locals, in case a random monitor listened in. So we had to watch enough vid to give us a background to chat.

That was another necessity. We had to have vid and comm access for every admitted residence and business. It would be so unEarthy not to that it would be an instant flag. We made a point of programming for certain series of shows and adjusted the schedule in part according to ratings. Periodically, someone would flip through the channels in the break room at Storage Center, just to make it seem as if we were paying attention.

All this took time and money. Think about it—maintain the life you have now, learn a new culture's idiosyncracies, support five of your friends, hide the illicit money, keep an arduous schedule of physical conditioning (done inside where no one can see) while wearing weights to compensate for the low G, eat bland, boring local food you aren't used to and plot the overthrow of the most repressive regime in existence. Do you understand why I'd picked the people I had, and why I dreaded some mistake bringing everything tumbling down around our ears?

It wasn't more than a few days before additional problems reared their ugly heads, spread their hoods and hissed. I was upstairs in the break room, flipping channels with one hand while loading maps on flash chip from the library into my comm with the other. It was an Earth comm, black marketed with its codes changed so as to be hard for the police to trace as stolen, then Kimbo had done some diddling so its feedback circuit was completely missing—*all* Earth comms are plugged into the nets so they can be traced. This one officially didn't exist. That also meant I had to load all data manually.

The maps were civilian grade only, of various dates. We had to scour libraries one by one, but not too often, because that was not in character for Earthies. They have expensive, well-staffed libraries with lots of mediocre, out-of-date info that hardly anyone uses. Really. So we had to sneak around something as mundane as going to a library. And no, we could *not* log on through the nets for this data, lest a pattern was drawn. However, since we had created personae that *did* use libraries, we had to log on periodically and look at meaningless crap as another method of cover.

Back to these maps. They were mostly old, mostly travel oriented, did not have decent grid coordinates (what they had were accurate enough to call a recovery vehicle or the cops, assuming your transponder and implant had failed), did not show relief or contour. They were very unsuited for military purposes. For the cities, we had to try to determine traffic flow and density of occupancy and chart it over time and location. It was a task to take months, which had to be done when not doing other things, such as the interruption that morning:

"Boss, get down here," Tyler said over the intercom.

She sounded urgent, not desperate. I saved data, vaulted over the back of the couch and made quick work of the first three flights before slowing to a professional pace for the last one. I kept aware of my senses as I opened the door.

There were five punks in the office. They had weasel-in-the-henhouse expressions on their faces. They were dressed in pop icon style of spiked hair, polymer coats and velvet tights with platform shoes bedecked in rhinestones. I looked them over, sized them up and fought the battle. That done, I decided to break it to them gently that they'd lost.

"May I help you?" I asked.

The alpha-twerp stepped forward, and said, "I'm Cutter." He had what he imagined was a predatory grin on his face.

"First name Fart?" I asked.

"Don't be lagging me, man!" he said. I was glad for our course in slang from Kendra Pacelli.

"What do you want, punky?" I asked him.

"We're security consultants, do," he said. The last word was as meaningless as "yeah," "eh?" or "right?"

"And?" I asked. M1000 a month. That's what he was going to ask for.

"Well, this old building isn't the tightest, do?" he said, sauntering closer.

"So?" I asked.

"So, we can assess it for you, and work on plugging gaps." He nodded as he said it, figuring the deal was done.

So I said, "I prefer to discuss business in my office. This way, please," and turned for the door to the first level. There'd be room in there. Mister Cutter and his largest goon followed close enough to crowd me, with the rest far enough back to envelope.

As soon as I heard it close, I faced them again, and said, "How much?"

Cutter grinned and said, "Two-half kay Marks, first of the month."

Greedy little bastard, trying to sooch me. ("Sooch" is Earth slang for a con game that insults one's intelligence. I have no idea where it came from.) Or maybe he figured I'd beg for a better rate, so as to amuse his asslickers. I nodded and said, "And how will that be paid?"

"Oh, cash, of course. Cash gets things done, do?"

If he only knew how pathetic he sounded.

"Fine," I said. "Will you bring it here, or do I have to come get it?"

You could see the wheels turning in his head. This was not the sharpest knife in the drawer. Not even the sharpest butter knife. I Boosted.

He got angry. "Don't be fuckin' wid me, pokey!" he yelled, and moved to get in my face.

I felt Boost take hold, with that brightening of vision. What I did was tactically foolish against a trained opponent, but he was no threat. I grabbed him by the throat and heaved him off the ground. Then I drove my knee into his gonads hard enough to see them displace his eyeballs, which rolled back out of sight. I dropped him, catching him in the solar plexus with my boot hard enough to paralyze his diaphragm, bruise his liver and lungs and stun his heart. He imitated a fish out of water and I turned to his buddies.

The tendonhead was moving in close, and I started the object lesson. I brought up both feet in a crescent kick combo that cracked teeth and jaw, broke his nose across his face, massively contused his right cheek and smeared his lips to goo. I lit, bounced, and caught him in the right kidney with my left toe and in the collarbone with my right as he fell.

The other three were confused and motionless, and I stepped in among them. Shortly, they joined their buddies.

Now, Mister Cutter had barely a scratch on him, even though he was still gaping for air. He'd pass out soon, and would wake up sore but unmarked. The others were hamburger. This lesson

would be repeated as necessary, until they figured out that hanging with Fart Cutter was painful on the joints.

Just to make the lesson stick, I wire tied their scrotums. I threatened, but didn't cut them off, but did warn them that they had
only a few minutes before the tissue started dying. They hunched
over and took off, swearing at us as they went. I laughed. They'd
have to drop trou and have a trusted friend break the ties with
wirecutters, or burn through them with hot metal. Embarrassing
and painful, either way. I had Tyler mop the floor while I went
to sterilize my hands.

CHAPTER 20

Gradually, by twos and threes, we brought everybody in. The twenty-six of the total admitted on work visas were squeaky clean. I would never contact them, they'd simply take their cues from their own private messages, or from the initiation of hostilities. They were warned of other activities that might occur, and to ignore those. We wanted them only for the big event. Miranda Kirlan slipped out of the embassy and joined us. I felt sorry for her—she hadn't, and wouldn't see the outside anywhere a camera might catch her, unless and until we could black market another chip for her. I was trying to avoid that as a security issue. After a few days, we shuffled her off by night and private car to St. Louis.

We also brought in a nuke. I almost went gibbering insane from the associated risks. We had a specific need for a low-yield mining device, but with the huge numbers of security personnel and equipment on Earth, it seemed certain it would be found. It would be an obvious terrorist device, as they don't allow nuclear charges to be used for mining on Earth, ever. Really. They have a phobia about it. Well, we'd give them a reason for that phobia, even if after the fact.

So I made a long, lonely, unarmed drive from my HQ in the FDC area out to a still remote spot in the mountains of West

Virginia, where a large tract of World Heritage Forest would cover me, I hoped. I was followed by Kimbo in another vehicle. Both of them had transponders that could be shut off in a moment, and three different IDs. I was still worried lest someone note us turning them off, but we timed it closely enough and the system assumed we'd left zone control or made a legitimate stop. Kimbo would stay out as watch and support, while I went in. I hid the car, penetrated the fence—you wouldn't think trees would be protected by a double cordon of bare earth, razor wire and sensory mesh fence, but Earth is just nuts—and scrabbled quietly between the boles in dark. Getting captured would mean compromise for a lot of Operatives.

It had been too damned long since I'd done any wilderness crawling. I got tired in a hurry, and made enough noise that the animals would go silent around me. My hands got raw from the dirt and the coarse roots, I sweated and muddied up and quickly was a mess.

After several hours, I was at the right locus in time and space, in a flattish meadow just below the steep crest of a hill. It was still woody, but had fewer trees than most of the surrounding area. It was a warm, humid night in the thick air of Earth, but I cooled off quickly, lying on the ground and not moving.

Above me in space (okay, some distance around the planet—picky, picky), a stealthy assault boat should be making a very specialized approach. I wasn't sure if it was *Ninja*, *Black Watch*, *Ranger*, *Legionnaire*, *Zulu* or *Speznaz* that was up there, or even if anything was there, but I'd know soon. Aboard should be ten more Operatives and a package. They'd been crammed into a tub for twenty days and would likely not care about the risk of death, so long as they could get out of the box.

The boat (well, "ship"—it had interstellar capability, after all) should be phasing into normal space . . . now. And it should be phasing back into hyper . . . now. Ten Operatives should be doing the ultimate in insanity, a drop from orbit to a precise target on the planet below. Too low in mass, density or threatening material to trigger alarms, too insane an idea to consider. They would have been braked by a heavy thrust of degenerate hydrogen, the fluffy cloud of polymer strings around them burned off by the friction of the fall into atmosphere. Deployable shields would ablate slowly as they fell, and we hoped the trace would be too low-energy to detect, or that it would be assumed as mere debris, as there was insufficient mass at too low a velocity for a strike.

If we were wrong, ten Operatives and my surprise package were about to be fried into vapor. That assumes that making a phase jump that insanely close to the gravitational field of the Sun, and to the mass of Earth, was accomplished without a multi-dimensional shockwave that would be invisible in regular space but would smear the atoms of the ship and crew from here to the edge of the universe. Our boat crews are as nuts as we are, and get even less publicity. I'll always spot them the first beer when I meet them.

Less than an hour later, I heard the faint rustling flap of parachutes. They were opening at two hundred meters with fast opening canopies. They each had two set to trigger independently, had manual releases as well, *and* a spare canopy in case one of the others failed. They'd be fully open at about fifty meters, have time to look down and hit the ground. It redefined "suicide drop" and if anyone lived through this war, that would be a story to beat all stories. "No shit, there I was. Thought I was gonna die—"

Ahead and above in the clearing, dark shadows were shifting and drifting. I heard them land with soft thumps and sporadic low crackles of weeds and brush. It looked to be about ten figures. They tumbled down, wrapping their canopies in their arms as they did, a maneuver I'd trained in but never thought we'd have to use. They went silent, I waited until the animal noises resumed, then I signaled them.

It was just an infrared flash, in a simple pattern that said it was safe. I got a double flash in response, and three minutes later I had ten bodies counted as they ghosted past and went back to ground. I was elated. Considering that three of them had only had the training jumps we'd given them, it was quite an accomplishment. I rose and scuttled through the formation and took cover in a thick tangle of bush, wrapped around the clump of limb trunks. They moved again. In that fashion, we made it back to the fence and then to the cars.

They eased into the vehicles, which had no internal lights.

Shuffling and shifting indicated they were changing into the civilian clothes we'd had ready for them, and in my car I heard a single "Oh, blast," as someone realized they were in the wrong seat and had clothes that didn't fit. I hoped they'd hurry. The canopy was starting to fog up. While that would hopefully be taken as a couple scrocking in the woods, it might draw some cop who wanted a ticket for his monthly tally.

The nuke should be in the trunk, heavily shielded and sealed. I had no intention of checking it. Either it worked or it didn't. Frankly, I wanted it gone as quickly as possible. There are places on Earth one can easily hide the stray emanations from a nuke. Eastern North American was not one such place.

They finally finished dressing, and Tim Blankenship spoke. "Damn, that was a rush."

"I'll bet," I said. "Sorry I missed it. You got the other gear?" I was only half sorry I'd missed it. The glory of doing it had to be something. The excitement, too. But the risk . . . no, thanks.

"Sealed and ready," he assured me. Mostly what he'd brought was hermetically sealed explosives and a bit of nerve agent. We could manufacture both on site, and would, but it was easier to smuggle it in here and through the embassy in increments. I see no need to do it the hard way, when I can simply drop people in from a jump-capable craft in orbit, through the atmosphere and to the ground with chemicals that are sealed so as not to be detected by the UN's sensors that are present in every town.

Four other drops took place over the next month. We lost two troops going into Africa, scorched into vapor by ablation problems. Operatives Burkett and Mandall. They were our first mission casualties. None of the ten for Australia made it. I can only assume the ship was lost doing that insane dropout so close to the conflicting G fields of Earth, the Moon and Sol. Warne crashed in in Russia, one canopy failed, the other streamered around it, and his reserve not deployed. He landed hard enough to shatter his body, and they perforce left him in a hole, sans gear and clothes. If he was ever found, he'd be a John Doe murder victim and never associated with us. Thirteen deaths of fifty insertions was a hell of a casualty rate, and I cried over it, locked in my room. I was killing my kids to get them in place so they could die, possibly to no avail. It was painful.

First of the month. I'll bet you thought I'd dismissed the incident with Fart Cutter, didn't you?

Wrong. I slid up to the outside of his pack's hangout around 2330 (24-hour clock, recall), and waited. I suppose this was a bit needless and egotistical, but I didn't want him imagining he'd grown a brain and coming back. This was to be Part Two of Lesson One: Thou Shalt Not Mess With Mean Strangers From Out Of Town. Frank and Tyler were with me, just like old times. We were bedecked with procured assets and improvised gear.

It was an apartment building, not that old but officially decrepit and abandoned. You'd think the cops would do something about the lights inside and the movement, what with power wastage and the environment and safety issues, but the cops were only thugs against unarmed peasants. Against weasels, they turned into rabbits themselves. Or were paid off. Or, some places, were part of the gangs, using the uniforms for cover. Everyone knew what went on, no one did anything about it.

We clambered up the wall on the alley side using gaps in the brick façade as hand holds. We'd pause periodically as pieces would crumble away, clicking down the side of the building to bruise one of us.

The room we wanted was clearly lit by a single tube, about 50 lumens. It was easy to locate, and we finally hunched around the frame like three spiders, me on the sill above, hanging by my fingers with my toes resting on the top ledge, and Frank on the broken remnants of what had been a fire escape, with Tyler hanging from the sill with her feet above the window below. Frank gave me a map of who was where, I whispered, "GO!" and in we went.

My feet broke the age and Sun-crazed polymer window into several shards, and I arched, bent and stuck the landing. Tyler vaulted in and across to my left, Frank shot in to the right.

"Hello, Fart Cutter," I said.

"Dogf—" he started to swear, recovering from the shock. He

clutched at his waist, probably for a weapon, and I shot him with goo from a stickyweb gun. I shot him in the face.

Tyler swarmed into Tendonhead and a buddy, and I heard the pop of breaking wrists. She's a nasty minded bitch, and I love working with her. A couple of screams were interrupted by cuffs to throats and jabs to solar plexi, and I continued with business while Frank sat on three others.

Fart Cutter was thrashing and yanking at his mouth and nose, trying to separate his hands and his face and the web. That wouldn't work, and I couldn't have him dying, so I spritzed just enough solvent on to let him breathe with difficulty. I relieved him of his "gun," which was a homebuilt muzzleloading piece of garbage. Kimbo could do better in ten minutes.

"It's now the second of the month," I told him. It was three minutes after midnight. "You didn't come round with that twenty-five hundred marks. So I'm here to collect."

He tried to be brave. "Dogfuck, I ain't paying you space. And I'll be by tomorrow to—"

"*You ain't fucking gonna live until tomorrow unless I see money, punky,*" I snarled. Then I kicked him in the head enough to rattle his brain around.

He was silent, and I continued, "Two five kay. Now. Or I slice off your fucking scrote." Yes, I use that threat a lot. It works. I clutched at his groin and he whimpered.

"Can, man. Do," he said.

"Where?" I prodded.

The cash was in a box behind the couch, under a floorboard, and inside some ratty quilts. I looked inside. Six thousand and a bit. Plus the thousand he was carrying and the two more from his buddies. "Two five," I said. "Plus late payment fee, interest, collection fee, and a bit for my friends. You'll remember next month, do?"

"You're going to fucking die by next month, dogfucker," he insisted.

Well, a lesson had to be delivered. These asocial little animals didn't even understand brute force. "Kill one," I told Tyler. "Not the Tendonhead." She did. Slowly.

There was a substantial dark stain under the body when she

finished. Facing the others, I used the illogic beloved of terrorists, five-year-olds and street punks, and said, "Fart Cutter killed him. And he'll kill you, unless he brings the money, every month. Do." That is such a stupid fucking slang.

Then we thoroughly beat the shit out of the others. I sprayed solvent on Cutter as we left. Other than a faint bruise, there wasn't a scratch on him. I figured the point had been made. I was right. He was found dead in a dumpster three days later. A pity. We could have used his chip. But we did keep the spare we got from the kill. A petty criminal's chip is better than none.

Are you wondering why we didn't buddy up to the local punks? It's simple. They have ties to the cops, who get kickbacks from them. Yes, the cops know who runs the operations, and often, you can get stolen merchandise back by bribing the right cop enough to pay his friends and himself. As long as you can beat the price offered by the fence, you're good to go. Or you can pay the cop to list extra things on your report, and insurance will pony up the matching money, to give you a little something for your trouble. Really. The cops are worse than the regular criminals, because they can hide behind the government and you can't stop them. I wanted nothing to do with that end of the "business," because it would take too long to get plugged in, would make it obvious when I left, and while they could be bought off on most crimes including murder, a hint that we were there for espionage or worse would make them be good boys and share that knowledge with people who would come looking for us. It was risky to fight them as I had, but I needed the money for operations. It took every penny we generated legally, everything we could import from off-planet, and everything we could illicitly transfer. And the cops wouldn't be friendly enough to the gangs to back them up on collections. So long as they got their cut of the money, they didn't care where it came from, and they wouldn't want to hear excuses.

Ironically, the real problem came a few days later. We took turns buying food, and tried not to fall into patterns. That avoidance itself would be suspicious, were it attached to us. We hoped to not get it attached to us by never appearing anywhere on schedule, thus making it harder for us to look suspicious in the first place. People get busted as suspects simply for having a schedule that matches a particular series of crimes. Concrete evidence is not considered necessary. So we didn't dare keep a schedule and we didn't dare not.

Anyway, I was at a local food store with a cart, buying what appeared to be a typical load of bland, pre-cooked, frozen, microwaveable shitmeals, cardboard bread, instant mix-with-chunky-tapwater glop and overpriced packages of flour and stale spice to mix with the two kilos of real food, or rather, soy protein and vat grown pseudomeat that I picked up. We had to look typical. We also couldn't eat most of this stuff and stay in shape. The carbohydrate load would bloat us into well-marbled chairwarmers. So we gritted our teeth, held our noses and choked it down.

I mindlessly drove the cart along the aisles, grabbed things as if comparing prices and appearing confused at the difference, occasionally snagging something seemingly on impulse, and doing my best to appear typical. I had a bored, vacant stare on my face as I rolled through the checkout and waved a cash card over the sensor, then unloaded the food from the store cart and into my little wire mesh pushcart. I was just turning to leave.

I saw a man shake, drop a bundle of boxed meals that scattered across the floor like tiles, then sag back against the front wall.

"You okay, guy?" I asked. It was obvious to me he was not okay. His face was gray, he was panting in pain and clutching at his left chest and shoulder. I was thinking "Myocardial infarction" as he dropped his remaining bag and collapsed.

In a second I was alongside, easing his fall and getting him laid out. I ripped open his jacket to relieve pressure on his throat and chest, pressed his neck to check his carotid pulse and said loudly and clearly, "Someone call an ambulance. Heart attack."

It was pretty severe, but he could be saved if they were quick. His eyes were rolling back in his head and his blood pressure obviously dropping as he went into V-fib, but he was still gasping for breath. I started chest compressions at once. All this was pure trained reflex. I've rehearsed similar scenarios so many times I could do it in my sleep.

I was so focused, I didn't notice what has happening around me until hands clamped on me and dragged me to my feet. An angry voice demanded, "What the hell do you think you're doing?"

I snapped back to my surroundings to realize they were cops. Two of them. Burly. Brown shirts, armor underneath, helmets and belts of gear that were appropriate to tank crew, not public safety officers. The one who had questioned me was wearing the practiced snarl that thugs learn to intimidate people. "Administering CPR to a heart attack victim," I replied.

"Are you a doctor on duty, wearing some uniform I don't recognize? Do you have proper authorization or a waiver? Or did you just decide to have a whack at playing doctor on this guy?" he asked.

"I'm— " I started, then my brain locked my mouth down. The only people here authorized to render medical aid were doctors or medics on duty, in uniform, usually after getting a waiver signed. There was no first aid certification, no emergency rules of succor, no Good Samaritan defense. As I remembered this, the victim curled up tighter and gasped. He twitched and died, just like that. Had I been able to stay on him, I might have kept enough blood flow to hold him for the ambulance crew, just now pulling up outside. He might still be revivable, depending on how fast they got him into a stasis box or hit him with drugs, but they'd have to "routinely" check his ID first. They'd killed him with their assinine rules.

"You killed him!" the other cop shouted. "Just because you interfered."

I just hate the way these sheep think. "If it's not in your training, don't try to do anything in case you make it worse." No one is allowed surgical tools, weapons or fire extinguishers in their homes or cars because "such things are best left to professionals."

The medics were crowding through the door in a hurry, but were going to be hindered by the circle of gawkers. I swear, people who stand around and stare at accidents should just be exterminated on the spot. "Heart attack, V-fib," I said to them.

They looked confused, then one smiled condescendingly and said, "We'll find out shortly, sir." It was that type of smug expression you just want to smash.

The cops were hassling me, spinning me around and preparing to slap on cuffs. Those would be followed by a locking belt, ankle shackles and a hood, and I'd be wheeled out to a van on a dolly. It takes time to break out of even a half-assed jail, and I couldn't have them running my ID. Holes would show up eventually. So I had to break out right now.

I Boosted even though most of this would be over before it kicked in, and took charge of the situation. I went limp enough to let them start tugging at me, then shoved in the direction they were pulling. My left arm went across the throat of cop number one, and I kneed him in his groin armor hard enough to break the plastic against the tendons of his thighs. Pain shot through my leg but I ignored it. As the second one tried to wrestle my arm down, I turned and punched him in the face. I danced my feet into a good stance and shot out a knife-edge foot to crack his rear ankle, then threw his front one out from under him for good measure. His face had that pained look people get as a hundred kilos drops onto a broken ankle. He fell. I continued the turn, dropped into a sweep that put my leg through those of number one, now bent over and gasping, who fell backwards and landed fat ass first on his partner. I swung the foot up and back and drove the heel into his face as hard as I could. I rolled back onto my shoulders and went into a back somersault with a half twist, landing on my feet and facing the crowd just as Boost kicked in. Everything took on that lengthened focus and the sharp edges that are symptomatic of the drug. Bliss! I enjoyed it far more than was healthy.

I didn't smash the face of the medic who'd given me that grin that deserved to be smashed. He just might save that poor bastard's life. I did elbow a couple of gawkers in the ribs and kick a couple of shins. It served two purposes; it got me through the crowd and it might teach them not to do that. Once through, I sprinted, dodging and hurdling obstacles. I cleared a baby stroller while doing a lovely ballet-like turn around the father pushing it, slipped between him and the mother and kept going. I went through the "In" door as it opened, cut through the incoming mob and ran faster than any out of shape wimp on this low-gee ball of mud could crank. Barring an Olympic sprinter, I was free of the local crowd. I changed pace to a walk as I hit the corner and turned left, hoping to confuse anyone watching by camera.

I found a cab, climbed in and said, "Fourteen hundred block of west Sixteenth Street," swiped my card as I opened the other door and stepped out. If they were tracking electronically at that point, I hoped the cab would cool my trail.

But I couldn't count on it. This was the most intrusive society in history, and I was wearing a tracer. I touched my phone and said, "Dial Jim Four," which gave me a one-time use connection we'd prepared for cover. On the second chirp, Tyler answered "Hello" and I said, "Trash, locations five or nine, now," and disconnected. The cab was pulling away and I crossed the street through the traffic, risking a jaywalking ticket. Either this ID would cease to exist in a few minutes, or I'd be captured. The ticket wouldn't matter. I got into an alley and sprinted—alleys are less monitored, and thank God and Goddess I was on the surface rather than above or below or in a box. It was dark, stank of urine and rotten trash and was a perfect place to toss the phone, behind a trash container where it would take a few seconds to find and a few more to approach with their police procedures. The alley T'ed, I turned left and heard that odd echo steps make in such corners. I slowed as I neared the next street.

I turned right and walked two blocks, recovering from the endorphin rush of Boost. It, adrenaline from the fight and the instinctive thrill of action were an almost sexual flood. A part of my brain thought of Deni for a moment until I pushed it back. A few deep breaths and meditation got me to a normal state again, except for a slight chromatic aberration around the edges of images and a thudding of my pulse in my ears.

I saw another line of cabs and pulled out my emergency cash card. Climbing into one, I gave it directions and swiped the card. It took off.

Here's where I was tense. Had they traced me? Had they IDed the vehicle? If so, it would lock me in and head for a police station, and we'd play this game all over again. But I needed the vehicle to get me a few blocks away at least. As it stopped at a traffic point, I stepped out. I grabbed the nearest slideway and took it one block back the way I'd come from, just to confuse any human watchers, then walked through another alley and took a different one.

It must have worked. I wasn't captured. Twenty minutes later, ready to have my own heart attack from exertion and fear, I was at Location Five. It was the corner of an apartment block in a neighborhood safe enough to be out in, trafficked enough by soft criminals for us not to be noticed. Cameras here were random, so I should be safe. No need to use backup location Nine.

It was a bit dirty by Earth standards, meaning the ground was littered in stale food packages and other drifting trash with dust ground into them. Graffiti was minor, only six gang "codes" and a halfway decent mural. A small strip of what had been grass had been abandoned to weeds and mud. And a rustle indicated someone approaching. Tyler.

She didn't say a word, simply came out from under stairs and nodded. I started walking. She'd follow a few tens of meters behind to keep me covered. Had the tracer been an immediate threat, she had an EMP device to burn it out.

Thirty minutes later we were back in our main safehouse. Everyone gathered around. I gave a brief rundown and everyone looked serious as I concluded, "So let people die. We have a cover to maintain."

Kimbo asked, "What are you going to do about your tracer, boss?"

"Stay here until we find out if I need a new one," I said. "I need you to try to find out how hard they'll be looking for me. I may have fucked the dog for all of us." If they took my fingerprints off any of the food packages, they'd get a null there, too.

"I'll look," he said. "Don't we have some spare tracers?"

"Yes," Tyler said, "but we have to match physiques and jobs closely. And Marquette will have to disappear if they come looking. Luckily, he won't show up on a DNA trace, as he isn't actually Marquette."

"So a lack of perfect cover will protect me," I laughed, mostly in relief. It also might arouse suspicion as to *why* I didn't show up on file. We couldn't have many incidents like this. I couldn't fathom how anyone could live in this shithole, or why they weren't killing cops, politicians and political scientists out of hand. I'd been secretly cheering the whole time when one of the overclass got gapped on the headline news. I'd stop doing it now. Being secret about it, that is. They deserved to die. Preferably slowly and painfully. The junior flunkies working for them I had mixed feelings about. Some of them had joined the gang just to keep themselves safe. On the other hand, if they had enough moral courage to refuse to help the masters, it wouldn't be as bad as it was.

I was still tense. My face couldn't be changed without surgery. Yes, there are nanos that can do that; I would be taking some. The effective change is small, however. I understood that the chances of them IDing me by face were very slim, but that still left a miniscule chance they would. That tiny risk grew in my brain and would continue to haunt me. I growled at the idea already. And what if they showed up here *looking* for Marquette?

Hell with it. I needed a drink and I didn't dare have one in case we had further repercussions that evening. I needed a blowjob and Deni was off limits, Tyler even more so and I couldn't waste the cash or risk a local. I'd have to settle for food and sleep.

I had a sandwich, bland as our covers required, and lay down. As I started to doze, I recalled an old joke: "Don't tell my mother I work for the UN government. She thinks I pimp six-year-old boys to spacers at Breakout Station." I chuckled myself to sleep.

CHAPTER 21

After determining that my ID was still good and I wasn't wanted, we did more recon and learned the difference between the fairly normal (from our view) cities and the megacities. The megacity dwellers referred to those from smaller towns as "Wides." Wides referred to their opposites as "Cubes" who lived in "Boxes."

Tyler and I made a reconnaissance tour of the Boxes in Washington-Baltimore. It's easy to visualize a 300m square building 1000m tall. It's not hard to calculate the materials and strengths.

Have you ever *been* in one? To borrow a phrase from Kimbo: "That's a huge fucking building. It doesn't even make any *sense*."

We entered at ground level late one night. Two sliding doors created an airlock, ostensibly to save energy. It also slowed people down. I made note of that. I could use it.

"Impressive," Tyler murmured. She had her hair trimmed into a crest with hanging tiny bells, short at the sides and dyed purple, which was the style at the time. It and her snug gray outfit made her look even smaller. The skates she wore affected her proportions even more. I probably looked just as goofy in a T haircut with a slashed black shirt over a T-shirt.

I made a barely perceptible gesture and we rolled off to our right, holding hands. We looked like a flirting couple as we dodged and wove carefully among the crowd, which even at this hour was heavy. Escalators were there, and we kicked the skates back onto their retaining springs on our calves so we could step on.

This place was a rat maze. Corridors ran north and south, east and west, a few diagonally, some sloped between levels, depending on where tall rooms and facilities might be. Open atria were crossed by slidewalks and escalators. Elevators and occasional dropshafts ran up and down skeletal frames in those atria, within hallways and outside the structure. Viewing platforms and windows clashed with each other. I was keeping a tactical map as we went, there were local screens with directions, and I was still lost in minutes. It was nuts. Each one of these monstrosities was a microcosmic city unto itself. Its residents might leave only to work in another, returning later. To that end, tubes like hamster trails linked them to each other, hundreds on a side. The streets below ran through tunnels, for all practical purposes.

It was remarkably quiet in our current location, two floors above a section where dance clubs and bars predominated. The music echoed up to us, the beats muffled to thumps and the highs sibilant whines. I made another signal to Tyler and we turned down a side passage. About five meters down was a sign that read "AUTHORIZED PERSONNEL ONLY." Service corridors. That's what I wanted.

The door was locked. Fifty meters away was another one. Locked. The one after that wasn't. We slipped inside.

I sped up, barreling down the hallway. Heavy tools and cleaning gear stood against the walls, in gross violation of building codes. The walls were cracked, with a sheen of age and occasional scribbles of notes from workers, to act as reminders or as messages to other shifts. There were occasional low-value personal items left around, like staff jackets and battered cases. All stuff that no one would bother stealing. We took it all in as we played chase, until we stopped near another door to grope and kiss before heading back out into the public areas, giggling and grinning as we did so. Any observer would assume I was interested in her skinny body, which would make me a freak by Earth's soft standards, but they wouldn't question it. It would never occur to them that I'd noted four different service elevators, one for heavy maintenance gear, two for moving household goods and store merchandise and one for the staff who cleaned the main areas. I'd gauged the locks, the apparent traffic flow from the wear on the walls and floor, the capacity of the elevators and the uniforms that were worn around here. Tyler nodded slightly. She'd seen what she needed to, and we'd compare notes later. We skated on.

Even within this microcosm were good and bad areas of different types. We came into a wide open space, built on several levels, that was devoted to entertainment. Different types of music and crowd noise echoed out to us, calling at the social animal within to join the festivities. I looked for and found the tiny logo that declared the entire complex the property of Universal Entertainment. Every arcade, every theater, every bar, club and restaurant within view plowed money into one huge conglomerate, that then plowed it into the government in taxes. So the 30% or so of income that people actually kept after taxes and thought of as "theirs" they were indirectly using to support the very mechanisms they resented. Ironic, and a weapon to be used against them.

We kept moving as crowds brushed past us. It was amazing. One of the clubs had "glass" fronts that slid open, allowing customers within to stare out at the passing crowds. In this case, all of the tenants were young women, dressed as custom dictated to show off their assets. Of course, they couldn't actually show them off by law. They could only hint. Sometimes blatantly. The scene made me laugh. I had a momentary vision of walking up to one, handing her a M500 cash card and asking, "Three-twenty a kilo?" Yes, it was that kind of meat market.

They had an odd morality here. Women would show off their tits, almost but not quite entirely bare, but it's socially, morally and in some cases legally offensive to mention the fact. One is supposed to pretend not to see her body, while being attracted to it. I found it safer to simply not get involved. And really, pale, low-G types are not my thing anyway.

"I see a dozen places that look good," Tyler said.

"Yeah," I agreed. We were thinking of places to cause mayhem, not places to be entertained. We wandered slowly through, spotting exits, service corridors, all our usual targets. Our jabber was meaningless after weeks of practice. Occasionally, we'd pretend to talk to someone on the phones built into our jewelry.

"Hey, that sounds like Weinrib singing," I commented.

"Yeah. Total do, man," Tyler replied. "Liddy. Catch the sparkly," she said, indicating a woman in a reflective ultraviolet lit dress, one of the few people with any color.

"Liddy," I agreed. "Kinda shifting in the lights."

We entered the zone around a bar called The Skybox. There were sixty stories above us and a hundred meters of offices in every direction, so I don't know which sky they were referring to.

Tyler yelled, "YO!" and snagged a server as he walked by. He was fresh and cute in a way that would be sexy if I got into men. I only noticed because he was one of the rare ones who didn't look as drab as the surroundings. He served us two drinks of something from the tank on his back. Tyler politely declined inhalants, paid him with a twenty and said, "Keep the change."

Speaking of the surroundings, it was obvious up close—this place was old and ragged. Old paint was chipped or had been overpainted instead of stripped. Repairs to hardware were with mismatched screws. It passed the five meter rule—it looked good as long as you didn't examine in detail. But those details were crappy. No good Freehold club owner would let his place get that worn. Yet this was in one of the upscale districts. I had to wonder what the seedy ones looked like.

We'd wasted enough time. We drifted back out of the maze via another route, keeping up the chatter as cover. We used another exit, and found excuses to slip through another twenty dim corridors as we did so. There was a slight risk of being seen and questioned, but there were a lot of slight risks, and the big risk would be having to tackle a battle without recon and intel in advance. We completed our tour and headed back to our base.

Once there, we recorded reports separately, then cross-examined each other and confirmed as much as possible. Every recon we did was analyzed for data and everything went into a private file we hoped no one could or would ever find, because it would damn us all. We were analyzing the culture and the environment, and most especially every city we were in.

As we undressed from the ridiculous getups dictated by fad, we gave everyone a brief rundown on what we'd seen. They were all attentive, getting the "feel" of it from us now, which they'd add to the briefing we'd do in a day or two.

Kimbo was at his console. He gave us half an ear while he dug for data on one of his projects. "This is unbelievable!" he suddenly interrupted.

"Yes?" I prompted. A quick glance showed the screen to be a political text load.

"Banks here are limited to seven percent interest, right? And they are talking about lowering it to five. You were wondering how they make any money?"

Grinning, I said, "Hit me." This promised to be amusing.

"They do it with user fees. The more they've been restricted from charging interest, the more fees they charge, and then some. Get this," he said as he itemized the list. "Late payment fee. Early payment fee. Payment by comm processing fee. Payment in person processing fee. Automated payment fee. Penalty for paying ahead on the account, penalty for excessive activity, penalty for insufficient activity, charge for business transaction, charge for personal account transaction, statement charge, monthly service charge, annual account charge, withdrawal charge, deposit charge, transfer fee, service representative consultancy fee, cash transaction fee, NSF fee, overdraft charge *and* negative balance charge, mandatory annual review and fee . . . and it goes on for another page," he said, too worn out and amazed to finish.

"Damn!" I replied, stunned. Nothing had prepared me for that. Considering for a moment, I said, "You can do nothing without being charged, and then they collect interest on the penalty. I'd rather pay an honest forty percent than that rat maze." And I wouldn't have to. Back home, we paid about fourteen percent on accounts.

"Boss," Kimbo said. "I want to go *home*! Or a nice, comfortable Nazi concentration camp! This place is beyond a toilet. How in hell can people live here? How do they stand it?"

It was worse even than that. There was so much we hadn't learned from research ahead of time. This was to be expected. Things are never either as good or as bad as you are led to believe, but in this case, the bad massively outnumbered the good. I was amazed.

Examples? Well, let's take some of their "safety" laws. I've already mentioned that knives longer than 10 cm are illegal, even in the kitchen. After all, they might be used as weapons. There's talk of selling all food pre-cut, and eliminating those, too. Bats for cricket, baseball, and even sluggerball are illegal to carry except in a case to or from recognized practice or school, and must be stored in a locked room at school under supervision. There's even some whacko proposal to ban belt buckles over 40 grams as "potential weapons." As if there aren't rocks and sticks lying around. As if anyone poor enough to be that type of criminal can afford a chunk of metal or ceramic that size as a clothing accessory.

Then, there's a law that no more than a three day supply of "non-prescription drugs" (many drugs actually require written permission from a doctor *licensed by the government* to dispense such. They have a higher accidental kill rate than our doctors, too. So much for "professional standards.") may be sold in a single package. The theory is that it reduces "accidental suicides," because a person wallowing in despair will "have time to think" while visiting enough stores to buy a lethal dosage.

It's my experience, as a professional in the subject of death, that people who really want to kill themselves will find a way. Those that don't really want to and are just drawing attention to themselves need therapy, and their friends and family should notice that fact. Of course, windows on Earth don't open above the third floor, and cars are centrally controlled. Despite all this, the suicide rate on Earth is ten times what we have in the Freehold.

I have a hint for the overlords, as no other term applies to them: People on Earth don't kill themselves because a knife happens to be lying around. They kill themselves because you have turned their planet into a festering shithole with no hope of escape, no hope of individuality, no chance of innovation and creativity, and not even the dignity of surcease in a clean death.

Of course the crime and violence rate is extreme. That's historically been true in most dungeons.

"To understand all is to forgive all," I've heard said. Well, I understood just fine and I would never forgive. The more I looked at Earth, the sicker I got. The history, the roots, the few bits of scenery left unspoiled, buried under antlike legions of ignorant, stupid, petty little bureaucrats determined to ensure that no one has a better lot than they themselves do made me want to vomit. The poor sheeple living under the yoke, flogged into basic modules to serve this machine filled me with despair.

This was a culture sick to its very roots, poisoned by government, crippled by those who had the hubris to claim that they knew better than the rest how to run people's lives.

And worse still was the impotent need of these creatures to impose their will on us. The theory that after 5000 years of raping the resources, sodomizing the human spirit, crushing individuality under hobnailed boots, Earth has developed an "understanding" and a "compassion" that gives them "insight" into "the problems facing the Freehold in its development" and the imperialist right to drag us into their pit.

To borrow a phrase from the North American old Southwest Expansion Era, "They needed killin.'"

The more I looked, the worse it got. Parents are *prohibited* from teaching their kids at home. There's a "set pattern of development" that educators follow and by breaking that cycle parents are hurting their children, so goes the logic. Children are slammed behind the bars of the State at age three. Most are in State-controlled and regulated day care before that. They are kept there eight hours a day, being taught by rote the simplest functions—basic literacy, basic arithmetic, use of comms (but only the superficialities, not how to actually get work out of one)—then kept there four more hours so the "parents can have some time to themselves," during which they are taught to be obedient cogs in the machine, and how bad it is to want to be independent; how everyone depends on you to do your part, how it's wrong to dislike, or get angry, or rebel, or goof off, or do anything else that is fundamentally human. There are no frontiers, no visions to work for, no aspirations other than to be a good part of the whole. They compete to see who can be the most mediocre. No wonder they rape, kill, suicide, riot, and drug themselves senseless. Denied any safe outlet of emotional overload, the brain goes into a loop that ends only when its basic functions collapse.

Now let's be clear: I have no space for bigots in my life. Every person should be judged as an individual, not as a class. I went through some serious soul searching on Mtali over that. But to *force* people to have the "right mindset" is more heinous than any ignorant bigotry, because it is intentional destruction of free will.

I had been wondering, since wealth and success were punished by taxation under the theory that "wealth is an asset of society, and a person merely its caretaker," why the body wasn't considered an "asset of society" and required to mate as directed to produce the ideal human. Well, it wasn't quite that bad—they weren't that logical. But they could prohibit "undesirable genetic codes" from reproducing. That included habitual, unreformable abusers and various incurable psychoses. While the idea stuck in my craw, it did make a certain amount of sense. The question is, who decides? Because they also included certain individuals as "mentally ill" who simply disagreed with enough bureaurats to be made persona non grata. Not that these people were given treatment, because there was nothing actually wrong with them. It was simply an administrative means to hurt them and discourage others. It was logical—society must protect itself from those who would reform it. They were destroying any rebellious mindset in any way possible.

Then I came across something so revolting I have no words for it.

Look, I was on Mtali. I have little use for rabid Christians. Many of the ones I met elsewhere were just as bad, many not. Officially, I belong to Grainne First Druidic Assembly. Actually, I haven't been to church in years and regard all religion as a sham. But that's my personal position.

On Earth however, certain sects of Christianity are regarded as a subversive threat. One has religious freedom, certainly, it's just that a few specific religions are inappropriate. The practitioners thereof are scrutinized and harassed, for the "safety" of society. So they practice in secret, thus arousing more suspicion. After all, why is one secretive unless one has something to hide?

Once on that list, one is marked forever. It is never believed that one changed faith, but rather that one must be a potential terrorist incognito. So parents actually bribe officials to *deny* their faith exists, so their children will not be so treated . . .

"Obscene" comes to mind, but doesn't even being to describe it. How Dantesque can you get? Pay someone to deny your heritage in order to make you safe. The Christians' Simon Peter must be spinning in his grave.

I dreaded the almost certain conflict ahead of us, because I saw only two outcomes. Either Earth, with its massive, grinding, soulless infrastructure rolled over us and made us just like them; or we smashed the roots of the tree of human evolution whilst we cut out the disease eating at the trunk.

That shopping for food issue came back to haunt us again. We'd been using various discount cards to reduce our expenses. It never occurred to us, though it should have, that the government monitored those, too. I'm surprised they didn't have cameras installed in toilets to monitor our feces. Then again, they just might.

I got called downstairs by Tyler, who phrased it so I knew it was a bureaurat. I neatened up and headed down, trying to look nonchalant.

The caller was suited in collarless polyester with current stylish hair. About thirty. No match physically. That last datum was never directly important to dealing with them, but was a habit of mine to assess. Also, physical presence can be used for intimidation. He started as soon as he saw me. "You're Mister Marquette?" he asked.

"Yes, can I help you?" I replied.

He whipped out his badge and holo. "Bart Petersen, UN Bureau of Agriculture. I need to ask you a few questions about your shopping."

"Okay," I agreed, suddenly flushed and nervous. Yes, me. It was the nature of the system. In my case, it was risk of a blown cover. In the case of the peasants, it was ingrained fear of authority.

"You seem to buy a lot of food, Mister Marquette," he said. "Your purchase records from ADaM Foods . . ." he said as he flashed a page on a comm, not enough for me to read, just enough to prove he had it, " . . . make it look to me as if you're feeding about three people. What's going on?"

"I eat a lot," I nodded, trying to appear casual. "And I entertain. I'm also sloppy and let food go bad sometimes," I said. I sounded properly panicked and as if I were trying to be overly explanatory.

He gave me The Stare. "Isn't it important to you to conserve resources?"

"Uh, yes. I'm sorry. I just get so rushed, working long hours—"

He cut me off. "You're buying a lot of protein. Makes me think you're black marketing it."

"Oh, no!" I assured him. Though it was an idea for fundraising, except we didn't have enough now. "No, I'd never do that. Please, even a suggestion of that could lose me my business."

"I know, that's why I'm here," he said. "You're already unusual enough without standing out on our files."

We went on like that, he speaking down from the Mount, I abasing myself before him. I would rather eat maggots than do that, but it was the only way out of the situation. "Sorry, Sorry, Yes, Master" was what he needed for his ego, so I provided it.

He said, "There are laws against wasting food, you know."

"Uh, yes," I said. "I didn't think I was pushing them? Am I? I'm sorry."

"Just what's with all the sweets?" he asked.

"Oh, that," I said. "When friends come to the apartment, we snack while we watch vid. And I keep some of it here to give to customers now and then."

"That's not a good business practice," he said, while handling the four bars of chocolate I'd brought out of the fridge to show him. He examined the labels. They were good brands by Earth standards. Heck, by standards anywhere. Swiss chocolate is incomparable.

"Am I being that illegal?" I asked.

"You are," he said. "Friendly advice: have your friends bring snacks with them, be responsible with your own stuff, don't give freebies not related to this business out to customers, and if you need to eat that much, see your clinic about your digestion."

"Of course!" I agreed. "I am really sorry. I just hadn't realized . . ." I tapered off as he nodded and headed for the door. My fear of discovery was the perfect base for the act of a fearful slave, and it came out beautifully. And all the bribe I'd needed was some chocolate. I held myself tight until I was sure he was gone, then heaved a sigh.

Our solution to that was yet more scheduling, since we couldn't get more IDs. We calculated how much food and sundries each of us should theoretically be buying as single adults, and set up a chart. We changed stores and hours every trip or two, so as to not leave a pattern or be noticed. We'd go in, shop, be asked, "Do you have a discount card? Would you like one?" We'd reply, "Yeah, sure," then toss the card in the trash outside and repeat at the next store. Consistent refusal might not be noted as aberrant behavior, but I was getting paranoid at this point. Every potential leak required that much more work to plug. Shortly, we'd all be twitching bundles of nerves. I was, already.

On top of all that was a personal problem. I'm essentially a loner. I can only handle so much input from the herd before I need silence for an equal amount of time, or to smash things. I get around this on duty by having a specialty that requires me to smash things. Here, I couldn't. It would not be good to let rage take over and destroy my command, either. I was a spring, bound and wound tight and getting tighter. Eventually, I'd have to uncoil or break.

CHAPTER 22

Even after years of experience, I was still amazed at the incompetence of the UN. I know, I've told myself for years not to be. But they never cease to make the wrong decision at the wrong time, and pile stupidity on top of idiocy. It was little different from the mass hysteria of Earth's 19th and 20th centuries. How the hell did we survive to get off this decrepit, marginally habitable mudball with Government "helping"?

They attacked the Freehold. More specifically, they attacked Grainne itself. I could see seizing the jump points and forcing a blockade, but to attack the surface with an undefended rear? It was archaic thinking that only a politician or a politically motivated general could come up with.

Tyler kicked my bunk and said, "Boss."

I woke, grunted a "Yeah?" and rolled out. It was 3 am local.

"Local news," she said.

I stumbled through the doorway behind her, coming awake and wondering what was so important at this hour.

Vid was on, and as I approached I heard "—no additional details at this time, but the 71st Special Unit is expected to have control of the capital city of Jefferson very shortly. Again, according to the UNPF Space Force, the carrier *Johnson* launched assault shuttles just a few minutes ago. The purpose of this mission is to have troops seize Grainne's capital of Jefferson and wrest power away from the military dictatorship that controls the planet—" They went on, but I tuned them out. No facts there.

"When the hell did we get a military dictatorship?" I asked. It's a laughable idea. Our constitution splits power between District and Freehold, and the entire reserve military takes its orders from the District councils. Any dictator would at worst create a short-lived bloodbath as the military fratricided, then be himself slaughtered by the populace. At best, he'd be ignored, shot and forgotten. And it's a silly idea. We don't have leaders who want supreme power. We're set up to keep that kind of freak in the private sector, where they belong.

"According to them, we've always had one," Deni said. "The Citizen's Council controls the military, which makes them a dictatorship."

"*Any* government controls its military," I protested. "Sorry. Got it now," I said, shaking my head and awake at last. "'We are at war with East Asia. We have *always* been at war with East Asia.'" How gullible Earthies were.

If you're not from Earth, have you ever tried to watch their news? "Something you're eating right now may be poisoned! We'll tell you what it is, right after a word from our sponsor!" It's not "news," it's "Entertainment," with a capital "E." They have so little content padded by so much repetition, crap, half-assed speculation by experts who know dick and hawking of worthless merchandise, it's hard for a rational person to pick out the few gems of actual intel. And it is tedious to wade through the junk to do so. They couldn't have made my job harder if they'd designed it that way.

Officially, it's a free press. In actuality, any media that doesn't suck up to the main source of info, the ruling bureaucrats, doesn't get any stories. They're mouthpieces, plain and simple. Every election there's a struggle among bureaucrats to control the news and among the media to control the source—the politicians. Yes, they're all part of the same power struggle. Madness.

It was tense, and we didn't sleep, rested only fitfully, and ate little. We had to maintain our business cover, not daring to pay undue attention to events. But inside, we were all wondering, was this how it began? Was Earth seizing our home? How would it play out for us? Was this assault force big enough and organized enough to defeat our defenses? What of our friends?

This could be the start of the mission that would kill us, and a large chunk of Earth's government and infrastructure, and we weren't really in place to do anything yet. What was happening?

We didn't know. No one knew. The day was a waste, and I wasn't even able to break loose long enough to send a "Don't worry, we're the best" pep message to the other cells.

The next day, footage and reports started coming in. With about ten hours of light speed lag at each end and relay time through the jump point, no one actually knew anything until then.

Then we got our revenge. We spent the next day laughing in hysterics.

They dropped ten assault shuttles, 1000 troops, with the intent being to seize commo and the Citizens' Council Building. Rather pointless; they are only there on formal occasions. Earth still meets in person to discuss matters. None of the colonies or star nations bother. That's what comms are for. That was Wrong Assumption Number One.

WAN Two was that they'd have the element of surprise. Orbital Defense Command and Grainne Defense Command conduct regular training missions, and we do get occasional criminals trying to sneak by to set up facilities in the Hinterlands. Our people are used to practicing, and occasionally actually burning targets out of space. The UNPF ships were detected, challenged and slagged. Only six made it down. Those six were pinned down by Starport security, the flight line crew on the military side of the port (Capital District Reserve 4th Aviation Regiment and their support), and a few City Safety Patrol and some Resident volunteers. People keep assuming that these hedonistic, colorful Freeholders are unarmed, helpless peasants. It keeps getting them killed.

WAN Three was that we wouldn't respond. Two of their ships were caught as they jumped through with follow-up forces for Westport and Marrou. They dropped out of JP 3 and JP 1 and were at once surrounded by massive firepower. Gunboat commanders used them as a live-fire training exercise, disabling star drives and pinning them in place. Then they were swarmed and seized. The *Johnson* was deep insystem, but a gunboat chased them down and intimidated them into surrender. Yes, an *assault carrier* surrendered to a lone *gunboat*. What cowardice and incompetence was that?

I really felt sorry for the 800 dead grunts. Those poor bastards had followed orders that sounded good, boarded in high morale and with good intentions (from their point of view) and had been scorched into ash or shot down like dogs. Of course, Earth blamed us for "unreasonable use of deadly weapons." What, they expected us to use stun batons and giggle gas? Apparently so.

It actually took me days to draw out that info. There was so little real intel on the news. Heck, I'd been tasked with finding such threats and I'd had no inkling. They actually were very good at keeping secrets. From their own people. I even had to get a few blanks filled in from our intel people, in a message I received a week later. Why? After the dog was fucked, the UN knew what had gone wrong, every commercial Freehold station had the reports, most of the star nations knew. The only people still in the dark were the peasants sucking mud on Earth.

It was two days later that I got a message for the DC area team, meaning my immediate HQ, to conduct "Doolittle." They wanted me to attack the UN base at Langley, wreck it but minimize casualties, and report back. It seemed rather foolhardy politically, but the real intent was to plant some of our programmed weapons and loot what intel we could get. It might blow our covers, of course. I sighed and got people to work. At least I could acquire more assets while I did so.

I'll skip most of the details of the raid. You've read what we did to the Caledonians when they expected us. Twenty of us unannounced at Langley was a brick through the crystal cabinet. We tore the base apart.

The high point for me was bypassing the guard and the alarm at the Installation Commander's house and squatting on his bed with two of my kids. We watched his wife and him snore and drool blissfully, until we got the signal. I prodded him in the chest with the Merrill.

He said, "Huwha?" and sat up. That let me press the muzzle against his lips. His eyes got wide as he started to track.

"Please consider yourself my hostage," I told him. "Wake up your wife and let's go." Yes, it was abrupt. I didn't have time for discourse.

We ran them outside and into a borrowed vehicle, then took them to the Security Force office which we'd commandeered. We shoved them into the cells in their underwear along with the growing number of terrified rabbits we'd acquired. I grabbed a handy young blonde contractor who was a beauty by Earth standards, too soft and pale for me, and frogmarched her down to the arms vault. The sergeant inside was refusing to open the door. I knocked, figured he could see us on the monitor, stuck the muzzle into her mouth as she whimpered most convincingly. I said, "We haven't killed anyone yet. Open the door and we won't start. Otherwise, I'll keep killing until you do."

Of course, it worked. The watch commander ordered him to open the vault, and he did. We took him down, added him to the tally and started loading weapons and ammo. We'd need some for our upcoming operation and we'd distribute the rest for money.

By the time we left the base in the early dawn, we had rifles, grenades and some hijacked explosives. We had reduced the facility to a shambles and uploaded all our software weapons. We'd copied as many files as we could and accessed as many more as practical, both to create a security risk and to give them more to search through. The base personnel were running screaming, the upper staff were locked up, the police were afraid to come through the gate lest we shoot at them again and the government was trying to sit on the press, unsuccessfully. No one noticed us slip away from the perimeter in twenty different directions, and none of us were followed. We had no casualties.

That left the minor problems of DNA traces, explosive sniffers, possible stray images on cameras, and a manhunt. We burned all those IDs, of course.

I wasn't sure why we had just done what we did. I knew the UN had conducted a botched raid against Jefferson, back home. This was obviously related, but I didn't know why it was necessary to give them a bloody nose like this. It seemed a terrible risk of our covers. I spent the following week not sleeping, not eating, and trying not to have a breakdown. Nothing ever did come of it. Our embassy was ejected right after that, and I suppose they assumed our embassy security had conducted the raid, or that we'd been smuggled in for that and then had departed. There hadn't been any real casualties, on purpose. That seemed to be the deciding factor. It's very hard to create a crusade against petty degradation. In fact, many people were laughing about it, and a news survey showed that most didn't consider it important.

Just over a month later, with fall descending and giving trees in the parks at least some taste of the passionate autumn colors we get back home, we got orders to deploy to our final positions. It was a sobering event. Frank and I said our goodbyes and split, him for the West Coast, me for the Midwest. The twenty of us split for four cities. The Atlanta squad split for four more. The European Platoon fragmented across the old cities of the Continent, and so on. In a matter of days, we were in twenty-six small towns, eleven of twelve medium cities and twenty-eight large ones of the thirty we'd planned for, allowing for the casualties we'd taken already.

CHAPTER 23

Our business was transferred to the team staying in Washington. I was still "owner," along with an investment company. They'd been making noises about buying my share and controlling it themselves. It was a pretty standard deal. I led them on a bit at a time. We needed to keep it, but I didn't mind signing deals for advertising, etc, as long as the only people who could access the property were our people, the police, insurance investigators, federal, state and local representatives and anyone with a court order. The investors would have to ask.

After that, my team trickled in the direction of Minneapolis, using fresh IDs from our bare few. The embassy had funneled additional chips to us as it received them from outsystem Earthies who were suborned. We kept our command people stocked with those and knocked off a few punks, including several of Fart Cutter's old gang for their chips. This wasn't unusual, apparently. Identity theft is fairly common, so it went unquestioned. Any petty criminal found dead and stripped was assumed to have his ID in use elsewhere, and it was shortly deleted. People went to great lengths to hide bodies. We buried them in remote dumpsters, or drained the blood and stashed them in the roof hatches of abandoned buildings. Those bodies would never be found. And the way the system worked, out of sight was out of mind. It only registered presence, not absence.

First was to set up our new business in Bloomington, which was coordinated by our investor, on the theory that we would be much more willing to start selling out as we developed more of them. This time, it was a commercial warehouse. Commercial warehousing was easier on the nerves than personal warehousing. We should have thought of it earlier. Of course, it took more startup and the potential clientele was smaller. And our old one in Washington was well-established now. The rough part was that it was much harder to sneak in funds from outside, with the Embassy gone.

We acquired four different safehouses, and arranged ways to tell if they were compromised. Deni and I set up the first one, acting as a disgustingly cute young couple who couldn't keep hands off each other. It wasn't much of an act. We chose an efficiency apartment (I call it a bach) in a suburb on the south edge of the metroplex. It had one window and a door, two outside walls, as it was at the end of a row, and would do as a bolthole during an escape. That was our first priority.

It was a nice little place. The apartment was on a side road off the entrance, and there were lots of speed bumps. An attack on the ground would be slow. The unit was on the back of the building, but that side was protected by, yes, an adjacent fenced-in personal warehouse facility. People on Earth have so much stuff they have to store it in locked boxes away from home. My thought is, if you don't need it enough to keep it at home, get rid of it. And for the price of the storage, one can lease or buy that much more dwelling space. At least on Grainne. Space was limited here, and I'm digressing. Any attack would have to be on foot, rather than drive up to the door and bust in. That was all to the good. We arranged payment to be by deduction from Deni's bank account, as she had one of our few legit IDs, and did a test at once. We left a few bank notes on the opened bed (it folded from the wall) and left the door unlocked.

Five days later, it was untouched. We'd hoped so. It was a clean, simple neighborhood of unassuming people, and no one hassled them much. They were too remote for the inner city thugs, not wealthy enough for the roving rural gangs to bother with. We stocked it with dry goods and cans and a few basics.

Kimbo and I found the second place, masquerading as a gay couple. We both wore a bit of makeup. He had trouble playing the role, and he swings now and then. I guess the act was just not him.

It was a small half unit not that far from downtown, attached to the back of a house, behind its garage. It had been built as an office for some forgotten business run from the garage. It was old and worn but not decrepit, and we put on The Act.

"So," I asked him as the landlord looked on. She was a sweet elderly lady, and smiled warmly as she reminisced as to her own youth. "Will it work, pal?" I brushed up against him and cupped his far hip.

He managed to turn his part into "not in front of others, you're embarrassing me!" and shied only slightly. "Well, it's small, but I won't need much when I'm in town," he said. "I won't have to go near the house."

"We can dress this up," I assured him. "Perhaps some of those purple whirls in the textured paint. That and some new furniture and some lighting."

The landlady said, "Please do. I'd love to have it taken care of. Good tenants are so hard to find these days. Not like when I was younger." She was so nice. She'd like this next part.

"Well," I said. "We'd prefer it if people didn't know Andry was here," I said. "If we could not sign a lease, I'd be happy to pay up front and add a little for your trouble. I know there's a hint of risk, but we'd *rilly* appreciate it," I threw the single slang word in there. A hint, not overkill, is all it takes.

"Oh, I'd be happy to, but the State has to have a copy for the property tax," she said. "It's so annoying, I know."

"Yes," I agreed. "Well, we'd really like, um, my family not to know he's here," I said, twisting the ring on my finger. "I mean, I care for them all, and I wouldn't want any friction. But I could cover some of it in cash." I acted embarrassed at the suggestion.

"I suppose we could work something out," she agreed. Cash was always good, even if illegal in quantity. The quantity I was going to give her would ensure her silence. It took only a few minutes to settle on a rent, pay her a month in bills now, and promise that "Andry" would meet her the first of each month with rent in cash, and we'd leave another three months with her in case he missed. She was either poor or greedy or rebellious or all three, because she jumped on it. I could see her buying a few luxuries here and there, and being glad of her secret tenants in the closet out back.

Tyler and I got the third one. We were acting as an established young couple in graduate school, and got one near the UM campus. The building might have been three hundred years old. It was picturesque, or picture skew more accurately, but was adequate. It would be a waystop and diversion more than anything. It had once been multiple locking rooms, sort of a private dorm, and had been just a house before that. They did build them well, if on the ugly side of plain in the 22nd century.

It looked for a while as if we might not be needed. Things steadied down to nasty messages and veiled insults. The UN called us everything but a limited-franchise republic. We ignored them. The stuff Earth wanted from us economically they got, if more expensively due to circuitous routes to avoid the impression of being bought from us. It was okay to buy a sub-license of a program from Novaja Rossia or Ramadan, even if the royalties went back to the Freehold, as long as no direct transaction took place. It was all politics for appearance. What Earth demanded politically we told them to stuff. They didn't like that of course.

I even saw one ridiculous Person on the Street interview where a shopkeeper defended Earth's demands with the statement, "Well, this is where civilization began ... so ... y'know?" as if that debatable criterion were relevant. Besides, even if it had begun on Earth, the rest of us had moved beyond the flea-picking and grunting stage.

No, we were going to be needed. This would play out shortly. Meanwhile, we got back to the business of being obedient little peasants while clutching every penny we could get toward our needed resources.

We had some deliciously ironic sources of income. For example, in Arabia, Aaron Livne of Jewish ancestry was running the Mtali

Relief and Development Fund, acquiring money from Muslims. Besides paying him and four other Operatives healthy salaries, due to the lenient local laws it was able to pay overhead for their lodging, food and travel, as well as "advertising," which included mass-market mail with encoded data for me. What was left of the donations was sent to Mtali, to a drop run by our Embassy (which we maintained for business reasons only), who funneled the money into purchases of equipment from our South American office in São Paolo, who pocketed the profit at that end, after paying taxes. And Noora Radosevic of Muslim ancestry, portraying an expatriate from the Iraq Province of the Republic of Israel, reduced her taxes by donating to MRDF. You might think it was risky linking the two like that, but it was so ridiculous that they'd never make the connection, just assume it was coincidence.

The news changed again shortly. The transit and shipping regulations started to be enforced to the letter of the law against Freehold Registry vessels, or more specifically, Freehold Registered vessels that were also owned by Freehold Residents, rather than foreign nationals using our system. Shipments were seized and a few crews detained. All that was annoying, but not critical by itself. It was a power game.

Six months later, it all went to hell. The idiots invaded.

At least this time it was competently done. They seized all three Jump Points then hit the major military installations with kinetic kills. We gathered around the vid and our blood ran cold.

Some bubblehead reporter was saying, "—and with that, the junta has been taken out of power. The UNPF plans to consolidate the planet and put down any insurrection, and the Colonial Commission will resume administration, the end goal being to bring this disadvantaged star nation up to speed in those areas it lacks so it can join the UN. I understand there's a lot of areas that need fixed. For that, over to Jack Raffi."

His fellow lackey took over. "That's right, Jewel. Let's start by reviewing recent history," he said as a chart and graphics came up. "After three hundred years of colonization and development, first as a possession and then as a member of the Colonial Alliance, Grainne declared itself a star nation. However, they took an unprecedented and outrageous turn by declaring independence from the UN and the rule of law. The courts still haven't reached a decision on whether or not it is legal for a nation to exist outside of UN law—" I tuned it out while reviewing our preparations so far. We likely had enough goods to handle a takedown at this point, but I always like extra hardware. Also, if the UN actually had control of communications, I might not get any signals from home. That left me the guy making those decisions. Also, it would be dangerous to be caught reading any messages that could be traced back to the Freehold. Though that was a risk I already faced. I snapped back alert as the mouthpiece said, "—will start by nationalizing the assets of the ruling class and imposing the basic infrastructure of government. Hard as it may be for many viewers to comprehend, the so-called 'Freehold' holds no elections, grants no rights to any basic human needs such as medical care or housing, and restricts rule to a tiny minority of incredibly wealthy despots—"

"Turn that shit *off*!" I shouted. Tyler waved her hand and did so.

I was seeing everything tinged in red through my rage. Not only had they attacked a tiny nation with overwhelming force, the cowards had used weapons of mass destruction, then had the sheer gall to claim they were "liberating" us from oppressors . . . oppressors who were a tiny minority because they had to prove their dedication by risking their lives and then coughing up their personal fortunes as ransom. The cleanest member of the UN wasn't fit to lick the shit off the boots of our least worthy Citizen. And since our Citizens surrendered their wealth to serve, what "assets of the ruling class" could they possibly refer to? And we don't "grant" rights. Human beings derive the rights they wish from nature, by their willingness to defend them.

Hell with the philosophy. It was a vicious military attack, an immoral theft of our history and culture, and outright lies designed to make us appear savage thugs. It was an absolute reversal of the truth.

I did my duty then, as much as it hurt me to do so. "We will continue with the mission until we get orders otherwise, or lose contact." It was an order second only to Mtali as the hardest one I'd ever given, even as simple as it was. Because inside I wanted to slag the entire fucking planet right then.

We all went to bed. I doubt anyone slept. I know I didn't. All I could do was think about the situation. Naumann had been correct again. He was always correct. It was uncanny his grasp of events and outcomes. Now I had the fate of at least two planets in my hands, and what I decided to do would determine how many people lived or died.

The rhetoric continued in the press. It seemed we were guilty of being successful.

It came back to economics again. The standard way of colonizing a system, once one had been found that was either inhabitable or terraformable was to send a science ship through to set up the Jump Point, then start shoveling gear through. As the science ship has to travel at sublight speed, this takes several years.

Then Freehold-based Brandt StarDrive Systems had developed the Phase Drive, allowing a ship thus equipped to translate to star drive without a Jump Point. They were expensive as hell: the year we started equipping our military ships with them, all other budgetary concerns were chopped to the bone. Very few civilian operations could afford them, but any who could were securing loans and buying drives. They intended to exploit the opportunity by finding as many planets as possible, taking the Jump Point gear with them, and basically owning a system. It made sense. It would help the human race expand.

The key was that word "exploit," which on Earth means "someone is doing better than I am, and that cannot be allowed because it isn't fair." Never mind that these operations were risking their fortunes and their lives on these jaunts. It wasn't "fair," that recurring whine of neofeudalists, liberals, terrorists and children. Life is supposed to be fair? I'd never been told that.

Beyond that was the fact that every year, more businesses moved to the Freehold, at least our Halo, because the low taxes and minimal regulations made business easier. It's called "supply and demand," and we discussed it earlier. We supplied a friendly business environment. They demanded it and paid for it. That's why we had almost no unemployment, and certainly not in the technical fields, and a tremendous R&D base for a small nation.

Yes, we were rich, getting richer, and all the UN propaganda couldn't hide that from the Masses. We were a threat and had to go.

On Earth, we continued our preparations. One of the reasons we'd picked an industrial operation as a cover was so we could get supplies. I'd never encountered societal paranoia as it existed here. Explosives are strictly controlled. Firearms are restricted. In theory, they are banned, but you can get them if you can afford one, the license to go with it, the "safe" to store it in against the theft that wouldn't happen if they weren't so rare and prized, if you can pass the psychological test, are single or in a "stable" relationship, because of course you might kill someone during a breakup, don't belong to a "questionable" group (any group the current politicos don't like) and if you can get a politician to authorize it. Translation: rich, politically connected suckups have guns and bodyguards. Peasants can beg for mercy and hope not to get their brains splattered. This is what Earth defines as "reasonable."

You'd think it stopped there. I'd thought it stopped there. Apparently, denied a market source of weapons, criminals arranged to have them built. Therefore, steel, ceramics, certain polymers, industrial mills, lathes and heat treating furnaces, laser, fusion, particle and force beam tools and chemicals that might be turned into propellants or explosives (any acid or nitrate and it got worse from there) requires licensing, certificates and inspections. You have to account for every scrap of the stuff.

So Kimbo's persona got investigated by a bureaurat to determine his fitness to handle materials for maintenance. He put on a good show, we bribed the suit with a case of liquor and some cash, and Tyler made the ultimate sacrifice and met him in a hotel room after he hinted. Worse than her life, she sacrificed her dignity. But we needed that authorization. I would have had sex with him myself to get his signature, if necessary. Six weeks later, we had a license for power equipment and restricted materials, even though we weren't a manufacturer. We would absolutely toe the line with that, using it as a cover for the materials we acquired elsewhere.

The news didn't get better. Marshal Dyson, our Commander in Chief, was brought back to Earth and imprisoned, pending charges. Not "pending trial," but "pending charges." Holding someone without charging them was a violation of the UN Charter. That didn't apply to us, though, since we weren't UN members. It was a legal gray area that I grudgingly had to admit was yet to be defined by the courts.

What was utterly outrageous was our captured troops who were being charged with "rebellion and sedition." They were soldiers in uniform, under orders from what had been a recognized government. Under the Geneva, Hague and Mars Conventions, they could be charged with war crimes for atrocities that violated the Conventions, but not for the civil "crime" of "rebellion." Of course they were rebelling by definition.

A large number, meaning a few hundred, of UN troops were being captured. They were not being exchanged, we were told. That was ludicrous. Our people would certainly swap one for one our captives for theirs. We couldn't afford to lose the troops we had. It would be to the UN's advantage not to swap prisoners. That would explain the illegal criminal charges against our people. But why make a stink about there then not being a swap? Something wasn't right there.

Kimbo was turning out assorted complex chemicals that were the basis of several hyper explosives and chemical weapons. All were being stored in the ceramic-lined drums he'd gotten authorization for. The small tools he had were cover as maintenance gear, but were actually being used to manufacture valves and delivery apparati. We lived in constant fear of either discovery, or an accident that would kill us. And we still had to continue business as usual. We were working 19- or 20-hour days, 7 days per Earth week, and it started to show. I reduced us to a maximum of 18 waking hours. We needed sleep.

One morning, a news load arrived that shocked us. Behind the reporter's preening face, we could actually see Jefferson.

It looked like hell.

Fires had gutted large parts of downtown. Traffic was mostly on foot due to damage to the roads and bridges. All air traffic had been grounded, forcing what was moving to squeeze about on the damaged roads. The signs of population looked very light. Those I could see looked drab and sad, much like the wretched peasants I lived among now. In short, it looked like something from 500 years in the past.

Then the reporter spoke of the "progress" that was being made . . .

They had destroyed my home, and dared to tell me it was for the good.

I swore at that moment that when the time came, I would make Earth pay a thousand times over.

That evening, it was just Deni and me in the office. I stared out the window at spattering rain and gray clouds, lost in my thoughts, and wasn't even aware of what I was pondering until her voice interrupted me.

"What are you thinking?" she asked.

I drifted back to the surface and replied, "That I want this op over with so we can go home. This is a sentence in hell."

"The place?" she asked. "Or the mission?"

"Yes," I replied. I had my head in one widespread hand. I felt better with my eyes covered.

"It must be hard on you, Ken," she said. "You're carrying the entire stress load of everyone, as well as your own."

I straightened up and nodded. "I keep waiting for one of these mistakes to get us nailed, for us to be caught by someone bright enough or dogged enough to follow up, who's dedicated to the cause of universal order. And then we're dead." I stared at her. She was tense about something. I could see it in her face, expressions familiar despite the sculpting that had been done.

Our fingers near each other suddenly touched, then wove together, then along each other's arms. "It's been a strain . . ." she started to say, and tapered off.

We drew back from each other. I knew exactly what we both wanted, and knew why it was a bad idea, and why nothing else would get us to relax, and why that relaxation would cause more problems than it would solve. I stood up and walked toward the window. Not much could be seen through most of the panes even before water rippled down them, but I could pretend I wasn't thinking what my body was thinking.

Then she was behind me, touching my back with a static discharge and her voice breathing through my nerves, "Ken . . ."

I followed her.

Deni's reaction was so unlike her. She was always passionate and intimate, but this was different. No sooner had I closed the door to my room behind me than she was inside my clothes and her mouth was on me. Then she pulled them off me completely, and stripped while still working me.

I suppose "frantic" is the word. She insisted I take her hard, and we kissed and touched and clutched at each other. Body hair does not improve oral pleasure either, but we didn't care. Then I was inside her again, eyes locked and thrusting muscles against each other. From training and solitude and long experience that was too far behind us, we felt each other build. The raging staccato rhythm of raindrops on the roof above matched our mutual climax. Orgasm stopped any worries, for a brief time.

I was still flushed after a shower, and was sitting on the couch contemplating sex and strategy. And yes, the two are related, except in one the conquest is over emotion, in the other over reason. Thumping on the stairs and a knock announced Tyler's return.

I was sure our indiscretion was obvious, especially when Deni came from the bathroom toweling her hair. We both had that sated aura, and that mated aura.

"Been quiet here?" Tyler asked, looking back and forth between us.

"Just the rain," I replied, trying to sound neither tense nor relaxed, but conversational. A news load was on, but I wasn't watching it.

Deni said, "Could have showered outside and saved water."

"Okay," she nodded, and handed me a ramchip. "That's what I have," she said. "Still not a word from back home. It's looking bad, Boss."

"So we continue to wait," I told her. "We don't want to move too soon, or without orders. It might be some months."

" 'Months,' " she replied. She continued, shrugging, "Well, if that's what it takes, I can let the back pay pile up."

She gave us both another appraising glance as she headed for her room.

One of the dangerous mundane duties was depositing our business funds to the bank every week. While most of the transactions were automatic, a few were run in person and a few more were done by cash card. Cash cards are like cash in that whoever possesses one can acquire the funds. Theoretically, it can be either traced or, if an anonymous card, blocked if stolen. In actuality the possessor has the funds. So every week one of us was subject to being dragged by gangers while making the deposit.

Officially, the government advises one to "discourage clients from using cash. Vary the schedule of deposit times. Consider paying a courier company to make the deposits . . ." Well, we needed the money that would be used to pay a courier. Since we were all Operatives, we did our own security.

We saw no problem with that. Another piece of their advice was to "consider a health and fitness class to give you more confidence against crime." I'm not sure what "confidence" someone in great shape is supposed to have against punks with clubs, but we've already established that they were illogical and morally corrupt. We took weapons, though camouflaged ones.

I enjoyed my monthly turn of taking the funds in. It gave me time alone, and time to think. I'd dress in local casual style and drive down. I'd at first expected to deliver the envelope to a drive through facility. Apparently, however, those are closed after normal business hours. Something about bombs and feces in the chutes, and the few personnel at 24-hour facilities being killed. Sufficient security was too expensive to justify it. So they didn't do it. And only a paranoid nut would think he needed a weapon to defend himself. Besides, it's not worth a fight over mere money, or so they said.

And no, we couldn't wait until the next business day to do it. By law, we had to have all funds in the bank before midnight. Don't ask me, because I don't know.

I only ever had one problem, and I rather enjoyed it. Call me an atavist.

I arrived at the bank and parked. The lot was empty, as I'd waited until the last minute. It had been well lit at one time, but someone had smashed the lights. It was a perfect place to be attacked. There was no one immediately visible, but I grabbed my stylish walking stick anyway. It was one of the things the cops had trouble objecting too, as it could be considered a medical aid, yet it could still serve as a weapon. Officially, I should have a prescription. In actuality, at worst they'd seize it.

The weather was clear, so visibility was good. There was enough traffic noise, however, that I couldn't hear any potential threats. I started the fifteen meter walk around the formerly decorative flower island, now dead and full of weeds, with my senses aware for anything.

And here they came. Why alleys and convolutions are allowed, with the threats they can hide, I don't know. It could be a conspiracy. It's more likely stupidity. There were only five of them, but at their pace, they'd be at my vehicle before I could get back. They were armed with those little kitchen knives, hard polymer knuckles and pipes or cables with tape wrapped as crude grips. Talk about your Homo habilis. The hope was that I'd drop the package and run. Barring that, they could "Teach me a lesson" if I delivered it, by beating the shit out of me and trashing my vehicle. I opted for the latter, sort of, and slid the envelope into the narrow slot that was just wide enough to hold it. The vacuum handling tools took it, and peeled off the polymer coating that protected the envelope proper and contents from the shit that had already been pointlessly smeared across the opening. I turned to walk back to the car just as the zeros arrived there.

"You better have a card, scrotebreath," one of them said. It's culturally traditional to have a cash card you can drop as you run. Yes, the locals reinforce the bad behavior by wimping out and paying the thugs. And as long as they do so, it will continue to happen. I was about to do them all a favor.

"Nope," I said. "Sorry. Now let me get to my car, please."

"You'll remember next time, asshole," the spokesman said as he charged me.

Of course, I was unarmed . . . mostly. You recall I was carrying a walking stick.

Well, it wasn't just a walking stick. Did I forget to say it had been made by Kimbo? Clumsy of me. It was solid carbon crystal pipe as used in starship fuel systems, rated for some ungodly pressure. It contained 150 grams of mercury in a vacuum. It was tipped with bronze, also. What I had was a disguised mace and then some.

As they approached, I lifted it slightly, holding it to check and block. The first one came in boldly, trying to psychologically over-power me. I flattened the stick at my side and drove it forward. The head hit him in the breastbone, then the mercury slammed home. He went, "Guuuhhh!" and staggered back, clutching his chest and falling to his knees. I caught him a glance with the tip as I brought it up, and when it came down, the tip cracked his skull . . . then that mercury thumped again. He wouldn't be getting up.

Moron number two was standing looking dumb, and I swung sideways, smacking him in the nose and letting the mercury do the work, then jabbing back the other way to catch a third asshole in the trachea. He gurgled and dropped. I came overhead, gripped it like a ball bat, and made a delayed swing, holding my wrists until the last moment then exploding into the turn with a snap. I timed it just right, and the bronze finial smacked into another clown's head just as the mercury arrived for backup. I won't bother you with the gory details, except to say that he would need plastic surgery before his casket was opened for the viewing.

I slid the shaft back in my hand, stepped forward and smashed it like a ram into the ribs of the last goof, then again. I dropped the tip and drove it down onto his right instep. In training, this thing broke bricks. On his foot, it was spectacular, and his shoe pulped open. The head smacked his chin as I brought it up, break-ing his jaw, and I stepped over and kept walking. Ten seconds later I was driving away. It actually was an accident that I drove over the shin of one of them.

Sure, I could have used my bare hands, but why break a sweat if you don't have to?

r r r

More scary things came about from that prisoner of war issue. I got a message inquiring about it. As it required wasting a standard contact to ask, as well as using a code that would have to be scrapped, I knew they were serious.

Decoded, it read, "Can you confirm numbers of UN POWs repatriated to Earth since commencement of hostilities?"

I encoded a message back that said, "No mention of such in Earth news."

That was disturbing. We had released UN prisoners, but said prisoners had not come home triumphantly in the news.

THEORY: The UN didn't want them admitting how badly we were kicking their asses. Unlikely, or I wouldn't still be here; we would have won and I'd be home. The strategic calculations said we couldn't win under the present conditions, anyway.

THEORY: The UN didn't want its troops speaking of how well they were treated, after the crap they were still telling the masses, that we were not feeding them and keeping them in unpleasant environmental conditions. But that wasn't a huge deal. Admit that early reports were in error. Print a new Truth that everyone knew was True. Boast of how we'd "morally improved" and "acceded to decency" under their guidance. It was easy to spin it to their benefit.

THEORY: Any returned prisoners would give us an element of humanity in the news, so those troops were being held incommunicado by their own people for leverage. That wasn't reasonable. What would happen after the war? Assuming they won, the deceit would be obvious. Unless they never intended to repatriate their own people. That was silly.

Hadn't there been mention on Mtali of unreturned prisoners, whom the factions insisted they knew nothing about?

No, that wasn't a practical concept, no matter how screwed up the logic a politician might use. They couldn't assume a loss on their part. It was unthinkable. Therefore, it was unnecessary to jump through all these hoops.

Only . . . where were those released POWs?

I was being made paranoid by my environment. Because I could not think of a good reason for them not to be in the news.

I watched Earth's elections with fascination. We don't bother with them. The idea of counting noses is silly. Given the education level on Earth, it's even sillier. Those illiterati are not competent to decide an issue. Besides, if it's humiliating to be ruled, how much more degrading is it to choose your masters?

Our public comm got election ads from all the politicians. Multiple times a day. They started as mindless pap about how many billions of marks they'd taken from the taxpayers and were giving back to them as services they wouldn't need if they'd had the money in the first place. Silly, yet convincing to these sheep.

Then they got nasty. Candidate Henke alleged that Assembly-woman Julie Larson had cheated on her taxes. She alleged that he was a "muckraker" for the comment. He replied that she was "attacking" him and somehow wrong for doing so. She called him a "racist," even though they were both the same race. He called her a "gender-unification bitch."

The whole debate was amusing to me, and I'm sure to the voters, who, when this was over, would give one of these people the win, and thereby lose themselves either way.

What I was able to find about Larson was that she was on the Subcommittee on Housing Costs, while owning four condemned buildings she was waiting for the city she allegedly represented but hadn't lived in for fifteen years to seize and dispose of using its taxpayer assets. She was, in fact, delinquent on her taxes for ten years, which she blamed on caring for her ailing mother, who had died four years before the trend started. Though somehow, she was on the Committee on Financial Services and the Com-mittee on Tax Policy. (How many committees did these clowns have? I did a quick check: 4132 assemblypersons and 6000+ committees. Really.)

Eventually, she won. The week before the election, trailing in the polls, she blubbered and whined about how unfair "those people" could be, then claimed the voting programs were rigged against her. After winning, she stated that "We've sent a message that only good people belong in the assembly and the bad people can stay home." She was a very gracious winner.

And the UN wanted to bring us the "right" to participate in

this stupidity. They might as well simply hold us up at gunpoint and steal all our resources.

Then I remembered they were doing exactly that.

We didn't have much luck finding useful AI weapons on the nets, though we did find a couple. It was a chase game. There are a few rebels on Earth, and some use their tech skills to create worms, virii, punches and other effects. Sadly, they are uncoordinated. Either they throw one out as a protest, or they do one as a boast of their skills. Very impressive. About as much as graffitiing a building. We planned to show them what organization could do.

Several of our people, including Kimbo, played network tag to glean useful tools. He did that from "our" apartment behind the house of Ms. Dortch, that sweet old lady. While he did that, he was on the phone to Melanie Chastain in Australia, who was watching him to see if anyone probed his operation, and Carlos Mendyk was watching Chastain from Germany, to cover *her*. A word would have Kimbo fleeing and the place abandoned, with no identifiable DNA for a trace.

We thought we'd hit pay dirt with a group called The Democratic Underground. They sounded like revolutionaries. It turned out instead that they were political ranters. The average IQ was around 85, the education level that of 7-year-olds, and all their technical links were garbage. They were simply trying to impress each other with bullshit. As far as their politics, everything was Earth's fault, including the expansion of the universe. Sadly, they weren't even a good political ally for us, because they were such pathetic losers.

There were no permanent sites on network weapon design, of course. What we found were sites tossed up on short notice, hinted at on newsgroups using an ever-shifting slang as code, that were deleted by the government as soon as they were found, with traces run to every system that linked. Kimbo was running through multiple cover IDs, anonymous remailers and cutouts. While we eventually put the tools he found to use, I think in hindsight it was a terrible risk and waste of time for very little real effect. Brute force applied in the right places was a hundred times more effective than any electronic attack on the decentralized nerves of the planet.

One of our worst fears finally caught up with us: Employment. We were a private corporation, so we could hire whom we wanted, right? Well, not on Earth.

All jobs had to be advertised for "fairness." All qualified applicants had to be considered. Some bureaurat noticed we hadn't posted any ads lately, and came by to investigate.

My choice of teammates paid off. With two women and Kimbo's obvious African ancestry, they simply fined us for not filling out the proper admin and left. I tossed a note to everyone else to watch for similar garbage. I'd been fortunate in choosing the right people for the job at hand, based on their ability. According to the UN, I should have hired them based on race, faith, preference and color, without being allowed to ask about their race, faith, preference or color. These rules were necessary, because people were "prejudiced." (Yes, I admit it. I prefer competence.) But these rules made it harder to fire employees who'd complain about being treated unfairly. This raised the standards to hire, thus increasing the education requirement, which increases the taxes paid for education, which means higher wages, which requires a better employee, which were all irrelevant if you were one of the 83% of the population who belonged to a minority, that the hirer was discriminating against.

Don't ask me to explain it. It had been going on for centuries. And there was no recourse against the bribery, stupidity or petty intrusiveness. There was the upper caste—those in the government in any capacity, or those rich enough to bribe them, a gray area of middle class, and those poor who had no say in anything, despite the mythical right to franchise. The bad part is that there are provisions in place that make it impossible to take legal action against those government agents. A corrupt agency chief (as if they have any other type) can literally order a person arrested, raped and beaten to death, and the family can *not* pursue criminal or civil action against him, because to do so would "Interfere with the official's ability to perform his or her duties." But they will take your complaint and review it internally. Likely thereafter, you'll wind up dead in a ditch with three bullets in the base of the skull, having "committed suicide." And I'm not being sarcastic; that was a headline I saw the same week.

I simply gritted my teeth, apologized and filed documents as required, and yet again hoped we'd be gone soon.

Ironically, I had few financial inquiries. Because I was doing it on the cheap and not asking for loans I'd have to guarantee with personal information I didn't have, we never came to anyone's attention. They were too busy dealing with the inquiries they had to worry about those they didn't have.

CHAPTER 24

Deni came in from the back, looking worried. "We need to talk, boss," she said.

"Sure, what?" I replied.

"Privately," she insisted.

My eyebrows went up. Whatever it was was bothering her immensely. "My office," I said. Kimbo was in the room and looked surprised, too.

I let her lead the way, feeling a tension from her. It wasn't friendly, but it wasn't distant, either. Something felt odd, was all.

My office doubled as my bedroom. I had a single cot in the corner, my suitcase and duffel, and the rest was comm gear. There were two chairs. We didn't use them. She turned as I closed the door, paused a moment, and said, "I'm pregnant."

I felt adrenaline ripple through me. "Ohhhh, shit." It wasn't eloquent, but it summed up the situation.

I tried to come to grips with this as a flush ran through me. This was not a good thing. This was not a plot complication. This was a tactical nightmare. "What happened? Your nano expire?"

"*Both* our nanos failed, Ken," she said sharply. "I had help, remember?"

I understood her being upset and didn't argue the obvious.

Mine had probably expired first, now that I thought about it. I said, "If I'd known you were close to deadline..."

"If I'd known *you* were close to deadline..." she said.

Then we were laughing. It was a huge problem, a potential disaster, but it was so ridiculous that we had to let it out.

Then we came back to reality. "So what do we do?" she asked.

The first thing we did was to tell the others. Tyler just nodded and looked thoughtful.

Kimbo exploded. "How the fuck did that happen?"

"Pretty much," I agreed.

"I'm not joking, 'boss,'" he said with an edge to his voice. "Who gave us the lectures on professionalism?"

I said, "Everyone needed to be informed. Now the question is what we do next," I said.

"The question is, what were you bloody thinking? Or were you?" he shouted.

"The question is what we do next," I insisted.

He persisted. "Goddam, man!" he said, using Earth colloquial slang. "Do you have any idea what you've done to our mission? How could you be so goddam careless?" He was scared, and I didn't blame him. This could blow our cover, and we'd all wind up dead or worse. But he was pissing me off, nevertheless.

"BECAUSE I'M A HUMAN BEING!" I roared at him. "I screwed up, okay? We both screwed up." He stepped back at the blast and sat, looking chagrinned. "Lacking a time machine," I said, "we are limited to after the event solutions. Now, what do we do next?"

Tyler spoke, and saved us from going at each other. "Is there any way to do a personnel transfer for another... person?" she asked.

"Not bloody likely," I said as I shook my head. "We are in a state of war, now. We'd have to find another qualified person, smuggle someone in through a third party carrier, with adequately secure ID to get them here, then have them disappear, or try to whomp up some valid ID to let us do a swap for Deni. We're looking at several months to do that."

"And we don't have several months," she noted.

Kimbo put in, "We can't get her into a hospital without an ID chip and a history, but we can probably manage an abortion here."

"No," Deni said. She didn't raise her voice at all, but I've never heard her be so firm.

"What do you mean?" Kimbo asked. "Of course we do."

"No," she said again.

"I don't believe that's your decision to make," he said.

She was out of her chair. "It sure as *fuck* isn't yours, pal!"

He stood too, and for a moment I was afraid there might be blows. "You aren't under orders anymore, Sergeant?" he said sarcastically.

"Enough," I said. I was obeyed. They turned to me. "Covers, please."

"Sorry," he acknowledged. We no longer worried about names, because we changed them so often. But we hadn't used rank terminology for the duration, and wouldn't. "So I guess it's your call to make, boss. What do we do?" He had trouble meeting my eyes. He avoided Deni's.

Deni said, "We continue as we are, I have the baby here if need be, and we deal with it as it happens."

There was silence for several seconds. "Why not abort, Deni?" I asked. My voice was soft. "It would be safer."

"It's my child, I'm not killing it, and there's nothing in law or reg that allows you to make that decision, Ken," she said.

Kimbo said, "That's ridiculous. He's the boss."

"And he doesn't have that authority," Deni repeated.

She was right. Under regulations, I could relieve her from imminent danger, transfer her on a medical waiver, but I had no basis to decide whether or not she carried a child to term. It was her body, the child was in an undefined legal status, but by being in that status was not subject to military orders. It was a can of worms I wasn't going to open. "She's right," I said. I didn't like it. I didn't like *any* of the potential outcomes of this, so I didn't try to argue for one over another.

Acceding to the inevitable, Kimbo said, "So then, for the record, what's our position?"

I dictated my decision as unit commander. "Deni continues with her duties until physically unfit. She handles the admin load here after that. The baby will be born here, barring problems. After that, we play it by ear. The mission has received a potential minor and temporary casualty, and it will be so noted in my reports. But the mission will continue."

The situation continued to degrade. More prisoners were being brought back. More troops were deploying from the UN. But I noticed there were casualties. Not that they admitted to most of them, but there were "live-fire training accidents" and "injuries from vehicle mishaps." As the UN never before had done live-fire exercises, I wasn't convinced. I think our surviving troops were making them pay the ferryman. Indicators from Grainne were that the UN troops had bad morale. I could guess how badly they'd screwed up and how unwelcome they were being made to feel. Even worse than in previous engagements, this time they'd attacked a very wealthy and happy society, and were dragging it down into the mud. It wasn't a temporary gain of assets for the "liberated," followed by economic stagnation. In this case, they'd picked the one nation that was prospering. There was nothing they could do to improve the standard of living or wealth, and it showed. So the locals were putting up a furious fight.

And those locals had centuries of experience being arrogant, self-reliant jerks, in an environment that was unpleasant to Earthies and most other star settlers. I could almost feel sorry for the invading troops. Almost.

Here on Earth, Kimbo made several trips to other elements, setting them up with assorted software and providing tools for distillation and refinement of chemicals. He installed new circuits on vehicles, so we could override the ubiquitous central control every city forced upon travelers.

We settled into a dull but reassuring routine. Of course, we still had periodic excitement, such as Bureau of Commerce inspections. We'd frantically shuffle gear around, ensure nothing incriminating was in sight, that the admin for all the space we were renting to our cover identities was complete in every detail. The last irony we needed was for some minor detail to get us busted for unfair or questionable business practices and units opened up for inspection—units that contained deadly weapons, toxic chemicals and unauthorized weapons grade steel and ceramic.

The economy wasn't good. Allegedly, wars improve business. Perhaps things were better overall, but not for warehousing of industrial supplies and records. Our income shrank, which reduced what we could acquire for our mission. We kept at it.

One of our necessary tasks was to stock our safehouses with supplies. Any obvious military rations or commercial bulk food containers would be an indication of forethought, so we had to buy lots of the grocery store crap and decide how much and what we needed. All of us except Deni cut our food intakes; we'd been gaining bulk on the crap we were eating anyway. Deni needed the food and all the extra nutrients we could get her. Pregnant women need some body fat to cushion against the shock of delivery. Deni had very little fat and even lost weight the first six months. Kimbo assured me it was okay. So did Tyler. So did Deni. I had to take their words on it. I'd not planned on being a parent soon, and my medical training was limited to delivery and care afterwards, not to nutrition and physiology beforehand.

We had to acquire supplies for the baby, but slowly. The incident with the Bureau of Agriculture goon harassing me over purchases was still in my mind. We could occasionally buy a pack of diapers or some formula and claim it was for a "friend," but only occasionally. I wasn't sure we were going to have sufficient stocks on hand.

I also wasn't sure delivery was going to be safe, nor that any of us were getting out of here alive. The baby was really going to be a problem.

Deni continued well enough. Her belly swelled a little, but she kept most of the growth close to her torso. Everything seemed okay; no thyroid or other hormonal issues, minimal morning sickness, baby in good position, very active and with a reliable heartbeat. I was still scared as hell at the thought of a battlefield delivery relying on bare hands and crude instruments with no modern backup. The "natural birth" people are idiots, if you ask me.

We caught every newsload from Grainne we could, looking for clues as to the situation in the background. There were very few reports from the Halo, and not enough information to tell us anything. Everything we had came from the surface. Jefferson was enemy territory, though the increasing damage we saw behind the reporters indicated it was still being disputed. Westport was garrisoned but not heavily, and a fight was still openly going on there. I wondered how my family was doing? Marrou was too small to resist the forces dropped on it. All in all, I estimated there were five million Unos on the mission. That was good news. Five million of them versus 300 million of us equaled five million dead Unos. Though they might take thirty million civilians with them. They'd already used nukes or KEs on half a million near military installations, and the economy was a wreck. People were starving because food could not be reliably shipped from grower to city. Part of that was incompetence and part security concern about weapons being smuggled in. And to be fair, part was our fault for sabotaging everything if doing so might kill an Uno. It was a hell of a fight. Even if we lost, they'd know they'd been hurt.

The Halo was harder to get intel on. The jump points were all under control of the UN, though for some reason I never discovered, Jump Point 1 was not being used. All flights were going through Caledonia and Novaja Rossia to JP2 and JP3. Either there were serious technical problems at JP1, or we still controlled it. I couldn't determine and marked it in my calculations as a likely friendly but unknown. The odds came out 70% in our favor for that objective. Most of the orbital industry was UN, and being run badly by what jokingly passes for "Unions" by their rules. Production was down what appeared to be 60%. Of course, much of that was due to sabotage by the press-ganged workers. The planetoids and outer Halo weren't reporting much, but those hardy miners would have to be taken one by one; they wouldn't surrender. There was every chance they'd sell their ore to the UN, however. While mercenary in attitude, their concern was likely more urgent and immediate: food. They wouldn't be happy, though.

The communiqués I got shrank in number. Every few days I'd get another one telling me to stand by, await orders, have gear at Stage 2 readiness, Stage 1 will follow. I sighed and complied.

There was nothing else to do. I kept a tight lid on my urge to scream or smash things and trusted for advice and orders to a screen with some officer or other at the far end who might or might not be Naumann. I simply had to hope they knew what they were doing, because I had little enough to go on.

We carried on as we had, building up stockpiles of munitions a few precious kilograms at a time, then stashing them where we could reach them but deny them if needed. That's as tough as it sounds. We stashed some in a warehouse space we'd rented to ourselves using long-gone ID we could deny, but had to keep it a low enough quantity to avoid the aerial sensors picking it up. While being able to deny association with the hardware was good, the idea was to be able to use it. We couldn't push the issue. Some we had buried far out beyond our area of operations, where it couldn't be associated with us without long, careful observation.

We had a very good idea of when Deni was due. Kimbo cracked a joke that made me laugh hysterically and want to strangle him at the same time. It's a talent he has. "So, we know the date and time of conception. In the shower, from behind, facing north? On the bed facing east? All could be factors."

While I tried to figure out how to respond, Deni said, "Typical rich girl position. Facing Bloomingdales," with that beautiful, subtle, wry smile on her face. Situation defused, we all laughed. It stopped the nerves we all felt, at least for a moment.

It was later that week that she went into labor. Babies always arrive when it's least convenient to everyone else and the perfect time for them. I was asleep and relaxed, able to ignore the stress in between terrifying dreams. A disturbance jarred me and I came awake fast with a weapon in hand, as I always do. My brain sorted through unconscious memories and decided it had been a knock at the door. "Yes?" I asked softly.

"Boss, it's time," Deni said. She sounded a bit out of breath.

"Right," I agreed, rolling to my feet and grabbing my pants.

Everyone was up in seconds. Bleary-eyed, I took in the time from the vid screen; I hadn't done so in my room. I'd been too groggy to track. It was 0517 local. I'd slept for two hours.

Deni was walking laps around the room to hasten the event.

Everyone else was moving smoothly, gathering the hidden supplies we'd need. I hit the bathroom, took care of business, scrubbed up thoroughly and came back out. First labors were often false. They were also often days long, resulting in a baby.

She was still walking at a good pace, clutching her distended belly and gasping, panting for air. She was obviously flushed and pained and that scared me. It was perfectly normal, but Deni is *not* normal. I forced myself to calm down.

At nine, Tyler went down to watch the office. Periodically she'd come back up. "No change," we'd report. Deni was sipping water and not eating, waiting for the ordeal to firm up, take shape and resolve.

At 1205 she said, "My water broke." It wasn't as messy as I expected; it was just a trickle. Still, things were starting. We put her down on her bed, built up behind her with thick foam pillows and waited to get to work. Babies are like battles. You wait for ten hours for ten minutes of panic.

Tyler came up as soon as she locked the doors at 6pm. "Are we ready?" she asked.

"Soon," I said. Deni was panting away, sweating, ashen-faced and tired-looking. I'd caught a nap during the day. She hadn't.

I reached up inside her birth canal with a gloved hand and felt. "Maybe three centimeters," I said. It was the oddest feeling. A part of her that had been a snug sleeve for my pleasure was now a swollen hunk of flesh, twisting and distorting as it prepared to release a burden larger than we had ever evolved for. It must have shown in my face, because Kimbo said, "Boss, have you ever done this before?"

"No," I admitted. "Only classes, but lots of them. And my share of trauma medicine."

"No real childbirth, though?" he asked again.

"No."

"Then I know more about this than you do. Swap places," he said.

"I'll be fine, just advise," I told him.

"I am," he said. "I'm the closest thing to an expert, and your ladyfriend needs you to comfort her. Swap."

Shrugging, I agreed and peeled off the gloves. Deni looked like hell, face stretched from pain, gaunt, pale, drenched with sweat and scared. Sure, she was strong. She was also passing a bunch of coconuts through a garden hose. She gripped my hand until I thought she'd break knuckles. "Thanks," she muttered, and went back to breathing.

"Two minute interval," Kimbo said. "Want to give it a try, Deni?"

"Sure," she said through gritted teeth.

"Okay," he said. "On the next contraction, bear down for twenty seconds. Ready . . ."

She hunched up and grunted, straining until cords showed on her neck. Nothing. It unnerved me slightly, but I got it back under control. It seemed so strange under bright lights with her all exposed. It seemed like one of those things that should be done in private.

"Going to be a bit longer," she said, interrupting my thoughts.

"No problem," Kimbo agreed. "We've got time."

Either she or the baby wasn't wasting time, though. Less than half an hour later, during one of his regular probes, Kimbo said, "Baby's coming."

Tyler took her right shoulder, I took her left. We each grabbed one of her knees. As the next contraction started, which we could clearly define by Deni's restrained scream, I yelled, "*Push*," and helped her raise her shoulder. "One, two, three . . ." I counted, Tyler and Deni joining me, though Deni sounded weak. At twenty, she collapsed back against our grips and we lowered her.

Childbirth with no trank field, not even drugs. No proper monitors, no neural tools to control the contractions, and only the basic tools should a Caesarian be needed, unlikely as that was. Still, at least we had sterile procedure and a warm place. How the hell did the human race survive all those Ice Ages, wars, civil strife, colonization eras, famines and local disasters?

It was time to push again. We helped her up, she clenched her teeth and strained as she had for that five hundredth leg lift in SW training, and we counted to twenty. Hell, I was sweating myself, and I was barely exerting. Poor Deni. I'd been throwing out jokes to distract her. I now said, "I told you we should have practiced with that canteloupe."

She snickered while looking at me in disgust, but for that moment she wasn't hurting. It was the best I could do for her.

"I've got the head," Kimbo said. He was sweaty, but calmer than I was, his face a relaxed mask of concentration. "Want to feel?"

I was curious, but decided I could do without. "I'll take your word on it. Good job, keep it up and all that."

He cracked a bare smile, nodded, then said, "Deni, we're likely to get the baby in the next push or two. Give it everything you have."

"Sure," she agreed. Her voice was still steady.

"Of course, it might be several more. I'm guessing, and it's in part up to the baby."

She cut him off by starting to shove as the contraction hit her. She lost count at three, instead saying, "Arrrrrrrrrhhhhhhh-hhhuuunnnnhhhh!"

And the baby came out. The head protruded first, and seemed to stop there. Kimbo gave a slight twist to release the shoulders, and suddenly had his arms full of live, slimy, twitching baby. The baby did two things upon arriving on the planet Earth—squawled and shit. I couldn't say I blamed it.

Kimbo flipped the concealing umbilicus aside and announced, "It's a little girl. Looks healthy. Stand by."

He grabbed two loops of Dacron dental floss, tied them around the rubbery cord and handed me a pair of shears. "You want to cut?" he asked.

"Go ahead," I nodded. He shrugged and snipped, wrapped the baby in a towel and stuck her in the makeshift incubator. Then he came back and finished.

Cleaning up after a baby is born is a disgusting mess. Deni squeezed and the placenta came out, looking like raw liver. Well, that's about what it is. There was more blood. Kimbo pressed on her belly and a tidal wave of urine came out. Deni felt none of this, her nerves overloaded from the ordeal. "Are we done?" she asked, breathless and panting still.

"Just beginning," I told her. "Baby's fine, you'll be fine, and we're back to work. After you lie on your ass and recover for a few days."

She nodded. "How do I look?" she asked.

"As if you lost both chutes and hit the ground face first," I said.

"Screw you, asshole," she joked. "How's the baby look?" she asked.

I didn't say, "Like Winston Churchill," even if that was accurate. "Just wait and see," I told her.

Only a few minutes later, Kimbo walked over, nodded to Tyler who was still washing off the baby with cloths, and helped wrap her up. He brought her over and presented her to Deni, formally and with what appeared to be a huge weight lifting off his shoulders. "Your daughter," he said. "Got a name ready?"

Nodding while eagerly taking the bundle, Deni said, "Chelsea."

"Jelsie?" Kimbo asked. He thought he'd misheard.

"No, Chelsea," she corrected. "The old spelling." She stared in at the baby's small, pinched face. She was smiling. Supposedly, babies are cute. I missed the "Cute" part. The baby still looked like Churchill.

Kimbo nodded at her comment as we all gathered around. It was that kind of bonding moment.

That's why the human race has survived.

We left Deni and Chelsea to recover while we gently brought the lights up, gingerly moved Deni so she could watch vid and then cleaned up the tools. I asked Kimbo, "Where'd you learn childbirth procedures?" He seemed giddy and exhausted, both at the same time. Everyone did.

"I delivered a baby on Earth once," he said. "In a warehouse, with only rudimentary tools."

It took me a moment to decipher it, and I gave him a Look.

"Sorry, boss," he said, "But you looked unsure, and were emotionally involved, and Deni *did* need you."

He was right. "Kimbo," I said, "if anyone ever doubted your qualifications as what we are, you've just proven them wrong." The man was an Operative. No question. I'd had few doubts myself, but there would be none now, and I'd quash any from anyone else. Taking charge, acting confident as things go to hell, never letting anyone know you're terrified, those are all good soldierly qualities. Doing those while pushing your commander aside as his exec and ladyfriend delivers a baby is one of the defining levels of worth, even if it's not in the book.

He smiled tiredly and said, "Thanks."

I tried to go back to sleep. Everyone else thought it was crass of me, but baby or not, we had a mission, and I needed rest to maintain my cover and run my ops.

No good. They were cheerfully loud, and I'd had too much excitement. I got back up and came through to hit my list of daily cover maintenance, local chores, local work and real mission.

Tyler cornered me at once, walking briskly over from where everyone was still gathered. "Boss, you have to come and see your little girl!" she said.

"No, I don't," I snapped, a bit too loud. She stepped back with a look of hurt surprise on her face. "Deni can handle the baby, she can call if she needs help, and we have work to do. Now get to it," I said.

"Uh . . . okay," she replied. Her expression was hurt and confused.

Whatever. I wasn't going to explain. And I wasn't going to see the baby.

Things calmed back down again slightly. Deni stayed hidden in back, doors closed. There was no real reason to hide the presence of a baby from customers, except that they might talk and we were paranoid. On the occasions when anyone asked about "Laura" or "the red-headed lady," we'd make excuses about her taking a leave of absence.

While she could handle the routine flipping of channels, chattering aimlessly on the phone with some acquaintance from the nets and do the real admin we had to have done, her state left us with three people to handle the visible work and the military mission. That lost us much sleep. Fussy babies cry at a frequency resulting from seven million years of evolution, that is annoying as possible, so as to get attention. That lost us all sleep. Deni couldn't go around the clock like that, and Tyler spelled her during the day, Kimbo at night. He was good with babies, cycling through the basics and delivering bottles, changes or snuggles as needed. His already damaged opinion of me sank lower when I flatly refused to get involved. "I'm running the show, I need my sleep," was all I said. There was no reason for me to waste time on an infant.

"You could at least cuddle your daughter once or twice a week," he said in disgust.

"It will distract me," I said.

"You really are an asshole, you know that?" he said.

I didn't argue. He did his job and did it well. That was all that mattered.

Not quite a month later, I slipped down to the library to check on reports and messages. There was the usual garbage and one that was official. It was entitled "hi son."

It was the mail I'd been craving and dreading:

"Hi well join you thursday. I think its around 9am your time but check to make sure Im lousy with time zones. Itll be good to see you again. Love mom."

Well, that was it. 0900 Earth Zone Six Thursday, several Earth-shattering kabooms would presage the collapse of a civilization. I had almost no assets, little notice and an exec with an infant. I've learned that when things get that bad, there are things you never do. So I didn't ask what else could go wrong. It would probably happen anyway.

In theory, all my team leaders had gotten similar messages, and several hundred bogus ones had gone out to confuse any observers as to how many of us there were and as to our actual identities. To ensure the message went out, I would now start a tree. I would send out five different messages from five different locations to my five continental commanders. In twenty-four hours, I'd get back confirmation from one and only one source that the message had been received and confirmed by all, some or not at all. If it had not been received clearly, I'd have to reschedule to the best of my ability, or settle for a partial attack, or fake it. Lives of literally millions of people, including me, in several star systems now depended on me. And on the vagaries of Earth's commnets.

I was only sending out five messages, and would only get back one, because the more I sent, the more cover addresses I'd have to use, and the more likely it was that several hundred similar messages in one file would trigger an investigation. My people were relying on me as commander, I was relying on them as my unit. We all did this properly, or we all died. No pressure.

We'd thought about targeting military targets exclusively, but it wasn't practical. Much of their space-based facilities were unreachable to us without years to build cover. The juggernaut of the UN forces was spread across tens of systems, and most of what we'd have to hit were stations and ships. There was no way to do so. What we had to do was hit them politically, destroy their desire to fight, make their military too busy worrying about their homes to attack Grainne or any Freehold target. It meant attacking Earth, as the majority of UN forces were from there, especially command staff. It meant making them feel a greater need to chase us Operatives than take revenge on our system. We had to stick our necks and dicks onto the chopping block and dare them to chop.

But first we had to get their attention. That meant hitting civilian targets and hitting them *hard*.

Back at our warehouse, we made a last manic shopping trip, figuring no one could respond to an irregularity in less than a week. Baby supplies topped the list, as did additional prepared food for us. Cold packaged soup is no treat, but it can be eaten unheated. We had no idea what things were going to be like afterwards, assuming we survived, so we did what we could.

Then it was time to gather our remote supplies and bring them in. We had to dig them up or drag them out, bring them back and hide them as well as we could onsite, watching nervously around for any sign of betrayal. We also had to trust everyone else to be as cautious. One discovery would lose us a city's worth of Operatives. Two discoveries would alert them to a larger operation and kill us. We'd take as many of them as we could with us, but it would be death for certain.

That night, we all sat soberly, Deni feeding and caring for Chelsea while alternately laying out supplies and weapons. She would stay here and make us appear to be doing business as usual, and hold down the fort. The other three of us would do the work. I allowed everyone one drink, and led everyone in the Oath of

Blades, despite their insistence that it wasn't necessary. Religious rituals are never "necessary," but are often essential. None of us had real swords or knives with us, so we substituted those crappy little kitchen blades. They were symbolic, they served just fine.

But that last line of the ritual, of "Our blades, our bodies, our souls. For God, Goddess and the Freehold" had an awful finality to it. I doubt anyone slept. I know I didn't.

The next day I secured reports up the tree that everyone was ready. There was no message telling us to abort.

Black Operations was about to enter the war.

CHAPTER 25

Blister agents aren't really that hard to produce, if you don't care about purity and long-term storage. We didn't. Kimbo had brewed us five containers of the stuff. Each container would handle a typical city building of 80 stories or so. That was a good start for what I planned.

Delivery was only slightly difficult. Tyler drove the truck, he and I swapped off on handling and placement.

Tyler drove us through town in a rented box van. Since we planned to ditch all our IDs at once, it was no problem at all renting it. She used a credit card, a bogus address and her implant. No questions asked. We loaded the stuff up and went for a late evening trip.

The streets were quiet, which had nothing to do with driving, since once the destination was selected, Tyler was largely along for the ride. Once we entered the service drive for our first target, the comm chimed a warning and slowed. She switched to manual control and took us up to the loading dock. She backed in like a pro and we jumped out in our basic oversized coveralls, hats low over our faces. It was dark, so there was little to see of us, especially with cheek inserts and scruffy, unshaven faces. By the time the security guard came out to inquire what was going on, we had the first tank, thoughtfully labeled "dry nitrogen," strapped to a dolly.

He asked, "What's this?"

I replied, "Nitrogen for the maintenance department." I used a flat, slightly raspy voice.

"What for?" he asked. Idiot.

"I think they use it to pressure test the AC. Hey, I'm just the muscle, okay?"

He frowned. He had the perpetually frowny type of face that goes with the potato sack body. He scratched at his chin and said, "I wasn't told about this."

"Prolly didn't write it down for you," I said. "Look, can we drop it off out here? Should we take it back? Or take it where the manifest says so?"

"Where's that?" he asked.

"Um . . ." I said, pretending to look at a screen in front of me. "Says here to take it to the 57th Floor Equipment Room."

"Shit," he said. "That's going to take a while, and I have to come along."

"You're getting paid, aren't you?" I asked reasonably.

"Yeah, but 'Your Police At Work' is on," he said.

"New episode?" I asked.

"Yeah," he said. "And my recorder at home is broken, I can't afford to reserve a showing, and we can't record here," he said.

"That sucks," I said. "I'm going to catch it later. Any good?" I could chat all night, if it would soften this guy's brain any more than it was already. He wanted to be a real cop and could never qualify, so he watched vid instead. He was soft enough in the head, but likely too squeamish about clubbing people to be a real cop.

"They're in Lvov, Russia. Lots of drunken Russians and a few riots." He sounded as if he really wanted to get back to it. How ironic. Lvov was on our list.

"Sounds hilarious," I said. "But you're missing it while we talk."

"Damn," he said, the candle flickering above his head. Moron. "Look, do you guys know where to go?"

"Yup, do this every six months or so," I said, figuring that was long enough he either would have forgotten, been on another shift, or not have worked here.

"Oh, yeah, I remember," he said as he didn't. "Well, if I sign you out a key, can you handle it?"

"Sure, but I'll use this to bring a safe down with me, and clean the cash out of any jackets I find lying around."

He snorted. "I don't think you can move a safe, and serve them fricking right." He turned to the service door, reached inside and hit the switch for the bay door, and said, "Hang on, I'll get a key."

So we went up unescorted. Kimbo hadn't said a word the entire time. The rent-a-fool hadn't looked at him once. No description there for him to give.

We rode the service elevator silently, faces averted from the camera. At the 57th floor, I rolled the dolly and Kimbo walked quickly ahead. He had the door open by the time I got there. Yes, it was late, but there might be a worker in an office somewhere, and we didn't want to be seen. The fewer witnesses, the better. Once inside, I unfastened the drum and he started rolling it. The rumble of large fans would mask any noise we were making, even assuming anyone was around to check.

I left twenty minutes later. By then, he had it inside one of the air handlers and I'd helped him hoist it up behind a bend in the ducting where it wouldn't likely be noticed. He finished attaching it with professional mountings, so that even if found it might be mistaken for a storage location for unauthorized excess or illicit goods.

While he finished, I went downstairs, returned the key and chatted with the guard, who was ignoring his scanners and watching vid. I made a few comments about the show to keep him occupied until Kimbo arrived. Then I said goodnight and we left.

We managed to get three of our other primary buildings. The guards at the other one insisted they had to verify the delivery. We refused. They demanded a call to our boss. We discovered we had the wrong one, looked embarrassed at the "error" and slunk away to their laughs.

Then we hit our secondary list and planted it in another building.

As soon as we got back to our base, we loaded up again. Deni had our weapons and explosives laid out and we went right back to work.

The effects of our attacks were varied intentionally. We wanted to create in people's minds that nothing was safe—work, home, food, water, transport. Whether large town or small, they were targets. Helping others would expose them to attack. Nowhere to run or hide, no safety. We intended to throw an entire planet into panic. We would be merely a catalyst. They would destroy their civilization for us. Also, we had to use the resources at hand.

So we all took different approaches, some planned, others improvised. Very few of the preparations would be at all suspicious—commercial gases and vehicles, tools and basic computer gear was all it took, as long as those wielding the tools were human weapons.

My buddy Warrant Tom Parker had a great idea that was put to use in Melbourne. His few people, their insertion being the team that died, had visited eight buildings over a few days, dressed as maintenance or inspectors. Most buildings' air handlers have access areas for fans and filters big enough to walk into, that are odd-shaped and have dark corners, despite being lighted. In these, they set up gas-burning space heaters with triggers for Zero Hour. The environmental controls adapted for the temperature and increased "air" flow, and the system was designed to balance CO_2 and O_2 levels, not CO. The CO sensors were a separate circuit in the alarm system and easy to bypass. It was well over an hour after the flames lit before the symptoms—nausea and headaches—registered as a problem, and even longer before anyone realized that *everyone* in the buildings was suffering.

They tried to evacuate through the elevators, which also double as ventilation shafts. The first crowded loads down were unconscious at the bottom, and collapsed bodies jammed the doors open. Then the emergency elevators were disabled the same way. The older buildings with stairwells became clogged the lower one got, as people tried to scramble over piles of corpses-to-be. Some beat themselves to death trying to get through rooftop hatches to fresh air. A few made it out onto vertolpads and outer rooftop gardens, for the time being.

The treatment for CO poisoning is pure O_2 and exercise. Not even every rescue vehicle and crew in the city had enough masks to treat everyone, or could transport people fast enough. They sat weeping in frustrated rage as their patients died by the thousands, cyanotic tinges on their faces. The ones they reached last were the higher-ups on the upper floors, meaning that thousands of key business and government people were dead. I'd thought to destroy the rescue vehicles too, but he'd decided against it. The utter helplessness was a *huge* psychological weapon.

Then the power and backup generators to the hospitals failed . . .

I was impressed at the response overall. Some genius acquired fittings from hardware stores, and split the O_2 hoses into manifolds. They were able to treat a few more people that way. New generators were dragged to the hospitals in not too many minutes, but all those who were going to die had already done so. The police, rescue, and military reserves deployed to the downtown area in a hurry . . .

. . . just in time for the bombs atop the buildings to shower them with rubble with a thousand meters times mass of rubble of potential energy. That also took out the vertolpads and survivors who'd gathered there.

A couple of subway crashes, a power substation out, and damage to a water treatment plant meant Melbourne would not be a functioning city for the next several days. It was an absolute panic, and people were abandoning vehicles to run on foot. That made it even worse. Sydney and Auckland were no better off.

Chandra Ramirez pulled a related stunt in Mexico City. She used chlorine gas, which had been purchased at a swimming pool supplier's, with a basic chemical license. It was offensive at the least, lethal at worst. The victims hack and cough fluid and retch, while their mucous membranes burn. Tears and snot are disgusting and terrifying when seen on thousands of wheezing, drowning victims. The altitude made it worse. The upper levels of the towers were kept pressurized for comfort. It's not much, but little air is exhausted, mostly being scrubbed of CO_2 and reused, and the vertolpads are all reached by airlocks. No rush could get out there. While all that took effect, she staged driveby shootings of several nearby fire/rescue stations, shooting out the tires and engines of the vehicles. Panic ensued when no one responded. It's the nature of the serf to wait for the Master to help, and people on Earth had been discouraged from even considering rendering aid, remember. She managed to drug a breakfast delivery to a police station, and that didn't improve things for the enemy. Her troops created a traffic jam by the simple expedient of having four vehicles slew and park across eight lanes of traffic. Once the flow backed across the first intersection, it snowballed from there. Accidents made it worse, and no one was going anywhere.

We didn't do anything with Oklahoma City. It was a good target, but it was a favorite of terrorists, having been hit six times in five hundred years. We didn't need to bother. As soon as word got out, Oke City residents panicked and did the job themselves.

In Chicago, we went underground. Literally. There are ancient sewers, built 600 years ago for drainage, as deep as three hundred meters underground. They drew rainwater from the massive surface area out to the Sanitary and Ship Canal. Later, water mains were run through them. Some of those still exist, most of them are abandoned. The new water mains run nearby, with those old tunnels used as access. It's dangerous access, as several hundred thousand lurkers, criminals, homeless people and subversives live down there, in dark corners, dug caves and old utility niches.

Lawrence McGuinn and crew had slowly taken down on hoists and winches material to build a massive thermobaric charge. The first stage was a four component, self-oxidizing powdered solid that filled millions of cubic meters with the second stage, a self-oxidizing liquid slurry. It was not an "explosion," it was a "deflagration burn." The pressure built relatively slowly—about 120 milliseconds. When it was over, the old rock and concrete cracked from the appalling pressure. Everything in that section of shaft was tossed for kilometers, bashing into walls and tumbling along them to be ground into sludge, cooked by the heat. The cavernous water mains were torn open, and trillions of liters flooded into the passages, joined by inflow from Lake Michigan. The city had no drinking water to speak of. It had no way to get people down to effect repairs, unless it could find maintenance workers qualified to work in pressure suits, and find suits for them. The depths under the city were swelling or eroding from the flow, causing upheavals and settling that would destroy buildings.

The damage wasn't obvious at once, and the "explosion" had been slow enough that it wasn't recognized as a weapon until compared to other events. They thought it a natural phenomenon at first. But when incendiary charges ignited conflagrations in dozens of buildings, it became obvious what was happening. People would burn. People would be thirsty in minutes, dehydrated in hours, dead in days. The other events meant there was no way to get enough water into the city to matter. People would die, or drink contaminated water and sicken and die, or panic and die. Then the shifting tectonic activity would tumble rocks atop them as gravestones.

I mentioned Lvov, Russia. Belinitsky went for brute force and simply started detonating bombs. They were built into vehicles that were parked and abandoned, set atop buildings to blow down the elevator shafts, destroy the elevators and leave people trapped and panicking, and in upper offices to throw glass and shattered bodies onto the street for panic effect. Roaring fires were even easier, simply requiring good oxidation and a sticky flammable liquid. What value a few maintenance pass badges? Those and a few thousand kilograms of nitrates, flammable liquids and explosive gases. She'd picked her locations with exquisite care. The whole downtown and several outlying concentrations were aflame. Her element also hit Murmansk, Moscow, Leningrad and Kaliningrad.

Back out on the street in Minneapolis, we went to work. Our plain white van, with some quick painting, became a maintenance vehicle that covered us while we screwed the traffic control circuits. That would start the inconvenience, we'd start the panic. Right on schedule, the blister agent started to release. The timers on the cylinders ran down, acid ate through a small membrane, and pressurized nitrogen blew it through opened bottle valves. It filled the volume of the air plenums with finely vaporized liquid, which was blown through the buildings in a matter of a few seconds. Casualties would only be about 50% in those buildings, but that was better for us. Panic is what we wanted. The buildings triggered five minutes apart, which we figured was long enough for a panic, short enough for no response to be effective.

Tyler diddled with some phones and alarms. Kimbo cracked a primary water line from the plant by the river that would deprive people of water and flood a few streets. I tossed a rocket at a major power distribution point atop a shorter building. Several blocks and several hundred thousand people were without power.

We then brought out the rest of the weapons we'd acquired at Langley.

Quite honestly, we could do far more damage with vehicles, buildings, and improvised explosives than with basic infantry tools. But we used them for one overpowering reason: it scared people.

Pull out a gun in the Freehold, and you will be met by one of two reactions, depending on your attitude and body language. 1) People will rush over to see your cool toy, ask how much you paid and if they can handle it, or B) pull out bigger guns (there's *always* someone with a bigger gun) and kill you. People just aren't impressed by guns.

In societies where people are not familiar with them, however, and Earth is the worst, you become a leper. They've seen all the crap on vid where people get blown backwards with gaping holes from pistols, guns shoot for hours on end on automatic without running out of ammo or jamming, where every shot counts, where they "go off" rather than "being fired," and they are "taken away" from the good guys but somehow never from the bad guys. Crap. Garbage. Utter criminal stupidity from panty-wetting, idiotic freaks (I speak of vidwriters) whose technical educations stopped at six years old. Six Earth years.

Which made them perfect for us to use. "Familiarity breeds contempt," Aesop taught us 3000 years ago. People have never learned. We were familiar with weapons, they weren't, and they panicked when the shooting started. We hit very few, and only wounded those (screams add so much to a panic, don't you think?), but the cracks, bangs, breaking glass and chipping polymer and concrete had them throwing themselves on the ground or stepping on those who'd thrown themselves on the ground.

We started in the middle of a crowd outside the old Ventura City Building. There were security guards and cops nearby, of course. They were armed with incap gas and stunners. While there's the occasional punk inaccurately shooting things up to protest society trying his buddy for the minor crime of raping, killing and eating someone, professional shooters are unknown. Or were.

I pulled a UNPF issue American Small Arms Factory carbine from under my coat and started shooting. Tyler had a pistol. She'd wanted a rifle, but wasn't large enough to hide one. Kimbo had a standard issue antitank launcher as well as a pistol. That doesn't sound like a lot of hardware for three people, but it more than did the job, especially with the suppressors removed to get more noise out of them.

It was a steely gray sky over dirty gray buildings surrounding drab gray people and streets. The people were as mentally dull as the scene was visually dull and no one noticed when we first pulled the toys. After several seconds, screaming started, but we were already starting to shoot by then. Pity. Had they panicked sooner, we would have had a better crush of people.

Some air limo was just landing in front of the building, rather than on the roof. Whoever it was was a civilian, a moderately powerful one to have a chauffeur and aircar here, but not powerful enough for rooftop landing privileges. No matter. It was large, black, sleek and imposing. Two cops were directing the crowd back as the driver brought it down. Kimbo pasted it amidships, it exploded most impressively out the far side as the anti-armor charge slammed through the soft polymer monocoque. That debris caused cars across the street to slew as the onboard systems assumed an accident, and people to scream and duck, while the confetti of shrapnel up close shredded the two cops and damaged another vehicle.

I was on the left side of broad, flat steps with the carbine, waiting for the inevitable response. And waiting. And waiting. These were really not the brightest or best security goons. It was a full minute and more before thirteen cops came swarming out to grasp at their buddies and try to control the gawking crowd. Note for the record that that's all the crowd did—gawk. No one moved to help, administer aid or even direct traffic. They milled about like sheep. Then they started to run, the threat finally oozing into their molasses-slow brains.

I caught the cops at leg level with a sustained burst, then changed magazines and picked out specific threats if they tried to target me. Tyler was behind me as backup and I heard the loud, sharp reports of her pistol as she picked off additional targets exiting the building. Kimbo was across the street, shooting at cars and windows. I headed down that way, Tyler following. The denouement was a macabre, psychotic scene of us walking down the street, unmolested, pointing our muzzles at people to terrify them. Occasionally we'd shoot at a vehicle or large window for the sound effect. Without suppression, the muzzle blasts were deafening. Some people afterwards would report we'd been tossing bombs.

Twice, heroes with guts but no training tried to tackle me. A quick twitch and a squeeze pinged them each in the hip and the leg respectively and they went down screaming. A woman carrying a four-liter container of milk was a great target; it fountained all over her as the slug tore the carton, and she ran screaming. A street vendor was selling chili dogs, and a well-placed burst spewed lumpy dark reddish-brown liquid across several people. It was boiling hot, and the splashes as well as the surprise generated more screams.

By then we were low on ammo. Ducking into an alley, we dumped the weapons in a side passage and kept walking. There were a few terrified victims fleeing the carnage in with us, but most of them didn't notice. One guy whipped out a phone at that point to report our presence, but Tyler kneed him in the balls and smashed the phone under foot. He'd have a hell of a story for his grandkids, if he survived that long. He wouldn't have a story for the cops in time to matter. We scattered in three directions and dodged into the crowds to disappear.

Behind us, the firing continued. The Police Weapons Unit had arrived and was "firing back" at threats. I can't think what threats they saw, but I'm certainly glad we don't have fools like that on Grainne. Someone could get hurt.

Minneapolis was no longer a functioning city, and wouldn't be for days.

Baghdad and Tehran in the Republic of Israel got gassed, too, courtesy of Azweicz Ashe. It was rather appropriate. Before they'd been annexed by Israel, those had been the capitals of warring states. Their favorite weapons against each other had been chemical agents. Water is very critical in the desert, and we anticipated a great return.

Rex Weaver managed to detonate the nuke against the dome shell of Baja Pacifica. The blast took out the outer dome, the resulting cavitation and collapse of water shattered the inner one. Barring a few people out in suits or subs, a million people died just like that, crushed under tons of water. The SeaTrain tunnel was turned into a giant shotgun, the wave forcing trains and debris up to the surface. I don't know if he got away and was killed later, or if he died along with his victims. If the latter, I don't know if it was intentional or not. It seems unlikely he survived, though. I'd never ordered anyone on a planned suicide mission before. It felt odd. Disturbing.

Agua Azul off the coast of Spain fared marginally better by some accounts. Dean Karnu used conventional explosives to crack four airlocks and let water rush in, but it takes a long time to fill a dome that size. They were able to hold with increased air pressure, and only had a few people drown in the lower levels. But the effect was the same. There were fourteen submarine cities on Earth. In minutes, all thirteen surviving cities were full of panicked animals trying to escape.

New York and London both had their own megascrapers, and both were convenient for the precious few liters of nerve agent we had. A whuff of air and it was all over, with half a million people flopping like fish and rolling in their own shit as their nervous systems shut down. Only the cores of the buildings were affected; the ventilation was run in zones. Still, it was enough. Both cities also run in part on hydrogen power. Lee Finley didn't manage to set off the charge in New York. He was caught in the act. Much of the hydrogen came in on surface ships, and we'd hoped to crack a couple of those for fuel/air effect. Jerry Armentrout fired his in London, though. A few kilos ruptured a major line, and an incendiary ignited the cloud. The blast melted the power station and caused hundreds of hectares of scorched earth. It was enough of a drop in power to create interruptions of service. Not what we'd hoped for, but enough for panic. Nerve agent makes people shit their pants. So does the thought of it. Nasty stuff. But hey, Earth had used chemical weapons on us first, so fuck them. In actuality, only a few hundred died, a few thousand suffering long term effects and the rest needing short-term hospitalization. But in the aftermath, that would be impossible. The real death count was due to their panic reaction. The attack on Paris, Germany was almost totally ineffective. I have no idea why. It didn't matter. People panicked anyway and torched their own city.

Heinrich Kepasur used more thermobarics in Djakarta. Those megascrapers are hard to attack, because they are so huge. But overpressure does wonders.

He and his people snuck in with assorted IDs and planted drums containing the charges at the bottom of the central elevator shafts of one. The charges were fused from the bottom. The pressure wave propagated straight up the shafts, which contained it just long enough. The rising air pressure above served the same function. The charge burned and continued to do so, the containment increasing the burn rate until it almost reached detonation velocity. According to our calculations, the overpressure at the heart of the burn was over 7 billion gigapascals. That's over 85,000 kg per square centimeter. It takes less than 1 kg per square centimeter instantaneous overpressure to kill.

It was all over in a fraction of a second. The shafts ruptured, the wave erupted and slammed through the building. Every body was crushed into a dead, hemorrhaged paste. Every interior door blew away to smash like a pneumatic ram into whatever was behind it. Every window powdered into dust and disappeared, to be followed by a shower of debris, pieces of flesh, rubble and vapor. The shock was still lethal as it passed through the skywalks to surrounding buildings. Passersby were crushed like bugs as pieces of the structures collapsed and fell into the streets.

There was no immediate evacuation citywide. For one thing, those ants lived in them and rarely left. For another, the news from all over didn't hit at once. When it did, most people simply didn't believe it. Vid was at once real, but unbelievable. What happened on screen was The Truth, but also always worked out okay in the end. They stayed glued to their teats.

A bogus second one in another building, merely a few kilos of HE, triggered twenty minutes later. It created a small panic. Another false alarm followed it. Then a third. Just as people were starting to think it a failure, with only the first one effective, a second real one did fuze. Another building churned like a blender and spewed a giant people smoothie.

Five minutes later, a mob of forty million people were ripping each other apart to flee the city on foot, in any vehicle, however they could.

The charges along the transit rails were just icing on the cake. It created the impression there was nowhere safe to go. Panic turned to insanity.

That made twenty-eight large cities in shambled ruins. We took it yet another step. You'll recall twenty-six sleepers I mentioned? They were mostly in small towns. Eric Walden for example, was in Champaign, Illinois, North American Union. He was a contract programmer at the university there, and had been kept employed even after the war started. He'd been searched several times, and had been grudgingly accepted as an apolitical technogeek. After that, they ignored him.

He spent lunchtime hopping through buildings, hitting cafeterias. He waltzed down Green Street, then south to Florida Avenue, and in each building he left a present in a trashcan. Some time later, they delivered nerve agent, improv napalm, or plain old shrapnel to the bystanders. Shortly, people in classes and dorms were twitching or flaming or perforated and he joined the panicking crowd running in all directions. He even snuck a pressurized canister into a pizza oven, with most impressive results. Then his worms dug into the network and tore it down. His actual casualty count was low, but the secondary effect was staggering.

Newark, Ohio; West Boudville, California; Slippery Rock,

Pennsylvania; Aberdeen, Scotland; Bunbury, Australia, Salzwedel, Germany; Lagunita Salada, South America; Dhorpatan, Nepal; Kolwezi, Africa. A little place called Nowhere, Arizona was begging for it by name alone. Across the globe, small towns joined the larger towns in their panic. Jenny Bak took out the dot on the map called Sinanju, Korea. It was taken by the flock that nowhere was safe for them. Cities we hadn't touched began reporting suspicious people, terrorist acts, panic and evacuations. No pattern could be analyzed, because we'd picked many of them at random. It seemed that the entire planet was being attacked by tens of thousands of terrorists with a master plan. And there were less than two hundred of us.

One of the keys to all these attacks was that when people panic, they turn to authority figures. Everyone in the areas we hit clogged emergency phone lines, frequencies, saturated public offices and radio and vid stations with calls, swarmed the nets, and generally made it worse. Of course, that's when our worms and moles hit and dragged the comm systems whimpering to their knees before blowing their electronic brains out.

Being out of contact with friends and family in the thirty different ways technologically dependent people constantly use to chat and reassure each other was as terrifying to them as the disappearance of a chatty voice was to our primitive gatherer ancestors. It screams into the hindbrain, "PREDATOR!" and the response is to seek cover. And they did.

That increased geometrically the number of people seeking refuge physically at police stations, government buildings, hospitals and the like. The only practical response was for those facilities to lock their doors against what was an unthinking mob. Denied daddy to pat their heads and tell them everything would be alright, that mob howled like five-year-olds and began breaking things in frustration. The only things available to break were their own cities, and they did.

As it spread, the waves propagated into areas and cities we hadn't even been near. There were also the "FUCK SOCIETY!" anarchists of various political leanings, who mistake the difference between self-government and no government. They began shooting, looting, throwing bombs and starting fires of their own, cheering us on without even knowing nor caring who we were. It oscillated into a seething abattoir of screaming, panicked animals.

In less than a day, Earth was totally nonfunctional as a political power. Emergency meetings were called, and threats were made. Everyone knew the Freehold was responsible, but no one could prove it. They all hunkered down around the tribal fires in their warpaint to discuss how the gods were malign, and performed primitive rituals and chanted incantations to fix it, as they'd done from time immemorial.

CHAPTER 26

Back in our suburb, we locked the doors as everyone else did and sat down to watch the results. I'd rather have left at once to avoid the mob, but we needed to see if more action was warranted, and we had to be close by to do that. We had more weapons at hand, both small arms and simple bombs. Nothing else would be needed to cause additional fear. We had bags packed ready to evacuate, carrying only enough stuff to look like refugees. Well-prepared ones, granted.

The comm and vid were almost non-existent, as most of the major stations were in large cities. It was up to the secondary suburban units to fight their way in closer and get what data they could, swimming against the stream of fleeing rabbits. Pardon my mixed metaphor. There really wasn't much to go on, but I had the plans of each element on file, and the after-action estimates from some, and that combined with maps gave me a good basis to assess the incoming reports.

It was glorious! Scrapers in Washington were collapsing from the after-effects of the pressure waves and from internal fires we'd caused. Roiling fires created howling hurricanes in Chicago and Minneapolis, building the firestorms higher and incinerating everything organic into black, chunky goo. The mindless, panicking rioters were crushing and trampling each other to death.

All roads were gridlocked, automatics deadlined and most of the mass unable to drive on manual as it required the ability to think. They were mugging and looting for food and shelter, lighting fires for warmth and light, that would end up torching more buildings, beating and raping to reinforce in their own minds that they were superior to someone, anyone more helpless than themselves. And as the images went out, still more cities not yet damaged collapsed socially into the quagmire. Raw, naked truth was something they'd never been taught to handle, and there wasn't enough government left to filter it. The concept of shutting vid down totally was as alien to them as to us, but in our case it would be an unthinkable violation of right. To them, it was unthinkable to let people think. Vid must go on, no matter how bad it was.

Jeremy Hausen and Kent Shanks had handled the Moon city of Selene well. Two cargo pods had crashed into the exposed surface structures, a virus was eating the algae in the oxygen tanks, and several bombs had wrecked pressure doors. They'd survive, certainly, but it generated that much more fear. *Nowhere* was safe. A few cracked greenhouse panels in O'Neill got everyone into secure quarters or vacsuits and shut it down until further notice. I'd hoped to have an assault boat to make a pass for that attack, but it wasn't possible. Still, Burk Smith had done a great job, considering how tight and controlled the Trojan point habitat was. Ships were orbiting or leaving their docks and shuttles in launch stage were aborting to land at the nearest available facilities and going nowhere.

Baja Pacifica had left a macabre finale: millions of bodies and pieces of same, tossed by concussion waves, crushed by 200 meters of water pressure, bloated by lack of pressure at the surface, all being chewed into mulch by the largest school of swarming sharks ever seen. I didn't think anyone would live in submarine cities in the foreseeable future.

The next load brought me up short. It was local to Minneapolis, and I ordered up the volume and enlarged the image. They started showing the damage and havoc we'd wrought. I immediately started narrative, written and mental notes for my debriefing, and was quietly impressed by the carnage. This city and the others would not be in shape to do anything for at least a couple of years, and wouldn't fully recover for a decade or more, local clock. It was beautiful. Then the camera flashed across one of the debris-strewn and rubble-blocked streets. They were clearing the rubble and bodies with bulldozers to get access in. It focused for a moment and I dropped my gear. The image framed is still with me, and I'll never forget it. I see it every night in horrific visions. I shot a glance over at Deni, who looked white and reflective herself.

It was a baby, about three months old, dead in the street, bruised and battered by falling concrete. It must have died from shock, as the physical damage wasn't that great. Then I saw the mother sitting next to the pathetic little corpse, weeping and moaning as she rocked back and forth in anguish.

There were more pictures. A school class on a field trip had been pureed by falling glass. A day care center had been in one of the buildings we'd gassed, and they had laid out a row of helpless, blister-faced little corpses, some still clutching favored toys as talismans. I had known intellectually kids would die, and knew intellectually this was a sympathy grab on the part of the vid crew. But even before Mtali, children had been a sensitive spot for me.

A school near downtown had been buried under one of the scrapers, with more than 5000 students unaccounted for. I could account for them. They were dead. The Children's Medical Institute had been damaged, and hundreds of kids had died before power came back up. Others were injured or smashed and being dragged out of the rubble. One disgustingly bizarre image showed a young girl holding her crushed and severed right arm in her left hand, confused from shock and stabilizers and staring at it as a nurse tried to help her.

Congratulations, Captain Kenneth Richard Chinran. You've become a state-sponsored terrorist. I kept hearing it echo in my head.

"I have to take a walk," I said, and left before anyone could say a word.

Outside was a scene from Dante. There wasn't much damage in this area yet, but the streets were clogged. I'd seen that, noted it, but hadn't realized in my guts just how bad it was. Cars were bumper to bumper. Some people had managed to override the controls and those with aircars had even attempted to fly, only to crash into building faces and then into the crowds below. It was fucking dangerous here, twelve hours and fifty kilometers from where we'd hit. That was good strategically and bad for us personally.

I wandered away from the building, no particular route in mind. Any time I saw something disgustingly wrong, I stared in horrified fascination. I saw a family van full of kids. It must have been an attempt to evacuate a building, as it was crammed full and had only a single woman driving. Foolish. Brave. It was to no avail; it had been smashed as an aircar fell on it and the kids were screaming. I didn't want to know if any were hurt. I kept walking. Everywhere I looked, my mind focused on the kids. Killing politicians is a social duty to the race. Killing enemy soldiers may be a necessary evil in time of war. But this . . . was obscene. What had we done? How bad were things back home that this had been the last resort? Were things that bad, or was this a vengeful response? Who the hell *had* my orders come from? Did they have any idea what they'd asked, and what I'd accomplished for them?

There was a crowd gathered quietly around a building, and I sought it for intel. I wanted human intel, feeling. For the first time in my life, what others thought of me really mattered. I was part of this society and would be so until we extracted. I was unarmed, alone, cut off from all contact, and suddenly felt a rapport with this mass of humanity. I had to know how they felt.

It was a vid store. This far out and this much later, no one was looting. They were too shocked, or too sheeplike. Whatever the reason, they stood and stared. Every screen in the display window was tuned to the same news load. The volume was loud enough to hear outside. I could see live broadcasts in crispest, clear high-density imaging, with perfect stereo sound and full depth. I wanted to puke and couldn't.

Across the screens floated images of hell. They were the same ones I'd seen earlier. That didn't make it easier.

I was interrupted by a woman turning and yanking at my arm. I quivered alert and looked back at her. She stared at me with wide, empty eyes, tears streaming. "Why did they do this to us?" she wailed. With a step she had her hands on my shoulders and shook me. "WHY?"

It took me a second to realize it was a generic question, not aimed at me personally. I shrugged noncommittally. She threw herself on my shoulder for a moment, then staggered off.

There were people looting elsewhere. I avoided those areas. Others traveled in mobs, either for safety in the defense or for strength in the offense. I steered clear of them, not needing to prove a point and not wanting an altercation. Drifting smoke and dust was starting to settle over the area, even though we were theoretically upwind. I could only wonder how bad it was in areas that had been subject to greater fire damage. It coated my skin and filled my lungs.

I was out for hours, dazed, contemplative and meditating. We really hadn't thought about the aftermath, because none of us intended to survive. But what I saw here told me all I needed to know about the current situation, and I needed away from it. It was a filthy stain on my soul.

While I was walking, UN intelligence finally caught up with us. Either our pics or our DNA had been traced. Or else they'd put enough other data together for a pattern. It was too late for Earth, but not too late for retributions. As I returned to the warehouse, I saw tens of vehicles and vertols and hundreds of troops in urban gear, and faded back into the spectators to watch. Part of me wanted to charge into the fray, but the likelihood of me accomplishing more than twenty or so deaths including my own was remote, and that wouldn't help. I had to get the intel back if at all possible, rescue any POWs if possible, and more orders might follow. I clamped down on my emotions and watched in horror. Things were getting worse, and I felt my mortality, more than ever before.

They brought out bodies. Admittedly, there were far more than three, but the result was the same from my end. There but for a moment's anger go I, I thought. I shivered slightly. I shivered a lot. I had to stay alive to report in, and I left slowly, drifting away like a good gawker. My exterior was calm, but inside, I was cold and shaking. There'd been no need to kill everyone. It was sheer vengeance. I suppose I understood that, but I didn't find it any easier. I avoided further thought. I didn't want my mind working on Tyler, or Kimbo, or Deni. Especially Deni. And what about Chelsea? Was she dead? An infant killed in vengeance? Would she be raised by these rabbits?

I sought transport and a safehouse. No time to worry now. That's what I told myself. It was lucky things were in such a panic; I blended right in.

I was shaking uncontrollably by the time I got to our small apartment. It was a ten kilometer walk. It took two hours, and I was still shivering. It took three tries to steady the key enough to mate it up to the sensor plate, and I staggered inside. I ignored the lights, which probably weren't working anyway, and stumbled into the kitchen nook. I grabbed until I found the right cabinet latch, and snatched the first bottle I could find. I had six good swallows down before I could taste what it was. It was whiskey. A fairly decent blend, and one of the few luxury items we'd put aside, ostensibly as trade goods in this aftermath. Now, it was medicine.

I'd been stuck in so professional a thought mode, I hadn't even considered the effects I'd had. Now I did think about it, and I wanted to scream, kill, die, shit myself, laugh insanely . . . I had no idea what I wanted. My body was wracked with shivers, my brain spinning as if already drunk, my guts roiling with nausea. I could feel my pulse and respiration and knew I was in shock.

Minneapolis. Population pre-event, fifteen million. Population post-event, ten million and dropping. Four Operatives. My share of the initial casualty count was one million, two hundred and fifty fucking thousand people. The number was meaningless except as a strategic calculation and a sick, horrible comment percolated through my thoughts.

I. Am. A. Weapon. Of. Mass. Destruction.

What in the name of God and Goddess had I done?

I sat there in a stupor. I sat there all night, and killed the bottle, a ritual metaphor for the city I'd killed, and for my soul, and for my brain cells, dying in poison. And because I was a dedicated masochist, I had vid on (There was power. I hadn't even noticed the lights outside, I was in such shock) and watched as the story was repeated endlessly, there being nothing else anyone could do but relive the experience.

Please, I thought to myself, *at least let this* be *the end*. I couldn't imagine doing more than I'd already done. What if Earth still wasn't convinced?

There was surcease in booze and fatigue and depression and remorse and self-loathing and the sheer terror that the door might be kicked in any second . . . and I *not* be killed by my enemy. I could live a long time in a hospital, if they so chose, and my existence kept secret. Another thing I hadn't considered was what would occur after the attack. My part was over, I hoped and as best I could discern, but I was still here. This cold, enemy territory had just taken a turn for the worse.

I don't think words exist to describe what I felt. Even worse than someone dropping a bomb or a KE weapon, I had done this with my own hands. Maybe that caused the disassociation that numbed the pain.

The vid brought me back to the sick, sad, black comedy of human existence. A commentary and exchange started, and the words sunk in through the fog. The made me laugh in distress. It was the immediate clamoring that the "government must *do* something!" Here they had a perfect opportunity to be done with the institution that that trashed their rights, oppressed them, gotten them into a war over purely selfish motives and left the planet a shambles. Yet the first thing these fools screamed for was for *that same government* to "fix" the problems it had created, with more problems. Stupidity had got them into that mess. They wanted it to get them back out.

Folks, it is *impossible* for a government that size to do *anything* in a fashion and timeframe that will matter, and do it without making you a slave. Oh, you silly, silly sheeple.

The UN and the Colonial Alliance were too bloody eager to jump into this power vacuum and start slugging it out. There was nightly rhetoric on the vid about who had whose best interests in mind, and who should have been listened to, and who knew this would happen (odd that they made no effort to prevent us from doing so).

But I'm ahead of myself. Or maybe not. I can't describe it so you'll feel it, I don't *want* you to ever feel that way, and I don't want to think about it myself. How do I live with myself? With nightly nightmares and shivers.

The power failed about 4 am. That was good, I suppose. Being now a victim as well as an attacker, I shook in fear. How far would things collapse? Should I bug out now? Seek refuge in the rural areas?

But I couldn't. I had to determine what had happened to my team. There was the unresolved matter of a baby. I'd killed millions, but I was damned if that particular one would be on the list. Duty. Duty is what you do when you have nothing else to drive you. It keeps you alive in hell.

The power came on again about noon. I must have slept. I must have done a lot of things, but I can't remember. Shock. Sheer, overwhelming shock. Me. If I was this bad, I wondered, how bad were the sheep outside? A glance confirmed that I'd emptied an entire liter of liquor. No wonder my mouth tasted like a dead mouse.

I scanned through vid. I was confused at first, but slowly made sense of what I saw as my head throbbed. Recovery had started, even if uncoordinated. The culture was sick, the government a cancer, but within the rot and the filth there were still competent, decent people. People I'd killed along with the detritus. They were working on digging out the mass graves of the megalopoli, that held now more than a billion casualties, the press said. That would mean about three hundred million, after duplicate reports were crosschecked. Hell of a day's work. I watched crews digging, heaving, snatching at mass beyond reason and clutching at hope. Every time they showed a wan, weak but still living body being pulled from the havoc, I cheered along with them.

How ironic would it be if I joined such a crew, gathered intel up close as I worked to save the merely injured? I thought about it for a while. Fear stopped me. I knew if I was identified that I'd be ripped into bloody little bits where I stood. As unlikely as it was I'd be pegged, the fact was that they'd found our HQ. They might know who I was.

While I considered my position, the regular Freehold Military hit us.

CHAPTER 27

What Earth hadn't admitted in public, and may not even have known, was that their intel webs were a shambles. They were not seeing what happened, were seeing things that weren't happening, had random ghosts and intentional misinformation to deal with, and made the assumption that "terrorist tactics" were all we had. That assumption was what killed them.

In truth, I didn't know either—this was blind territory, but I at least understood the reasons behind it. I did hope for the planned conventional backup, and was almost orgasmic at the response. Training pays off. Training *always* pays off, and our people were better trained than anyone. Nukes rained down on Paris, Berlin, Tokyo, Toronto, New York, Washington, Delhi, Moscow, Beijing, Los Angeles and Rio de Janeiro. We'd hit the industrial cities, the regulars hit the political centers, and a few choice targets like Chicago and London got hit twice. Along with the nukes were Brandt StarDrives converted to be used as weapons. That was simple enough; they were pointed at the cities from orbit and translated into drive. With no navigation plot or clear space to translate, they simply converted into energy. Whatever was ahead of them burned. Mostly, they hit cities. Occasionally, one was mis-aimed and hit suburbs or farmland. One that was likely aimed at Pittsburgh made a perfect hit on the little town of Mannington,

West Virginia, leaving nothing but a perfectly round hole where the town had been. Raging fires added to the fallout from the nukes and threw the weather control into fits.

Earth has used tailored crops for centuries. It makes the growth more predictable, but also limits biodiversity. Tailored nanos and virii had been salted into the atmosphere, and in a few weeks, there wouldn't be any food, either. I was suddenly aware of stockpiles I'd placed. I'd need them soon. Luckily, I'd have plenty, not having to share. That threw me into another fit of depression. I was oscillating between pride and loathing. And I wasn't sure which side I was on anymore.

It was three days before I recovered from the shock. Three days. Me. I'd never felt this level of stress before. I'd not eaten or drunk, hadn't showered, had barely done anything but sit and stare at the vid or the wall. It's lucky for the Freehold I wasn't needed further at that point, because I couldn't function. I was a casualty of my own attack.

It had worked, at least for now. That was my only consolation. The attack had worked, I mean. The UN had frozen its forces in place and was begging for negotiations. The anti-Freehold rhetoric continued, but now we weren't poor, repressed victims of a nasty regime. Now we were a scourge to be feared, who had wiped out the forces on Grainne, destroyed the space based command and control and slaughtered people on Earth without provocation.

I saw some of the images from Jefferson and Westport. We'd had provocation. But they were standing down now, so let them mouth off.

I thought back to my family. My father was annoying, but he would have fought. My mother could be as vicious as a ripper. No question there. My little sister, now adult if she were still alive, would have done her share. I knew inside that they had their own body counts. A repressed, childish part of me looked at an image of Jacqueline and chanted, "I beat you!"

In my mind, she replied, "That's not fair! You cheated!"

Cheated? Outnumbered a hundred to one and I'd cheated? Outnumbered 150 million to one on Earth and I'd cheated?

Most certainly.

Thoughts of family brought me back to Deni, who was as

family as I could get after all these years and parsecs, and to Chelsea. I hadn't seen an infant come out of that building. For three days I'd been avoiding the issue, but I couldn't anymore. Someone had to do a search to confirm, and get any intel from the site. I was the only one available. I was also the commander and it was my duty.

But first I had to get myself in shape. I ate, drank lots of water from the supply, not spilling a drop because there might not be more, and found dark clothes that looked appropriate to the situation but not obviously intended to be clandestine. I didn't shower. Not only was it a waste of water, but I'd be getting filthy anyway, and a clean person in that abattoir would be very noticeable.

I grabbed my jacket and stepped outside into the chill. Some cold, rough dirt smeared on my face and hands added to the effect of my matted hair and grimy, unwashed body and I was indistinguishable from my victims. At least from those who'd survived. I tucked my hands into my sleeves and started hiking. Ten kilometers would take me about three hours under the circumstances.

There was again that feeling of walking into a nightmare. The fleeing crowds had stopped, but there were still mobs loitering in parking lots, wondering what to do. The skyline ahead was murky, broken by occasional still burning fires.

The roads were quiet, with only an occasional vehicle, usually trucks carrying debris or emergency gear, or loaded with people driving to help dig out any survivors. I moved onto secondary streets to avoid being seen. Who in their right mind would walk toward that disaster? Especially in a cold drizzle? I didn't want to be asked any questions.

As it grew dark it was easier for me. I slipped through yards and across fences. It took a conscious effort of will to do that, because back on Grainne during a disaster, people would be on the lookout and would question intruders at gunpoint if they didn't just shoot them outright. I had to recall: no guns here. No knives to speak of, only a few improvised clubs, and people trained to be like sheep. Nor would most people go out in this cold.

Our location wasn't near the city proper, but things were still a mess. Many buildings were abandoned, some smashed by rioting, others occupied but without power. There were small crowds lurking on streets. I avoided those. Overall it was dark and gloomy. I made use of that to get in close and unseen. Between damage and dark and piles of debris and trash, it was no real feat. I wound up just two buildings down and considered my next move. There were guards at the warehouse, though how many I couldn't tell exactly. I waited until late, then moved in cautiously, alert for any sign of awareness.

The guards might still have been in shock from the event. They might also have been zeros hired to look like guards and not do anything. Either way, I only saw one and he paid no real attention as I circled the block, across the street and hunched over. There appeared to be another down the back alley where our loading door had been. I decided to go in the side between them, in the service alley and off the street. I circled the rest of the block, removed my coat and reversed it to the black lining, shivering in the cold, then approached. I slid along the wall of the adjoining building with my back to it, then slipped around the corner while the front guard was looking the other way. I was perhaps ten meters from him.

It wasn't hard getting into position. Between smoke, dust and power trouble, it was dark enough I wasn't worried. My years of experience let me flit through the shadows unseen, from the alley mouth past the piles of old trash and new debris from the shattered windows. There was the guard at the back cargo door, but I dropped around an old trash bin, waited until he turned around in boredom to fumble with a reader or vid. He wouldn't see me on this side. Shadows swallowed me again.

If I were them, I would have lit the alley and had a double guard. They weren't expecting an Operative to come back to a revealed safehouse, and ordinarily I wouldn't, of course. The guards were to keep gawkers and squatters out until they could do another check of the building. The delay was easily explainable; they had a nightmare of their own to deal with.

It didn't seem as if they'd found Chelsea. I hadn't seen any mention in the news, though that proved nothing. There had been plenty of signs of a baby for them to follow. They weren't expecting a reconnaissance or rescue attempt, yet they likely knew one Operative was still at large. I kept going, still cautious. My nerves stretched out into the dark for any threat.

Entering the building was easy. I scampered up the rough block, gripped a window ledge and gingerly drew remaining shards of glass from the frame and brushed them from the sill, then did a pullup. I was impressed. That was armored glass we'd had, old as it had been it was still tough. They'd shot it out during the raid. Nothing came into view as I peeked over, so I rolled over the sill and inside. My feet eased onto the floor and spread out to take my weight without disturbing anything that might make noise or squeaking any floorboards. It was one of the most nerve-wracking penetrations I'd ever done, because any failure would mean death. There was no chance of talking my way out if IDed, no way to hope for an exchange of prisoners. I was the most hated man in modern history. It's doubtful I'd even make it into custody alive.

The best place to hide a baby would be in our second cache, used for paper documents and keys. There was nothing to trigger a sensor. And it seemed they hadn't yet come in with a DNA sniffer. Their whole mission had been incompetent, rushed and more vengeful than practical. But I'd known that.

I peeled back the floorboards and stared into the dark. I couldn't see anything, but there was a slight shifting of shadows and a tiny breath. I could smell baby, too. I wouldn't have believed it, but Chelsea was there.

Deni apparently had time to shoot her with a time-release sedative, and the dose was hopefully small enough not to cause brain damage. The goons had no reason to look for an infant at the time, so hadn't. Chelsea is not the only child whose mother sacrificed herself to save her, but I think the circumstances warrant special notice. For that matter, three Operatives had died to protect her. The other two had undoubtedly kept the attackers busy while Deni successfully drugged and hid a child in the midst of battle. Based on the cost and effectiveness of the troops involved, this baby girl was one of the most valuable items on this planet.

The poor little wiggler was wrapped in a towel, and it had gotten tangled over her head. I suppose that's a mixed problem at that age. On the one hand, it's scary to be trapped. On the other hand, she had no basis for comparison. I unwrapped her, and she squawled very healthily. I stuck a fingertip in her mouth to quiet her; I didn't need any undue attention. She had good reason to complain. She was undoubtedly hungry, and the towel was soaked and filthy. There was little enough to do anything with, so I gave up my jacket and wrapped her in it. It would be cold outside anyway. Why the hell hadn't I brought a blanket or spare jacket? I wasn't thinking straight.

Exercise problem. Remove an infant from hostile territory. The Operative must assume compromised cover, no assets, no backup. Capture will mean torture and death, the infant will be captured, disposition unknown. The territory in question is a war zone in chaos. The survival of the child is necessary. Once the child is placed in protective custody, the survival of the Operative is useful but not essential.

I now had a whole new timetable to worry about. This kid needed mother's milk or formula within the day. Diapers wouldn't wait much longer, but I had to have food. I kept her wrapped and close as I headed back to the safehouse. I'd have to leave it soon, too, and seek shelter away from here. Once they did an autopsy on Deni, they'd know to be looking for a child or corpse. Then I'd have to get off this planet sooner than I'd expected. Kids are a huge hindrance to clandestine movement. But she was a Resident through her parents, and I was one of those parents, and my legal and moral position was clear. She must be taken home. This was not and never should be home to a human being.

Now I had to get back out with a squirming, fussy baby in my arms. I bounced down the stairs, retraced my steps through the tattered second floor, paused a chilling fraction of a second when I kicked a piece of glass that skittered across the floor, crashing and tinkling with others. I let it spin to a stop, scanned around to catch any other obstacles in my vision, then moved quickly toward my exit. I spread my ears to catch any sound of reaction. There wasn't any. I either hadn't been heard—entirely possible, I was hyperaware and it might not have been that loud—or else the guards assumed the noise came from random shifting or rats or such.

Getting out was a bit more difficult. I had thought about the first floor, but nixed the idea. Too much risk of discovery. Once outside, I was on much safer ground to talk my way out of trouble, so I needed to get there quickly. I skated across the floor in a low crouch, scanned out the window for threats and saw none, swung up onto it and paused for a second. I took a breath, checked the bundle in my arms was safe and secure, checked the distance, and slid over.

My shirt caught on a sliver of window or frame and tore, as did my back. It was a fiery line up the back of my ribs on the right.

But I was down. It was the hardest damn landing I've ever done—letting my legs soak up momentum, keeping Chelsea balanced, avoiding crushing her between my knees and torso, *not* rolling out, which would be hard on her skull, taking the sting up my heels, feeling my knees grind, my ass bouncing off the ground and dinging my tailbone. But it was a good landing; I walked away from it. Now I had to go past the guard again, and there was only one way to do it, as sneaking, if I got caught, would be an obvious sign of guilt. So I loosened my stride and staggered just a little, letting my eyes appear to focus on nothing. I looked disreputable enough from days of angst and filth that I wouldn't be recognizable at once.

Sure enough, the guard noticed me. He couldn't *not* see me. I wasn't quiet, and stumbled along without apparent notice of my surroundings. "You!" he challenged me. "What are you doing here?"

"G-getting out of town, officer," I said. "My wife's dead . . . I've got to get my daughter to safety." This was where it could all come apart, if they'd found out Deni had delivered, and if this character had been told.

"How'd you get down here?" he asked. "The other end is guarded."

"I dunno. I wasn't stopped," I said.

He leaned closer, looked back down the alley, and muttered, "Asshole needs to wake up down there."

"Pardon me, officer?" I asked.

"Nothing," he said. "Get going. Good luck."

Nodding, I said, "I could really use some transport."

"So could ten million other people. Sorry, pal."

"Okay," I said with a sigh. "Goodnight."

" 'Night."

I ducked and ran, trying to act like a scared refugee. It wasn't that hard.

It was a long hike back out to the suburbs. It was reminiscent of Special Warfare training all over again. My ears went numb, then my lips, then the rest of my face. I was racked by shivers, my gonads froze, then my fingers and toes lost feeling, leaving only a warm lump against my stomach. Under the paralysis the cold caused, there was a biting, stinging pain in every nerve. Cold, ash-laden air misted, fogged and turned into filthy freezing rain. I occasionally stuck a fingertip inside the jacket to determine if Chelsea was okay, if she wasn't moving and crying at that time, and she seemed to be. I fought the temptation to stick my hands into the bundle to warm up. All I'd do would be to freeze her to death while still being cold myself. I simply kept slogging at a fast walk, alternating with jogs and sprints, taking shelter from the wind when I could. When I'd pass back onto a route open to the west, the wind would peel me raw again. It, burned the exposed skin, chilled the cold rivulets running down my spine and turned me to stone. I lived in a cold, gray world. Cold, gray buildings, roads, the few people I passed. I'd thought they were colorless before. They were absolutely frozen in clear monochrome now.

I staggered the last kilometer, leaned against the door and fumbled for the key I'd hidden. I was glad that I hadn't stopped earlier, because I probably wouldn't have started again, simply stayed still and died. Movement is your savior in the cold. I'd learned that long ago.

That thought revitalized me a bit. I'd done this before. I was an Operative. There was nothing here I hadn't trained for, nothing I couldn't handle. It would hurt, it would suck, and it might even kill me, but I'd get done what I had to. Rowan Moran had taken nine bullets in the chest and saved someone not even under his protection, while killing eleven terrorists. All I had to deal with was the environment. The bullets might come later, but all I had was environment. One problem at a time.

I'd already gone over all this. What I needed most of all was to think.

I stumbled in, closed the door with my back and put Chelsea in the shower stall. It was the best bassinet I could think of. I wrapped her in a warm towel, stuck her in for the support and restraint it gave, and dug into the meager emergency baby supplies. It was convenient, having the bathroom open off the kitchen.

I couldn't feel my hands and had to direct them by sight. That was what I was looking for—it was a small squeeze bottle I could adjust for minimum flow. I filled it with lukewarm water and rubbed the tip against her lips. She clamped on tightly and stopped yowling. I knew she needed to be held, but I was still cold enough to freeze her, so I propped the bottle up with her towel and set to work warming myself.

What I needed was a hot shower. What I used was a hot, wet towel. I peeled off my clothes, grabbed the towel, soaked it in the kitchen sink and started laying it over my torso and working out across my limbs. It was as hot as I could get it, and I hoped that I didn't have any actual frostbite. The heat on frozen skin would make things worse. But I didn't dare delay warming my core temperature.

The second steaming cloth went over my head. I hissed to avoid shrieking as it cooked my ears and scalp. A rush of bloodflow made me dizzy. I clutched at the counter and held myself up until it passed. Then I warmed my torso again. It took a while, but gradually the pain turned to ache to blissful nothing. Then I started wracking coughs. My lungs had been damaged by the cold and dust.

Chelsea was asleep again when I looked over. At least I hoped she was. She wasn't moving. I gently probed her shoulder with my finger, and she wiggled slightly. Good. Her temperature seemed okay. I was worried, though. She'd been in a coma, in dust, in frigid cold, without food or water for three days. I couldn't take her to a doctor, and had to hope she would be okay.

Once we were both warm, I ran outside to make a recon patrol. It only took me a few minutes to find what I needed.

Three doors down from me, the trash container outside the door had not yet been taken to the dumpster. There were diapers in it. The tenants there could help. I ran back home, bundled Chelsea in the only dry blanket I had, went back to the door, stepped up and knocked.

Soft muttered voices inside stopped. There was slight movement at a curtain as I was examined. Shortly, a muffled masculine voice called through the door, "What do you want?"

I said, "I'm Ron Draper. Three doors down. I've got a newborn and I need some help."

There were more mutters, a careful slipping of locks, and the door opened a crack. He was tall, dirty and needed to trim his beard. Well, I was in the same state. "What do you need?" he asked.

"Formula, bottles, diapers. Whatever you can spare," I said. It wasn't hard to look miserable. "My wife's dead. It's just us." Was Deni my wife? We'd known we loved each other, but was that what we were? Stupid thing to be wondering about. I suppressed it.

"We don't have enough to spare. Sorry," he said.

"Please," I begged. I wasn't going to kill anyone, though I was running out of options. This was my daughter.

He grumbled wordlessly, then said, "Wait." The door closed and I was left standing in the cold.

It wasn't long before he reopened it and handed over a bag. "All we can spare. Good luck," he said.

"Thank you . . ." I said. I'd almost added "Sir." He probably wouldn't have twigged, but I was shaky. I needed to get back in control.

"No problem," he said, nodded and closed the door.

I got back home and found the bag contained a baby bottle, a baby outfit, ten diapers that were too large but would have to do and enough formula to last a day or two. Considering the odds of anything else being available, he and his wife or ladyfriend had been more than generous. I hoped we'd all come through this.

The power was out everywhere, and even after it came back, it was sporadic. I was lucky in the choice of safehouse. Backing onto an industrial area, there were both scrub trees and scrap working timbers lying around. I used both as firewood. Our brazier was a small metal box with vent holes punched in it, and set on con-crete squares on the tiles inside the door. I laboriously cut a hole for a chimney, using a saw blade wrapped in my rag/towel/baby blanket. The chimney itself was a joint of pipe set at an angle. It smoked horribly, but vented enough to prevent suffocation. With the sheets tacked around to keep the heat in a two-meter square area, and us snuggled under the sleeping bag and quilt, it was warm enough to keep her alive and mostly healthy. I developed a brutal respiratory infection. Then she did. I could hear liquid bubbling in her chest as I held her close. It was frightening. I'd made myself a refugee in this war, and I had a sudden apprecia-tion for the nightmare.

Infants are so tiny. I'd forgotten what my sister had been like at that age, but that was sixteen Freehold years previously and I'd been young myself. I never did roll over and suffocate her by accident, but the risk was real.

I got to experience first hand what it's like to be a refugee in wartime. I had no ID, and had to come up with cover story after cover story to explain why my implant wasn't working. The Sul-livans (the helpful neighbors) agreed, without too much prying as to why, to break in and take Chelsea if I was gone more than two days. It was a terrifying adventure.

There was a refugee point nearby, and it would have baby sup-plies. I had food for me, and water still flowed out here at the edges of the city, at least when the power worked. And I had a few containers ready at all times. My survival wasn't an issue. What was important was my little girl.

I dressed her in her outfit, a task akin to stuffing an octosquid into a sack. The cleaner towel of the two turned into a carrier with some creative tying. I stuffed clothes and paper around her as extra insulation. Paper is a wonderful insulator. Remember that in case you ever need it. I had a proper jacket for me, and braided a headband of socks to keep my ears warm. She was asleep when I finished.

The distance was only a couple of kilometers; they were set up in the parking apron of a mall. What they called a mall. It was a cast concrete excretion surrounded by hectares of parking, tens more large buildings, countless small buildings and twisted, confusing access roads. Esthetically, it was a good thing it would soon be lost to history. The weather was cold and overcast but dry. That was fortunate.

The crowd started some distance back from the trailers and vertol that were the supply point. There were a lot of guards doing traffic control, trying desperately and unsuccessfully to stop these panicky rabbits from gridlocking their vehicles. They'd actually broken programming and not used the marked and edged parking spaces, rather just stopping the vehicle where they found convenient and leaving it. Some of them didn't bother to lock them, even leaving the doors open and motors on. Idiots.

I waded through the crush of drab humanity, Chelsea held high on my shoulder, clutching at my shirt for reassurance, then crying. Yes, baby girl, Dad's here. Dad is going to get you fed. I pulled her under my arm but still high up from the people pressure, and slipped the bottle to her. I rearranged blankets to hold it in place and didn't stop my forward momentum to do so. I progressed through the crowd's Brownian motion gently enough not to anger people, urgently enough to get up front. You do this by pressing in the direction you want to go, slipping in a knee or elbow wherever a hole opens up, and never backing off. Some few tried to push me away, just as gently. Some of them yielded to the baby on my shoulder, others gave me the "Tough luck, pal, me too," look and forced me to detour.

Eventually, after an endless patient but anxious time, I was near the front. All the way there I'd been listening to their orders, echoing by speaker across the area. "Stay calm! The vertol will return shortly with more! We have plenty for everyone. *Please* try to form a line, people. *You*, stop shoving or we'll pull you out! Okay, folks, when you get here, we'll need your ID and we'll give you enough for your house for two days. If you have casualties, please don't be greedy. We need this food for other people. It won't seem like much, but if you're careful, it'll last. Split it into six servings and spread it out. There's also a book with directions for water and staying warm. We have to urge you again *not* to start fires inside. Between the poison gas and the risk of setting the buildings on fire, it's a no no. I'm not sure how most of you are starting fires, but you have to stop! There isn't any fire response right now, or any emergency response at all. Yes, there will be shortly. We're told there will be no more attacks. The government has it under control and we're discussing peace. You need to get what you need and go home. You will be taken care of—" and on it went. Do nothing, stay helpless, come here for food like cattle at a feedlot. I had my doubts about the peace talks, but it wasn't something for me to worry about right then.

Then I was in a chute between two rows of plastic barrels, armed guards with joltprods on either side. I didn't try to shove past, just waited until they waved me into line, nodded and stepped forward. I ignored the guy who squeezed past me. The guards screamed at him but did nothing, and someone else shoved in behind my left shoulder. Then they actually had to shock a few back to make them wait. I'd seen it earlier, and realized that in this case, the thugs were doing the right thing and that it would be best to go along with the program.

One of the guards wound up alongside me, which instinctively made me nervous. Between jabs at the crowd, he glanced over and deduced that the bundle was a baby. "How old?" he asked.

"About a month," I said.

He nodded. "Mother?"

"Dead."

"Shit," he said, shaking his head. "Oh, I am so sorry, pal."

"I guess we'll manage," I said. I didn't want to talk about it.

"Yeah," he agreed. "Ain't it terrible what some people will do over politics?"

I grunted an affirmative and we parted ways as I stepped forward and he back. Yes, it's terrible. Pity you assholes didn't think of that before nuking our towns, slaughtering my brothers and sisters in service and trying to enslave my people. I felt fresh loathing for these bleating sheep, for my orders, for myself and for the human race in general. What had we come to?

Then I was up front. From the trucks, rescue workers were handing down armfuls of supplies, just shoving it off for the runners on the ground to take to the supervisors up front. I looked at their capacity, shot a glance at the crowd from this angle, and figured they'd be at this task forever. And there was no reason for it. Out here, where people had grass and trees, there was plenty to eat if they only knew how to harvest it. Fools. The basic human skills had been so suppressed, along with the intellect and instincts that this was, in fact, a pack of domestic animals.

"Baby?" I heard a male voice ask.

"Yah," I agreed.

"Anyone else?"

"Neighbors," I said. It seemed a fair thing to do.

"Can they walk?"

"Yes," I admitted, being honest before being smart. It would lessen the load on these poor but decent bastards if I kept people out of line. But this was their program.

"Then they'll have to stand in line like everyone else," he said, with a pause before he softened it with, "sorry."

He handed me a bottle of water and a food pack, a small blanket and a box with diapers and other baby stuff. He said, "Lemme see your hand," as he held up a scanner.

Here we went. I shifted the entire armful around, prepared to drop it all if I had to. Chelsea went under my left arm like a football. I held up my right hand, splitting my attention between him and the scanner, watching for clues. He waved the scanner over my hand. Then again. It wouldn't read anything because there was nothing there to read. "Your safety chip is broken," he said.

"W-what do I do?" I asked, trying to sound confused and scared.

"Step over there and we'll do a DNA trace and get you a temporary one until we can ID you and replace yours," he said, thumbing over his shoulder toward a van set up behind him and far to the right. I glanced over. The occupants were classic goons. As for a DNA test, not a chance in hell.

"Oh, okay," I said, and started to shift along the shoving, elbowing edge of the crowd, as if actually complying.

"Go ahead and take the food," he said. "It'll save you a second trip."

Why, how thoughtful, practical, non-reg and momentarily unlike an ant of him. "Thanks," I replied as he nodded.

Once at of the edge of the crowd, with him too busy to notice, I merged with it, ducked under the rope and slipped back through the crowd. Twice I had to stomp feet to stop people plucking at my loot. That it was only twice was an indication of how helpless they were.

Once clear of the press, I headed away at exactly the same speed as others. No way was I giving out DNA evidence on me or Chelsea. If I had to scavenge, scramble, hunt or steal to feed us, fine, but I would not risk the system finding us.

I supplemented the horrible emergency rations in several ways. Dandelion greens and such broke the monotony, as well as providing a little sugar, little enough of them there were, this early in the spring. With the brazier, I was able to cook salvaged packaged goods I found. I built a blowgun from a scrap of pipe, and used heavy wire and paper to make darts. It's one of the easiest primitive weapons to improvise in the modern world, is dirt cheap and almost totally silent. It's also one of my best. I could ease the end out a window, puff a dart downrange and knock prey off a fence at twenty meters. Despite hundreds of years of "development," squirrels and birds still run loose in Earth's cities. Both roast well. I nailed a cat once, and I won't apologize; I was hungry.

Late nights, with Chelsea asleep and snuggling in the blankets, I'd sneak under the fence and loot the warehouses. No one responded to the alarms, and most of the thieving going on was for cars and jewelry. Truly valuable stuff like books and food and clothing was left behind at first. I took the best. Outer garments I had aplenty, underwear and socks were scarce. Chelsea had more than enough clothes, and I planned for her growth. I even found her some shoes for months down the road. A security camera setup was a rich find. It was a civilian door model, with no enhancement capabilities, but it ran off batteries and I might need it.

I grabbed a stash of books to keep myself amused. There were some classics I hadn't read, including some Hemingway and Hugo. I can't recommend either as cheerful. There were a handful of kids' books, including one diabolical piece called *Fox in Socks*. This Doctor Seuss character was a literary sadist, but hysterically entertaining. I decided to keep that one, too. I realized I was thinking of the future, and that I intended to survive. At least at that moment. I dropped into the dumps again shortly.

I found more fuel, including a mixed case of liquor to fuel me. I suppose I drank too much, but I had a lot of pain to cauterize. Oh, Deni, whatever possessed us to be martyrs? What possessed us to assume the right to execute six billion people?

Yes, I thought of suicide. The pain, the anguish, the agony. How many words do you want? Do you know what it's like to kill? Do you know what it's like to exterminate? Do you have any idea what six billion dead people, three hundred million of them children, amounts to?

Yes, I personally was only involved with two million total casualties, after all was said and done. Thank you for making me feel much better. It had all been on my orders and intelligence, though. And I'd thought the village on Mtali had been bad.

I suppose it had to be done. My own people were being slaughtered, and I swore an oath to protect them, and do believe our way of life superior. That doesn't mean I feel a need or desire to kill those who aren't quite as enlightened. They're still human beings, and their lives still matter, even if only to them. And I'm babbling. This is just history to you, right? Unless you're on Earth, in which case you want me dead. Well, first you have to catch me. I'm not suicidal anymore, just remorseful.

One of the first things those assholes did was to repair the implant ID system. Really. Apparently, being able to track people was more important to them than feeding the masses. And those masses seemed to agree. Granted, the press were cheap whores, owned body and soul and sucking off bureaurats for headlines, but the interviews they did had tens of people stating how relieved they were that an important system would soon be working again, and how it was proof of recovery.

It didn't bode well for me. I'd have to scavenge to feed my daughter first, and take whatever I could find that was left over. If their intent was to catch the few Operatives still at large, it was a pretty piss-poor, incompetent and economically infeasible way to do so. So I have to assume they needed control of the masses in case those serfs woke up to the true threat. It didn't bode well for Earth's future.

And I realized I was in a quandary. The war was over. We'd won and the UN was suing for peace on our terms. Nothing required me to enable the deaths of more Earthies. At the same time, I needed to maintain my cover. I had a duty to report back, but an oath to help those in need. Should I share the food and expertise I had, or not?

First was to see what orders I had. Or even an offer of a ride home. It was a nice idea. The nets were down, however. Official traffic and authorized business accounts were operating. None of the civilian ones were. Mass mailings had stopped. All out-system messages were being scanned and any "not relevant" were deleted. I was cut off.

Sighing, I went "home" and worked on staying alive.

I acquired more clothes, food, some bedding. Toys I improvised—sterile plastic is fine for infants to chew on, and it would be some time before more was necessary. Things like blocks and such wouldn't be hard, and I could write and draw simple children's stories. It doesn't take a lot of money to raise a kid, if you aren't obsessed with name brand goods.

Chelsea started as a wiggling blob, turned into a baby a couple of months later, and progressed into a toddler. It had been a long time since my sister was that small, and I was glad to see that all the caregiving came back to me. I got to spend all day every day with her, which is almost worth being dirt poor and having to scramble for everything. I was cold and hungry more than once, but I never let my little girl miss anything. Snuggling with her was very cathartic, and it's amazing how much heat a baby puts out. That's useful when the power keeps failing all winter.

The twigs I'd gathered for fuel were running out, in part because I'd shown some of the neighbors how to build braziers. It was now necessary to devise some method of chopping wood. Mario Sullivan and I spent a long day using pieces of scrap metal wrapped around wood to make crude wedges, which we hammered into deadwood with small logs. Every few strokes the tools would break apart and we'd start over. Blisters, nicks and dings were the order of the day, but we kept at it.

"Ron?" he asked after a few hours of frustrating labor, "How do you know so much about this? Gathering, hunting, cooking, medicine?"

I'd prepared for that question, though my answer wasn't the best. It was all I had, though. "I was in the Forces. A Special Unit," I admitted, trying to sound as embarrassed as a UN vet would. "I learned a lot on Mtali." And it was all true, too.

"That must have been nasty," he observed with a slight shiver.

"I managed," I said as I banged another log into two pieces and lost another wedge. It landed in the dead, brown grass but was broken anyway. I grabbed another sliver of wood and started grinding it to shape on the concrete walk.

A few minutes later he asked, "Any idea why they did this?"

That was one line of inquiry I didn't even want to start on. I grunted noncommittally.

He said nothing for a while. When he finally did speak, he said, "I suppose when you're a small country being beat on by a large country, you get desperate. But I think they overdid it."

I left that alone and considered it. Was this idle curiosity? Or was he putting my competence together with the situation and coming up with a conclusion? "When I was on Mtali," I responded at last, "we usually over-reacted to everything. If you take fire, you call for artillery and air support, maybe even an orbital strike. Because if you don't, you may not have enough power to do the job, and even if you do, most of what you ask for won't arrive."

"I suppose," he said. Then he met my eye as I stood up and added, "But I think this was obscene."

I stared back at him and said, "I agree."

"And even understanding why they thought they had to," he said, "if I thought I'd found one of them, I'd want them dead." He tossed a split piece at my feet. The expression on his face was dark and his teeth were clenched.

"Can't blame you for that," I said, stacking it. "There's a list of people I want dead, too. It's not politic, but it's human."

"Yeah," he said. "Makes me wonder about the people they sent to do it. Hard to imagine they had families of their own."

"Things are different now that I have a kid," I agreed. "Chelsea and I were lucky to get out when we did."

"Sorry your wife didn't make it," he said.

"Thanks. So am I," I said. Oh, damn, was I sorry Deni didn't make it. If it wasn't for Chelsea, I don't think I'd have had any reason to stay alive myself. I tried to control the pending flush of heat to my neck and ears, and hoped he wouldn't notice.

"Are you going to be staying around here?" he asked.

A ripple ran up my spine. "Probably not much longer," I said. "I need to try to get hold of her family and move closer, where I have more support."

"That's probably best," he said. "It's still pretty bad around here, and it might get worse. Especially since they don't know if the terrorists are dead or just being quiet."

He knew. The man was no fool. My high-G build was hard to hide. The odd schedule Deni and I had kept. My competence in disaster skills. He didn't know about the food we'd stashed, and that was good, as it was a dead giveaway. There was the odd, archaic name my daughter had that I wasn't about to change because it was Deni's legacy. My intelligence. My lack of family locally to ask for help, since most everyone on Earth had friends or relatives nearby. He'd put it all together, probably along with the guilt that had to emanate from me, and he knew. Chelsea had saved my life by giving me a reason to live, and was saving it now because he figured I had to have some redeeming characteristic within my own soul if I was caring for her. He realized I'd had my own reasons for doing what I'd done, but he couldn't forgive the carnage I'd wrought.

So he was giving me a subtle warning before he called the Unos.

We resumed chopping, keeping the conversation light. We quit at dark.

That night I left.

I had to abandon most of what I had acquired. I took all the baby clothes and formula I could manage. I grabbed the Dr. Seuss book. One bottle of whiskey would work as bribe goods. I had the clothes on my back, extra underwear and shirt. The little remaining ID and a few cash cards would have to do me.

I was in quandary over the food. If I left it, it might be taken as a bribe, or used as evidence against me. If I burned it, it would be obvious. I couldn't think of another way to get rid of most of it quickly. They might think it poisoned and avoid it. They might be angry that I hadn't shared before. There was no good answer.

I left it. I closed the door softly and left it unlocked. The food would be useful, I hate wasting resources, and it wasn't that big a clue. Besides, Mario and Becky deserved it. I turned and walked off, Chelsea tugging at my hair and quietly staring around at the scenery. She hadn't been outside much; her world had been a six meter box. I'd have to remedy that.

I walked south and east. There was little in that direction, but less in any other at this point. It was slightly less chill. It seemed a warm front was moving in. I looked at the clouds, backlit by an early moon, and saw impending rain in them. Not good. I should have paid more attention to them before I left. On the other hand, I hadn't had much choice.

Traffic was light. Apparently, cities not hit and farther suburban areas were resuming operation without too much hassle. They were busy enough straightening out their own problems to be able to provide only the barest help to survivors. Earth would be digging out the rubble for another year or more, and not worrying about anything else in the meantime. The UN Star Nations and the Colonial Alliance were grinding their political axes on the husk of Earth. We'd succeeded. Somehow, I still didn't feel good about it. Perhaps if I knew how bad things were back on Grainne it would be different.

I watched the few cars drive by. None would stop to offer a ride, of course. It might prove dangerous. In the aftermath, they were cooperating with each other, but only close friends and neighbors warranted that help. Strangers were still a threat. *Plus ça change . . .*

I was not paying attention. I didn't notice the police car pull up along the roadside. "Hey, buddy," a voice called.

I snapped to attention, tried not to show any panic and said, "Y-yes?"

The cop was getting out of the car and asked, "Where you going?"

"Nowhere particular," I said, and realized it was the wrong answer. Evasion wasn't the way. "Eventually my folks' place," I said.

He looked at me. His driver sat and waited, not getting out yet. That was a good sign. Unconsciously, he heaved at his gunbelt, low on his soft belly. That wasn't a bad sign; they all did that. "There's a curfew of dark. Hadn't you heard?"

I'd heard, but hadn't seen it enforced. This looked bad. I felt everything around me, from slightly gusty wind to spongy ground to buildings too far away and too separated for cover. "Ah, I guess I forgot," I said.

"Why are you out in the dark?" he asked, still probing.

"Dunno." It was all I could think of. Playing stupid often works.

He shook his head, looking slightly bewildered. "Get in back," he said, turning and opening the door. "We'll take you to a shelter."

I did not want to get in that car. I would be trapped and helpless. But if I didn't, he'd know something was not right. It was almost certain he had an image of me on his gear. That image would go to everyone and might match up with a file from their patrol cameras.

"Wow, thanks," I said, and stepped forward. There was nothing else to do at that point. I climbed in and sat down, awaiting the sting of a baton that never came. I awaited a high-speed drive to a building with more cops. That didn't happen either. They actually took me to a shelter. It was set up in that local mall. An old department store had been converted and was lit up from within.

We arrived and he let me out again, then walked me to the door. "I'm fine, really," I said.

"It's no trouble," he said. "I'm supposed to help people." There was also a hint of "I'm not letting you sneak off again, you loon." He figured the stress of the events had gotten to me, and he wasn't far wrong. At least he left after opening the door for me. I'd have to check in then leave out the back in a hurry.

"Here y' go," he said to both me and a harried woman running the admissions desk. Then he was gone.

"Name?" she said. It was an actual desk. They had only a portable comm and one data line.

"Uh, Martin Lee," I said.

"ID?" she asked.

"Broken," I said. "I have a card, but no chip. Got to get it fixed." I was still sizing up escape routes surreptitiously. Escaping here wouldn't be the problem. Not being IDed for file would be.

"We've had some of those," she said without suspicion. "What's your daughter's name?"

"Melanie," I said. She was asleep on my shoulder by this time.

"All we've got is cots and soup," she said, sounding apologetic.

"Oh, soup sounds so good," I said, sounding relieved.

"Great. Well, Lara here will show you where to go," she said. A teenage girl came around, all cheerful.

"Hi!" she said. "This way."

"Thanks."

She chattered as we walked. "That is such a cute little baby. Girl?"

"Yes," I agreed. "About six months." She was eight months, but always the cover story.

"Good! She'll be big before you know it."

I said, "She's getting heavy now," while casually looking around. Large open area, lots of people on cots and occasional vids. Pillars. Several cops. I'd have to be subtle.

Giggling, she said, "Well, we'll put you right here in the middle. If you need help, just let me know. I'm roving around helping."

"Thanks," I said. I tried to sound grateful.

I laid down and snuggled Chelsea, trying to act as if I was resting. Had Mario made that call yet? Would I get associated with the description? How would I get out of here?

A bathroom break seemed like a good idea. I stood and looked. None were immediately visible. "Restrooms?" I asked in the general direction of a family nearby. I shouldered my bag. I wasn't leaving anything lying where it could be swiped.

"Up the escalator," I was told. "Sucks."

Nodding, I wandered that way and up. There were lots of side rooms and staff offices down here, but all were in use as nurseries or such. None of them appeared to have outside doors.

Near the escalators, I met Lara again, as she was coming the other way.

"Need a hand?" she asked.

"Just going to the restroom," I said.

"Oh, okay. I can hold her for you. What's her name?"

"Melanie," I said. "I'll be fine. Really. I hate putting her down."

"Oh. Okay," she said, looking crestfallen but not suspicious. "Well, let me know, huh?"

"Sure."

I turned and rode up, along with a couple of other people. Upstairs was about the same, but more open. There were lots of back passageways. I hit the stinking, overused restroom first, then started to patrol.

Yes, indeed. Lots of exits. All three roof hatches near the restrooms were locked with padlocks. I might be able to kick one open, especially Boosted, but where would I go? There were three other roof hatches at corners, behind "MAINTENANCE ONLY" doors. There was a service conveyor that went down at an angle. It was locked off. The warehouse areas were dark and guarded by cops. Without lights, they were deemed unsafe.

I wandered downstairs. I'd have to sneak out one of the two regular sets of doors. Easy enough. Fresh air or some other excuse should do it. I grabbed some soup as I passed, needing food.

I'd reached our cot and sat down, Chelsea starting to stir a little. I mixed her a bottle and sat back to consider. Then I stopped considering, because the choice was made for me.

A news load came on one of the channels, showing a flashing "TERRORIST ALERT" at the top of the screen. I couldn't hear and tried to move closer, then realized that might not be too bright. I was just close enough to hear, "—suspected terrorist may be traveling with a baby. Everyone should be alert for a young Caucasian male adult with an infant—" The rest was lost in a stir of voices.

Sometimes, sheer gall is your best weapon. "Hell, that description could be anyone!" I said aloud.

"Even you," a man replied, looking levelly at me.

I replied, "Yeah. Even me. Watch it. I've got a loaded baby and I'm not afraid to use it!"

Laughs scattered across the area, including the man who'd been momentarily suspicious.

But it meant I'd have to stay here tonight. Leaving now would be a clear sign. I sighed. It would be a long night and I wouldn't dare sleep.

I lay there under the lights, dreading every passage of the security, cops and staff. When would they swoop in like vultures and take me?

I knew they'd get me sooner or later. Every time a guard trudged by, staring at faces, I cringed inside. When would it happen?

As soon as it was light, I grabbed one of the offered breakfast pastries and checked out. "Leaving already?" the current staffer asked.

"Yeah, got to find my folks," I told him, trying not to seem too eager.

"Was your stay okay?" he asked.

"Oh, sure. Warm, dry, fed. I can't complain, can I?" I said.

"You'd be amazed how many do," he said, shaking his head.

I muttered a goodbye over my shoulder and headed out.

A week later I was in another efficiency, trying to collect resources to move further. I was south and east of town now, near Zambrota. It seemed that every time I gathered enough stuff to make a good move, something came along and kicked it. Still, I'd learned patience. I could take as long as necessary.

My enemies weren't patient, though. They wanted me dead. A current load on the news had a half-assed sketch of me. Mario was still giving me a fighting chance, and I owed him. I just wished there were some way I could talk to him. There were some really decent people in this rathole, if you could find them.

I needed to keep moving. I also couldn't stay in a shelter, that one night had decided me. I could hop hotels, but not more often than I could apartments. Every move meant a different ID and I had two left. If I could just get a week to scavenge a few items, I'd be fine. The point of an apartment was to appear permanent and stable. I figured they'd look at the more itinerant population first.

I was hardly sleeping. At any moment, they might show up to grab me. I was running out of time and resources. I considered myself expendable, expended in fact, but I had to get Chelsea off planet even if I died to do so. This was not her home and I didn't want her living in this hole, nor being reviled for her father, the butcher. Nor killed outright as one of "them." And if you think people won't kill children out of blind, stupid hatred, I invite you to spend a few months on Mtali.

My paranoia was necessary, but it kept me from sleeping, eating, showering. I did everything in short spurts, and kept an eye out the door. I'd picked an apartment on the back of the building again. While not wanting to fall into a pattern, it would give me a good escape route as it backed onto an industrial zone. I just hoped I wouldn't need it.

It worked for a month. I'd acquired a few of the items I needed for the next step, and was ready to leave. Then my hand got forced.

My hyperaware danger sense was alert for any input, and it got one. I must have heard a door slam, or a weapon clink or seen the reflection of vehicle lights pulling into the lot at odd angles. Whatever it was, I suddenly was that more alert, the way one knows a real threat from simple nerves. If you've ever been in combat, you know what I'm talking about. If not, you're fortunate.

You'll recall that one of the things no one had wanted that I'd stolen were security cameras. I had one outside on the corner, small and invisible, with a tiny screen inside for me to monitor. It was showing a police tactical van in the parking lot. I quivered, shook, and became alert. I'd known they'd ID me sooner or later. Here it was, and I needed to move, fast. The complication was Chelsea and support gear. Ugly.

A careful glance showed they weren't outside my door yet, but were still forming up. Modern technology, professional paranoia, and a bit of luck in keeping late hours had arranged to save my ass. I turned, scooped up Chelsea and started bail-out procedure.

"DAaaaaad!" she shouted as I grabbed her, happy for more attention. It was one of her few words so far.

"Shush, little girl," I said with a quick smile and a bump of her nose. She giggled. She thought it was great fun when I stuffed her into my rucksack. It took a few precious seconds to lash cord over her shoulders and snug the straps around her middle, then

I grabbed the four bottles of water I kept prepared, the formula mix and a couple of toys and slid them into the side pockets. Her towel wrapped around her neck as cushioning, and she was able to only wiggle. She'd get frustrated and complain shortly, but this should all be over by then. I grabbed a couple of items including a pair of old kitchen shears which I twisted into two separate blades, and headed for the door while lugging the ruck to my shoulders and fastening the chest straps.

They were outside already. I'd been afraid of that. Well, the only thing to do was to go through them. If you do it fast enough, the shock factor keeps them from reacting. We'd find out just how good Earth's best agents were. And we'd find out right now.

I triggered Boost, ripped the top off a tomato sauce bottle, and splashed it all around me over the door, floor and walls. A pause with eye to peephole showed them lining up in standard entry fashion and preparing to swing a battering ram at the knob. I watched the swing, stepped aside, and threw the door open.

The nearest goon stumbled in, as he'd been expecting resistance. I reached up and drove the sharp scissor blade under his faceplate, into his chin and up through the roof of his mouth to his sinuses and possibly brain. He shrieked like a warning siren, and dropped convulsing. I left the blade in him. He'd most likely survive, but would be in excruciating pain until they filled him full of narcotics.

I was already stepping over him, and with the other blade I ripped a vicious slash across his partner's hand. The fool had neglected gloves, probably for a better grip on his weapon, probably due to insufficient training. After all, what were the odds that an arrestee would slice his hand open? Well, in this encounter, 100%. He screamed, blood ran, and I stepped aside while shoving him backwards into the line of troops.

The fall and splashes of red all around and agonized howls rending the air distracted the rest for a few seconds as they tried to figure out what had happened. Meanwhile, I stepped lightly on the environmental unit heat exchanger, then the windowsill, and hopped over the fence to the neighbor's porch, dinging my hip and knee as I did so. I heard the thuds of stickywebs and the crack of bullets thumping the fence, and trained reflexes decided it was better to make another pass than to try for the next fence. So I clamped down on the pain, turned left, twisted out of the gateway while reminding myself that I could *not* roll with a baby on my back—she whipped against one shoulder from the turn—and found the two trailing agents blocking the gateway to my porch. Others were still trying to crowd into the apartment, the distraction having drawn attention away from my escape.

I was behind the first of the rearguards, and drove the shear blade up from behind, between his legs, behind his cup and into his groin. He kicked like a pithed frog and dropped. I stumbled, recovered, and faced the molasses-slow turn of the other. Before she could yell a warning, I was on her, and twisted her weapon aside. Her fingers popped and cracked as I did, I jerked back to dislocate her elbow, and left the improvised blade jammed in her chin as I had with the first. She fell forward and landed on it, ululating like a siren. All the running had Chelsea giggling with glee. It was just another twirl with Dad to her, but the macabre laughter had to confuse them further. That was one minor casualty and three criticals, one of them possibly lethal, in about four seconds of combat. They were armed, I wasn't, and if all had gone well, the remaining four should be totally confused and helpless for a few more seconds. I didn't want to get near their van, as they undoubtedly had backup and a medical team. I needed to disappear, so I dodged downhill across the dew-sodden grass while the twelve kilos on my back laughed and bounced, scrambled the fence into the dock area of the post office distribution center situated there, recalled once again and just in time that I couldn't roll with Chelsea hanging on, and tumbled. The downed branches and debris hurt like hell, but didn't cause any major injury. Behind me, the screams of pain continued. Good.

The fence absorbed the next two shots of web, mostly, but I felt goo splash across my back and left arm. As long as it hadn't smothered my daughter, and I was fairly sure it hadn't, we'd be fine. I ran between the buildings, keeping them between pursuit and us and got to the front quickly.

They would be expecting me to keep running, so I slipped out the one-way metal people gate that was next to the truck entrance, and dodged across the street quickly. That was a four lane, edge of city route, and most of the few cars were still on autocontrol, so they were easy to judge. I ducked into the auto food place located right there through its side door, and hit a restroom. A women's restroom. They'd not look there first.

I locked the door, tried to recover my breath, all drenched with sweat from the boost, and doffed the pack and my jacket. I still had my regular knife, and used it to cut open pockets rather than reach through oozing goo, and pulled out my survival gear. It went into my pants and shirt pockets, then I carefully sliced the bottom of the ruck and eased out a wigglin' little weasel. She was fine, barring a few strands of web in her hair that I'd deal with later, and grabbed me in a big, laughing hug. I reached in and retrieved her bottles and formula, pulled some disposable towels from the dispenser, abandoned her regular towel because of the web on it, flushed my ID, rolled the jacket and ruck into a ball with the web inside, and we left.

I ran lightly down the alley with her clinging monkeylike to shoulder and hip, stuffed the bundle far into a trash container that looked as if it was it due to be dumped within the day, turned onto a side street, and resumed walking normally. I was down to my last identity, and wondered how long I could keep up this fight. The war was over, I could demand to be repatriated, but it was clear that everyone thought me dead and the UN was trying to fulfill the belief.

Somehow, I'd have to find assets to get me off planet, and take it from there. No problem, to a person with plenty of assets. I had a few hundred in cash, a low-limit credit chit, the clothes on my back, and a knife. I was among 20 plus billion people who'd rip me apart bare-handed if they ID'd me, and didn't dare show up anywhere my face might be photographed.

And if anyone thought that would stop me, they'd find I still had mental resources I hadn't used yet. I just needed to be left alone long enough to get them rolling.

I snagged a bus, deciding I was far enough away to be safe for now, and sat down in the back. It was quiet, I was undisturbed, and it took only a few moments to gum the web in Chelsea's hair with towel so as to not get me stuck, and cut out the con-taminated hair. She'd look a bit funny until I could style it a bit better, meaning, shorter, but the obvious signs of trouble were done away with.

We would spend the night in a classy hotel, I decided. It was convenient, I had the money, and it would actually be good cover now since they thought me out of assets. I broke open my last ID, credchits and related stuff, plus two cash cards, and waited for the regular stop at the corner. No need to draw attention by getting out early.

The hotel I had picked was second tier. It was a luxury commercial operation, not one of the overdone palaces used by people living out royal fantasies. Ironically, the really wealthy are quite happy in the second tier, and real royalty won't touch the snobby dumps, but rather reserve mansions. This place had obviously been nice before the war, I thought as I entered through lifting doors that mostly worked. Now, it was a bit shabby. Glass and mirrors on the lobby pillars were scratched. Brass rails were dull and fittings had broken loose. The carpets were worn and threadbare. Hey, at least they were still standing and had electricity. That put them in better shape than a lot of the planet.

The desk staff looked at me a bit funny as I checked in, but I had a great credit rating, and I told the clerk I'd had an accident. There were still enough odd happenings because of the war and they didn't question me further. I'd chosen an expensive place because they are far more tolerant than the lower echelon, as long as you pay and are quiet. They hate having flashing lights outside. It's bad PR. They get political deals, organized crime, etc. Cheap hotels scream to the cops if they see anything suspicious. *Really* cheap dives I don't want to use if I don't have to. Besides, why would they look for me in the most expensive chain in town?

I paid too much at the hotel micromall for more clothes, a manicure kit with scissors so I could trim Chelsea's hair, one shirt and a pair of pants and other accessories. The front desk sent up a complimentary toiletries kit at my request. We showered, cleaned up and dressed.

Once fed by the overpriced mediocre crap from room service, I teased Chelsea into giggles and exhaustion, and got her to sleep. After that . . .

I'd been dealing with this for near an Earth year. Life had been a living hell. I'd been shot at yet again. There was no way to get what I needed, which was off this stinking shithole of a rock, so I sought solace in mindless pleasure.

I called for an Earth escort. Since it's illegal, they use euphemisms. I found "massage" listed in the directory, called for one to come visit, paid the fee and while waiting made a quick dash downstairs to draw a few extra UN marks in cash as tip.

The girl arrived, and I mean girl. Legal age was 20, she was no older than 22. Pretty, but with no style of garb, just vaguely disaffected and dressed to not clash with the décor and guests. Nice blonde hair. Pity she'd dyed the roots black. She was cautiously friendly but unsophisticated, although she warmed up a bit when she found I was free with cash, decent-looking and not wanting to abuse her. Conversation was not a practical option—she couldn't hold a light one and I didn't want to talk reality with her. The sex was okay. What the hell, it was relief, human contact and body heat. I tipped her a bit extra, got her stage name and said I'd call next time I was in town.

Chelsea had stayed asleep in the corner, hidden by chairs, and I never mentioned her. She might have hurt my cover and I just hadn't been interested in the sympathy ploy. I felt a bit better, a bit braver, and refreshed. The UN could fuck itself—I would get out of here yet. I turned on the vid. I craved alcohol, but quashed the urge. I needed my wits and I'd been drinking too much.

There wasn't anything on the news, which confirmed my opinion. They didn't want to admit I was still alive, they didn't want to admit they'd failed miserably, and they didn't dare let the Freehold learn about the issue. That was all to my advantage. No pictures on the news kept me safer.

Sighing, I picked up the little bundle and crawled into bed. I wrapped an arm around her. How she could put out that much heat I'll never know. But it was comforting, and I slept. And I managed not to dream.

CHAPTER 28

It was another long march. I was getting used to them. But with Chelsea on my back, curled up deep in the new ruck, I had one less thing to worry about and her radiated heat was a comfort to me. The tools I had were wrapped in the ubiquitous blanket to hide my intentions, except the small shovel I carried through the straps.

Far south of the metroplex, I sought a cache that had been hidden for us when we were only in the prep stages. It would have more than I'd need for this problem. The trick was to get there.

Outside the cities, there are grids of roads, unlike back on Grainne where we have only a few. They're paved too, rather than being fused. I found the mark I needed at the edge of the southernmost suburb of Preston. Now I would head four squares south and three east: 11,200 meters.

The dark was a comfort, as it closed out visibility. Operatives live by night. Of course, criminals do, too. I slipped down into weeds the three times vehicles came by. I might cadge a ride from one if I looked helpless enough, I also might be questioned or attacked. It was still chill; spring comes late to those latitudes, and the environment was still a mess. Every time I lay down, I could feel the cold seeping through the wet spots on knees and elbows and eventually chest. It didn't matter. This trip here should set me up.

My ears were on automatic, picking up the occasional bird amid the rustling, sighing, whispering trees. What did the trees make of this? They had CO_2, a cool environment, and were being left alone out here, but stripped to the ground in their few remaining camps in the cities. Above, or below all those natural sounds was the pervasive, muted and barely audible soft rumble of the city. Even this far out, the omnipresent reminder of humanity intruded. How could one live on a planet like this?

I was suddenly alert. Something was wrong, but what? Bird sounds stopped. Threat, but what and where? Footsteps in soft ground, behind and to the right. About fifty meters. Closing. Run, or engage? Engage. My brain, trained as a battle comm, sorted through what it needed almost without me thinking about it. The ripple of natural adrenaline was followed by the surge of Boost, and I turned with the short shovel in hand.

My attacker was surprised as I spun. He'd been sure he had the edge. The tape-wrapped chunk of cable in his hand made him a threat, not a supplicant, and I struck, the edge of the shovel batting his crude sap aside before shattering his right shoulder as I brought it down. "No!" he yelled in denial. Scream. He collapsed. Whimper. "Fuck you, asshole, you shoulda been *mine*." No hope of salvation in this piece of shit. Cock back for a lethal blow to the skull . . .

. . . turn and keep walking.

I couldn't do it. He was no threat mentally or physically. He was a waste of my time and his death would serve no purpose.

Behind me, there were animal cries of pain. I was used to them by now. I kept walking. Shortly, I turned east.

From the mark I'd sought, I followed a buried hydrogen line by its markers for 150 meters. From that bend in the line, I continued ten more meters. It was a dangerous spot, so close to a farmer's field, but northern wheat didn't grow that deep. The harvest I sought was far below.

I dug. Digging is meditation for a soldier, because we do so much of it. I kept Chelsea in the ruck, and had it on the ground next to me, always at hand. I stopped periodically to refill her bottle, check her diaper and drink a few swallows myself. Then I returned to digging. The small shovel, E-tool really, made it slow work, as did the need to keep the fill pile low. I acquired blisters right through my gloves, but at least I was warm from the exertion.

Then she started fussing. Baby cries travel a long way, and I had to stop them. I picked her up and she clung like a monkey, heels and fingers clutching my jacket. She quieted down at once.

But I had no luck in giving her a bottle and putting her down. She wanted to be held. One cannot argue with an infant, they have no higher functions. I couldn't have the noise. I had no way to sedate her and would be reluctant to do so anyway. So I turned the blanket into a sling and placed her under my right arm, a hindrance but not an incapacitance. I just hoped the digging wouldn't take much longer.

Two meters should be my depth. I was at two meters. Nothing. I hoped I wouldn't have to try again another night, or dig laterally. Perhaps additional soil had been laid above by the farm.

That was the case. At 220 centimeters, I struck crate. Eager now, frantic even, I cleared away one corner. There were stress lines that could be broken in an emergency. This was an emergency. I snapped off the corner.

Riches! I had more clothes. I had at least four IDs that would work passably. I had weapons. Everything but a Q36 nuke was here. Even this far out, Earth's sensor field would have found the anomaly, so we hadn't left any. Which was fine. I wasn't here for weapons.

I looked longingly at a Merrill Model 17, the brand new 11 mm killer. Lovely, but a dead giveaway. My weapons were my wits, these mere tools. I left most of the tools where they were, except for a good folding knife. I took the clothes, the IDs and risked a double armful of battle rats. I took cashcards and credchips that matched the IDs. I wanted a standard military shelter, but that, too would reveal me if found. I settled for the plain but adequate inflatable civilian tent within. I abandoned the cheap backpack for a better grade of camper's ruck. The whole process took minutes.

Then it was time to exfiltrate. I rigged fuses to a five-kilo demolition block and shoved it far back into the case. I rigged fuses on three Magburn incendiaries, the proprietary mix that was evolved to cut titanium struts, hardened concrete and weaken structural whisker composites. It had been so long since I worked with professional explosives, but my fingers were sure in trained muscle memory. Insert fuse to detonator, butt, crimp, insert, place. Rig a second detonator for every charge as a backup. Uncoil fuse. I couldn't test burn the fuse, but it should be 300 seconds per meter. I'd have to rely on the estimate, and I'd need approximately twelve meters of fuse for each of eight detonators.

I climbed out, piled the dirt back in as fast as I could, using it as quick fill and not worrying about compaction. There was no visible fill pile to indicate anything, and hopefully no one would look for yet another few weeks. There was bare gray in the east when I finished. Looking around for observers and seeing none, I spoke aloud, the textvid safety formula now a ritual to remind me of who I was.

"I am ready to strike. The area is clear. Fire in the hole. Strike, strike, strike, strike, strike, strike, strike, strike." At each "Strike" I clicked a fuse igniter. As soon as I confirmed them burning, I pulled the igniters free with the tip of my knife. I scooped them up and wrapped them in a rag, still hot. Then I began walking.

An hour later, I was five squares east. I glanced at my watch. Right now. In that cache, the magburn was melting the unused explosives, the crate, the weapons and the ammo. The ammo would be sputtering as its matrix decayed in the heat. And right now, the explosives to the side would be blowing the molten pool into slag mixed with dirt. Should anyone find it, they'd assume it had been caused by a gas leak. The hydrogen utility would check, see it wasn't their problem, and ignore it. If they recognized signs of explosives, they'd call in experts. After some days of checking, the experts might deduce it had been a cache. That would tell them there were infiltrators on Earth. Which they knew. Very careful checking might show the possibility that the cache had been used after the attack. That would tell them that at least one Operative might be alive. Which they knew. I reminded myself again that I was safe. Then I turned and kept walking.

Later that day, I came to a small town called, of all things,

Caledonia. It had four small hotels. I had a cab take me to the cleanest-looking. They were glad to see me, after I knocked long enough to make them realize they had a customer. They took cash with no questions and I slipped into a room. I scrubbed and soaked—they had hot water, the power working reliably out here. And lucky for them—this far from anything, they'd have all died without it. Or maybe not. They were less antlike than the city dwellers. I cleaned Chelsea up well, scrubbed our old clothes and tossed what was damaged beyond use. Then we slept. I sprawled in a comfy bed and wrapped myself around that little bundle of heat. She was stirring and excited, but I calmed her down with whispers and caresses of her head and spine, until she conked back out the way small children do. I slept like a log. I was so out of it, I didn't notice her get wet, until I woke in a puddle. Oh, well. I'd lain in worse things.

Our new persona was not "refugee." It was "slightly inconvenienced survivor." I dressed decently and would travel likewise. More walking followed by rented single autocar took us to Eau Claire, from where we took surface train down through Illinois, taking side routes to avoid Chicago. I had an idea what Chicago might look like. I had no wish to confirm. Louisville had not been hit, and was in a better environment. It would do for now. I still had a duty to recover other survivors, and it might take time to do that. Along the way, I could use public comms if I could find any.

I found one in Rockford and risked using it, changing trains after the fact just in case. There were still no messages from anyone. Their orders had been to send me a quick, "Dear Bill, we're okay. Just a quick note. Please call when service resumes. Love, whoever." There was nothing. That meant they were either dead, or so woefully out nowhere that there was no net service. Unlikely. Either they'd died in the attack, or they'd been hunted afterwards. Or maybe some of them had managed to sneak off Earth. But if so, I should have messages relayed through various locations and a "We're home" message. Nothing equaled nothing. They were all dead.

It was chilling at first. Then I wondered how everyone would feel about it, and perhaps they'd feel better dead. Then I had to give credit to the odds; two hundred Operatives, likely *three billion* casualties were our share. One Operative, one city. I really couldn't blame anyone who wanted us dead. We'd succeeded beyond anyone's dreams. Nightmares. Hell, part of me wanted to arrange to wipe out my own planet as a threat to the species.

Louisville hadn't been hit. It had still had some rioting, and a spate of refugees from Cincinnati, Indianapolis and even Memphis. It was intact but crowded and depressed. I found us a small efficiency far out in the Taylorsville suburb. It was musty but adequate, almost a twin of the one in Minneapolis. A cookie cutter planet. I paid for a month, signed a lease for five more, and mentally burned the ID I'd used. I'd leave when it was convenient and they could charge off on the debt. Yes, the debt collectors on Earth were still in business. Scavengers and parasites are always the hardiest of lifeforms.

Ironically, I was slowly making my way back to Washington, that being the best place to arrange travel off planet. I was thinking again now, and plotting my exfiltration. There was no more intel to gather. Anyone still alive I wouldn't be able to help from this distance, and we'd known that beforehand. Exfiltration was on our own authority. No one would expect me to head toward the center of government, and I'd move toward it, taking my time, waiting for a Freehold or Caledonian or Novaja Rossian military contingent that could pull us out. Or maybe a humanitarian mission I could con into lifting us.

I took it a town at a time, a few weeks at a time, asking locals for intel and checking maps on the nets as I was able. I'd check for reports, too, just before I actually moved location. It was frightening how few people knew anything about anywhere other than where they squatted. On the other hand, that made me safer. I was asking about towns in all directions, which would slow down pursuit. I switched from adequately well off to poor and back, staying in small apartments or back rooms but never in shelters, because the government goons running them might happen to be alert enough to notice me. I was alternately growing and shaving my beard. Yes, with a shaver. Earth has always been that primitive. Nano and chemical depilation just never caught on. I don't know why. I used every trick of accent, cosmetics and misdirection to make myself invisible and throw the most astute tracker onto a dozen false trails.

The problem was that Chelsea couldn't help being what she was—a bright, cheerful little girl with hair that coiled manically in back. I might be hard to track, she would not be. I did what I could. She got her hair bobbed and became a boy for a while. I dyed it several colors with shoe polish, which would wash out in a few days. The stuff was cheap; no one was using it. It was cheaper than the bleach I used on my hair.

It's been almost two Earth years now, and there's enough infrastructure back up that I can actually plan for our departure. I've been amazed at Chelsea's development recently, as she picks up a new word every day and learns to solve problems and get into things. She brushes her teeth before bed, picks up after she eats and is quite neat. It must be a trait from Deni, because I tend to be a slob. She built a tower of boxes and chairs up to the counter the last week, and came back holding a kitchen knife. Clever kid. Typical, I suppose, but I'd forgotten to expect it. I told her she was a bad girl, and she curled up on the floor, sobbing. After a while, she unwrapped herself, stood up, threw herself on me and said, "Dad, Ah'm cryning!" She was still sobbing in remorse at upsetting me.

How can an adult with any humanity be mad at a kid when they say things like that?

I was able to do some research of what was unclassified about the war. Casualties were horrific, but we kicked the crap out of a force nearly a hundred times our size. Training, logistics and sheer bloody-minded determination won that war. Our people simply wouldn't back down, no matter the odds. Naumann ordered Operatives and Blazers to blow UN ships and space installations. Every one of those was a suicide mission and almost every one of those soldiers accepted his mission. Virtually everyone I knew in the military is dead. If one of those self-styled, hypocritical "pacifists" ever tells me that soldiers don't understand the true cost of war, I'll likely rip his jaw off on the spot and piss in the hole. I owe it to my brothers and sisters.

I discovered that Kendra Pacelli, our invaluable source on North America, joined the FMF and advanced to warrant leader. Not only that, she was awarded the Citizens' Medal for selfless bravery, holding off UN infantry long enough for more than 250 troops to fall back and regroup. Most people back home will never know just how much they owe her for her technical data and innate knowledge of the UNPF mindset and operating philosophy, in addition to her actions at Braided Bluff. I owe my life at least twice to data she furnished me. Thank you, Sergeant Pacelli. I'm glad you survived.

Sorry about your hometown.

So far, no Operatives have reported in to me. None. How many others are hiding as I am, afraid and ashamed? Few, I presume. Most must be dead.

And I had to fight parasites recently. Fleas, lice and worms. Must have wandered by on a stray animal and been tracked in. I found these disgusting little black dots doing handstands all over Chelsea, and over my lower legs. Along with them came lice. Filthy lifeforms, both of them. I've never understood the slobbering sexual fantasies surrounding vampires that crop up in literature every few years. To me, a person who gets off thinking about bloodsuckers needs a swift whack alongside the head with a club to shake their brains up. I shaved my head for the lice and went through hers with a comb and kerosene—it was still impossible to find basic medicine in stores. It took chemicals, garlic on the skin, and regular plucking with tweezers to kill the flea infestation.

Worms I didn't get, but Chelsea did. Common enough. What wasn't common yet again was any medicine. I finally did it the hard, battlefield way, and force-fed her a hundred milliliters of kerosene. Yes, kerosene. It's being used in heaters until the power grid comes back up totally. She screamed, spat and howled, but next day she spewed into five diapers and the little bastards were gone. It stank like you wouldn't believe. She'd been drinking water to get the oily taste out of her mouth, so she didn't dehydrate, fortunately. I don't think they teach any of this in basic parenting class. The more primitive the conditions, the tougher it is to raise kids. Anyone who wishes for the simple days of the village and all the mothers staying home to care for the commune of chillun is living a misguided fantasy. I want modern technology, modern drugs, prepared foods and a support staff, as I would for any combat operation.

CHAPTER 29

And now we're going home. It wasn't that hard to arrange, and I could kick myself for not doing it sooner. On the other hand, the only office until recently was near DC, of no help to me in the Midwest, and I had to remain in the field in case my people needed me.

I met with one of the Freehold contingents here to help recovery. Most Terrans won't go anywhere near them, so there was no worry about being seen, nor any need to wait in line. Their office was small, discreet, and well guarded: an entire squad was stationed there. It bothered me that my own people scanned for weapons. That's an ominous trend for a society based on personal freedom, but it did seem a good idea, under the circumstances.

I used my best Capital District accent, and explained that we'd been here on business for a Jefferson based company. I told them Chelsea's mother was dead, and since the little weasel looks older than she is anyway, they didn't question me. "You'll have up to a year to arrange residency without penalty," I was told.

"Oh, thank you!" I said, sounding even more relieved than I was.

"You're welcome, Mister Ravahan. Can we give you a ride to get your possessions?" the aide asked me.

"I have everything that matters," I told her, and it wasn't hard to look rueful. "We're ready now."

It was so easy. They didn't even charge for the lift to the spaceport. I took one last look back in pity at the mudcrawlers of Earth, waiting for someone to "do something," while we Freeholders simply did whatever had to be done and moved on. I said a quick prayer for Deni and Tyler and then for everybody we left behind. I shouldered our bag in one hand, carried Chelsea in the other arm, and she waved, "Bye-bye!" to the techs as we entered the terminal. Everyone loves a grinning, cheerful child. They make great cover if you want to be unseen. Just please, in the name of God and Goddess, get them out of the line of fire before it gets ugly. With a Freehold diplomatic pass, we went straight through a nearly empty concourse and boarded.

I suppose a few readers are amazed at how much effort I put into the kid. Others may think I had some sort of epiphany over the children on vid who caused me so much discomfort, or over finding Chelsea alive. Well, both and neither. I've always loved kids. I didn't avoid Deni's pregnancy and Chelsea's birth from distaste. Deep in my soul, I was terrified that I would have to kill, or worse, *order* killed, Chelsea to maintain cover or to let us escape with our data. I knew I couldn't do that if I didn't remain remote. Seeing other kids killed to prove a political point, no matter whose, made me ill. Doing it was a torture straight out of hell.

I've recorded this narrative in part for Naumann, who is still alive. Consider it my final addenda. Fuck you, you bastard. You'll never send me to slaughter civilians for you again. Do your own killing. I've attached my final debriefing, I'm retiring, and I don't think you have the means to find me. Part of me would rather die than return to Grainne, but that's the place I know best and the easiest place to hide and still have modern facilities for Chelsea. Of course, I may be lying and headed somewhere else entirely. I'm not looking forward to what I'll have to do to get set up and hidden, but for this little girl, I'll do it.

She sat on the seat next to me during takeoff, snuggled in a fluffy jumpsuit and clutching her towel—the same one she's had her whole life—strapped in her harness. The seats were a bit worn on this Earth-based craft, another indication that they'd be some time recovering and would never again have the political clout to push others around. We had done an amazingly thorough job. Sometimes I even scare myself.

Chelsea's shout of, "Dad! Shuttews!" brought me back from introspection, and I saw her pointing out the window at the row of similar shuttles from various lines. A warning sounded, and she gripped my hand and was momentarily wide-eyed and quaking as we lifted, but she didn't cry. Every other kid in the bay was screaming in terror, but she took it and dealt with it. When we reached orbit she kept me informed of events and asked questions all the way to our transport.

"Dad! Wazzat?"

"That's Earth from orbit, Little Girl. It's called a 'planet.'"

"P'anet," she said. Whirling around in my lap and squirming to reach other ports, she made a discovery. "Look! Dad! Sips!" she said, yanking my sleeve and pointing enthusiastically. She bounced away in emgee and laughed delightedly. Her long coils bounced around her head, and she laughed at that, also.

"Yes, those are ships. We're taking that one home."

She stared where I pointed and wiggled in glee. "Yes!" she agreed, with a single nod of her head. It was a quirk of hers.

We left the shuttle with the crew ready to adopt her. "Bye-bye, Jeri! Bye-bye, catpin! Bye-bye pi'ot!" she shouted at the purser and flight crew while waving over my shoulder as I swam out. There's few prouder feelings than knowing you're raising a good kid. I'm optimistic.

That's my next task. Chelsea may not grow up rich, and she may not have a mother, but I'll ensure she has a good upbringing and a happy childhood. Any person, entity, or government who tries to stop her from doing so will arouse my ire. They do not want to see me angry.

Remember, even retired, I'm still an Operative. We took a lot of casualties in the System Battle, Braided Bluff and here on Earth, but we are without question the best soldiers in human history.

Twelve hundred and eighty-seven Operatives have died in the line of duty. At the end of time, the forces of evil will form ranks and march to the last battle. When they reach the gates of Heaven, they will find those Operatives guarding it . . . Rowan, Tom, Frank, Neil, Tyler, Kimbo, all scarred and grubby and laden with Death . . . and Deni in front, a calm, imperturbable look on her face, hunched over her rifle and ready to deliver immortal wrath. And if the legions of evil have any brains at all, they will about face and leave.

And one little girl has her own personal Operative as bodyguard, teacher . . . and father.

AUTHOR'S AFTERWORD

Despite his misgivings, Captain Chinran is not a terrorist. He is a soldier following orders over a defined enemy, with a collateral casualty count that is truly horrific, but nevertheless an act of war, not terror. Obviously, he feels dreadful guilt over the event and its aftermath. This is one of many differences between him and cowardly terrorists, who cheer the deaths of innocents as an accomplishment.

Most of this novel was plotted and written before September 11, 2001. As horrific as those events were, they could have been a lot worse. I hope no one will attempt to draw parallels between the events of that day and this book.

Hopefully, we will learn from those events and not mistake repression for security.